OTHER BOOKS by KASSANDRA LAMB

<u>The Kate Huntington Mysteries</u>
Psychotherapist Kate Huntington helps others cope with trauma, but she has led a charmed life...until a killer rips it apart. (10 novels)

<u>The Kate on Vacation Mysteries</u>
Even on vacation, Kate Huntington can't stay out of trouble. (4 novellas)

<u>The Marcia Banks and Buddy Cozy Mysteries</u>
Marcia Banks trains service dogs for veterans, and solves crimes on the side, with the help of her Black Lab, Buddy. (13 novels/novellas)

<u>The C.o.P. on the Scene Mysteries</u>
Eight days into her new job as Chief of Police in a small Florida city, Judith Anderson finds herself one step behind a serial killer. (spinoff from the Kate Huntington series; 2 novels–more to come)

<u>Romantic Suspense</u>
written under the pen name of Jessica Dale

FAMILY FALLACIES

A Kate Huntington Mystery

Kassandra Lamb

a misterio press publication

Published by *misterio press*, LLC

Cover design by Melinda VanLone, Book Cover Corner

This book is dedicated to:

My mother,
from whom I learned more about psychology and writing
than I ever did in any classroom,
and who literally gave me the idea for this book.

And to my cousin,
because she liked this one best.

PROLOGUE

Darkness. What woke her?

A shadow moves. Terror freezes her throat.

Get up! Run!

She runs, knowing it will do no good. The shadow will follow, will find her, no matter where she hides.

It looms over her. She screams.

Hands grabbing for her, holding her down. She tries to scream again. A big hand descends across her face. She fights against it. She can't breathe.

Big hands on her arms, gently shaking her. "Babe, baby..."

The shadow never calls her that.

"Babe, wake up. You're dreaming."

Audrey opened her eyes. The bedside lamp shone on Ted's worried face.

"It's okay. You're safe. It was just a dream."

She nodded.

Ted sat up next to her. He rubbed her arm. "Same one?"

She nodded again.

"Did you call Kate?"

"Yeah. I've got an appointment next week."

Ted nodded. "Can you sleep now, do you think?"

"Yeah. Uh, Ted..."

Could she make herself ask? Damn, she was such a wimp.

"What, babe?"

"Could we leave the light on, for a little while?" Her voice was just barely above a whisper.

"Sure. Come on, cuddle up here. You're safe with me."

CHAPTER ONE

Kate fumbled with the button at the waist of her favorite slacks.

Damn, I'm nervous.

The realization surprised her. She wasn't an anxious person by nature. Nor did meeting Skip Canfield for what she had jokingly dubbed *non*-dates normally make her nervous. Today, however, was different. She would be introducing him to her eight-month-old daughter. No matter how much she was attracted to the man, the way he interacted with little Edie would be a deal breaker.

At the thought of her daughter, Kate felt a stab of guilt over returning to work. She had barely begun her usual litany of reassurances–*it's only three days a week, Maria's a great nanny*–when her late husband's soft baritone broke in.

Now stop that, Kate. You're a great mom. Our little girl is just fine.

The guilt was replaced by a much sharper pain that took her breath away. She sat down hard on the side of her bed and struggled not to cry as the familiar anger and longing washed over her. It was so unfair. She and Eddie had tried to have children for six years without results. Then after he was gone, senselessly murdered, she had discovered she was pregnant.

One of the tears building up in her eyes broke loose. She gave her cheek an irritated swipe with the back of her hand. "I miss you, Eddie," she whispered.

I miss you too, love, his voice echoed in her head.

The only thing that had made her grief bearable had been these little conversations with her dead husband. Perhaps they were just figments of her imagination but they eased the loneliness, made her feel that Eddie was still with her, in spirit at least.

Of course, she hadn't mentioned these internal chats to anyone, not even Rob Franklin, who was her closest friend. As a psychotherapist, it would not bode well for her career if it got around that she thought she could talk to dead people.

Her little girl wasn't the only stumbling block to the non-dates with Skip becoming true dates. As long as she had moments like this, when she missed Eddie so much she could hardly stand it...well, it just wouldn't be fair to Skip.

He had reassured her that he was a patient man.

Kate glanced at her watch. If she didn't get a move on, she would be trying that patience further by keeping him waiting at the restaurant.

———◆———

Skip spotted his lunch date negotiating her way awkwardly through the crowded restaurant, baby on one hip, diaper bag dangling from her opposite shoulder.

The picture Kate had shown him hadn't done little Edie justice. She was cute as a button, a tiny replica of her mama with her dark, unruly curls and bright, blue eyes.

He stood as they neared the table. Despite the noise in the restaurant, he could hear the woman at the next table suck in her breath. His cheeks warmed and he silently cursed both the woman and his tendency to blush easily.

Intellectually he knew that at six-five and two hundred-thirty pounds of mostly muscle, he was considered a hunk. But emotionally he'd never quite gotten used to the idea. He'd been short and scrawny most of his youth, until a late growth spurt had blessed him with his current physique. He still did a double-take sometimes when he passed a mirror.

A couple times, Kate had fretted over her perceived discrepancy in their levels of physical attractiveness, saying that she "wasn't in his league." He'd assured her that he was interested in the whole package—brains and personality, as well as appearance—and he preferred her whole package to those of the more classically beautiful women who sometimes threw themselves at him.

She shuffled sideways between the diners at two adjacent tables, then turned toward him with a smile. The diaper bag strap perched on the very edge of her shoulder, threatening to slide off and land the bag in their neighbor's salad plate.

He reached out and snagged it. Even that limited contact sent a jolt through his system. He dropped the bag onto an empty chair.

Her fair skin flushed as she fussed over getting Edie settled in the highchair the waitress had brought to the table.

She'd no sooner sat down than the baby made a grab for the tablecloth. Water sloshed out of the glasses on the table as Kate struggled to pry chubby fingers loose from their death grip on the fabric. "Sorry–"

"She's adorable, just like her mama."

Her flush deepened.

The waitress came and took their orders.

Kate fished a toy out of the diaper bag and offered it to the baby. The child played with it contentedly while they made small talk. But as soon as their food had arrived and they'd taken their first bite, she began to fuss.

"Sorry." Kate brushed her napkin across her lips and rose from her chair. "She's the Energizer bunny. Doesn't deal well with inaction."

Skip held his hands out toward the highchair. "May I?"

She unbuckled the strap holding Edie in the chair, and he scooped the baby up. "Go ahead and eat," he said. "Your soup'll get cold. My sandwich will keep."

The little girl, now perched in the crook of his arm, had stopped crying and was giving him a solemn look. He balanced her on his knee and started bouncing her up and down, making quiet giddy-up noises. The child blessed him with a smile.

His hair flopped down on his forehead. He left it there, using it as a screen so he could watch Kate while she ate. An errant curl had snuck down her cheek. His hand itched to reach over and tuck it behind her ear.

But that was against the four-foot rule. He mentally berated himself for suggesting that damn rule. He'd thought it would make it easier to resist kissing her if they kept their distance, but not being able to touch her at all was agony.

She glanced up before he could wipe the longing from his face. Her gaze quickly dropped back to her soup bowl.

He couldn't help himself. In a low voice, he said, "I know we're not supposed to talk about it, but I gotta tell you that I'm *not* just looking for a romantic fling."

She coughed, choking a little on the sip of soup she'd taken.

He paused, searching for the right words. "Let's just say that I'm, uh, interested in a serious relationship, and I know you and Edie are a package deal."

She froze, staring at her bowl. Then she brought her eyes back up.

"I know." He grinned at her. In a high falsetto, he said, "It's too soon, Skip!"

"Good heavens, I hope my voice doesn't sound that screechy."

"Darlin', your voice is pure music to my ears," he drawled, letting his native Texas creep into his speech.

Edie started complaining that he was neglecting his horsey ride duties. Skip resumed jiggling his knee.

Kate hastily ate another spoonful of soup, then pushed the half-empty bowl away. "Here, let me take her awhile so you can eat."

"What, Kate Huntington, the woman with the appetite of a grizzly bear, isn't finishing a meal?" he teased, as he handed the baby to her.

"Comes with the territory, I'm afraid."

Skip picked up his sandwich and took a bite.

She asked, "So what can I give you to celebrate the opening of your own private investigating agency?"

It was his turn to choke on his food. He coughed, then carefully swallowed and took a swig of iced tea. "You might want to rephrase that question, 'cause I'm real tempted to say a congratulatory kiss." Although that hadn't been the *first* thing that had popped into his head.

"Well, actually I was thinking more in terms of a small investment to help you get things started. I have a good bit of money tucked away, from Eddie's life insurance."

He tensed, narrowing his eyes at her.

"I'd like to make things a little easier for you..." Her voice trailed off as she caught his expression.

"Thanks for the offer, but you keep that money for the baby's education. I've got a good reputation established. Already have a half dozen clients lined up."

An awkward pause, then she said, "Well, I'm treating you to lunch, at least. So tell me about these clients."

After another Edie exchange so Kate could finish her soup, he told her the gist of some of the cases he had landed already.

When they'd finished eating, she paid the bill. Then she started putting toys and other baby paraphernalia back into the diaper bag.

He hated to see their lunch come to an end so soon, but then the time he spent with her never seemed like enough. He stood up, handed her the baby and grabbed the now bulging bag.

Outside, the blast of late-August heat actually felt good on Kate's skin, after the aggressively air-conditioned restaurant.

She'd managed to snag one of the few shady parking spaces, along the outer edge of the lot. As they walked toward her car in companionable silence, she tried to analyze his reaction to her offer of money. Had she found the male ego he kept well hidden behind his easy-going grin?

Yet another stumbling block.

She hadn't told him yet that she was a moderately wealthy woman, thanks to her late husband's foresight. That insurance policy had been for a million dollars.

By the time they reached her car, the heat no longer felt so good. Kate was grateful to move into the shade. She started to juggle the baby around to her other hip so she could get to the keys in her pocket.

Skip took the child from her. This time Edie gave him a big grin and bounced up and down in his arms.

"I do believe you've made another conquest, Mr. Canfield." She fought the urge to reach up and brush back the straight brown hair that had fallen across his tanned forehead.

The baby now tucked in the crook of one arm, he leaned toward her. "Don't suppose I'm gonna get that congratulatory kiss, huh?"

Her nose picked up a hint of citrus from his aftershave and the faintest whiff of male sweat. She found the latter oddly reassuring. He might look too good to be true but he perspired like ordinary men.

She dropped her eyes, which turned out to be a mistake. On the side where he was holding the baby, the loose hem of his shirt had hiked up, revealing a glimpse of taut abs above the waistband of his slacks.

"That would be against the four-foot rule, wouldn't it?" she whispered, mesmerized by that tantalizing wedge of flesh.

He sighed. "Wish I'd never suggested that rule."

Bracing herself to back him off, she forced her gaze away from his exposed skin and looked up at him.

His eyes were soft above a gentle smile.

The lack of lust on his face threw her. She cared for this man. Why not move on in their relationship?

Guilt and grief clogged her throat.

That's why not.

She swallowed hard, trying to come up with something to say. But her mind was blank.

Skip handed Edie back to her. "How about a group hug then." Without giving her time to respond, he wrapped his long arms around both of them.

Despite herself, she let out a sigh. It felt so good to be held by a man again.

It didn't take long, however, for the baby to get restless. Kate reluctantly pulled away from him.

He suddenly dropped a kiss on the top of her head. In a strangled voice, he said, "I'll call you later." Before she could react, he had turned and was loping across the parking lot toward his SUV.

By lunchtime of her first day back at the Trauma Recovery Center, Kate was beginning to wonder why she'd been so eager to return to work.

Leaving Edie that morning had been harder than she'd expected, even though she knew her little one was in good hands. Family or not, her friend Rose never would have recommended Maria for the job of nanny/housekeeper if she didn't have total faith in her cousin's abilities and trustworthiness.

Still, Kate had made several false starts before she successfully got out of the house. Maria Hernandez, only recently arrived from Guatemala, spoke very little English. But she had found other ways to communicate through gestures and facial expressions. She had used one of those eloquent facial expressions when Kate had headed back from the front door, for the *third* time. "Did she just cough? Do you think she's coming down with a cold?"

The plump little woman had stood, arms crossed, between her and Edie, who was playing on the living room rug blissfully unaware of her mother's attempts to leave her. Maria's face was set in the no-nonsense look she gave Kate whenever she was being an overly anxious mom.

The rest of the morning had been a mixed bag of experiences with clients. There were the things she had always loved about being a psychotherapist. The sense of connection with her clients and the intriguing task of sorting through what people said—and didn't say—to get to the heart of what was bothering them. And the satisfaction when she saw the dawning of an important insight on a client's face.

But she had conveniently forgotten about the negatives while she'd been on maternity leave. One of her morning clients had neither shown up nor bothered to call to cancel.

Then Kate's last client of the morning had been Tammy Wingate, the financially pampered but otherwise neglected wife of a well-to-do businessman. Sally Ford, the center's director, had taken over her case while Kate was out.

Tammy had swept into the office—her slender figure clothed in a chic designer dress and her honey-colored hair pulled back in a French braid. She had thrown Kate off balance both figuratively and literally by dragging her into a hug. Expensive perfume wafted around Kate's head as the young woman aimed air kisses in the direction of her cheeks.

Tammy was basically a nice person, but she often failed to deal well with anger. Today had been no exception. The smiles were quickly replaced with passive-aggressive barbs. Sally, of course, was a great therapist, but Tammy felt that the director's blunt style was not really right for her. She hadn't made much progress in the last few months. And of course she understood how important it was that Kate stay home with her baby—after all she was a stay-at-home mom herself— but it had been so disruptive to her healing process.

Kate wasn't sure that her concept of stay-at-home motherhood and this woman's were quite the same. Tammy had a household staff of four people and she rarely mentioned her three-year-old son, with whom she seemed to spend very little time.

Don't get defensive, go with the resistance, Kate had reminded herself.

Clients often felt abandoned and angry when their therapists got sick, took vacations or went on maternity leave. It was illogical but somewhat understandable, since the therapist was a major source of support and sometimes their main lifeline to sanity. And the very nature of the one-way therapeutic relationship encouraged clients to *not* think about their therapist's life or needs.

Ignoring the barbs, she had told Tammy that she was glad to be back at work, and then had asked how the young woman was dealing with her dysfunctional extended family. That had successfully moved the focus off of her and onto the client's life where it belonged.

As Kate ate her sandwich, she shifted mental gears to her first client of the afternoon. She was particularly fond of Audrey Spaulding. She'd worked with her two years ago on issues related to verbal and emotional abuse by her parents. Astute and down-to-earth, Audrey assessed the problem, looked for a solution and then implemented it.

Her father had also been physically abusive when he'd gone on one of his frequent drinking binges. The old man, as Audrey called him, had been sober for the last five years, but he was what Kate's colleagues in the addictions recovery field referred to as a *dry drunk*. He was sober but had done nothing to understand or truly recover from his addiction. Both he and his codependent wife were still very unhealthy people.

When Kate went out to the waiting area after lunch, she was shocked by the young woman's appearance. Audrey's jeans and cotton shirt were wrinkled, her short brown hair uncombed. There were dark circles under her eyes, and she had lost weight that she could ill afford to lose. Kate struggled to hide her alarm at the client's disheveled state as she ushered her into her office.

It quickly became apparent that Audrey's personality hadn't changed even if her grooming had gone downhill. After a short exchange of pleasantries, she got down to business. "Here's the problem. Ted and I have decided it's time to give Alicia a little brother or sister. But ever since we started trying to get pregnant, I've developed less and less interest in sex... And then about a month ago, I started having weird dreams. I wake up, and can't get back to sleep."

"What are the dreams about?" Kate asked.

"Well, the first ones were all different kinds of situations where I felt threatened by something, and I'd try to hide, but I'd have this feeling that whatever it was would still find me. Then two weeks ago, I dreamt that somebody was trying to force something down my throat. I woke up choking and sobbing. Totally freaked Ted out."

Audrey dropped her gaze to her lap. "I've had some variation of that dream almost every night since then. It's all a bit shadowy. I can't tell who it is. It's like a big giant or monster, and I'm real small by comparison. Whatever's going on..." Desperation crept into her voice as she looked up again. "I just knew I couldn't face it by myself. I'm so glad you're back."

Choosing her words carefully, Kate asked, "When you were a child, did anyone ever physically do anything to you, or with you, that made you uncomfortable?"

One side of Audrey's mouth quirked up in a half smile. "Come on, Kate. You don't have to beat around the bush with me. No, I don't remember being sexually abused as a kid."

Kate had a short debate with herself. The symptoms the client described certainly suggested the possibility of sexual abuse. But these days, when therapists were being accused of planting false memories in people's minds, it was dangerous to probe too blatantly.

On the other hand, she hated that such considerations got in the way of doing good therapy. She knew this woman. Audrey would not think that she was trying to influence her memories.

"I wouldn't normally say this so bluntly with most clients, but sexual abuse would explain the problems you're having. And there is such a thing as traumatic amnesia, when an event is so upsetting that the person's mind blocks it from normal awareness. The memories are still in there somewhere, but the person can't access them."

"Is that what you think is going on with me?"

"I don't know, but it's a possibility," Kate said. As blocked memories started to surface, they did sometimes show up first in dreams. But by themselves, dreams were not a reliable source of information.

"You said all this began when you decided to have another baby?"

"Yeah." The young woman looked down at her lap again. "It started feeling like I *had* to have sex. It wasn't spontaneous anymore, and I started feeling resistant. And then I'd say to myself, 'Well, you can't get pregnant without having sex' and I'd try to push past the feelings, but it just got worse."

That made sense to Kate. If indeed Audrey had been forced into some kind of sexual activity as a child, feeling like she was now *forced* to have sex might very well stir up those old feelings and memories. But she decided not to say anything more for now. She didn't want to sound like she was pushing the idea of abuse.

"Audrey, whatever this is, we'll figure it out. But for now, I would suggest that you stop *trying* to get pregnant, at least for a month or two, until we get a handle on this stuff. Just relax and don't worry about that for a while. Okay?"

The woman nodded reluctantly.

"I'd also like you to keep a journal. Write down any thoughts, feelings, dreams, anything that's the least bit unusual or disturbing. We may begin to see a pattern that will help us sort this out."

Kate ended the session with more reassurances that whatever was going on, Audrey didn't have to face it alone. They would get through it together. It was a promise she frequently made to her clients, that she would walk the path with them, sticking by them until they didn't need her anymore.

But in this case, she wondered if that promise would be harder than usual to keep.

CHAPTER TWO

Wednesday morning, the baby slept a whole half hour past her usual wake-up time.

Oh, bliss!

Kate had never sufficiently appreciated a full eight hours of sleep until she became a parent.

While feeding the baby her cereal, she planned her day off. Maybe they would start with a walk around the block so she and Edie could both get some fresh air before the heat of the day became too intense.

The little girl was gobbling down her last spoonful of oatmeal when the phone rang. Well experienced at maternal multitasking, Kate reached back to the kitchen counter to snag the portable phone while her other hand scattered bite-sized pieces of fruit on Edie's highchair tray. The child would only eat about half of them but she would entertain herself by smearing the others on her face and into her hair.

"Girl, you don't waste any time," the counseling center's receptionist said in her ear. Pauline's tone was teasing. "One day back and you've already got folks falling apart on you."

Kate sighed. *So much for a peaceful morning with Edie.*

This was yet another downside to her job, having her personal life interrupted by client emergencies. "Who is it and what's their number?"

"Audrey. But she didn't ask that you call her back. She wanted to know if she could get in to see you before her appointment next week. You have a hole in your schedule tomorrow but I wanted to check with you first." The sixty-two-year-old woman had been the center's receptionist for well over a decade and had picked up on some of the nuances of counseling, one of which was the need to not encourage too much dependency in clients.

But Kate had no such concerns with Audrey. She wasn't the type to become overly dependent on anybody. Indeed, the woman's independent nature was one of the reasons she and Kate clicked so well; they shared that trait.

"Yes, plug her into the opening tomorrow."

When Audrey arrived for her session the next morning, the young woman looked even worse than she had two days ago. After a quick greeting, she abruptly said, "I think you're right. I think I was sexually abused."

"Oh?" Sometimes the less a therapist said the better.

"Yeah, I've started having flashes of images, like the dreams, but it's when I'm awake. Do you think those are the memories coming up?"

"Possibly. But we need to go cautiously here. Human memory is a bit fickle and susceptible to suggestion."

"Wait a minute! First you tell me you think I was abused, and now you're backpedaling?"

"No, not at all," Kate said. "But I don't want you to force the issue and *try* to remember something, because then you may not be able to trust whatever comes up."

"All I know is that since I started having these memories, images... whatever the hell they are, I've been incredibly anxious. Tuesday, after our session, I felt like I was jumping out of my skin. Then that evening, I actually started running from room to room as if I was trying to get away from something. Fortunately, Ted wasn't home and Alicia was in bed."

"Well, that does support the idea that something real is trying to surface. Something you were imagining wouldn't have that strong an emotional charge on it."

"Either that or I'm just plain losing it." The young woman paused. "Sorry for snapping at you, Kate. You're not the one I'm angry with."

"Who are you angry at?"

"The son of a bitch who did whatever he did to me!"

"Is it like in the dreams, you can't see the face?"

"Yeah, just this big body looming over me. But it looks like a man's body." Audrey closed her eyes for a moment. "Actually it's... he's built like my father. Or it could be creepy Uncle Phil. He looks a lot like my father. But my gut says it's the old man."

"Again, we need to be careful not to jump from speculation to reality here."

"I know, I know." Tears sprang into Audrey's eyes. She slammed her fist down on the arm of her chair. "Damn that son of a bitch! Here I had all that stuff about him and Mother all put to rest, tied up in a nice little package, and I was getting on with my life. Really feeling *good* most of the time, and now this crap."

Kate wasn't surprised by her outburst. It was called trauma recovery, rather than cure, for a reason. You were never sure if you'd gotten through it all. The past could come back to haunt you again, as new issues came up or buried pieces of the trauma were triggered by life events.

She reassured Audrey that her reaction was normal and understandable, then said, "One thing I never have to worry about with you, like I do with some of my clients. You don't have any trouble getting in touch with your anger."

That got a small smile out of the woman.

"But we need to proceed carefully, not jump to conclusions. Your father could be the abuser, or your uncle or someone else entirely. We just don't know yet."

"I do understand all that," Audrey said. "But I really need to figure this out. I can't wait forever to have a second child. I'm already thirty-three."

"I know you're not the type of person who waits around for something to happen; you make it happen. It's one of the things I admire about you." Kate leaned forward. "But you may have a bit of a challenge here. You may have to learn to be patient."

Audrey snorted. "Yeah, not exactly one of my strengths. But I'll try."

As the session was winding down, she told Kate that she had decided not to let her parents babysit her daughter anymore. Kate wholeheartedly agreed with that decision.

Then Audrey said, "Can I see you twice a week for a while? Ted just got a raise and he said he wants me to get whatever help I need to get through this."

Kate suppressed a smile.

So much for patience.

Out loud she said, "There may be times when it would be better to let something percolate for a while. But yes, for now, we can do that."

———◦———

At noon, Kate was sitting in her favorite booth at Mac's Place in the center of Towson. Both Rob and Liz Franklin were joining her for what Liz had dubbed her return-to-adulthood luncheon.

Kate had arrived a bit early. Enjoying the opportunity to relax for a few minutes, she closed her eyes and took a deep breath. She loved the way the restaurant smelled. There were the delicious fragrances of Old Bay seasoning and crabmeat that made her mouth water for one of Mac's excellent Maryland crab cakes.

But the non-food smells were part of the bouquet for her as well, even the slight mustiness of the stuffing peeking out of a crack in the brown vinyl of her bench. They evoked pleasant memories of the days when Mac Reilly's parents and her own had been best friends. Kate and her siblings had often played hide-and-seek with Mac amongst the booths and tables of what had then been called Reilly's Pub.

Rose Hernandez broke into Kate's reverie about childhood games by dropping onto the bench across from her.

"Hey, Rose, what's up?"

"Just hanging around, helping Mac out," Rose said. Her black silky hair was pulled back in a tight bun and her short, compact body was encased in snug jeans and a peach knit top that made her skin glow.

Come to think of it, whenever she wears that top, Mac glows as well.

"Rob coming?" Rose asked.

"He should be here any minute. Liz, too."

"Skip told you the news, right?"

"Yes." Kate grinned at her friend. "But I'll let you tell them."

"Tell us what?" Rob asked.

Rose got up and moved around the table to sit next to Kate, giving Rob the opposite bench to himself. At six-two, with middle age spread gaining on him, he took up a fair amount of space.

"You're looking at the proud co-owner of Canfield and Hernandez, Private Investigations." Rose flashed one of her rare smiles that transformed her rather ordinary face into a vision of radiant beauty.

"Wow! Congratulations," Rob said. "But I thought you didn't have your PI license yet."

"I don't. Skip insisted on putting my name on the door anyway. Figuratively speaking that is. We don't have an office yet. We get established, then it's bye-bye Baltimore County Police Department, hello independence."

She stood up. "You guys want your usual?"

"Yeah, and a duplicate of Kate's for Liz," Rob said.

Rose went off to place their order.

Liz arrived a moment later and slid in beside her husband. As Rob told her the news about Skip's and Rose's new venture, Kate studied her friends from across the table. Petite Liz looked almost like a child next to Rob's bulk. Her smooth complexion, mischievous green eyes and short strawberry blonde hair belied her age–just a year younger than his forty-eight. Indeed the salt that now dominated the pepper in his hair made Rob look a bit older than his years. But he refused to dye it, saying the distinguished look gave him an advantage in the courtroom.

Kate and Rob had started out as work buddies. His law firm was just down the hall from the counseling center, and through the years he had helped many of Kate's clients deal with the legal messes in their lives. As the relationship had evolved into friendship, they'd started socializing outside the office, along with their spouses. Then in the weeks after Eddie's death, when his murderer had made multiple attempts to kill them as well, Kate and the Franklins had been to hell and back together. Like soldiers in combat, they had forged a bond that was sometimes hard for others to fathom.

They explained their relationship, when they felt someone merited an explanation, as that of brother and sister, but Kate was actually closer to Rob than she was to her siblings, even her sister, Mary. After what they had been through together, they were more like twins, or at least what she imagined most twins experienced–a sense of connection that often did not require words.

She realized that Liz was talking to her. "Have you seen their new office?"

"They don't have one yet. They're working out of their apartments, trying to save on overhead. Rose is staying on the force for a while, but Skip has already quit his job." Kate hesitated for a beat. "I tried to lend him some money, to ease the squeeze while they got things rolling, but he wouldn't take it."

Skip's refusal of her money should have reassured Rob of the man's good intentions, but he was frowning. Liz made eye contact with Kate and rolled her eyes. Neither of them quite understood why he was having so much trouble accepting Skip.

Liz changed the subject. "So how's it feel to be back at work?"

"Good, well, mostly good," Kate said. "It feels great to be making a difference in people's lives again. I mean, being home with Edie was making a difference in her life, but... I'm not saying this very well. I guess it feels like I'm doing my part to make the world better, one psyche at a time."

Rob reached across the table and gently poked her chin to move her face to the side, then nudged it around to the other side.

She pulled back a little, laughing. "What are you doing?"

"Trying to decide which is your best profile for the publicity photos, when the governor names you Caped Crusader of the Year."

Kate stuck her tongue out at him.

Liz chuckled. "Now children, behave."

A waitress arrived, depositing their crab cake sandwiches on the table, with fries for Rob and side salads for Kate and Liz. Rob stole the pickle slices off both women's plates to add to his own pile.

A short, wiry man with a brown buzz cut and bright, blue eyes appeared next to their booth. The apron that covered a good part of his T-shirt and jeans provided a visual guide to the day's specials. "Hey, Rob, Liz," Mac greeted them. "So you're back in the saddle, huh, sweet pea. How's it goin'?"

Rob started singing the Batman theme song. "Dinna-dinna-din-na-dinna, dinna-dinna-dinna-dinna, Caped Kate!"

Snorting, Kate inhaled part of the bite of crab cake she had just taken. As she coughed into her napkin, she located Rob's shin under the table and gently kicked him.

She took a sip of iced tea. "It's going good, Mac, for the most part."

He nodded, just as a busboy frantically waved at him from the kitchen doorway. "Later, gang." Mac took off to deal with whatever calamity was brewing behind the scenes.

Rob raised an eyebrow at her. "For the most part?"

"Well, I'm totally enjoying the stuff I've always loved about my work. But I had forgotten some of the not-so-fun things, like the no-shows and the emergency calls on my day off. I feel like I've jumped back in the water at the deep end of the pool instead of easing in at the shallow end."

———◦———

Kate was reminded of that comment the next morning when she arrived at the center. She had been anticipating a short and relatively easy Friday, but Pauline informed her that Tammy Wingate had called in a panic, demanding to be seen today. "I told her you might have an opening but I would have to get back to her."

Kate heaved a sigh. "Okay, see if she can come in at four."

There goes my short, easy day.

At noon, she was ushering her last morning client out of her office when she spotted Tammy in the waiting room. The young woman rushed over.

"Kate, I'm sorry, I just couldn't wait until this afternoon. Can I take you out to lunch?"

"Uh, I brought my lunch today. We can talk for a little bit while I eat." It was against the code of ethics for a therapist to socialize with clients, and Kate wasn't about to encourage this woman to start thinking of her as a friend.

Tammy followed her into her office. Rather than going to the sitting area in the corner where she normally talked to clients, Kate sat down behind her desk and made a show of unwrapping her sandwich. She had no intentions of eating while dealing with a client in crisis, but she wanted to make the point that Tammy was crossing a line by intruding on her lunch break.

As soon as the woman was seated next to Kate's desk, she put her face in her hands and burst into tears. "Mark wants a divorce. I just know he does."

"Did he say that?"

"No, but he said I was driving him crazy and he had to get away from me." Tammy looked up, streaks of mascara on her cheeks. "I was just trying to get him to understand that he needs to spend more time with me." Her voice broke on another sob.

Kate was not the least bit surprised that the man found his wife's moodiness crazy-making. She suspected, however, that Tammy was overreacting.

"So what happened after he said he had to get away from you?"

"He left for work."

"Did he give any indication that he didn't intend to come home again?"

"No," Tammy said in a small voice. "He, uh...said he'd be late tonight."

"So maybe he just meant he had to get away temporarily before you got into a bigger fight."

"Well, the big fight had already happened."

"Oh?"

"Yeah, we'd been yelling at each other for a while when he slapped me."

Kate sat forward in her chair. This was a whole other kettle of fish. "Has he done that before?"

"Only once. A long time ago. I, uh, threw something at him. I wasn't really aiming at him, but my dumb luck, it hit him. And then he... Well, he didn't exactly hit me. He grabbed my arm and shook me."

If that was truly all that had happened, did one grab and shake plus a slap, over a five-year marriage, make Mark Wingate a wife-batterer? Or was he just an average guy who was having difficulty dealing with his wife's volatile moods? Although there were parts of Tammy's personality that Kate found endearing, she had trouble imagining anyone being able to tolerate the woman 24/7.

"Okay, Tammy, this is what I would like to do. I want to schedule a couples' session for the two of you so we can hash this out."

And so I can figure out if this guy's a wife-beater.

She handed the client a tissue. "In the meantime, I think you could both use a little emotional space. I would suggest that you *not* try to force him to pay attention to you. I plan to address with him the fact that you need more of his time and attention. He may hear it better coming from a third party."

After Kate had ushered the young woman out of her office, she put Tammy's file in her briefcase. Although she sometimes worked on insurance forms in the evenings, she rarely took other aspects of her work home. The only way you could stay sane yourself, doing this kind of intense work with people, was to compartmentalize.

But tonight, after Edie was in bed, she was going to sit down with Tammy's file and give some serious thought to her diagnosis. It was looking more and more like the woman might have borderline personality disorder. The neediness and volatile moods, the rather distorted perception of reality and lack of awareness of interpersonal boundaries were all signs of that disorder. And Tammy certainly had the family history that could cause it—a physically and sexually abusive father and a cold and controlling mother, both of them hard-core alcoholics.

Borderlines were tough cases to work with, but Kate was usually able to see beneath the annoying symptoms and connect with the more loveable but very wounded child inside the demanding, volatile adult.

She glanced at her watch. *Damn!* Only ten minutes left in her lunch break, and she had a phone call she absolutely had to return. Kate wolfed down half a sandwich as she punched in the number on her desk phone.

The following Tuesday was Kate's first long work day. She saw clients from ten a.m. until seven-thirty p.m. The evening hours were necessary to accommodate those clients who worked nine to five.

Her last session of the night was with the Wingates. It produced mixed results.

Mark was definitely a Type A who spent way more time at work than at home, but he came across as a nice guy who seemed to genuinely love his beautiful but intense wife.

Kate brought up the slap during their fight the previous week.

His response was quick. "I'm really sorry I lost my temper like that. I was raised to never hit a woman."

He sounded sincere—no defensiveness nor blaming his wife for provoking him. Either he wasn't abusive by nature, or he was clever enough to hide the telltale signs.

Kate explained to Mark that Tammy's roller-coaster moods were mostly about the feelings being dredged up from her abusive past. He seemed to understand that, nodding sympathetically while he held his wife's hand.

But she wasn't sure he got it that Tammy needed more than pretty baubles from him. Kate knew she might not get the workaholic to agree to another session, so she took the risk of being fairly confrontive with him. She pointed out that his inattentiveness was rubbing salt in the wounds from his wife's childhood, when her parents had essentially met none of her needs.

Mark Wingate listened politely, a serious expression on his face. Again, no defensiveness.

But Kate had no idea to what degree her words had sunk in.

CHAPTER THREE

Kate was having an intense Friday. What had she been thinking when she'd scheduled her two toughest cases back to back?

Her ten o'clock session with Tammy had not gone well. The benefits from the couples' session two weeks ago had been short-lived. The Wingates' marriage had deteriorated into a series of screaming matches that often ended with flying objects and an exchange of slaps. Kate had strongly recommended couples counseling. She'd also suggested that the client consider a temporary separation before the violence escalated further.

Tammy had been offended that Kate would even suggest such a thing.

Then Audrey Spaulding had come close to having a full-blown anxiety attack during her session, while recounting the flashbacks she was having. The face was still fuzzy but Audrey was convinced, based on the shape of his body and the way he moved, that the abuser was either her father or her uncle.

Suddenly the woman had started trembling violently. Her voice child-like, she'd said, "He keeps saying he has a lollipop for me, and I'm so scared."

Kate had held Audrey's hand to ground her, repeating over and over that she was safe now, until the anxiety had finally subsided. Then she'd attempted to assuage the young woman's embarrassment by explaining that regression was common when one was experiencing a flashback.

She waited until Audrey went through the outer door of the center, then she blew out air. Pauline waved her over to her desk and informed her that her one o'clock client had cancelled.

Kate was secretly relieved.

Deciding to take a walk, she pulled out the sneakers she kept in her bottom desk drawer for just such rare opportunities. Between bites of her sandwich, she tugged them on and tied them.

The mid-September day was gorgeous. Looking forward to these few weeks of Indian summer was all that made the oppressive heat and humidity of August bearable for Marylanders. Kate ended up walking all the way to Mac's Place. She waved at him through the plate glass window, then strolled into the park across the street, in front of the Towson courthouse.

As it so often did these days, her mind turned to Skip. She was trying to figure out how she felt about him, but the intensity of the physical attraction was making that difficult. Did she love him, or was it mostly lust she was feeling?

After all, she'd been celibate for a year and a half, so naturally she would be getting, well, hungry. Her mind's eye conjured up an image of the man—soft hair flopping down into hazel eyes, easy-going grin, broad shoulders and muscular chest slimming down to narrow hips. She sucked in her breath and bit her lower lip.

Hungry, hell, I'm starving!

Skip's personality was a good complement to hers and she felt like she could be herself around him. But sometimes she would catch him looking at her with a longing expression that made her a bit uncomfortable. Were those looks just a sign of his attraction to her? Or were they indicators of a deeper unhealthy neediness? She definitely did not want or need a neurotic man in her life!

She wished she could talk to Rob about this. He was always her best sounding board, but he continued to be less than rational where Skip was concerned. Her chest ached a little at the thought that she couldn't discuss this important issue with her closest friend.

Wait a minute. Liz! That's who I can talk to about Skip.

As she headed back toward her office, she took out her cell phone and called Liz to set up a lunch date.

———◦———

By the end of the day, Kate was exhausted. She'd only been back to work a few weeks and hadn't completely adjusted yet to the new routine.

Not to mention you're pushing forty, she reminded herself as she stood next to her desk, trying to decide how many insurance forms she was willing to take home over the weekend.

Pauline knocked lightly on her half-open door. "Someone must have dropped this on my desk while I was in the ladies' room." She handed over a sealed envelope that had KATE written on the outside in big block letters.

Kate opened it. On the single sheet of paper inside were two sentences, also in big block letters. It took her tired mind a moment to digest the meaning of the words. Feeling lightheaded, she sat down hard in her chair.

"What? What is it?"

Kate put the note down on her desk and turned it around so the receptionist could read it.

Pauline's eyes went wide. "Shit, Kate!"

"My sentiments exactly. Has Sally left for the day?"

Pauline nodded.

"Can you check to see if she has any time in her schedule on Monday to meet with me?" Kate hated to think what her boss's reaction would be.

A few minutes later, Kate came out of her office with only the note in her briefcase. Having lost all motivation to do paperwork over the weekend, she had locked the insurance forms in her file cabinet.

"Sally has a hole in her schedule at two on Monday," Pauline told her.

"Fill it with my name. I'll call her over the weekend but she's going to want to see the note and discuss it in more detail."

Pauline patted her arm. "Try to have a good weekend."

Down the hall, the hustle and bustle in the law offices of Bennett, Stockton and Franklin was only beginning to wind down for the weekend. Not that a law office is ever completely closed. Lawyers usually put in fifty to sixty-hour weeks, once they reach partner level. Associates pretty much live at the office.

The receptionist had gone for the day so Kate went directly to Rob's office. His door was ajar. She stuck her head through the opening.

Rob was standing at his desk, rummaging through papers. Glancing up, he said, "Come on in, Kate... Damn, I can't find that phone message." He looked back at his desk; then her grim expression must have blatantly registered. His head jerked up. "What's wrong?"

She headed for the chair in front of his desk. Halfway there she changed course, walking straight into his arms instead. Trying not to cry, she told him how the note had arrived and what it said, while he gently patted her back.

After a minute, she stepped away, shaking her head. "It's probably hitting me harder than it should because I've had such an intense week. Must be a full moon or something. Everybody's falling apart on me at once."

Rob steered her to his desk chair. "Can I see the note?"

She took it out of her briefcase. He held it by the edges and read it, saying the words softly out loud. "She lies, you know. She's tearing us apart with her lies and your helping her."

"*You're* is misspelled," Kate said lamely.

Rob perched on the corner of his desk, laying the note down next to him. "Do you know who might have sent this?"

Kate shook her head. "Not a clue. I'm going to meet with Sally on Monday. Maybe if we go over my cases we'll be able to figure it out."

"You should call the police," Rob said.

"I can't do–"

He held up his hand. "I know, I know. It wouldn't do much good."

She shook her head in frustration. She couldn't violate client confidentiality and give the police any names unless she was sure who had sent the note. And maybe not even then. The message wasn't overtly threatening.

"What do you want to do?" he asked.

"Besides change careers?" she said, only half joking.

"Yeah, besides that."

"Not much I can do. Can you think of anything?"

"Not really. You might want to file a report with the police, just in case anything else happens."

"Maybe. I'll have to wait until I talk to Sally. See if she wants to do that."

Rob invited her to come over to the house for dinner and some moral support. But she was too exhausted to think about going out that evening. She thanked him for the thought.

Halfway home, Kate was wishing she had accepted the invitation. After Maria retired to her third-floor rooms and the baby was in bed, the evening would be long and lonely.

She pulled up in front of her house but didn't get out of the car. Digging her cell phone out of her purse, she called Skip. When he answered, she said without preamble, "If I ask you to come over this evening, do you promise not to take advantage of my weakened state?"

He chuckled. "I try not to make promises I'm not sure I can keep, but I'll make every effort to restrain myself."

Kate didn't say anything.

"You okay?"

"No."

"What's the matter?" Alarm in his voice.

"I'd rather not get into it over the phone. I just need... a friend."

"Be there in fifteen minutes."

When Kate opened her door, Skip tried to read her face. Other than looking unhappy, her expression gave no clue as to what was going on.

"What happened?"

She shook her head and stood back so he could step inside.

A short, plump woman bustled into the living room. She looked enough like Rose that he deduced she was Maria Hernandez even before Kate introduced them.

He chatted with Maria in Spanish as she herded them around the corner and into the kitchen. Edie was sitting in her highchair, happily smearing some food substance on her chubby cheeks.

"She's asking me to stay for dinner. Is that okay?" he said to Kate in a low voice.

"Of course. There's plenty, and don't worry, she made it." She gave him a rueful smile. "Cooking's not in her job description, but she took it over in self-defense. She always makes enough for an army on Friday nights, so I can eat the leftovers over the weekend."

"What's the matter?" he asked again.

"It can wait until after dinner." She paused, her eyes flitting away from him, then back to his face. "No point in spoiling our appetites. I, uh, feel better now that you're here."

Skip was surprised by the warmth that spread through his chest at those words.

Maria was setting another place at the table next to Edie's highchair.

"*Gracias, Maria.*" He sat down, then reached over to tickle the baby's neck. She rewarded him with a giggle and a big grin.

Kate helped Maria bring several fragrant bowls and platters to the big oak table. As they ate, Skip asked about the ingredients in the dishes he didn't recognize and translated Maria's replies for Kate.

She smiled at him. "Most of the time these days I have no clue what I'm eating. I just relax and enjoy."

He took advantage of Kate's lack of Spanish to ask Maria if she would be willing to put Edie to bed when they were finished eating. He was a patient man but there were limits.

He suspected that Kate understood some of the discussion. She narrowed her eyes at the word *bebé*, and didn't seem surprised when Maria wiped Edie's face and hands, then scooped her out of her highchair.

"You tire, Kate. I put *la niñita* bed. You talk *Señor* Skip."

"Tire-*d*," Kate gently corrected her English. "Thank you for putting the baby *to* bed, Maria. *Gracias.*" She leaned over and kissed Edie's cheek, then snuggled the child's neck. "Goodnight, little one."

As the stout little woman bustled out of the room with her babbling burden, Skip stood up and started clearing the table.

"You don't need to do that," Kate protested.

He ignored her and carried the stacked dishes to the sink. "Dishwasher dirty or clean?"

"It should be empty." Kate began putting plastic wrap over the leftovers.

When the dishes were rinsed and loaded, Skip said, "You *are* going to tell me what's going on eventually, aren't you? The suspense is killing me."

"Come on in the living room."

Kate motioned him to an armchair and pulled a sheet of paper out of her briefcase. She handed it to him, then sat down on the sofa.

He read the words on the paper.

SHE LIES YOU KNOW. SHE'S TEARING US APART WITH HER LIES AND YOUR HELPING HER.

He read the note, then held up the sheet, unsure where to put it. "You have any idea who sent this?"

Kate shook her head and pointed to her briefcase sitting on the floor. He slid the note into it.

"I'm probably overreacting," she said. "It's been a long and stressful week. It's not like the note's really threatening. I guess it's just disturbing, is all."

"I'll say it's disturbing. They won't be able to do anything about it, but you should file a police report, just in case."

"Yeah, that's pretty much verbatim what Rob said."

Skip tried to suppress the frown, but apparently he failed.

"Look, I'm too damned tired tonight to deal with–" She stopped, then continued in a more neutral tone. "Sorry. Look, he works right down the hall from me. I wanted his legal advice. *And* some emotional support."

Then her voice lost all of its annoyed edge and dropped to a whisper. "But when I started for home, I..." She trailed off and looked away from him.

Skip stood up and walked to her chair. He squatted down beside it. "I'm honored, Kate, that you wanted my advice and support as well."

She stared at him for a beat. "Damn it, how is it that you always manage to say just the right thing?"

He gave her one of his slow, easy grins. "It's a gift." Then softly he added, "What can I do to help?"

"I don't know. Well, actually I do, but everything I can think of involves touching. It's already helped a lot just having you here."

"Darlin', first and foremost, I *am* your friend. I will *always* be here when you need me."

She gave him a small smile. "Thank you for putting up with me."

They decided to watch a video. Kate apologized that all she had were sappy chick flicks. "When I watch TV, I want total escapism."

"Sappy chick flick works for me. Here, you stretch out and get comfy."

The movie was actually fairly entertaining. She chuckled once at the antics of the characters.

He glanced her way. Her eyelids were at half-mast and she looked totally relaxed.

He quietly blew out air.

By the time the credits were rolling, she was sound asleep. He called across to her. "Kate, oh, Kay-ate."

She opened her eyes.

"I'd offer to carry you to your bed, but I'm assuming that would be a bad idea."

She smiled and sat up on the sofa. "Good idea, wrong timing."

"I know, still too soon," he said, without the falsetto this time.

She stood up to walk him to the door, opening it and stepping back to put a few feet between them. When he was out on the porch, she said, "I meant it, Skip. I really appreciate you putting up with me. I wish..." Her voice trailed off and she dropped her gaze.

Again, the warmth spread through his chest. He reached out and put a finger under her chin. When she looked up at him, he smiled. "Kate, the waiting is hard to put up with, but you're not. I enjoy every minute I spend with you. Goodnight, darlin'."

CHAPTER FOUR

The next morning, Kate tried to convince herself the note had just been a bad dream. Reality came crashing back when Edie crawled across the floor toward her open briefcase by the sofa. Lifting the case out of the baby's reach, Kate took the note out and sat down on the sofa. She stared at the big letters, but they told her no more than they had the night before.

Oh, Eddie, what should I do?

After a minute she decided he wasn't going to answer her. What did she expect? The two flesh-and-blood men in her life had no suggestions other than filing a police report, so why did she think her dead husband would be able to help?

She put the note back in her briefcase and pushed up off the sofa. Scooping Edie up, she headed for the nursery to change her. They were meeting Liz for lunch.

At least there was one less thing she needed to sort out. Skip's actions last night had convinced her that he wasn't the neurotic one. If he seemed to be occasionally, it was because *she* was driving him crazy with the waiting.

An hour later, Liz was carrying the baby on her hip across the restaurant parking lot while making faces at her. Edie was chortling with delight.

"Why didn't you want to go to Mac's Place?" Liz asked as Kate opened the restaurant door for her.

"I wanted to talk to you about something that I don't want Rose or Mac to overhear." They joined a short line of people waiting to be seated. It was a little before noon but the Italian restaurant was already a bit crowded.

Liz nodded. "Do you think it's too chilly to sit outside?"

Kate glanced at the almost-deserted patio. "Good idea. Then we don't have to worry so much about her making noise and disturbing people."

They followed the hostess to the patio and took a table in the warm September sun. Kate dug sunscreen out of the diaper bag and put it on the baby's face.

"So what did you want to talk about?" Liz asked, once they had given the waitress their drink orders.

"Skip," Kate answered succinctly.

"Oh, ho!"

"Yeah, oh, ho. I hope you don't mind me using you as a sounding board. I can't–"

"Of course not," Liz interrupted. "To my mind, one of the best things about being a woman is talking about men with other women. They are such fascinating creatures, aren't they?"

Kate laughed out loud as she was breaking up a cracker on the highchair tray to keep Edie occupied. The child started obliterating the pieces with her little fist.

"And the one I'm married to is being a bit obstinate, in my opinion, about not accepting that you and Skip are an item now," Liz said.

Kate resisted the temptation to probe Liz's thoughts on why Rob was reacting that way. She wanted to get her feelings sorted out about Skip first.

"Well, that's the question actually. Are we an item now?"

"Looks like a duck. Quacks like a duck."

"Yeah, but the ducks never touch each other."

Liz raised her eyebrows. "And whose choice is that?"

"Mine at this point. Although I'm not sure *choice* is the right word. It's just too soon to go there."

"And where would you be going, besides to bed?"

"That's the crux of the matter."

The waitress arrived with glasses of iced tea and bread sticks. They ordered their food. Kate wiped most of the oil and garlic off of a bread stick and gave it to Edie to gnaw on.

When the waitress had left, Liz repeated her question. "So where would you be going?"

"I think we would go from zero to sixty faster than a NASCAR driver. I know holding him at arm's length is the right thing to do, until I've finished letting go of Eddie, but the side effect of that is we're..."

"Building up a lot of desire," Liz finished for her. She paused, then asked, "So how do you feel about him when you're *not* craving his body?"

"That's what I'm not sure about. It's hard to get past the lust, to sort that out. I enjoy his company. He's easy to be around. And he almost always gets me. He understands who I am."

"Sounds like a good start," Liz said. "How well do you know him?"

"Fairly well, I think, although you never know somebody completely."

"Tell me about it! Every once in a while, Rob still surprises me, even after all these years. His reaction to Skip, for example."

Again resisting the temptation to discuss Rob, Kate said, "We've been getting together almost every week, and we talk most evenings. I think we've talked about everything under the sun by now."

"Do you miss him when you can't get together for a while?"

Kate nodded.

Liz grinned. "Quack, quack."

The waitress arrived with their soup. She smiled at Edie as she handed Kate a pile of extra napkins.

Kate returned the smile and thanked her.

"So have you found anything about him that you don't like?" Liz asked, once the waitress had gone.

"No, and trust me, I've been looking. I see enough rotten relationships in my office to know what to watch out for. He's not the least bit controlling or possessive, although he gets a little jealous of Rob sometimes, of how close we are. But when I call him on it, he immediately backs off. He's just this incredibly nice, easy-going guy, with a great sense of humor and a quick mind."

Liz had been watching her face closely as she talked. Now she put her spoon down and covered Kate's hand on the table. "Sweetheart, you sound and look like a woman in love to me. And from everything I've seen, Skip is a great guy."

Kate squeezed her friend's hand, then let it go to wipe down another bread stick for Edie. The child had turned the first one into soggy pulp, ingesting about a third of it and smearing the rest on her highchair tray.

"Yeah, I keep telling myself I'm half in love with him, but I think I'm all the way there."

"And how does it feel to say that out loud?"

Kate laughed. "Liz, if you ever get tired of being an actuary, you should become a therapist. You'd be great at it. But to answer your question, it feels okay. Good even. Somehow it's not so scary to admit it. Not as scary as thinking to myself that I *might* be in love. Is this making sense?"

"Yeah, it is, but don't ask me to explain it back to you. So then why is it still too soon?"

Kate scooped up a spoonful of minestrone to buy some time. The answer to that was because she still talked to Eddie in her head, but that wasn't something she was willing to share, even with Liz.

"It just feels like I need to let go of Eddie more. It would be so unfair to Skip, if we *officially* became an item, and he was still in competition with..." She couldn't make herself say *a dead man* out loud. "With my late husband."

Liz nodded.

Of course when their entrees arrive, Edie chose that moment to get fussy. Kate pulled out a toy. The baby started happily banging the ring of oversized plastic keys on her highchair.

Trying to ignore the racket, they worked on their food for a few minutes. Then Liz said, "So you don't want to talk about Rob, huh?"

"Actually I'd like to hear your take on why he's reacting the way he is. I just wanted to sort out my thoughts about Skip first, knowing that the munchkin here would only give us so much time for serious conversation."

"I wish I had a good take on it, Kate. It's something he's been resistant to talking about."

"With me as well. Last summer, my sense was that it was a knee-jerk reaction like a father or brother would have. Who is this guy who wants to date my sister?"

"It doesn't have that feel to it anymore, though," Liz said. "Best read I can get is that he's just plain terrified that you'll get your heart broken."

"It's funny but I'm *not* afraid of that. It's possible that things won't work out with Skip but I know he would never do anything to hurt me."

The baby started to fuss again. Liz stood up. "I'll get her. I'm finished eating." She lifted the baby out of her highchair and started walking back and forth, bouncing the child in her arms.

Kate's fork froze halfway to her mouth as another thought took her breath away.

Liz glanced her way and stopped walking.

Kate whispered, "There's another reason I've been holding Skip at arm's length."

"What's that?"

Her heart pounded in her chest as she looked up at Liz. "I'm not the least bit afraid that Skip will hurt me. But I'm *terrified* that he'll die on me, like Eddie did."

———◇———

On Monday, Kate could no longer ignore the issue of the note. She made a special trip to the center for her meeting with Sally.

After examining the note, her boss said, "Any clue who this is from?"

"Actually, yeah. A few possibilities occurred to me over the weekend. I have two clients who are in the process of getting a divorce. Could be one of their soon-to-be-ex-spouses. Or... Do you remember Tammy Wingate?"

Sally caught herself in mid eye-roll.

Kate suppressed a grin. Her boss–a tall, elegant black woman with a cap of curly gray hair– was the quintessential professional, and she was the most no-nonsense person Kate had ever known. At the moment, those two aspects of her personality seemed to be in conflict.

"Tammy doesn't lie *per se*," Kate said. "But she often over-reacts and misinterprets reality. And she and her husband have been fighting like cats and dogs lately."

Sally's eyebrows went up. "She's exhibiting borderline tendencies?"

"Actually she meets the criteria for the full-blown disorder. I've only met the husband one time. He didn't strike me as someone so unstable he would send anonymous notes to his wife's therapist, but I did confront him about his emotional neglect of his wife. And Tammy's reported some violence, slapping and throwing things, on both their parts."

"So he's an abuser," Sally said bluntly. "That would qualify him as unstable enough to send nasty notes in my book."

Kate paused to choose her words. "I know it's not politically correct for therapists to ever excuse or minimize a man raising his hand to a woman. But, quite frankly, Tammy is pretty damned intense. And isn't it a bit sexist of us to expect the man to remain nonviolent, when his woman is hurling objects at him? Maybe Mark Wingate is an abuser, or maybe Tammy just drives him to distraction."

Sally gave her a small nod. "Good point."

Kate passed along Rob's suggestion that they file a police report. Sally was resistant to the idea, for fear it would bring negative media attention to the center.

She got up and pulled a fresh file folder from a box on a shelf. After writing *Note to Kate* on its label, Sally slipped the sheet of paper inside and put it in her desk drawer. "Try not to worry about it, Kate. Whoever sent this is probably just trying to shake you up."

"I hate to admit it, but he's succeeded."

CHAPTER FIVE

It took awhile for Kate to put the note out of her mind. After two days of obsessing about it, she asked herself, *What would I tell a client to do?* After that, when thoughts of the note popped up, she recited the Serenity Prayer in her head, reminding herself that this fell into the category of that which she could not control.

Driving to work the first Tuesday of October, Kate realized she hadn't thought about the note at all the previous weekend. Not wanting to start obsessing about it now, she deliberately cast about for something else to occupy her brain.

Skip's smiling face immediately popped up in her mind's eye.

I'm really looking forward to Friday evening, Eddie.

Oops! That was a no-no. For some reason, Eddie never answered her when she tried to talk to him about Skip. Could ghosts get jealous?

I love you, Eddie, Kate reassured him.

I love you, too, came the echoing reply, a bit fainter than usual.

At the center, Pauline informed her that Audrey had called, practically in hysterics, asking if she could get in to see Kate that day.

"See if she can come in during my four-thirty break," Kate said. It would make her long day incredibly intense to work straight through the afternoon and evening, but Audrey was not the hysterical type. This could not be good.

When the woman arrived at four-thirty, she looked like she'd been in a train wreck. Her clothes were rumpled, her hair sticking up, her face tear-stained. In a shaky voice, she said, "I'm sorry, Kate, but I just had to see you."

"My God, what happened?" Kate led her to the sitting area and settled her on the loveseat.

Audrey's voice gradually steadied as she talked. The previous afternoon, she'd had yet another argument over the phone with her mother, when she'd refused to let Alicia spend the weekend at her grandparents' house. Her mother had kept demanding an explanation.

Audrey had finally told her that she was having dreams, and sometimes little flashbacks during the day, that her therapist thought might mean she had been sexually abused as a child. Then, not sure where to go from there–she didn't dare imply to her mother that she thought her abuser was her father or her uncle–she'd ad-libbed. The memories were vague and she didn't know who it was, but she thought it might have been one of her friends' fathers, during a sleep-over. Until she and her therapist could sort out the memories better, she just felt too uncomfortable letting Alicia spend the night away from home, even at her grandparents' house.

This explanation had seemed to appease her mother, but not her father. He'd called an hour later, yelling his usual litany of insults, that she was stupid, crazy, an ingrate.

She'd hung up on him, but the verbal abuse had set off her worst anxiety attack yet.

"When Ted came home from work, and saw the state I was in, he suggested I go out for a while. Go to Starbucks, get a latte and read." Kate knew this was something that often helped Audrey get herself grounded again.

"But when I got there, this man... He was sitting alone, minding his own business. But I could have sworn he wasn't wearing any pants. Just a tee shirt. I was afraid to look at him. I knew any minute he was going to turn toward me and..." She choked back a sob.

"I get the picture. Did you report him to the staff?"

"But that's just the thing, Kate. He *was* wearing pants. After a few minutes he got up to throw his coffee cup away and he had on khaki slacks. I had an anxiety attack, right there in Starbucks. It was all I could do to get home.

"And then it happened again. When we were getting ready for bed. Ted started to take his pants off and I freaked out. I went out and slept on the couch, or tried to sleep. I couldn't be around him, couldn't see him, couldn't stand the thought of him touching me." The words were coming fast now. "Oh, my God! I can't do this to him."

Kate went over to kneel beside Audrey's chair and gathered the sobbing woman into her arms. "Sh, sh, it's going to be okay. We'll get you through this. Ted and I are going to help you get through this. He's a good man, Audrey. He'll understand."

When she was finally relatively calm, they went over her journal entries from the weekend. There was one, about the man in the flashbacks wearing a plaid shirt, that Audrey didn't remember writing.

"That's not totally unusual," Kate reassured her. "I've had clients remember an entire memory one session, and by the next week, their minds have pushed it away again. That's why I have you keep the journal." Also when the client saw the words in their own handwriting, they couldn't say that Kate was making stuff up.

At the end of the session, she reminded Audrey that she should call the emergency number if she needed to talk the next day.

***

On Friday, Kate stood at her office window, admiring the reds and oranges of the changing leaves in the trees scattered around the back parking lot. Sighing, she turned and sank into her desk chair.

Thank God it's Friday!

She kicked off her shoes, then propped her feet up on the corner of her desk and unwrapped her sandwich. As she ate, her mind turned to her two toughest cases. Audrey was scheduled to come in that afternoon for her second session of the week. Hopefully her unconscious mind would cough up more pieces of the puzzle soon. Kate was toying with using an imagery technique she'd learned at a workshop a couple years ago. She would see how things went.

Tammy had recently had one productive session, right after the note incident. Kate had planned to ask if she'd mentioned the temporary separation idea to her husband. But Tammy had run into her abusive parents at a family wedding that week. The encounter had stirred up her anger, and for once she'd directed it toward the appropriate parties.

Kate had hoped the young woman would stay focused on the past long enough to get some issues resolved. But by the next session, she and Mark had fought again, and Tammy was back to ruminating about his neglect.

A light rap of knuckles on her door startled Kate back to the present. "Come in."

Sally entered the office, closing the door behind her. She was holding an envelope.

Kate tossed the remainder of her sandwich onto her desk. Suddenly she didn't feel so good. She dropped her feet to the floor.

"Came in today's mail," Sally said. "No return address. Postmarked at Towson's main post office."

"Which tells us nothing." Kate tried to match her boss's matter-of-fact tone. She held out her hand.

The envelope was addressed to Sally Ford. The words on the sheet of paper inside were YOU NEED TO FIRE THAT KATE BITCH. SHE FILLS PEOPLE'S HEADS WITH LIES AND DESTROYS FAMILIES.

"Now I'm starting to wonder if this is the false memory crowd," Sally said.

Kate shuddered at the thought. In the nineties, several parents, who had been accused by their grown children of sexual abuse, had banded together to counter the accusations with the claim that false memories were being planted in their offspring's heads by inexperienced or unethical therapists. Since then many similar groups had sprung up around the country.

Sally flopped down in the chair next to Kate's desk. "I figured it was only a matter of time before they targeted us." Her tone was dejected.

Kate was a bit alarmed. Dignified and professional Sally Ford did not flop nor become dejected.

She wasn't sure what to say. If some local false memory group was sending the notes, then things were likely to get a lot worse. Some of these groups had gone after therapists in the trauma recovery field, filing lawsuits, picketing their offices. A couple therapists had even received death threats, although these could not be officially linked back to the false memory groups.

She sat silently, as she would with a client, but Sally continued to stare morosely out the window. Finally Kate said, "What do you want to do?" She wasn't afraid that Sally would fire her. She and her boss were not close but they had tremendous respect for each other and she knew Sally would not succumb to threats.

"I don't know. These notes are awfully vague. This could be about any of our cases, past or present."

Kate thought for a moment. "Has to be a current case. The first note was in the present tense. 'She lies. She's tearing us apart.' But you're right. What the notes are saying could apply to almost all of my cases." She was seeing a dozen survivors of childhood physical or sexual abuse, plus three women whose husbands were verbally and emotionally abusive. One of the things most abusers had in common was a phenomenal ability to distort reality, while accusing their victims of lying.

Sally pushed herself to a stand. "All we can do is hope that they stick to nasty-grams." She picked up the note and envelope and headed for the door.

At some point since Tuesday, Audrey's anxiety had shifted to anger. Kate spent the first half of their session that afternoon trying to convince the young woman that it was too soon to confront her parents about sexual abuse. She pointed out that Audrey's anger was natural and even healthy, and then spelled out her concerns about having such a confrontation.

Although Audrey was fairly convinced her abuser was her father, the face in the memories was still not clear. Something could come to light later that would point toward her uncle. *Hey, Dad, I think you molested me when I was a kid* weren't words one could easily take back.

Kate, unlike some of her colleagues, did not believe that direct confrontation of their abusers was the best way for abuse survivors to re-empower themselves. She pointed out to Audrey that all too often such confrontations backfired. The survivor could end up re-traumatized when other family members sided with the abuser, joining forces against the one who threatened their denial and the *status quo*.

She extracted a promise from the client that she wouldn't say anything to her parents until Kate felt she was ready to deal with the potential repercussions.

Kate paused for a moment, evaluating one last time whether or not the guided imagery technique she'd been contemplating was the best approach. She decided to go for it, hoping it would help the young woman vent some of her anger.

She explained what they were going to do. "Keep in mind now, that this is just in your imagination. I'm not advocating doing any of this in real life." This was not a technique she would use with someone who was unstable or the least bit violent, but she felt comfortable using it with Audrey.

Kate instructed her to close her eyes and take some deep breaths to relax, then visualize her father in her mind's eye. "What do you need to do so you feel safe venting your anger at him?"

After a pause, Audrey said in a low voice, "I need him to be tied up and gagged."

"Okay," Kate said softly. "Visualize him tied to a chair, and gagged. Now tell him exactly how you feel about him. Not out loud, but inside your head."

Eight minutes ticked by as Audrey silently yelled at the man.

When she saw her client's face begin to relax, Kate quietly said, "When you've told him everything you want to say, let me know how you want to end the scene."

Another pause. Audrey said, "I want to have him hauled away to jail."

"Then do that. Call the police and invite the little girl inside of you, the one that he hurt so much, invite her to stand beside you and watch him being dragged off to jail where he belongs. Hold her hand and watch the police arrest him and take him away."

Slowly a big smile spread across Audrey's face.

"Now give that little girl that you once were a hug, and tuck her back away inside of you," Kate quietly instructed.

Another moment went by. Then Audrey opened her eyes. "Wow, that was cool! How does that work?"

Kate hesitated, wondering if demystifying the technique would lessen its impact. Probably not for practical Audrey. "We don't know exactly. Often we stumble on therapeutic techniques that work, and then it takes researchers years to figure out why they work. But here's the theory."

She paused to figure out the most succinct way to explain it. "The right hemisphere of the brain tends to be more visual, and it's also where many emotions, especially the negative ones, are processed. So when we visualize something and then change the emotional charge on that image, the right hemisphere is satisfied. The left hemisphere is more language-oriented, and more logical. It knows what happened in the imagery isn't real, but the emotional charge is still changed."

Audrey grinned at her. "I'll say it's changed. That's the first time in my life that the old man *had* to listen to me."

Kate grinned back. She decided to wait until their next session to point out that confronting abusers in imagery is a lot safer and less stressful than real-life confrontations.

The imagery technique had been a success on two levels. Kate's earlier distress about the nasty-gram, as Sally had called it, had been displaced by the sense of accomplishment that comes with a job well done.

———◦———

When her last client was out the door, Kate grabbed her purse and briefcase and raced home. She and Skip were going out to dinner.

At the house, Samantha, the Franklin's seventeen-year-old daughter, had already arrived to babysit for Edie. Sam and the little girl were playing on the living room rug. Kate greeted the teenager and then hurried to her bedroom to change her clothes.

Skip was there when she finally emerged, after agonizing over what to wear—she wanted to look attractive, but not seductive. She'd settled on her favorite black sweater, dressed up with a string of pearls, over a simple gray skirt.

Skip gave her an appreciative smile.

After checking that Sam had her cell phone number, Kate headed out the door. "Did you have a restaurant in mind?" she said over her shoulder.

"Café Bianca okay?"

Kate froze at the top of the porch steps, then forced herself to move again.

Skip descended after her and fell into step with her on the sidewalk. "You used to go there with Ed," he said quietly.

Kate nodded mutely. They had reached Skip's Explorer at the curb before she felt she could trust her voice. "It was our favorite restaurant. We went there on our last anniversary, two weeks before he was killed."

Skip took her hand. "I'm sorry, Kate."

An electric jolt ran up her arm. She closed her eyes, fighting the urge to collapse into his arms. "It's okay. You didn't know."

He let go of her hand and opened the truck door for her. "Not exactly the way I'd planned to start the evening."

She smiled at him, feeling more secure now that the door was between them. "Want a do-over?"

He grinned back at her. "So, Kate, where would you like to go this evening?"

They decided on Chinese.

When their food arrived, Kate laughed at Skip's attempts to use chopsticks. He finally tossed them on the table and waved for the waiter to bring him a fork. "My hands are just too big and clumsy for those things."

"Your hands are not clumsy. I love your hands!"

Skip froze, his teacup halfway to his mouth. The gold flecks in his eyes danced.

Okay, that might not have been the best thing to say.

She changed the subject by asking him a question about his childhood. She never tired of hearing his stories of growing up in a small town in Texas. She especially loved the look in his eyes when he talked about his father, Reginald William Canfield, the second, after whom Skip was named.

When there was a lull in the conversation, Kate asked a question that had been on her mind for some time. Now that she was surer about her own feelings, she felt brave enough to ask it. "I've been wondering. It sounds like your folks had a great relationship, so I'm kind of curious as to why you've shied away from commitment?"

"Classic case of never met the right gal." Skip paused, then added, "Until now. Closest I ever came was the last woman I dated seriously."

His expression grew sad. "We were living together when my father got sick. I thought I should move back to Texas, but when I brought it up, she flipped out. How could I consider giving up my good job with the state troopers, and ask her to abandon her career? We fought about it, off and on, for a couple months. Then my sister called..." He looked up at the ceiling. His Adam's apple bobbed as he swallowed hard.

Kate only debated a second before reaching across the table and taking his hand.

"They never told me how far along the cancer was. My father didn't want me to disrupt my life, they said. So they'd pretended that he had more time than he did. I never even went home to see him, before..."

He pulled his hand free to search his pockets for his handkerchief, turning his head away from her.

She waited quietly.

He swiped at his red-rimmed eyes, then put away the handkerchief. "Can I have your hand back, by any chance?"

Kate reached across the table again. He put his palm against hers and their fingers entwined. A surge of energy–not sexual this time–flowed between their clasped hands. Her breath caught in her throat. She'd never felt so connected to anyone in her life.

Not even Eddie.

She tried to ignore the stab of guilt.

"I got a little crazy after my daddy died." Skip's voice was now thick with Texas. "Broke up with Carrie. Quit the force. Had me a good ole-fashioned mid-life crisis, a decade early. Bounced from job to job for a while. Eventually ended up as a bodyguard. I had finally gotten my act together and was working on getting my PI license, around the time Rob hired me to protect you from your husband's killer."

She'd already known a little about that period of his life, but he hadn't told her the whole story before. She gently squeezed his hand.

Neither spoke for a long moment. Then, so quietly she almost didn't hear him, he said, "Do you feel that?"

"Yes," she whispered, as she gently tugged her hand loose.

"Kate, I–"

"No! Don't go there yet." She reached over to touch his lips with her fingertips, then drew them back. "Soon... but not yet."

After a long pause, he asked, "Can we at least stop pretending that we're not dating?"

Her emotions were so stirred up, she couldn't think straight. "Can I get back to you on that?"

"Do I have a choice?" Frustration had crept into his voice.

"Yes, you do have a choice," she said softly. "But I'm praying you'll keep choosing to be a patient man."

"No, I do *not* have a choice. I could no more walk away from you than... fly to the moon."

"Oh, Skip, I'm sorry. This is so unfair to you. Of course it's silly to pretend we're not dating. But..." She stopped, not sure how to explain that she still wasn't ready for a physical relationship with him, not until she got Eddie out of her head.

His smile was gentle. "It's okay. We can leave the four-foot rule in place for a while."

She bit down on her lower lip, struggling with the temptation to reach for his hand again. Her heart wanted to reassure him that she loved him. Her head was saying that was a bad idea. Once those words were uttered, by either of them, there would be no backing up, except over the poor man's heart.

"I wish it didn't have to be this way," she said, her voice barely above a whisper. "But I think that's what we need to do, for a little while yet."

CHAPTER SIX

As Kate left work the last Friday of October, she was really looking forward to the weekend. The next night was the Franklins' annual Halloween party.

It was a tradition that Liz adored and her husband tolerated. Every year she came up with costumes for them. Rob's usually made him cringe. One year, she'd poked fun at his pickle addiction. His costume had been a kosher dill, hers a baby gherkin.

They had skipped last year. No one had the heart for it after Eddie's death. But two weeks ago, Liz had asked Kate how she would feel about resurrecting the tradition. Kate had insisted that she do so. Liz had countered by insisting that she invite Skip.

Kate detoured from her normal route home to make a stop at a costume store. As she drove, she thought once again about getting some grief counseling, to speed up the process of letting go of Eddie. It had been a month since she had admitted to Liz that she loved Skip, and three weeks since they had *officially* started dating. She was afraid he would run out of patience if she kept him at arm's length much longer.

But the thought of breaking the connection with Eddie once and for all made her heart ache. "Well, that's the point, Kate," she said out loud.

She'd tried to just not talk to Eddie, but she kept forgetting. Without forethought, she would find herself conversing with him again.

I love you, Kate, echoed faintly in the back of her head. Tears sprang to her eyes. She blinked them away and shook her head in frustration, as she turned into the shopping center's parking lot.

Once inside the store, she recalled how Rob had teasingly called her Caped Kate. She headed for the superheroes section. She was looking skeptically at a Wonder Woman costume, wondering if she had the nerve to wear the revealing outfit, when she noticed a Batman costume next to it on the rack. Thinking about Skip in that black bodysuit kicked her heart rate into overdrive.

About half the people at the party would be in costume, but the other half would be in normal attire. Probably safer if she and Skip joined that half. Kate left the store empty-handed.

———◦———

When Liz answered the door the following evening dressed as Tinkerbell, Kate had a real bad feeling.

Skip snickered softly behind her.

As they entered the Franklins' living room, she whispered, "Get it out of your system quick, *Skippy*. It would probably be dangerous to laugh when you see him."

A low chuckle was his only answer.

The Franklin daughters descended on them to ooh and ah over baby Edie, in the pumpkin costume Maria had made for her.

Samantha, who was just coming out of a long rebellious stage, was dressed as a devil.

How appropriate, Kate thought.

Out loud, she said, "I love your costume, Sam."

Edie loved her outfit too. As the teenager held her, the baby stroked the red satin and stared at the funny little horns on Sam's head. Then she leaned over, almost flipping sideways out of the girl's arms, when she caught sight of the sequin-covered, pointed tail that curled and bounced around Sam's knees.

But the baby was afraid of the older daughter's costume. She cried at the sight of the witch's face.

Shelley took off the fake, wart-covered nose. Then she used it to play peek-a-boo, putting the big nose in front of Edie's face. "Where's Edie? Where did she go?"

The child's tears morphed into giggles at this new game.

Knowing her daughter was in good hands, Kate, with Skip in tow, went in search of Rob. They found him in the family room, talking to Mac and Rose. All of them wore street clothes.

Kate sidled up next to Rob. "She went too far this time, huh?" she whispered.

"Oh yeah."

As she was getting dressed for work on Tuesday, Kate smiled to herself, recalling the Halloween party. Her little pumpkin had been the hit of the party. Liz had the guests vote anonymously for best costume, exempting herself as hostess.

Edie had won first place, with Samantha coming in second. The teenager had accepted her red ribbon graciously, joking that it matched her costume. Kate, however, felt Sam had been cheated. Her costume was excellent, but how could she compete with a cute little baby.

In the car headed for her office, Kate's mood sobered as she contemplated her schedule for the coming week. Today was her long day, and her toughest session was likely to be Tammy's, right before lunch. The woman had been in crisis almost non-stop for the last two weeks. The frequent emergency calls were getting annoying.

She reminded herself that this was the nature of the woman's disorder. Tammy wasn't trying to be annoying. The catch-22 of working with borderlines was that their issues from the past tended to fuel crisis after crisis in the present, and then those crises interfered with their ability to focus on and deal with the past. As the therapist trying to help them, you often felt like you were running full tilt, in a tight little circle.

Kate was anxious to see how Audrey was doing when she came in on Thursday. More details of the memory with the lollipop had surfaced during her session the previous week, but the face of the man involved was still fuzzy. Audrey's sense was that this scene had occurred repeatedly over time. The man would say, "Come here, sweetie. I've got a lollipop for you." He would then coerce and cajole her into having oral sex with him.

"Yick!" Kate said out loud, shuddering as she turned into the parking lot behind her office building. It never ceased to amaze and disgust her how depraved some people could be.

At eleven, she braced herself before going out to the waiting area to usher Tammy into her office. If she couldn't get the woman stabilized, she was going to recommend an in-patient treatment program.

The client spent the first fifteen minutes reporting in gory detail every fight she'd had with her husband that week. Kate's attempts to break into the flow had been unsuccessful. Tammy just talked over her.

When she finally wound down, Kate said, "Quite frankly, I feel like we're just going around in circles here. Actually a downward spiral would be a better way of putting it. As long as you're so angry, you and Mark are going to keep fighting. And as long as your marriage is in turmoil, you aren't in a good place to work on the abuse that's helping to fuel the anger."

Tammy launched into a defense of her position that she had a right to be angry at her husband for neglecting her.

Kate held up her hand in a stop gesture. "I never said that you don't have a right to be angry with him. It's the intensity of the anger that's the problem. Your reactions in the here and now are intensified by the unresolved feelings from the past. We need to get those old feelings resolved, and then you'll be able to deal with Mark more rationally. And he'll probably be more willing to listen to your viewpoint."

Knowing it was likely to cause her already intense day to get worse, Kate took the plunge and suggested a thirty-day in-patient program for sexual abuse survivors, pointing out that it would provide Tammy with a safe, calm environment in which to face those old feelings and deal with them.

She got the reaction she'd expected. First, Tammy accused her of wanting to get rid of her as a client. Kate repeatedly assured her that was not her reason for making the suggestion.

Then Tammy shifted gears and said that she couldn't possibly be away from Mark that long. Belatedly she mentioned her son as well. Was there something like that, but it would only be for a week?

Kate pointed out that a week would barely be long enough to get in touch with the feelings. Then she would be coming home to her neglectful husband, with those feelings totally raw. Not a good idea.

The client finally agreed to think about it, but she didn't look happy with Kate when she left.

That evening, Kate got home just in time to put Edie to bed. Maria had given her a bath and put her in her pajamas. Kate took the baby from the nanny and headed into the nursery to enjoy her favorite part of motherhood, snuggling with her sleepy child and breathing in the scent of clean baby skin.

Once the baby was settled in her crib, Kate flopped down on the living room sofa. Kicking off her shoes, she let out a sigh. Much as she liked her work, it still felt good when the day was done, especially on Tuesdays.

As she lounged on the sofa, letting her mind become deliciously empty, her eye was caught by something out of place in the baby's portable playpen, tucked into a corner across the room. Edie didn't like being in it anymore, but they still used it to contain her temporarily while answering the door or doing some other brief chore.

Kate squinted, trying to make out what the object was. Finally curiosity overcame inertia and she got up to investigate. A piece of white paper, folded in half, lay in the bottom of the playpen.

How the hell did that get in there?

She leaned over, picked it up and unfolded it. Her heart pounded as the words on the paper registered. She jammed a fist against her mouth to keep from screaming.

SEE HOW EASY IT WOULD BE. YOU NEED TO LEAVE OTHER PEOPLE'S FAMILIES ALONE!

She raced into the kitchen where Maria was making herself a cup of tea.

"¡Dios mio! What wrong, Kate?"

"Who left this here?" She held the note by its corner, as if it were coated with poison.

"Leave *qué*?" Maria said, confusion on her face as she attempted to see what was written on the paper in Kate's trembling hand.

Kate took a deep breath, trying to calm herself. "I found this in Edie's playpen. How did it get there?"

Maria shook her head, her eyes wide. "Not see again...before?"

Another deep breath. "Maria, did anyone come to the house today? Did you let anyone in?"

"*Sí*. Lady come, from *iglesia*, church. Want clothes, for *los pobres*. I give bag in closet. Iz okay?" Maria had helped Kate, a few weeks before, sort through her closet to weed out clothes she never wore. The nanny had taken a few sweaters. The rest had been put in a bag to be given to Goodwill.

"You left the woman out here with Edie while you went in the bedroom!"

"No, no, Edie wid me." Maria mimed carrying a baby on her hip. "Not okay give lady bag?" She was now looking distinctly anxious.

Kate tried to muster a reassuring tone. "Yes, it's okay that you gave her the clothes. But you can't let people in the house, ever!"

Maria shook her head in confusion.

Kate dropped the note on the table and grabbed the portable phone from its charger on the counter. She punched in Rose's cell phone number.

"Hernandez."

Kate tried to report what had happened, but she was having trouble coming up with coherent sentences. Finally, she said, "Here, just explain to Maria." She thrust the phone toward the nanny.

"Wait! Explain what?"

Kate put the phone back to her ear. "Maybe you need to come over, Rose, if you're not busy. Sorry to disrupt your evening, but it's kind of an emergency."

"That much I got. I'm at the restaurant. I'll come over while Mac finishes closing up. Be there in ten minutes."

Kate disconnected, then called Skip's cell. It went straight to voicemail. She left a message that she needed to talk to him right away. It was urgent.

He hadn't called back by the time Rose arrived.

After exchanging a short greeting in Spanish with her cousin, Rose turned to Kate. "So where's the note?"

Kate took her into the kitchen and pointed to it on the table.

"And it was in the baby's thing, out in the living room?" Rose said.

"Yes, and the only way it could've gotten there was from this woman who came to the door, supposedly collecting clothes for some church."

Rose asked Maria something in rapid-fire Spanish, followed by a lengthy answer from the latter. "She says the woman was nice but kind of ugly. Had thick glasses. Tall and maybe fat, but hard to tell. She was all bundled up.

Heavy coat. Hat pulled down. Scarf around her neck. Covered her chin and part of her mouth."

Rose asked another question in Spanish. Maria said a few words.

"Little bit of hair she could see was black, coarse. Real bright blue eyes."

"That sounds like a disguise," Kate said. "Maybe a wig and contacts."

"Distinct possibility," Rose agreed.

Maria chimed in with another comment in Spanish.

"She says the woman had some dark hairs sticking out beside her mouth and a couple above her upper lip."

"Hmm," Kate said. "Tall, bundled up to hide their build, stubble on the upper lip. Sounds like a man trying to look like a woman."

"Could be, but to Maria, many women would be considered tall." Rose's cousin was even shorter than she was. "Can't rule out a woman. *Mi madre* has some chin hair, and a bit of a moustache, since she's gone through menopause." She turned to Maria and asked another question.

Maria thought for a moment, then shook her head and said something back. Rose asked another question. Maria shrugged. "*Es posible.*"

"She can't honestly remember how tall the lady was. Just had the impression that she was tall. I asked if it could have been a man. She said maybe." Rose walked over to the table, picked up the note by its edge and slid it into a plastic bag she produced from her pocket. Then she studied the note through the bag.

"We've been getting notes at work, too. But my boss doesn't want to involve the police. She doubts they would do much since the notes aren't blatantly threatening."

"She's probably right," Rose said.

"But this can't go on. Not when whoever is doing this is invading my home and making veiled threats against my child! Rose, I want to hire you and Skip to find out who it is."

"Can't do it. You're a friend."

Kate's face fell.

"I meant we wouldn't take your money," Rose said. "We'd do it for free. And before you start feeling guilty, remember I need the hours of experience to get licensed. I can probably get a buddy of mine at the police lab to check the note for prints. But don't get your hopes up. Paper doesn't show prints well."

"Should we get the handwriting analyzed?" Kate asked.

Rose's eyebrow shot up to almost a forty-five degree angle. She had the most eloquent eyebrows of anyone Kate had ever known. "Can't say I've ever been impressed with handwriting analysis, unless it's to determine if two samples were written by the same person. Which we're already assuming here."

She turned to Maria again and said something in Spanish. "I told her not to let anybody into the house from now on except me, Mac, Skip and the Franklins."

Kate nodded approval as Rose said something else in Spanish.

Maria broke into a big grin, not quite as beautiful as one of Rose's, but close. She threw her arms around her cousin. *"Gracias, muchas gracias, Elena Rosa."*

"What did you tell her?" Kate asked, pretending not to notice Rose's discomfort. Her friend was not big on displays of affection.

"That I'm going to try to find out who the lady with the note was." Rose attempted to wiggle loose from her cousin's grasp.

Maria squeezed her tighter. *"Te quiero, prima mia. ¡Muchas gracias!"*

A red tide rose in Rose's cheeks. She squirmed again, then whispered, *"Te quiero también, Maria."*

The phone rang. Kate jumped, then grabbed it quickly so it wouldn't wake the baby.

"You okay?" Skip demanded before she could even say hello.

"Yes, no. I mean we're safe. But..."

"I'm on my way."

"Thank you, sweetheart!" She breathed out a sigh.

Kate's face was pale when she opened her front door.

Skip instinctively reached out to gather her into his arms, then stopped himself. She might have called him *sweetheart*, but the four-foot rule was still in effect, until she said otherwise.

"You okay?" he asked.

She nodded mutely.

"I'm sorry I didn't have my phone on. I was in a meeting with a potential client." He vowed to himself to never turn it off again. Even during surveillance work, he'd put it on vibrate.

"What happened?" he asked as they moved into the living room. He nodded a greeting to Rose and Maria.

Kate gestured toward the sofa. He sat down and she sank to the floor in front of him. She turned her face up to him and held out her hand.

He enclosed it in both of his. His chest ached at the fear in her eyes.

Rose cleared her throat. She was standing at parade rest a few feet away. Maria hovered behind her.

Kate shifted to one side and tilted her head toward the armchairs. "Sit down. You too, Maria." She swiveled back to face Skip. "There's been another note. Only this one was delivered here. I found it in the baby's–" Her free hand went to her throat. Her eyes flicked across the room to a small playpen.

Rose took over and reported on what had happened.

Skip asked Maria a couple questions in Spanish. Her answers fleshed out Rose's succinct summary. Looking down into Kate's worried face, he said, "We're not going to let anything happen to Edie."

He turned to Rose. "You got some time to work on this?"

"Every minute that I'm not on duty."

"Good. I'm going to stay here during the day when Kate's at work. If this gal, or guy, tries to deliver another note here, hopefully I'll catch 'em in the act. I think maybe a security system is in order as well."

Kate nodded. "But what about your work? You can't get a new business off the ground if you're babysitting Edie and Maria. I'm going to take a leave of absence."

"No, you can't do that," Skip said. "If you give into these vague demands and stop working, we'll never figure out who's doing this. Not to mention the fact that you love your work and your clients depend on you."

"It'd help if the asshole was more specific," Rose growled under her breath.

"But the question remains, Skip, how will you do your work if you're here all day? I insist on paying you two for your–"

"Not necessary." He held up a hand before she could protest further. "A lot of investigating is done on the computer these days. All I need is an internet connection. Any field work needed, I can do when you're not working."

Kate's face brightened. "You can use my study." She tugged her hand loose and gestured toward the back part of the L-shaped room. It had been filled with lounge chairs and a TV back when he'd been camped out on her sofa, protecting her from her late husband's killer. Now it was set up with a desk, computer and bookshelves. "That way, you'll always be near Edie. She's usually in here playing or next door in the nursery."

"Okay. Any new thoughts on who might be sending these notes?" Skip asked.

She gave a slight nod. "At first Sally and I assumed it was related to one of my cases, but now she's convinced they're coming from the false memory crowd. I'm inclined to agree with her."

Skip felt a little queasy as he listened to her description of the false memory movement. "Fun bunch," he said as she wound down.

Rose had been taking notes. She closed her pad. "I'll start checking them out tomorrow."

Kate flashed a grateful smile, that didn't quite reach her eyes. "Thank you so much, Rose, but please go carefully with these people. Try not to mention my name or the center's. If it's not one of them sending the notes, I don't want to draw their attention to us."

Rose nodded. "I'll find out if there's a local group first. There are ways for me to check them out without bringing you all into it."

Skip leaned forward and plucked Kate's hand out of her lap. She'd opened the door to at least that level of contact, and he intended to take full advantage, unless and until she slammed that door shut again.

"If you don't mind," he said, "I'd feel better if I slept here on the sofa tonight." If she said no, he would watch the house from his truck all night.

Kate squeezed his hand, then let it go. "Thanks. I think that's the only way I'll be able to get any sleep."

CHAPTER SEVEN

Rob learned of the new note, and where it had been found, when he called Wednesday morning to tell Kate something had come up and he couldn't meet for lunch.

"My God, is the baby okay?"

"Yes, Maria took Edie with her when she left the room, but it's totally freaking me out that someone came into my house and–"

He heard her suck in air.

"But things are under control now. I called around first thing, and a security company's installing a system this afternoon. And you know those wrought-iron filigree bars I've been talking about getting on the windows. They're coming tomorrow."

It's about time. She'd been talking about making her house more secure for months.

"And," Kate said in his ear, "Canfield and Hernandez, Private Investigations, are on the job. Rose is investigating who might be sending the notes, and Skip's going to stay here with Maria and the baby whenever I have to be away from home."

Rob paused, digesting the fact that she had called Skip instead of him. Finally he said, "Well, that's a relief to know they're going to look into this. Did you call the police?"

"No. What could they do? There's no direct threat, only an implied one, and Maria willingly let the woman into the house." There was a tremor in her voice.

"Are you okay?"

"No, not really. I mean I'm better than I was last night, but... I feel kind of helpless. How do I fight this, Rob, when I don't even know who's doing it? Or even what they're talking about!"

He felt his own surge of frustration that he had no answer for her. "Give Skip and Rose some time, sweetheart. They'll figure it out," was all he could think of to say. "I'll call you later to touch base."

He'd been walking to his car while talking to Kate on his cell phone. Now he sat in the driver's seat without turning the key, trying to sort out what the hell was making his stomach queasy and his chest hurt.

Last time he'd ignored those feelings, his knee-jerk reaction to them had almost done permanent damage to his friendship with Kate.

Something had threatened her child and she had turned to Skip first, not him. On a logical level, that made sense since Skip could actually do something about the threat, while all he could do was provide moral support.

But Rob knew that wasn't why she'd called Skip instead of him. The main reason was that Skip was now her... Her what? They weren't lovers yet. Saturday night, they hadn't touched each other the whole evening, even though the sexual energy between them was almost visible to the naked eye. Nonetheless, Skip was becoming her partner.

Okay, the queasy feeling was worry for her. Rob didn't totally trust Skip Canfield, even though the man had never really done anything to merit that distrust.

It was his looks, Rob finally decided. Kate was an attractive woman, but Canfield was movie-star handsome. Rob couldn't help wondering if the man had some ulterior motive.

And the ache in his chest, he admitted to himself, was because he wasn't first in Kate's life anymore. Which was pretty selfish of him, to expect to be first in two women's lives. But, as Kate had also pointed out to him on several occasions, feelings aren't always logical.

He was truly happy for her, that she had found love again. That is if this guy turned out to be on the up and up.

Rob shook his head and started his car. He needed to get to his meeting with his client.

The bottom line was he'd better get used to being a close second in Kate's life again, because he was fairly sure Skip Canfield, for better or worse, was going to end up a permanent fixture.

Audrey was Kate's last client before lunch on Thursday. By that point, Kate was already dragging. She hadn't slept well Tuesday night, despite the fact that Skip was sleeping right outside her bedroom door, or perhaps *because* he was sleeping right outside her door.

Then Wednesday night, she hadn't slept well because he was *no longer* sleeping outside her bedroom door. Even with the new security system, she was nervous being in the house with just the baby and Maria.

Kate quickly forgot her fatigue once Audrey's session began. The young woman was obviously avoiding eye contact as she settled into her chair.

In response to Kate's routine inquiry about how things were going, Audrey said, "I blew it."

"Blew what?" Kate asked.

"Actually, I blew *up*." She finally made eye contact. "At my parents. I did what you said not to do yet. I confronted them."

"What happened?" Kate's voice was gentle.

"I know you said to wait, you know, until we had more information and then I could make a rational decision about how I wanted to deal with them. But my mother..." Audrey shook her head in disgust. "She insisted I bring Alicia over in her Halloween costume before I took her trick or treating. When we got there, she had this big dinner ready. I told her we'd already eaten and we needed to get going, in order to trick or treat before Alicia's bedtime. She started in with the guilt-tripping, and then my father started telling me what an ingrate I was, and I just lost it.

"I started yelling, 'You wanna know what I have to be grateful for, Dad? Well I'm back in therapy, thanks to you. I'm spending hundreds of dollars of my husband's hard-earned pay, thanks to you, either you or that creepy brother of yours!'

"Somewhere during my tirade, my mother took Alicia into the kitchen, so when my father kept insisting that I tell him what the hell I was talking about, I did. I told him about the memories, which of course he denied. Said I had a lively imagination, or maybe I'd been watching too many soap operas when I should be cleaning the house."

Audrey paused for breath. Tears were trickling down her cheeks. She gave them an irritated swipe with the heel of her hand.

After a moment, Kate gently prompted, "Then what happened?"

"I yelled, 'Of course, Dad, because I'm *stupid and lazy* as well as an ingrate,' and I went in the kitchen and got Alicia. I told her to say goodbye to her grandmom. Mother must have realized I meant forever, because she chased us all the way to the car, yelling at me to come back and be reasonable."

Kate allowed a bit of a pause to make sure Audrey had finished her story. Then she said softly, "How are you feeling about them at this point?" She was concerned about the effect the whole scene may have had on Alicia but decided to come back to that.

Audrey thought for a moment. Finally she said, "I think something shifted inside after all that. It's like the last few threads that were tying me to them had broken. I actually forgot about it for a while, when we were trick or treating, and when I was telling Ted what happened later, I was crying a little but then I realized I felt lighter inside, like some burden had been lifted."

"A sense of freedom?"

"Yeah, exactly! But I feel bad for not following your advice."

Kate ignored the apology for the moment. "Do you really want to never see them again? That's not just something you felt in the heat of the moment?"

"Nope, I'm done. I have absolutely no desire, no need to ever be around them again."

"What about your sister and brother? What if they take sides?" These were the questions Kate would have preferred to have asked *before* Audrey confronted her parents.

Her client thought again for a moment. "You know, if they side with the old man and Mother, then the hell with them too."

"That makes you an orphan, with no family."

"Sorry, all I can drum up at that thought is relief." Audrey was actually starting to smile. "Some families you're better off without. Besides, I do have a family. Ted and Alicia are my family, and I get along good with his folks and sibs."

"Then no harm, no foul," Kate said. "You jumped the gun some, but it sounds like it's ended up being a therapeutic experience overall. I'm a little concerned about how Alicia might be taking this, however."

They spent the next few minutes discussing the best way to handle the little girl's reaction and the inevitable questions she would ask about why she wasn't seeing her grandparents anymore.

Then Audrey raised another issue. "I suspect you're not going to like this idea, but I'm thinking about suing them."

"In court?" Kate didn't even try to hide her surprise and dismay.

The young woman nodded.

"You're right, I don't like the idea much. You might have been ready for the confrontation you just had but I don't think you're anywhere near ready to deal with the stress of a lawsuit, not to mention the fact that we don't even know who your abuser is."

"Oh, I'm pretty sure it's my father. Otherwise, why would he protest so much?"

Kate shook her head. "No, he'd be just as likely to deny that his brother did that. He's not going to admit that stuff like that happens in *his* family. And, the way he is, he would be likely to say it wasn't true just because you said it was."

Audrey paused. "True. He'd probably claim the sky was purple if I commented that it was blue. But I want to check it out, about suing, anyway. It doesn't have to be about sexual abuse *per se*. I want to get them to pay for my therapy, past and future. It just isn't right that our money, that should be going toward our lives, our child's future... We haven't been able to save hardly anything for Alicia's college yet. Instead of going toward that, our money's paying for the damage *they* did. I figure that since they broke it, they should pay to fix it."

"I'll tell you what," Kate said. "If you're willing to pay for a consultation, I'll set you up with a friend of mine who's an attorney. He can tell you what your options are and the likelihood of success. But I am going to ask you to promise me something."

"What's that?"

"That you will not take any action on this until I say you're ready. I doubt you can even imagine how hard it's going to be, to tell your story in open court, in front of a skeptical judge, and then be cross-examined by their attorney who will do everything he or she can to tear you apart and make you look unstable."

Audrey was quiet for a moment. "Okay, I can live with that promise," she finally agreed. "But I think I do want to talk to the lawyer, maybe have a game plan in the back of my mind."

Kate gave her Rob's card and had Audrey sign a waiver of confidentiality allowing her to discuss the case with him.

After the young woman left her office, Kate called Rob. She got his voicemail. "Hi. I just referred a case to you. Her name's Audrey Spaulding. Call me and I'll fill you in."

———⋄———

At noon on Friday, Kate was headed for Mac's Place for her re-scheduled lunch with Rob. She was more than a little ready to celebrate the end of an intense week. She had a couple of clients still to see that afternoon, but they were relatively easy cases.

When she arrived, Rob was already ensconced in their favorite booth. After ordering their lunches, he asked how Skip and Rose were doing with the investigation into the notes and the strange woman who'd come to her house.

"Not much happening there yet," Kate said. "They talked to the neighbors. Nobody saw anything Tuesday. Rose is discreetly checking out the local false memory group. So how are things at your salt mine?"

"Pretty darn good," he said, looking smug. "Had an emergency custody hearing this morning for a case Sally referred. Pushed the husband and the jackass actually blew up at me in court. That was all it took for the judge to give the wife sole custody and supervised visitation for the father."

"Congratulations!"

"Thanks. Oh, I met with the young woman you referred."

"Already?" Kate was surprised, especially since she hadn't heard back from him the day before.

"Yeah, I had a client cancel a meeting yesterday afternoon and your gal seemed anxious to see me so I squeezed her in." Rob leaned forward and dropped his voice slightly. "I gotta tell you I have some reservations."

"What do you mean?" she asked, somewhat annoyed that he hadn't returned her call before meeting with Audrey.

"Well, first off, she hasn't got a snowball's chance in hell of making the case for sexual abuse when she doesn't even know for sure who her abuser was."

Kate nodded. "That's what I told her. But she wanted to talk to you anyway about the possibility of suing for emotional and physical abuse."

Rob shook his head. "I told her I'd look into it. See what the precedents are in the case law for that, but frankly it sounds a little flaky to me to think you can sue your parents because they yelled a lot and didn't totally meet your needs."

She tried to rein in her temper. Rob tended to be a bit brusque right after court, until his natural personality reasserted itself over his more aggressive court mode. But despite her best efforts, there was still an edge to her voice. "If you'd returned my call, I would've had the opportunity to tell you about this client, before you jumped to conclusions."

He sat back against the bench. After a pregnant pause, he said, "Okay, so tell me about her."

"First of all, *flaky* is the last word I would use to describe this woman. She's one of the most down-to-earth people I've ever known. Her rationale for considering a lawsuit is that she and her husband should not have to pay for the damage done by her parents. She wants to recoup the substantial amount of money she's already shelled out, and will be continuing to shell out for a while longer on therapy. Secondly, having to hide under your bed at night because your drunk father is likely to beat the crap out of you if you show up on his radar isn't exactly just failing to have your needs met."

At that moment, the waitress appeared and deposited plates in front of them. Rob had the good sense not to steal her pickles as he normally would.

"She didn't tell me that," he said. "She just talked about her father calling her names and the possibility of sexual abuse."

"Well, I'm not surprised she wasn't more forthcoming if you approached your meeting with her with the assumption that she was a flake."

Rob pulled out his handkerchief and waved it in front of him. "Can we have a cease fire, please? I'm sorry I didn't call you before meeting with her and I'm sorry I jumped to conclusions. And I didn't say any of that to her. I was gentle with her."

Somewhat mollified, Kate nodded. "Okay. Can you let *me* know what you find out about the case law precedents *before* you call her back, please?"

Rob nodded. They ate in slightly strained silence for a couple minutes.

"I really would prefer that Audrey not pursue this, and she's promised to wait until I say she's ready to handle it," Kate finally said, putting her pickle slices on his plate as a peace offering. "She has no idea how stressful a lawsuit will be. No doubt her parents' attorney will try to make her look like an hysterical nutcase with an overactive imagination."

"These are hard cases to present," Rob said. "It's difficult to get a judge or jury to understand, especially when you're dealing with... what do they call them now, *delayed* memories? It's hard for people to understand how you can *not* remember something horrible that's happened to you, and then later you do remember it. Quite frankly, I don't really understand myself. First, you don't remember and then, poof, you do?"

Kate blew out air. "It's a complicated topic. I do an hour-long guest lecture for a friend's psych classes at the university, and that's barely touching on the main points. The short version is that the human mind is programmed with all kinds of defenses to keep us sane. When a memory's so emotionally overwhelming that we can't cope with it, one of those defenses–it's called dissociation–can block the memory out."

"That's just so hard to... grasp."

She put down the fork she'd been using to poke at her salad. "Okay, I'm willing to talk about this some more. But only on one condition. I'm *not* willing to *debate* the issue."

He cocked an eyebrow at her.

She sighed again. "Rob, I can't begin to tell you how frustrating this issue is for trauma recovery specialists. Okay, as a lawyer, you know that some things are known. They're facts. And other things are not known for sure, so there can be opinions or theories about them. You can debate about theories and opinions, but not facts."

He nodded.

"I get really tired of *debating* about the validity of something that I know, *for a fact*, is real."

"But how do you know that?"

She glared at him.

He held up his hands in a gesture of surrender. "Why's this such a minefield for you, sweetheart?"

"I'm sorry. It's been a long, intense week... Okay, imagine what it would be like if a bunch of people, who were *not* lawyers, kept refusing to believe you when you told them again and again that it was illegal to marry your sister?"

Rob gave a short bark of laughter.

"That is illegal, isn't it?"

"Yeah, in most states, and I get your point, Kate. I will put skepticism aside. What's the evidence?"

"Okay, short synopsis. We've known about dissociative amnesia since Freud and his cohorts stumbled on it around 1890. But Freud got cold feet when things got controversial, so he back-pedaled and called the memories wish-fulfillment fantasies. That set things back for awhile.

"We've had *proof* of dissociative amnesia as far back as World War I, in the form of thousands and thousands of *documented* cases of it in combat vets, rape survivors, and later, Holocaust survivors."

"Holocaust survivors," Rob echoed, more statement than question.

"Yeah, roughly twenty percent had amnesia for all or part of their time in the concentration camps."

"I'm surprised that number isn't higher."

Kate nodded. "Especially since the rate is close to sixty percent for incest survivors. Nobody's all that shocked by amnesia in combat vets or Holocaust survivors. But in childhood sexual abuse cases, *that's* when it gets controversial and suddenly people don't want to believe it."

She paused to take a sip of iced tea. "What they *really* don't want to believe is that adults sexually abuse children. If a combat vet says he was so overwhelmed by the horrors of war that he blocked out all memory of a battle, we're amazed that his mind could do that, but we don't disbelieve that he was *in the battle!* But an adult says that they're now having memories of somebody sexually abusing them, the reaction is, 'Naw, that didn't happen. You're imagining things.'"

He nodded as he took another bite of his sandwich.

"And, as you pointed out, it's difficult to grasp because it *is* counterintuitive," Kate said. "Normally you can remember the bad stuff that happens to you all too clearly, so how could it be that some of the bad stuff you can't remember at all."

"So how is it?" Rob asked. "Why does some stuff get blocked out and other stuff doesn't?"

"That we don't know yet. But there are several theories about it. The one I think makes the most sense when it comes to sexual abuse is that, when it's better for our survival to not remember than to remember, we block it out."

He shook his head slightly. "Huh?"

"If you have a vicious dog in your neighborhood, it's beneficial to your survival to remember that and avoid going near that neighbor's property. But if your own father, on whom you depend for survival, does something bad to you at night, then tells you no one will believe you if you tell, and the next morning you have to sit across the breakfast table from him..."

"It will make life easier if you can forget what happened in the night," Rob finished for her. "And that would explain the lower rate for Holocaust survivors. They *did* need to remember who and what to avoid, if possible, in the camps."

Kate pushed her salad away. He dropped the remnants of his sandwich onto his plate. The subject of conversation was not conducive to a good appetite.

"It doesn't help," he said, "that there have been all these false memory allegations and lawsuits in the news the past few years."

"Yeah, and the way the media portrays them isn't always accurate. In one case, the jury found that there was no *proof* of the abuse and awarded the father *only* his back pay because he'd lost his high-profile job when the abuse accusations were made public. The jury denied punitive damages, however, because they did not *dis*believe the daughter. There just wasn't any concrete proof. But the news media presented it as the jury found that the young woman's memories *were* false and that the therapists *had* planted them in her head."

"Hey, I remember that case," Rob said. "Her mother and her sisters *all* believed her, but still it came down to her word against his in court. And her therapist, who was just doing his job, got caught in the middle."

"Yet another reason why I don't want Audrey to pursue this. Taking this sensitive issue into the adversarial arena of the courtroom has just served to make it more controversial. Then the media makes things worse by reducing a complicated situation into twenty-second sound bites."

He nodded. "The scary thing about the media is that it can influence us without our realizing it. After all, that's what advertising's all about."

"Yeah, and we're not using as critical a filter when we watch the news as we might when we're watching commercials."

"Very true." Rob looked at his watch. "Gotta run. Partners' meeting this afternoon." He pulled some bills from his wallet to cover his half of the check and stood to gather up his coat and briefcase.

Then he stopped and looked down at her. "Are we okay, Kate? I shouldn't have jumped to conclusions about the case until I'd talked to you."

"Yes, we're fine." She smiled up at him. "I forgive you for being human, just don't let it happen again."

CHAPTER EIGHT

When Kate got home Friday afternoon, she couldn't ignore the little back flip her heart did when she walked through the door and saw Skip. He was down on all fours in the living room, with Edie stretched across his broad back and hanging onto his collar. He romped around in a circle then raised his head and neighed like a horse. Edie chortled.

He looked Kate's way, his hair hanging down in his eyes, a big grin on his face. He reached up to pluck Edie off his back. In one smooth movement he flipped over and held the baby up in the air at arm's length. She giggled and grinned down at him.

Skip sat up, gave Edie a kiss on her button nose, then handed her up to her mother. Edie looked at her and said, "Ma muh."

Kate smiled and hugged her daughter. She caught a whiff of something. "Uh oh, time for a diaper change."

Maria appeared out of nowhere and scooped the baby out of her arms. "I change. You talk *Señor* Skip."

Kate hesitated. She looked forward to caring for Edie when she was home, but changing poopy diapers wasn't exactly her favorite chore.

Maria ignored her belated and half-hearted protest as she bustled through the nursery door.

Skip was propped up on his elbows on the floor, long legs stretched out in front of him. Kate sat down in an armchair a few feet away.

"I was planning to go to Texas, to my mom's, for Thanksgiving," he said. "But now I'm thinking I should cancel that."

"Oh, no. You don't need to do that. My folks are coming up from Florida. And my brother and his family will be here. Mac and Rose are coming for dinner. We'll be fine. I'm only working Tuesday that week."

"Okay, that should work. I'm flying out Wednesday morning. Coming back Sunday evening."

Kate had been toying with the idea of inviting him for Thanksgiving, and introducing him to her family... as her what? Probably just as well he wasn't available.

It dawned on her that she hadn't felt the painful longing for Eddie in some time, not even when she thought about the upcoming holidays, a time when she had missed him horribly the year before. She still had moments of missing him, that were eased by talking with him in her head, but the pain had subsided to a dull ache.

------◦------

From his position on the floor, Skip looked up at Kate, wondering what the play of emotions across her face meant. It was sheer agony, loving this woman and yet not being able to have her. The odds were good that she would someday love him back—maybe already *did* love him—so the idea of leaving her was unthinkable. But being around her in the intimacy of her home, then going back to his lonely apartment was getting harder and harder to do.

He sat up, cross-legged in front of her chair. "Kate, I know this is going to sound like I'm pushing you, but that's not my intention. I'm just trying to understand. I know people have to grieve for a while, before they can move on, and you haven't grieved for Ed long enough yet..." He trailed off when Kate started shaking her head.

"Uh, the grief, isn't all that strong anymore," she said. "And what's left is mostly just missing Eddie at times."

Hope surged in Skip's chest, followed by a wave of anxiety. "So where does that leave us?"

She looked at him for a long moment, a riot of emotions again doing battle on her face. Then she swallowed hard and ducked her head.

"I, uh, really care about you, Skip, but I'm still not quite ready to... but, well, I don't think it will be too much longer..." She trailed off.

Skip shook his head in confusion, wondering if he had totally misread this woman. In a gentle voice, he said, "Grief's such a vague thing, or at least not very concrete. How will you know when it's not too soon anymore?"

She surprised him with her answer. "Actually there is a concrete way that I'll know that." Kate leaned forward in her chair. "Skip, you're about to hear something that even Rob doesn't know."

His eyebrows shot up.

"Indeed, I had sworn to myself that I would never tell anyone this. And I know you're going to think I'm crazy, but I assure you that I'm not."

"Hey, you're the expert on crazy, not me," Skip said with a half smile.

Kate took a deep breath. "I talk to Eddie, and he talks back."

Whoa! Didn't see that *comin'.*

"It started about two weeks after he died. I was just making up conversations in my head at first, scripting his answers for him, but then it actually started to feel like *he* was talking back. And sometimes he starts the conversation. It's usually only one or two exchanges. I think something and he answers me, or he says something and I answer him."

He remained quiet, his eyes on her face, trying to digest what she was saying.

"These conversations, they're what kept me sane after he died, because I still felt connected to him. He was still with me in a way. And they've helped me get through the grief more quickly than I ever thought I would... I never imagined that I would ever date again, or at least not for many years. But here it is, not quite two years later, and I'm dating. And not just casual dating, mind you."

Skip couldn't help smiling at that.

"I never hear him in my head when I'm around you, or when I'm thinking about you. That's what's made it possible for me to spend time with you, while I've still been grieving. At any given time, I'm *either* connected to him *or* to you. So I don't feel conflicted, or like I'm being disloyal to either of you. Is this making any sense?"

"Yeah, I think I get it. But how does all this relate to how you will know—"

"I'm getting there. I know this is a rather long-winded explanation."

"You, long-winded? Naw, never," he gently teased.

She smiled. "Oh, be serious, you! This is the important part. I know that it is too soon *now,* because I still have those conversations with him. So if I let myself, uh, be with you completely..."

"Is that a euphemism for letting me make love to you?" he asked.

"Yes, but may I point out that the phrase 'making love' is also a euphemism. Are you going to let me finish?"

"Yes, I believe you were discussing the possibility of eventually trading in some euphemisms for the real thing," he said with a grin.

Kate tried to scowl at him but didn't really pull it off.

He schooled his face into a more sober expression.

"*If* I let myself be with you completely," she continued, "I'd feel like I was cheating on him. And then when I talked to him in my head, I would feel like I was cheating on *you*."

"And then you would feel conflicted."

"Yes, and I'm afraid that would come between us, somehow tarnish what we feel for each other." She paused. "But I've been hearing from Eddie less often lately. So, here it is. How I will know when it is no longer *too soon*."

"Drum roll, please," he said softly as he smiled at her again.

"It will no longer be too soon when I stop hearing from him completely."

He digested that for a few seconds, then said, "So how long will you have to go without hearing from him, before you will know that he's... that it's stopped completely?" He was trying to avoid saying, "you'll know he's gone"–words he knew would cause her pain.

"I was afraid you were going to ask that. That answer's not quite so concrete. I think I'll just know."

Skip laughed out loud. "Darlin', *that's* the answer I expected you to give me fifteen minutes ago." He pushed himself to his feet and started to lean down to take her hand, then caught himself.

Ah, screw the four-foot rule!

He grabbed both of her hands and pulled her out of her chair. They were less than a foot apart. He still felt the urge to kiss her but resisting it was bearable.

Quickly, before he gave in to the impulse, he dropped a kiss on top of her head instead, then stepped back and put his hands in his pockets. "Kate, I started this conversation because I needed something to hang onto. You've given me that. I can be patient a while longer."

———◦○◦———

On Tuesday, as Kate was ushering her last morning client out of her office, she was debating what to do with her longer than usual lunch break. Her one o'clock client had the flu and had called to cancel.

The decision was taken out of her hands when Pauline beckoned her over to the reception desk. Nodding toward a nondescript man sitting hunched in a chair, Pauline whispered, "He wanted me to knock on your door and interrupt your session." She rolled her eyes. Interrupting a therapy session for anything less than the news that the building was on fire was just not done. "Wouldn't tell me what he wanted but he's got some papers in his hand. He insisted he would wait."

Kate had a bad feeling as she turned to the man, the only person in the waiting area at the moment, fortunately. "I'm Kate Huntington. You wanted to see me?"

The man jumped up, thrusting the papers at her. "I'm here to serve you with these."

Kate took them reluctantly and glanced down at the legal jargon on the first page.

The man headed out the door at warp speed.

"Are those what I think they are?" Pauline asked, dread in her voice.

Kate could only nod. It was a health professional's worst nightmare. She was being sued for malpractice.

She raced down the hall to Rob's law firm, praying that he hadn't already left for lunch. He was walking across the reception area when she rushed through the door.

"Whoa, sweetheart!" He smiled at her. "Where's the fire?"

Kate just waved the papers in the air and kept walking toward his office.

He followed her in and closed the door, no longer smiling.

She flopped into a chair and threw the papers on his desk.

Rob sat down in his chair. He picked them up and started reading.

"Who the hell is it?" she asked.

"You didn't recognize the name?"

"No, I only looked at the first page. I don't remember ever having a client named Wells."

He read a little further, then said, with a sigh, "They're Audrey Spaulding's parents."

"Shit!"

Rob didn't even glance up. "They're suing you for putting false memories in their little girl's head." Still reading, he added, "Interesting. Their attorney has the same last name."

"Probably the sleazeball uncle. I seem to remember Audrey saying he was a lawyer."

"Hey," he said, with mock offense in his voice, "just because he's a lawyer, doesn't make him a sleazeball."

She appreciated his attempt to lighten the mood, but it didn't work. "No, he was already a sleazeball long before attending law school."

Rob glanced at his desk calendar. "What's your schedule look like this afternoon? I'm free at four."

She thought about her afternoon schedule. Her four o'clock client was doing quite well lately. "I can cancel my appointment for that hour. Then my next client isn't until five-thirty... Actually I may cancel the rest of the day. Suddenly I don't feel so good." She slumped further down in her chair.

Rob was scanning the document again. "Okay, here's what I'd like to do. I want to have a strategy session. You, me, Sally if she's available, and Audrey. Can you call her and see if she can come in at four? She's going to be your star witness."

"Wait, you're going too fast for me." Kate sat up. "The center's malpractice insurance company will provide a lawyer. And I guess it's up to them to decide whether to take it to court."

Rob looked up at her. "Not entirely. You have a right to have your own outside counsel as well, and if they want to settle but you don't, you can still defend yourself in court. But they're likely to cap whatever they will pay at what the plaintiff had agreed to settle for."

"How much are they suing for?"

"Not all that much. $200,000."

"Why so low, I wonder."

"I have a theory about that," he said, "but I'd like to save it for the strategy session. Can you see if Audrey can come?"

"I'm not real comfortable with involving her. The therapeutic relationship is, by definition, one way. I can't ask her to testify on my behalf."

"Even when her crazy parents are suing you?"

"Even then."

Rob tapped his pen against the desktop. "Look, I have some ideas swimming around in my brain. Can't we at least meet with her and let me present my plan, and then see what she says?"

Kate thought for a moment. "I guess, but if she's the least bit hesitant, I don't want her testifying." She called Pauline to get Audrey's number.

"Is she who's suing?" Pauline asked, incredulous.

"No, her parents are. What's Sally's schedule look like at four?"

"She's got a client then."

"Okay, I'll have to catch up with her between clients at some point this afternoon. Don't let on that we've been served. It will just drive her crazy until she can hear the details from me."

Kate disconnected, then punched in Audrey's number. As gently as possible she broke the bad news.

"That son of a bitch!" Audrey seethed. "Why can't he leave me the hell alone."

Technically her parents weren't going after Audrey, they were coming after her, but Kate understood what Audrey meant. Her control freak of a father was going to jerk his daughter around anyway he could think of.

"I'm in Rob Franklin's office at the moment. He wants to know if you'd be willing to sit down with us, this afternoon if you can get a sitter, and talk about some possible responses to this?"

"Sitter's not a problem. Alicia's on a play date. I'll call Joyce and ask her to keep her at her house until I can pick her up later. What time does Rob want to meet?"

"You don't have to be involved in this," Kate said. "I don't want this to set back your recovery process."

"Why the hell wouldn't I be involved? *My* crazy parents are suing *my* therapist over what is supposedly going on in *my* head. Sounds like I'm pretty damn involved already."

Kate decided to let it go for now, until she heard what Rob had in mind. "Can you come at four?"

"No problem."

"In the meantime, is it okay if I talk to Rob about your therapy, as it relates to this case? I know you signed a waiver, but that was under different circumstances."

"Of course it's okay. I like Rob, and you said he's a good friend of yours. That's good enough for me. Tell him whatever he needs to know."

Rob had been watching her while she was on the phone. When she disconnected, he asked, "How are you doing?"

Kate shook her head. "Got a whole bunch of feelings jumbled together. Can't begin to sort them out yet, but I can tell you they're all bad."

He nodded sympathetically, then punched a button on his desk phone. "Fran, could you do me a favor and get Kate and me sandwiches from the deli? What do you want?" he asked Kate.

She shrugged. She didn't feel the least bit hungry.

"Make it two ham and cheese on rye, mustard, extra pickles," he told his admin assistant, then hung up and turned back to Kate. "I hate to do this to you when you haven't had a chance to sort out those feelings, but I need to ask you some questions before we meet with Audrey this afternoon."

She nodded.

"Okay, when and how did Audrey's memories surface?"

Kate told him about the young woman's dreams and flashbacks.

"Did you, at any time, tell her the dreams were memories of something that might have really happened?" he asked.

"No. But the whole pattern of her symptoms, including the dreams, pointed toward sexual abuse."

Rob frowned. "Did you tell her that the flashbacks were valid memories?"

"Yes and no. Look I have a standard response to this kind of situation. I tell the client that the essence of the memory is probably valid, because the human mind is just not programmed to make up bad stuff out of nothing. The exact opposite. We have all these defense mechanisms to ward off knowledge of bad stuff that really did happen.

"But I also point out that human memory is very fallible and the details may not be totally accurate. That's another reason why I discourage clients from pursuing lawsuits, because I really can't, in good conscience, get up in a court of law and say that a particular memory is accurate."

He made no comment as he wrote some notes on a pad. "What techniques did you use to help her enhance her memory of what happened?"

"None. Usually once the memories start bubbling up, they get clearer over time on their own, which was happening with Audrey, slowly. But she just wasn't getting any more information about who the abuser was, other than he was built like her father and uncle."

"No hypnosis, no relaxation techniques?"

"Well, yes, I taught her how to relax herself to help her cope with anxiety, but I didn't use relaxation or hypnosis to do any memory recovery work. I did use guided imagery recently to facilitate her healing, but we weren't working directly on a specific memory."

Rob grimaced and made another note on his pad. "So you're telling me that you in no way, shape, or form tried to help her clarify her memories?" he asked brusquely, unaware that he had slipped into court mode.

She narrowed her eyes at him, but he was still looking down at his pad. Taking a calming breath, she said, "I did not use any specific techniques to clarify her memories, but of course we talked about them. Often, while the client is working on a memory in a session, it comes back full force, with all the little details. Because that's where it's *safe* to remember, in the therapist's office."

"Is that what happened with Audrey?" he asked, looking up.

"Yes, several times snippets of images evolved into a full-blown memory during a session."

He frowned as he jotted another note. "We're going to have to work on how to avoid saying all that in court, or at least how to say it in a less damaging way. Before the memories became more full-blown, did you ever suggest to Audrey that she might have been sexually abused as a child?"

"Actually yes, I told her that her symptoms tended to point in that direction and asked if she remembered being abused."

"Crap, Kate! You can't be saying that to clients these days." Rob threw his pen down on the desk.

"Damn it, I can't do my job otherwise," she snapped back. "If a client has certain symptoms that indicate they're depressed, I have to ask them about suicide, and likewise, when the client's symptoms indicate they might have been abused, I have to ask them about that. Otherwise it's like trying to do therapy with my eyes closed and my mouth sewn shut!"

Fran picked that moment to open the door, a brown paper bag in her hand. When she saw their faces, she froze. "Sorry. I should've knocked first."

"No, it's okay." Rob waved her into the room, then thanked her for getting their sandwiches. He busied himself with getting them out of the bag until Fran had closed the door behind her.

"I'm sorry. I shouldn't have snapped at you." He handed her a sandwich. "But in the current climate, you've got to be careful what you say to clients."

"I am careful, but in Audrey's case, I trusted her not to turn around at some later date and accuse me of planting memories. It never dawned on me that her parents might do that."

Rob nodded that he understood, then took a bite of his sandwich.

She ignored hers, still in its wrapper in front of her. "Besides, isn't all that semi-irrelevant. I never used any so-called suspicious techniques, such as hypnosis. And by the way, even hypnotically-retrieved memories are as reliable as those we recall normally, if the hypnotherapist does it right. I'd prefer to take the tactic that I discouraged Audrey from confronting her parents because human memory is not infallible."

"Hey," Rob said, a joking note in his voice, "You don't have to tell me how to do my job. Figuring out the best tactics for this is my problem."

One eyebrow arched in the air, she said, "Seems you were just telling *me* how to do *my* job."

"Oh, yeah, I was, wasn't I?" He raised his hands in surrender. "I just meant that you don't need to worry about how to present all this in court. That's my headache."

More to buy time than out of any desire for food, Kate unwrapped her sandwich and took a bite. It tasted like cardboard. Without looking at him, she said, "Maybe I should get a different lawyer for this."

Rob stopped in mid-bite to stare at her. "Why the hell would you want to do that?"

"Because I don't want this to damage our friendship."

"What do you mean?"

Kate looked up at him. "I need my *friend* to believe me when I say that, in no way, shape, or form, have I ever planted memories in anyone's head!"

After a beat, he said, "I believe you."

Kate frowned at his brief hesitation. "I'd better go try to catch up with Sally." She shook her head at the thought of that discussion. A vise had clamped itself around her chest, making it hard to breath. "What a nightmare," she whispered.

Rob got up and moved around to perch on the front corner of his desk. "Hey, I know you're the shrink here, but can I offer some advice? When something bad like this is going on in my life, I tell myself, 'In a few months, this will just be a bad memory.'"

Kate managed a small smile as she stood up. "That's actually very good advice. Can I steal that and use it with clients?"

"Be my guest."

She leaned over to give him a peck on the cheek.

He stood and drew her into a hug instead. "I always believe you, sweet-heart. We'll handle this, and in a few months it'll just be a bad memory."

CHAPTER NINE

Kate managed to catch up with Sally mid-afternoon when both of them were between clients. She quickly filled her boss in on what was happening.

Sally shook her head. "With the work we do here, I'm surprised this hasn't happened sooner. I wonder now if this is related to the notes we've been getting. These people might have contacted the false memory group for information and support, and now some fanatic has us in their cross hairs."

Considering how passionately protective Sally tended to be toward the center, Kate was a little surprised by her stoic response. She told her about the strategy session that afternoon with Rob.

"Our insurance carrier will provide a lawyer to handle this," Sally said. "You don't have to pay for one."

"Rob's worried that the insurance lawyers are only going to look out for their client, not us. And he'd be highly offended if I ever suggested that he should charge me or the center for his services."

Sally grimaced. "Unfortunately he's probably right about the insurance lawyers. Tell him I'm very grateful for his assistance."

At four, Rob offered chairs to Kate and Audrey in the sitting area at one end of his office. "I have a couple thoughts about this," he said, as he took a seat himself.

He turned to Audrey. "First, there's the issue of whether or not your parents even have the right to sue your therapist. Normally they wouldn't since they have no contract or direct relationship with her. But the Ramona case in California–that's the one we were discussing the other day at lunch, Kate. I looked it up. That case has been used successfully as an argument for allowing such suits. However, some aspects of that case don't really apply here. So I'll be asking for a hearing before the judge to argue that the case shouldn't even be heard."

"Is that likely to work?" Audrey asked.

"Depends on the luck of the draw. What judge we get. How smart he is, and what attitude he has toward sexual abuse."

Audrey nodded, but Kate knew the odds were poor that this tactic would work.

"The amount of the lawsuit is quite low. Ridiculously so, actually," Rob continued. "That says to me that maybe their lawyer doesn't have a lot of confidence in their case, and he's hoping the low figure will seduce the insurance company into settling out of court.

"And indeed, without you on their side, Audrey, they have a weak case. How can they claim that certain things supposedly happened in your therapy sessions when you're saying that no such thing did happen? I'd say they have about a fifty-fifty chance of winning if we went to court. Those are not great odds from where their lawyer is sitting. By the way, is this guy your uncle?"

"Yeah, he's creepy Uncle Phil."

Rob gave her an encouraging smile. "Well, I may just have something up my sleeve that will *not* make Uncle Phil's day, but more on that in a minute. It has also occurred to me that your parents may just be trying to scare Kate into dumping you as a client."

Audrey turned to Kate, horror on her face. "You wouldn't do that, would you?"

"Of course not. But that makes sense. They probably figure that if you don't have my support, then you'll cave under their pressure and come back into the fold."

Kate looked at Rob. "One of the dynamics of abusers is that they can't believe their victims actually have the gumption to stand up to them. They assume that, if *they've* lost control of the victim, it must be because someone else has taken over that control, that a spouse or a friend, or the therapist, is now pulling their victim's strings."

"That pretty much fits my father to a tee," Audrey said, disgust in her voice. "I've been yellin' back at him since I was fourteen, but he always blamed my rebellion on other things. My friends, usually. He absolutely refuses to acknowledge that I might have a mind of my own."

"This could also be about your mother not wanting to be cut off from seeing Alicia," Kate pointed out.

"And," Rob said, "if they can cast doubt on the validity of your abuse memories in a court of law, which would happen if they won this suit, they could sue for grandparent visitation rights, and they might just win."

Kate reached out and took Audrey's hand. The young woman had gone quite pale.

"Then if *we* only have a fifty-fifty chance of winning," Kate said, "maybe we shouldn't let this get to court. We can't let them get anywhere near Alicia, especially unsupervised."

Rob shook his head. "Agreeing to an out-of-court settlement could be construed as an admission that you did plant the memories and they aren't real."

"Then we've got to fight them," Audrey said.

"I'm glad you feel that way," Rob said. "Because here's what I propose we do. Sometimes the best defense is a good offense. We counter-sue, and for a lot more than a couple hundred grand. Audrey, you sue them for damages from childhood abuse and Kate, you sue them for defamation of character. For a million or so each. That might just scare them into offering to withdraw their suit if we withdraw ours."

He sat back in his chair. "Are you willing to do that, Audrey?"

She had brightened considerably. "Hell, yes! I was the one who wanted to sue them in the first place, remember? But I thought you two were against it."

"Well that was then and this is now. I was against it because we would've had a weak case, and Kate was against it because of what you would have to go through in court, and she's right to be worried about that. It's going to get very rough. But since your parents are forcing the issue, then we've got nothing to lose.

"And there's a subtle but important difference here," Rob continued. "If you sued them out of the blue, then they could play the underdog. The poor put-upon parents who were just doing their best and don't understand why you're attacking them. But now they're the attackers and we're the ones saying, hey, why are you doing this to us? Now we're just standing up for ourselves."

"Cool! I like it," Audrey said. "I like your plan a lot."

Meanwhile Kate had been mulling over the pros and cons in her head. There was a risk that they would be throwing fuel on the fire. Abusers didn't like to be challenged. Indeed, that was probably why Audrey's father was suing in the first place, because Audrey had confronted him.

But then again, what choice did they have? Let themselves be intimidated into going along with an out-of-court settlement that might end up jeopardizing Alicia's safety if it was used as ammunition in a grandparents' visitation suit?

Audrey and Rob had grown quiet, waiting for her response.

A slow smile spread across her face. "Yeah, I like the plan too. It will send a message to other abusers who think they can drag their grown children and their therapists through the courts with false memory charges, with no risk of consequences to themselves. Another thing about abusers is that they don't play by the rules, but they assume everyone else will. So, yes, it's time to stop playing nice and go after them with everything we've got."

"Great," Rob said. "Can you two come up with a justifiable figure for how much Audrey has already spent and is likely to spend in the future on therapy? Then we will add a nice chunk of change for emotional pain and suffering, and then some more for punitive damages. Kate, I'm thinking an even million for your suit. How does that sound to you?"

Kate nodded.

Rob stood up. "I'll start writing up the papers, and let you know when I have them ready for you two to look at and sign. I'd really like to get them filed by Friday. I want to hit back fast and hard."

Audrey shook hands with Rob, then she and Kate exchanged a hug.

After the young woman had left the office, Kate turned to Rob. She gave him a big hug. "It's a great plan. I think all those emotions I was having earlier were mostly about feeling like a helpless victim myself. I feel a lot better now. Thank you!"

Rob managed to get the counter suits filed by Thursday afternoon. He called Kate on Friday to report that the judge assigned to the case was a decent one, but not very savvy about abuse issues. He was going to allow the Wells' suit to be heard.

Kate decided to put the whole mess out of her mind for now. The gears of the judicial system moved slowly and it would be awhile before they would have to deal with depositions and such. In the meantime, she wasn't going to let it spoil her enjoyment of the upcoming Thanksgiving holiday with her family.

Not all the O'Donnell clan would be there. Her sister and her family in California and her brother Jack in Chicago weren't able to come. But everyone had agreed they would all fly to California for Christmas at her sister's house.

For Thanksgiving, it would just be her parents and her oldest brother, Michael, and his family, who lived in Silver Spring near Washington, DC. They would be joined for Thanksgiving dinner by Mac and Rose. It would be quite crowded around Kate's big oak table.

On Sunday, Skip came over to escort Kate and Edie to the grocery store. Kate had a long list, dictated over the phone, of the supplies her mother would need to make turkey and all the trimmings.

As they carried the groceries into the house, Skip drawled, "You sure do know how to show a man a good time, ma'am."

Kate gave him a chagrined look. "Sorry–"

He cut her off with a chuckle. "I'm joking. I loved every minute of today. But I'm afraid I've gotta go. Some surveillance work. Insurance fraud case."

Her mood plummeted at the word *insurance*.

"What's the matter, darlin'?"

Kate sighed. "I didn't tell you because I've been trying not to think about it. I got served with a malpractice suit this week."

"Shit!" he said, then glanced at Edie who was playing on the kitchen floor nearby. "Oops, sorry. Guess I'd better learn to watch my language in front of the little one."

"Yeah, she's starting to talk. Don't want that to be one of her first words."

"So who's suing you?" Skip asked, sitting down at the table.

She sat across from him. "Parents of one of my clients. They're accusing me of planting false memories in their daughter's head."

"Could this be related to the notes?"

"I don't think so. Not directly at least." Kate couldn't see the Wells sending the notes, not when they'd chosen the lawsuit path and no doubt self-righteously believed they would win. "If it came out that they were sending harassing notes, that would seriously undermine their case. But Sally was speculating that they may have contacted the local false memory group for information and that might have drawn their attention to us."

Skip nodded. "Guess you can't tell me their names, can you?"

She thought for a moment. "My client's married, has a different last name. And the lawsuit's public record. No reason why I can't tell you the parents' name. It's Wells."

"I'll pass that on to Rose. She'll see if they're in that group."

After Skip left, Kate called her sister-in-law to suggest that she and Michael and the kids stay overnight at her house on Thanksgiving and they do a girls day out the next day to catch the Black Friday sales. She had never been particularly close to her oldest brother and his wife, but they had been supportive in the aftermath of Eddie's death and she was trying to cultivate that relationship a bit more.

Phyllis agreed with her that showing up at the stores at the crack of dawn was not what they wanted to do. "I like to shop that day because it starts to get me in the mood for Christmas. Being part of a rampaging herd of bargain-crazed shoppers doesn't really do that for me." So the four women–Kate, Phyllis, Kate's mother and Phyllis's daughter, Amy–would head over to Towson Town Center around ten that morning. The merchandise would already be somewhat picked over, but the crowds would probably be a bit less horrendous and they would have more fun.

"And the boys can do some father-son-grandson bonding watching football at your house," Phyllis said, with an indulgent chuckle.

On Monday morning, Kate was feeding Edie her breakfast when the phone rang. She grabbed the portable and wedged it between ear and shoulder as she wiped the baby's face and hands. For Edie, eating was a contact sport.

Kate's stomach knotted when she heard Sally's voice. "Got another one. Slid under the outer door over the weekend. Just your first name on the envelope. May I open it?"

"Of course," Kate managed to get past the lump in her throat. She heard paper rustling. "What's it say?"

"'All you do is stir up trouble. You need to find another line of work, before it's too late.' In all caps."

Once again Sally was stoic. She was even more convinced that the notes were coming from some fanatic in the false memory movement.

Kate decided she wasn't going to let this latest note get to her.

Rose was investigating. She'd tracked down the contact person for the local group and had even attended a meeting, posing as the sister of someone who'd accused their father of sexual abuse. But so far, she hadn't been able to find anything linking the group or its members with the anonymous notes.

Meanwhile, Kate reassured herself, Skip would continue to protect Edie while she was at work. For a fleeting moment, she wondered if it was safe for her family to come for Thanksgiving. She shook her head at her paranoia.

Monday evening, Rose went to her second meeting of the local false memory group. It was an informal gathering. The twenty or so people mostly sat around and vented.

Some of them seemed genuinely confused by their grown children's accusations and wanted to figure out how to heal the breach in their families. But some of the others were quite spiteful and vindictive. Rose had no trouble imagining them as child abusers.

The worst of them was the self-proclaimed leader, Bobby Harris. He was in his early forties, tall and muscular, the owner of a bar in downtown Baltimore. His twenty-year-old daughter had sicced Protective Services on him once she was out of the house.

Rose had looked up the case. The two younger children had denied that their father beat or molested them, supporting the family line that the older sister was a nutcase. Without any concrete evidence, the social worker could only warn Harris that they had started a file on him and would be watching for any signs of abuse.

Harris dominated his quiet wife, as well as several of the more timid members of the group. If anyone started to waffle and dared to express the desire to make amends with their estranged offspring, Harris would go on a rant about ungrateful children and how they all had to exhibit tough love to get their kids back in line.

So far Harris had been nice to Rose. The thinly veiled sexual innuendoes told her why. He was hoping to get into her pants. Although the thought made her want to gag, she was not above using his interest to pump him for information.

After they'd gone around the room, everyone sharing whatever had happened since their last meeting, people started talking in groups of three or four. Harris got two cups of coffee from the refreshment table and came over to where Rose was sitting.

"Want some?" he said with a sly grin, waiting a beat before holding out one of the cups.

"Thanks." She took the cup and pretended to sip from it. She wouldn't put it past this man to try to drug and rape her.

"Is this helping?" Harris asked.

"Some. It's comforting to know we're not alone."

"You should encourage your parents to come, Elaine."

"I will. I just wanted to check it out first," Rose replied. "So is this all you do, just talk and support each other?"

"Well, this is mainly what we do at the meetings." Harris hesitated. "But sometimes we get more proactive."

"Like lawsuits against the therapists?" Rose said. Three of the couples had talked about having filed suits. But none of them had the last name of Wells.

"Yeah, that, but there's other things." Harris hesitated again. "Can't really get into it here." He tilted his head slightly toward the others milling around the room and chatting. "Some folks are more open to *proactive* activities than others."

Rose suspected what was coming.

Harris did not disappoint. "Wanna go somewhere for a nightcap? I can fill you in."

Rose forced herself to smile up at him, although the smile only had about ten percent of her normal wattage. "I can't tonight." She glanced at her watch. "Promised my mom I'd stop by this evening, but I could come to your place downtown tomorrow night, say about nine? Can't stay too late though. I've gotta work the next day."

Harris grinned and winked at her. "It's a date."

When she got home, Rose called her partner to report in. She repeated the conversation with Harris and told Skip about her plan to have Mac go into the bar and hang out nearby, in case she needed assistance.

He congratulated her on her rapid progress.

"Doesn't feel all that rapid. Wish I could haul the bastard in and have a long chat with him in an interrogation room."

He chuckled on the other end of the phone line. "Yeah, there are still days, after all these years, when I long for the power of the badge. But PIs have to learn to be patient."

Rose waited a beat, then said, her tone teasing, "I think I'm learning from a pro on that score."

Skip just chuckled again.

Perhaps it was all the anger and hate radiating from so many of the people in that room tonight that made Rose do something totally out of character.

"Don't give up on her, Skip."

A beat of silence.

"I have no intention of giving up, but thanks for the encouragement. *Buenas noches, Elena Rosa.*"

CHAPTER TEN

In her session with Tammy Wingate on Tuesday morning, Kate waited patiently through the woman's litany of complaints against her husband, watching for an opportunity to ask if she'd given any further thought to the in-patient treatment program.

When the opportunity finally came, the response was chilly. "I've decided that's a really bad idea. I think Mark may be having an affair. So leaving him on his own for a whole month is unthinkable."

Tammy then spent the next twenty minutes describing the vague indications that her husband might be cheating on her. There was no concrete evidence, but it did seem to Kate that Mark was withdrawing even further from his wife.

She finally found an opening to once again insert the suggestion that Tammy and Mark should start seeing a couples' counselor.

"Can't we see you for that?" Tammy asked.

"It would be a conflict of interest. I can have the occasional session with the two of you, to advise him on how to support you in your healing process. But it wouldn't be a good idea for me to work with you individually and then also with the two of you as a couple."

"Well, maybe we should just see you as a couple for a while, then."

"Tammy, you really need to still be doing your individual therapy. Yes, your marriage is in trouble, but that is not the only reason for the intensity of your feelings." Kate was getting really tired of saying that.

Dear Lord, give me strength.

Out loud, she said, "I'd like you to reconsider the in-patient program as well. I understand why you're hesitant about being away from home, but if you don't get some of these feelings from the past out of your system, then I am seriously worried about the future of your marriage."

This time, Kate couldn't even extract a promise from the client to think about it.

Audrey's session that afternoon was much more satisfying.

Before the client was even settled in her chair, she said, "I think Rob's strategy is working. Mother called Saturday. Ted answered the phone, and told her I wasn't willing to talk to her. I was so proud of him, Kate. She confronted him about our lawsuit and he said, 'Well, what did you expect, Frances, that we would stand by and let you and John run roughshod over Audrey's therapist when she's just doing her job?'"Audrey mimicked a deep voice.

"Then Mother said something about just wanting her daughter and granddaughter back and Ted pointed out that suing people was not exactly the best way to promote family togetherness. And *then* she hinted that they might drop their suit if we dropped ours."

"What did Ted say?" Kate asked.

"He told her they would have to talk to our attorney about that, and then he said, 'Have a good evening, Frances,' and hung up."

"He handled that beautifully," Kate said.

"I thought so."

Were her ears deceiving her or had no-nonsense Audrey just giggled?

"I jumped him as soon as Alicia was in bed."

Kate stared at her client for half a beat, then laughed out loud. "So a good time was had by all."

"Oh, yeah!" Audrey flashed her a big grin.

Kate grinned back at her.

For most clients, a legal battle with their parents would be psychologically difficult if not devastating, but for Audrey, it seemed to be having the opposite effect. The battle lines had been drawn in the here and now and this action-oriented young woman could fight a known enemy in a tangible way, rather than trying to do battle with a faceless abuser in dreams and flashbacks about the past.

Tuesday night at five of nine, Rose stood on the sidewalk in front of a topless bar on Baltimore's notorious Block. She looked up at the neon sign flashing *Girls, Girls, Girls.*

Why am I not surprised.

"Can't say I care for this set-up," Mac growled quietly from beside her.

Rose's gut was agreeing with his. "Kate'll be home by now. Go on in. I'll call Skip for some back-up."

When she entered the building a few minutes later, Mac was sitting midway down the bar, nursing a beer and looking straight ahead at the liquor bottles on the back counter. Rose eased onto a stool close to the door. Harris was behind the bar with another bartender, a curvaceous, scantily clad blonde. Harris spotted Rose and moved quickly in her direction.

Rose figured a certain amount of dismay at the surroundings would be expected. She pursed her lips and looked around the dim room, that smelled of stale beer and male sweat.

"I know." Harris tilted his head in the direction of the well-endowed and nearly naked brunette who was dancing on the stage at the other end of the room. "But it's what the customers want. Pays the bills." He gave a small what-can-you-do shrug.

"What can I get ya, Elaine?" He had to raise his voice to be heard over the outbreak of laughter around the pool table across the room.

"You got Coors Light?"

"Sure." Harris reached for a clean glass from the row behind him.

"Bottle's fine," Rose said.

He deftly flipped the cap off a long-necked bottle and handed it to her.

"Thanks." She took a small sip. "I can't stay too long, Bobby. Gotta work tomorrow. But I wanted to know more about these proactive things you were talking about. Maybe it's something that can help my folks. My mom was bawling her eyes out when I got there last night."

"Well, the key is," Harris leaned forward on the bar and lowered his voice, "ya wanna try to get to the therapist. Scare him or her off, or scare your sister into stopping therapy. You know who her therapist is?"

Rose shook her head. "It's a man, but I don't know his name. How does scaring the therapist help?"

"'Cause that's usually who's behind the whole thing. Young person's havin' problems, like we all do sometimes. Goes to a shrink. And the next thing ya know, the kid's accusin' his or her folks of doin' awful things to 'em. Gotta be the shrink convincin' 'em that it's all their family's fault. If ya can get the kid away from the shrink, ya can usually get 'em to see reason again."

"Okay," Rose nodded. "That makes sense." It actually sounded pretty crazy to her. What did this guy think people were, total sheep? But Kate had coached her on how this crowd tended to think.

"So how do you get to the therapist? Assuming I can get his name from my sister."

"There's all kinds a ways. Ya want another beer?"

"No, I'm good for now." Rose took another sip of Coors.

Harris opened his mouth but was interrupted by a loud shout from the other end of the bar. A man sitting on the other side of Mac was hollering, "Hey, Bobby, what's it take ta get 'nuther drink 'round here?"

"Hold your shorts on, Charlie. Can't ya see I'm talkin' to a lady here? Susi, get the man his drink, will ya!"

Mac used the exchange as an excuse to glance in Rose's direction. He raised an eyebrow, as if to say, *Where's the lady?*

Rose met his eye, the signal that Skip was on his way. If she had looked down he would have known they were on their own. Mac turned back to stare straight ahead again.

Harris leaned a little closer to Rose, a lecherous glint in his eye. "Now where were we?"

Stifling the urge to pull back, Rose gave him a small smile. "You were tellin' me how we could scare off my sister's therapist."

"Oh, yeah. Well, besides lawsuits, there's picketin' the therapist's office. That's usually real effective."

"I heard somebody at the meeting saying something about sending notes," Rose said. "Seems like that'd be an easy thing to do."

"Well, yeah, that's been done. But ya can't sign yer name or say nothin' real specific on account of it bein' against the law. Ya know, to 'harass' people," Harris made quote marks in the air, "through the mail."

He grinned. "That can be fun though, justa jerk their chain, but it ain't as effective as some of the other things."

Rose noted that here at his bar, Harris spoke fluent Balmorese.

She let a bit more Baltimore creep into her own voice. "So do you all, ye know, the group... Do ya ever help people even if they're not members?"

He looked a bit wary. "Why do ya ask?"

"Bobby, I tried to talk my folks into comin' to the next meeting." Rose pumped some desperation in her voice. "But my ma just bawled harder, and Pop kept mumblin' 'bout not airin' dirty laundry in public. So I was just wonderin' if you all'd be willin' to send some notes, or maybe organize some picketin', even if they won't join up."

"Well, now, you get the bastard's name from yer sister, and then we'll see what we can–" Harris was once again interrupted by loud voices, this time angry, coming from the pool table. He looked around and made eye contact with a very big, very ugly guy standing near the door. Harris tilted his head toward the noisy patrons, two of whom looked like they were about to square off with pool cues.

He turned back toward Rose. "Come on, we can't talk out here. Too noisy." He was around the end of the bar and next to her stool, wrapping his hand around her upper arm, before she could react. "Let's go back to my office."

When she made no move to get off the stool, his hand tightened on her arm.

They both glanced toward the door as it opened. Rose hid her relief.

Skip, his hair intentionally mussed and his normally neat clothes quite rumpled, strode over to the bar and plunked himself down on the stool between Rose and the back area of the bar, bumping against Harris in the process.

"Watch where yer goin', buster," Harris growled.

Skip turned toward them. "Oh, sorry, buddy." He gave Rose a slow, easy grin. "Who's the pretty lady?"

His eyes were on her, but Rose knew he was watching Harris in his peripheral vision.

"The pretty lady's with me, *buddy!*"

Rose used Harris's focus on Skip to pull her arm loose from his grip. "I need to get goin', Bobby."

He put his hand on the bar, blocking her way with his arm, but he was still watching the newcomer.

A bleached blonde, wearing a red dress that just barely covered the vital parts of her voluptuous body, had sidled up next to the big man and was suggesting that he buy her a drink. Skip was ignoring her.

The bouncer, having discouraged the rambunctious pool players from fighting, stepped over behind his boss. The noise level in the room dropped several decibels as many of the patrons sensed a brewing confrontation. The blonde scuttled away.

Rose suddenly leaned down as if to scratch her ankle. She deftly palmed the small pistol from her ankle holster hidden under the cuff of her khaki slacks. She wanted it in her hand, just in case things turned totally ugly.

When she stood up, she was on the other side of Harris's arm. "I'll call ya when I've got that guy's name. Thanks for the beer, Bobby," she said, as she backed toward the door. She gave Harris a big smile, managing to pump about eighty percent of her normal wattage into it.

It was enough. Harris and the bouncer stared at her, mouths slightly open, just long enough for Mac to slip past, acting as if he was ignoring all of them.

He and Rose got to the door at the same time. Mac held the door for the lady.

When Harris turned back toward the bar, his face red with fury, the big guy wasn't there. Skip was sauntering toward the men's room in the back hall, watching Harris out of the corner of his eye.

Harris looked at the bouncer and jerked his head. The two of them moved in his direction.

Skip ducked around the corner, then bolted down the hall and out the emergency exit in the back of the building.

He found Mac and Rose leaning against the front fender of his Explorer. "Towson Diner. Coffee's on me." He had no desire to hang around this section of town to get Rose's report.

Mac and Rose stood up and jogged down the block toward Mac's truck.

A scrawny teenager was crouched down beside it, bent on removing one of the Hummer's fancy chrome wheels. Mac picked the kid up by the collar of his jacket and the seat of his baggy jeans and tossed him across the sidewalk. A lug wrench clattered on the cement.

Skip chuckled as the kid's buddy, who'd been trying to pop the driver-side door lock, took off down the street.

CHAPTER ELEVEN

Thanksgiving Day was everything Kate had hoped it would be. The house was full of people and laughter and wonderful fragrances wafting from the kitchen.

She was flabbergasted by how much her niece and nephew had grown up, since the last time she'd seen them the previous Christmas. Mike was now a freshman in college and well over six feet. She looked up at him. "Don't you get dizzy up there, Mike?

"And look at you, Amy. You've turned into a young lady when I wasn't looking." The girl of last year, who had still had one foot in childhood, was now a full-blown teenager.

As the day progressed, Kate felt an occasional twinge of missing Skip. She imagined he was having an equally good time with his mother and his sister's family. He was probably giving his nephews and niece pony rides on his broad back at that very moment. She smiled at the thought.

It didn't occur to her until she was getting ready for bed that night that she hadn't thought about Eddie all day. That made her a little sad, and optimistic at the same time.

Friday morning, the "girls" were only a few minutes behind schedule getting away from the house. They had planned to take Edie with them, but she woke up with the sniffles so they left her in Maria's capable hands.

Kate had taken her father aside and filled him in on the notes and the possible risk to Edie. Dan O'Donnell was in his seventies but he was a big man, in reasonably good health, and the younger men would be there as well. Her father wouldn't let anything happen to his youngest granddaughter.

The three generations of O'Donnell women had a wonderful time for the first couple hours. But by lunchtime, Amy's interest in hanging out with her relatives was waning. She started whining that she was bored and wanted to leave. Phyllis pointed out that other people's plans could not be altered just because she was a bit bored.

Amy's face set in a stubborn look. Kate had trouble hiding her smile. She'd seen that look on her father's face quite a few times through the years. The girl was definitely an O'Donnell.

Finally Phyllis got tired of the whining and gave in when Amy suggested she could call her brother to come get her. "He's meeting me out front in twenty minutes, Mom," Amy said after making the call. "See ya!"

Phyllis just sighed and muttered, "Teenagers!" as the girl hurried away.

Kate clamped her teeth together to keep from saying anything. She wasn't sure it was safe to let a young girl loose in this crowd by herself. It would be far too easy for a sexual predator to target her. But she knew from past experience that Phyllis would scoff at such a warning. Michael's wife believed that her sister-in-law was paranoid about such things because of the work she did. But Kate knew that crowded malls were a favorite hangout for pedophiles.

Not my call, she reminded herself. *I'm not the girl's mother.*

An hour later the three women were rummaging through racks of clothes in Nordstrom's bargain area when Phyllis's cell phone rang. Her face went white and then red as she listened to whatever the caller was saying. "Stay there. I'll be right out," she snapped into the phone and disconnected.

"That girl is going to be the death of me yet," she said to Kate and her mother-in-law as she tried Amy's cell number. "Mike's been waiting out front for forty minutes and Amy hasn't shown up. He's been calling her phone and she's not answering."

Kate's stomach clenched. Had her earlier dire thoughts become reality?

But Phyllis was still bent on convincing herself that Amy had just gotten distracted by some cute outfit in a store window and had lost track of time. Phyllis left an angry message on the girl's voicemail and they all headed toward the mall's main entrance.

Amy was nowhere in sight.

Kate suggested they split up and check the other entrances on the ends of the mall, in case Amy hadn't realized which one was the main one.

After they had checked the entrances and searched all the stores' juniors' departments and shops that catered to teens, Kate said for the third time, "Phyllis, we need to call the police."

Bridget O'Donnell nodded her agreement. Her face was pale and her lips were trembling from the effort to resist crying. But Phyllis's face was still set in a resistant frown.

"Look, Amy's in a strange mall, and this place is mobbed. She could've gotten totally turned around, may be frantically looking for us. But in this crowd, we might never find her, or she us." Kate was terrified that Amy wasn't just lost. But telling Phyllis her daughter might have been kidnapped would probably not get the desired reaction.

"She has her phone," Phyllis said.

"Which obviously isn't working for some reason. Maybe the battery's dead."

Phyllis finally nodded and Kate led the way toward the mall's management offices to find the security staff.

Phyllis might not be ready to believe something bad could have happened to her daughter, but the security chief knew better. She took Kate's report seriously. After calling the police, she asked if anyone had a picture of the girl on them. All three women produced photos from their wallets. Phyllis's was the most recent. The security chief photocopied it to pass out to her staff, and to the uniformed officers who arrived a few minutes later.

As the three women and Mike sat in anxious silence in the security office, a man in a rumpled navy business suit strode into the room. He introduced himself to the security chief and the others as Detective Randolph of the Baltimore County Police Department. The thickening around his waistline and the gray heavily sprinkled through his rust-colored hair pegged him as middle-aged. His expression was sympathetic.

Chief Brown filled him in. "My officers and your uniforms have started a systematic search of the mall. Couple of my best people are going through the security camera data for the last three hours. No luck so far."

"I'll get some more uniforms to help with that," the detective said. He asked Phyllis several questions about Amy's personality and habits. Kate knew, even if Phyllis didn't catch on, that he was trying to ascertain how friendly and naive the girl was. Both traits would make her more susceptible to the tricks pedophiles used to isolate and then subdue their prey.

Kate called Mac and Rose. They came to the mall to help with the search.

Three hours later, the detective told the family that he was issuing a nationwide Amber alert and it might be best if they went home. Phyllis and Michael refused to leave, but Kate's mother was visibly sagging. Kate wanted to get her out of there. She asked Mike if he wanted to go home with them. He hesitated, then decided to stay with his parents.

By seven o'clock there was still no news. Dan had insisted his wife lie down, but Kate doubted her mother was actually napping in the guest room upstairs.

Kate's cell phone rang. The caller ID showed Skip's number. She rushed outside to the front porch for some privacy.

Skip's cheerful voice said in her ear, "Hey there, Mom and Suze are heatin' up leftovers so I thought I'd–"

"Oh my God, Skip!" She burst into tears.

"What's wrong?"

Kate couldn't stop sobbing. She sat down on the front steps and leaned against the end post of the porch railing, clutching the phone to her ear.

"Darlin', please tell me what's wrong," Skip begged in a choked voice. "Is Edie okay?"

"Yes, she's fine."

Finally Kate managed to get the story out.

———◇———

Thirteen hundred miles away, Skip was headed for his mother's kitchen to tell her he had to leave. "I'll be on the next plane," he said to Kate. "Be there tomorrow morning at the latest."

"No, there's nothing you can do that isn't already being done. Don't cut your trip short. That's not fair to your family."

I can be there for you, Skip thought but didn't say out loud.

He wasn't quite sure what to say out loud. What do you tell a woman whose niece was missing, possibly kidnapped by a sexual predator?

He turned back toward the living room. His nephews were romping around on the opposite side of the room, playing some kind of game of their own devising. His little four-year-old niece was trying valiantly to get them to let her play.

His eyes stinging, he said, "Oh, darlin', what can I do? How can I help?"

"Just talk to me for a while. Tell me about your visit so far."

So that is what he did. He talked to her for over an hour, trying to find things to say that would give her hope, or at least distract her.

"That sounds like fun," she said in response to his description of their Thanksgiving feast.

Fun?

She wasn't really paying attention to what he was saying, and there was a tremor in her voice.

"Are you okay?" he asked.

"Yeah, just cold. I'm outside, walking around the block, so my folks can't hear me."

"That's not really safe, darlin'."

He got no response. After a few seconds, he said, "What are you wearing?"

She let out a choked laugh.

He grinned in spite of the grimness of the moment. "I didn't mean that the way it sounded. Are you wearing a coat?"

"No, a cardigan. I'm okay."

Frustrated, he went back to trying to distract her with a description of his nephews' earlier improvised game of space aliens, from which they had so determinedly excluded their little sister.

Suddenly Kate yelled, "Dad, come quick! I think I see Amy!"

Skip heard feet pounding. She was breathing heavily in his ear.

"Kate, be careful!" He clenched his phone.

"It's her, Skip. Dear God, it is her! I'll call you back."

CHAPTER TWELVE

Kate raced toward the bedraggled figure she had spotted stumbling through the circle of light under a street lamp. Suddenly she was calm. Her clinical detachment had kicked in. She punched 911 on her phone as she ran.

When she reached Amy, she was already giving her name and address. The dispatcher asked what the nature of the problem was.

"My niece is hurt. Just get an ambulance here. I need to tend to her." Kate thrust her phone into her pocket as she struggled to support the staggering girl.

Between them, Kate and her father half-carried Amy back to the house. They settled the girl on the living room sofa.

Bridget O'Donnell was punching a number on her cell phone. "Michael, we've found her."

Kate tuned her mother out, focusing on her niece. She knelt beside the sofa. "What happened, sweetheart?"

"That you, Aunt Kate?... I don't feel so good." The girl's head lolled to the side. Kate felt her neck for a pulse. It was slow.

The ambulance was there in nine minutes, but the police detective beat them by two. He pulled up in front of Kate's house, his flashing light still revolving. Michael and his family were right behind, Mac's Hummer at the end of the parade.

Phyllis was out of the car before her husband had brought it to a complete stop.

The next few minutes were pure chaos. Phyllis raced over to the sofa where Amy was lying and started begging her daughter to "talk to mama." The detective was asking Kate questions. Dan was telling his son and grandson that Amy didn't seem to be seriously hurt. Edie had woken up and, reacting to the tension and noise, was now wailing in Maria's arms. Mac and Rose were trying to stay back out of the way.

The paramedics came in the still-open door. They looked around, trying to determine in the crowded room who their patient was.

Suddenly a female voice boomed across the room. "Shut up!"

Everyone turned and stared at the normally soft-spoken Bridget. Even Edie stopped crying, letting out a soft hiccup as she looked across the room at her grandmother.

"Let the lads take care of my grandbaby!" Bridget's voice broke on a sob. Dan was next to his wife in an instant, steering her to a chair.

Kate tapped Detective Randolph on the arm and gestured toward the kitchen. Once there, she said in a low voice, "My niece is a good kid. She wouldn't just take off like that and it looks to me like she's been drugged."

Randolph nodded. "For now, I'm handling this as a kidnapping."

Kate was relieved, but also surprised. She'd expected him to assume the worst about Amy, that she'd taken off to do drugs with her friends.

A corner of his mouth crooked up in a half smile. "I've got a grand-daughter who's not much younger than her."

Kate warned the detective that her sister-in-law was the queen of denial. She might very well be resistant to what needed to be done.

Back in the living room, a paramedic stepped over to Randolph and Kate. In a low voice, he said, "Symptoms are consistent with Rohypnol, sir."

Kate's heart stuttered in her chest. She blinked back tears.

The detective nodded, his expression grim. He took Phyllis and Michael aside. Kate unabashedly eavesdropped as he gently explained to the frantic mother and shell-shocked father that their daughter may have been given a date rape drug and might have been molested.

When Phyllis registered what the policeman was saying, she shot across the room and sank to her knees in front of her daughter. Amy was now sitting up on the sofa but was still fairly out of it.

"Is she okay?" Phyllis asked in a sharp voice, without taking her eyes off her daughter's face.

The paramedic next to her cleared his throat. "Uh, hard to tell, ma'am. We need to get her to the hospital and let the docs check her over."

"Do you hurt anywhere, baby?" Phyllis said to her daughter.

The girl shook her head and then said in a small voice, "I think I'm gonna be sick."

Phyllis jumped up, lifting Amy to her feet by her arm. She raced the girl down the hall toward the master bathroom. "Michael!" she yelled back over her shoulder. "Get our things. We're going home!"

Michael gave the detective and his sister a helpless look and followed his wife into the master bedroom, where they had slept the night before.

Kate noticed that Maria and the baby had disappeared. The nursery door was shut.

"Mike, can you get your sister's things, along with your own, please," she said to her nephew. The kids had slept in spare rooms on the second and third floors of the old Victorian.

"Okay, Aunt Kate." The boy swallowed hard, suddenly looking a lot younger than his eighteen years.

"Bridget, let's give the lad a hand," Dan said. As he walked past his daughter, he whispered, "Try ta talk some sense into her, lass."

Kate let out a soft snort. "I'll try."

"We should probably get out of the way," Rose said.

"Thanks for your help, guys," Kate said without looking at them. Her mind was grasping for something to say that would sway her stubborn sister-in-law.

"Keep us posted, sweet pea." Mac and Rose headed for the door.

Phyllis and Amy came out of the bedroom a couple minutes later. Michael trailed behind with two small suitcases.

Detective Randolph stepped forward. "Mr. and Mrs. O'Donnell, could you sit down for a moment, please."

Michael moved toward the sofa to comply, but his wife stood firm. "Thank you for your help, Detective. But there's nothing more to talk about. My daughter doesn't remember what happened. She's upset and I'm taking her home."

Phyllis glared in the direction of her husband. "Where's your son?" At that moment, Mike descended the stairs with two backpacks in his hands.

Before Kate could say anything, Phyllis had steered her daughter out the front door, with Mike in tow. Michael started to follow.

Kate stepped in front of him. "Don't let her do this. Amy needs medical attention." Her brother just gave her a defeated look. Then he stepped around her and out the door.

Kate flopped down in the nearest armchair. "Holy Mary, Mother of God!"

Her parents were just reaching the bottom of the stairs. "Don't blaspheme, Katie," her father said.

"I wasn't. I was praying for divine intervention, that God'll strike your eejit daughter-in-law with lightning between here and their car!"

Detective Randolph motioned the two elder O'Donnells toward the sofa. He sat in the other chair and faced them. "I'll call the sexual assault crisis center in Montgomery County. They'll send someone out to talk to Amy's parents tomorrow. When they've calmed down, maybe they'll see reason."

"Don't count on it," Kate said.

And by then all the evidence that would've told us what really happened will be gone.

Exhausted, she dragged herself to her feet. "I'll show you out, Detective." She needed to call Skip back, before his anxiety got the better of him and he headed for the airport. She didn't want him to cut his visit home short. There was definitely nothing he could do now. But she desperately wanted to hear his voice.

After seeing the policeman to the door, Kate turned to her parents. "Are you okay?"

They both nodded, although their sagging faces said otherwise.

"I'm gonna take a walk. Would you help Maria if the baby wakes up?"

"Aye," her father said.

Kate was not surprised when Skip answered on the first ring. She walked around the block as she told him what had happened, including the paramedic's comment that Amy might have been drugged with roofies.

The cold night air eventually drove her inside. The house was still, most of the lights turned out. Whispering into the phone, she went into the kitchen.

There was a note on the table, in her mother's handwriting. Grandma had the baby monitor, it said, and would tend to the wee one if she woke during the night. There was a turkey sandwich in the fridge and Katie was to get a good night's sleep.

At the mention of the sandwich, Kate realized she wasn't hungry, despite the fact that she hadn't eaten since lunchtime, over nine hours ago. She relayed this amazing fact to Skip.

"What, Madam Grizzly isn't hungry?" his teasing voice said in her ear.

"I think my stomach has gone into hibernation."

Skip shook his head. This was not good. He was glad he'd done what he had.

Kate was saying that she ought to go and to call her when he got home Sunday.

He'd toyed with the idea of making up a fib about the airlines messing up his reservation, but he knew she'd see right through that. "Kate, I changed my flight to tomorrow."

"You shouldn't have done that," she said, but he could hear relief in her voice.

"Well, it's done, so I'll see you tomorrow, late afternoon. Sleep tight, Kate. And if you need to talk some more, call me, no matter what time it is."

"Thanks, Skip."

"Goodnight, darlin'."

"Goodnight... sweetheart."

Skip rang her doorbell a little after four the next day. He had come straight from the airport, not even bothering to stop at his apartment first. When she opened the door, the look of pleasure and relief on her face washed most of the travel fatigue out of his system. This was the right thing to do.

He hesitated, then reached for her hand.

She let him take it and led him into the living room. "Ma, this is my friend, Skip Canfield. Dad, you remember Skip, I'm sure."

"I certainly do, Katie girl." Dan O'Donnell lumbered to his feet to shake Skip's hand. "Good ta see ya, lad."

"Pleased to meet you," Bridget murmured from the sofa.

As they all settled in the living room, Skip asked, "Where's Edie?"

"Taking a late nap," Kate said. "The excitement last night disrupted her sleep cycle."

They made small talk for a few minutes, but Skip was anxious to find out how Kate was coping. Had she heard from her brother? She had dark circles under eyes that were a washed-out gray instead of their normal sky blue. His heart ached for her.

The elder O'Donnells exchanged a look. "Well," Dan said, "I'm a bit knackered meself. While the wee one's still sleepin' I think I'll take me a nap." He stood and offered a hand to his wife

She rose to join him. "There's plenty of leftovers, Mr. Canfield. I hope you'll stay for supper."

Skip stood as well. "I'd like that, ma'am."

As soon as Kate's parents were halfway up the stairs, out of sight, he crossed to Kate's chair in one stride and pulled her to her feet. He wrapped his arms tightly around her and laid his cheek on top of her head. "I hated being that far away from you," he murmured into her hair.

She didn't resist. He felt her draw in a long, shuddering breath. She had started to relax against him, when the phone jangled in the kitchen.

Kate pulled away, giving him an apologetic look, and raced into the kitchen. He followed her.

She grabbed the portable phone from its charger. A frown creased her forehead as she listened to whoever was on the other end of the line. Then her expression morphed into something unreadable, but Skip guessed it wasn't good news.

"Phyllis, calm down," she yelled into the phone. "What about a note?"

Skip put his hand on Kate's shoulder. She was trembling.

Her parents hurried back down the stairs and into the kitchen. The baby started crying, but before her grandmother could get to the nursery, Maria was coming down the steps, baby monitor in hand. Mrs. O'Donnell turned back to her daughter.

"Phyllis, please, this is important," Kate yelled. "What exactly did it say?"

A brief pause. "I need that note, Phyllis. It's evidence... I'm begging you, please take Amy to a hospital. She needs medical attention, and psychological help."

Kate dropped the phone on the counter. "She hung up on me." She turned into Skip's arms.

"Kin we borrow yer car, Katie? I'm thinkin' we'll be makin' a visit to yer brother." Dan's brogue was thickened by emotion.

"Keys are in my purse," she mumbled from against Skip's chest.

"Take care of her, lad," Dan said softly as he and his wife headed for the front door.

"I will, sir."

Skip scooped Kate up in his arms and carried her to the living room. He sat on the sofa with her on his lap. She laid her head on his shoulder as he wrapped his arms around her. "What did your sister-in-law say?" he asked softly.

In a depressed voice, she told him. Phyllis had been doing laundry when she found a note in the pocket of the jeans Amy had been wearing the day before. The note had said, "Tell your aunt to stop destroying families, or I'll destroy hers." Phyllis had torn it into little pieces.

"Then she hung up when I tried to get her to take Amy for help. That woman is so infuriating."

"She's a mama mountain lion just tryin' to protect her cub, darlin'."

Kate stiffened in his arms. "Well she's going about it all the wrong way. If these notes are coming from some false memory fanatic, the odds are high that Amy was raped." Her voice was choked as she said that word. "They took her to scare me, but most of that crowd are parents whose adult children have accused them of child sexual abuse..."

"So these *alleged* abusers, who likely *are* abusers, wouldn't think twice 'bout molestin' a purty girl they had under their control," he finished for her. "Especially if they've slipped her roofies so's she won't even remember 'em."

A corner of Skip's mind noticed the extra helping of Texas in his voice after even a short visit home. He smiled a little, amused at himself. He considered mentioning it, to lighten the mood, but decided against it.

Then he considered lifting Kate's chin and kissing her. He regretfully decided against that as well.

She took a deep breath and let it out in a long sigh.

He tightened his arms around her. "You rest now, darlin'. There's nothin' more we can do tonight."

They sat like that for a long time, until Kate's stomach rumbled.

Skip swung her off his lap to set her feet on the floor. He stood up and took her hand. "Let's warm up some of those leftovers." He made her sit at the table while he put one dish after another into the microwave.

Maria came into the kitchen, Edie on her hip. She must have figured it was safe to resurface when she smelled food cooking. Without speaking, she put the baby in her highchair and set the table.

They ate in silence for a few minutes. Then Kate pushed her half-empty plate away. She bit her lower lip and closed her eyes. A tear leaked past an eyelid.

Maria stood and lifted Edie out of her highchair, without bothering to wipe the mashed potatoes and cranberry sauce from her face and hands. "I get dishes later, *Señor* Skip," she said quietly, then added in Spanish that she would bed the baby down.

Skip nodded. Maria took Edie off to bathe her.

Kate started to push up from the table to follow, but Skip said, "Maria's got it covered."

She nodded and sank back onto her chair. "I'm afraid I'm lousy company tonight. I think I just need to go to bed."

Skip walked around the table and took her hand to pull her to her feet. Once again, he wrapped his arms around her. She tucked her head under his chin. Despite the misery of the situation, his heart did a funny little flip. She was letting him hold her. It felt so right.

"I'm gonna hang out in the livin' room 'til your folks get back, if that's okay, darlin'?" He felt her head nodding, where it rested against his chest.

Reluctantly, he let her go and she shuffled toward the bedroom.

A half hour later, worry had him opening the master bedroom door a crack to check on her. She was lying on top of the comforter on the king-sized bed, still fully clothed except for her shoes. He tiptoed in and looked down at her sleeping form.

"I love you, Kate," he whispered under his breath. Then he found a quilt, draped over the back of an antique rocker in a corner of the room, and gently spread it over her.

Skip had lost track of time when a key rattled in the front door lock. He jumped up off the sofa, his hand instinctively going to the small of his back. But his gun was in his apartment, locked in a drawer, since he couldn't take it on the plane to Texas.

He relaxed when the O'Donnells came through the door.

Dan shook his head, his expression grim, and followed his drooping wife toward the stairs.

"Can I borrow the door key, sir? I want to go home and get my gun. Then I'm gonna sleep down here on the sofa. Just so y'all can sleep sound knowin' you're safe tonight."

"'Preciate that, lad," Dan said, handing him Kate's key ring.

On Sunday, Skip offered to take her parents to the airport. "I'd like to come back afterwards," he said to Kate, taking her hands in his as they stood in her living room. Her parents were upstairs packing.

She looked up into his eyes. They had darkened to a muddy brown. His face was pinched with worry.

"There's nothing I'd like more," she said. "But I need some time to think. Too much has been happening too fast. We'll be okay, with the security system and the window bars and all. Whoever this is, they're not likely to try anything so soon, at least not until I go back to work."

Skip lifted her hands to his chest, trapping them there under his own. She felt the solid beating of his heart through his shirt.

"So you are going back to work then?"

"I don't have much choice," she said. "The holidays are not a good time for people from dysfunctional families. I have several clients in crisis. I can't just abandon them. But if I can get them all somewhat stabilized, I may refer them to other therapists after Christmas, and take a leave of absence. That's one of the things I need to think about."

"Okay. But you need to be very careful. This guy's watching the house, at least some of the time. He'd figured out that Amy was your niece, had to have seen you gals leavin' on Friday and followed you to the mall. Then, later he must've dropped Amy off near here. It's unlikely she could've found her way back from the mall on her own. You've got to assume this creep is nearby and watching you."

Kate couldn't suppress the shudder that ran through her body. He dropped her hands and put his arms around her. She leaned her forehead against his chest.

"Do you have that detective's number?" he asked. "We should let him know about this development, even though the note was destroyed."

She sighed. "He gave his card to my brother. I didn't think to get one for myself. I'll call Michael... later."

"I've got some stuff to do tomorrow," Skip said into her hair. "But if you need to go out, run errands or anything, give me a call and I'll go with you. I'm not sure it's safe for you to be out in the world alone at this point."

She knew she should protest, but she couldn't drum up the energy. And she doubted she would go out anyway. She nodded against his chest.

He tightened his arms slightly and laid his cheek on top of her head. She let herself relax against him, wishing she never had to move again.

A few minutes later, she heard her father coming down the steps, his breathing heavy, a suitcase clunking against the wall.

Skip made no move to let her go.

Kate turned her head toward the stairs.

Her father had stopped at the bottom and was watching them intently. The corners of his mouth twitched upward. He cleared his throat. "We're ready to go, lad."

———————

On Monday morning, Kate couldn't shake the depression that had descended on her. She had to force herself to call her brother at work.

When he answered, she said, "Got a minute to talk, Michael?"

A pause, then he said, "Yeah. Let me close my office door."

She heard the sound of the door closing. "Michael, I love you." She bit her lip to keep from crying.

After another hesitation, he said, "I know, Kate. I love you too."

"And you know I love Amy, so please hear me out."

He listened without interrupting as she explained to him that the date rape drug Amy may have been given left women helpless and kept them from remembering later on a conscious level what had happened to them.

"But I know from the work I do that they're still traumatized by whatever did happen. They show signs of PTSD even with no conscious memory of the event."

"I hear what you're saying, but Phyllis believes that if Amy can't remember then it didn't do her any harm."

Kate took a deep breath to keep from snapping at him. "A lot of people think that, but that's not what we're seeing. You really need to get Amy into counseling. If she can deal with it right away, there's a much smaller risk that it will come back to haunt her later."

Michael was quiet for so long that she was afraid he had disconnected. Finally he said, "I appreciate your concern. I'll try to talk to Phyllis again when she's calmed down some more."

But Kate knew her brother was too much of a wuss where his wife was concerned to push the issue. "Michael, please!" she begged.

Another long pause. "You don't have to live with her. I do."

"Can you give me Detective Randolph's number?"

"Phyllis threw his card away."

She clenched her teeth to keep from raging at her brother.

After a couple beats, he said, "Take care, sis." He disconnected.

Kate sat at the kitchen table for a long time, staring into space, unable to quite fathom her sister-in-law's attitude, even though she'd certainly seen that level of denial before.

Maria paused by the kitchen doorway, Edie in her arms. Kate saw the worry in the nanny's face. She rarely left the baby in Maria's care on her days off, but today she couldn't even drum up the motivation to play with her child.

Maria frowned, shifted Edie to one hip, and went off to do some chore.

Kate got up to go into the bedroom to get something. Once there, she couldn't remember what she had come in for. She sat down on the side of her bed.

She thought about talking to Eddie for moral support, but realized that she really wanted to talk to Skip. She resisted the urge to call him, knowing if she did that he would drop whatever he was doing, no matter how important. She'd already disrupted his life enough recently.

She couldn't recall the last time she had talked to Eddie. It may have actually been before her confession to Skip that she conversed with her late husband in her head. When was that? At least two weeks ago.

Eddie? Are you there?

The minutes stretched out. Nothing happened.

"Eddie?" she whispered out loud.

No answer.

Kate didn't know how to feel. There was a dull ache of sadness in her chest, but much weaker than the longing and pain she'd felt off and on for the better part of two years. At the same time a small frisson of excitement ran through her. Did this mean it was no longer too soon?

Maybe.

Contemplating that idea made her feel a little better. She kicked her shoes off and stretched out on top of the comforter. She just needed to get rested up. She was so tired.

CHAPTER THIRTEEN

Tuesday morning, Kate still felt tired despite having slept a good part of the last twenty-four hours. She had to admit to herself that she was truly clinically depressed. Which shouldn't be such a shocker after all that had happened the past few days. She tried not to think about what it would mean for her family if the rift with Michael and Phyllis couldn't be mended.

She felt bad for her brother, but couldn't drum up much empathy for her sister-in-law. "Denial is not a river in Egypt," she muttered under her breath as she finished dressing for work.

When Skip arrived to stay with Maria and Edie, he insisted on watching from the front porch as Kate walked to her car. He'd arranged to have Rose come to her office when her client hours were over, to escort her to her car in the dark parking lot. He'd wanted Rose to hang out in the center's waiting area, as a bodyguard. Kate had told him he was over-reacting. He'd backed off.

On the drive to work, Kate had a little talk with herself. Depressed or not, it wasn't like her to let a man take care of her problems. Although it certainly felt good to have a man in her life again on whom she could rely. But still...

She was reminded of a thought she'd had the previous summer, when she'd first acknowledged the intensity of their attraction for each other. She could lose herself in a connection this strong.

It felt like she was doing just that, losing her sense of who she was. But how much of that was about the stress of her life getting to her, and how much was about Skip? Her mind blanked as she tried to sort that out.

Once she got to work, she perked up some. Nothing like focusing on other people's problems to help you forget your own for a while.

Pauline told her at lunchtime that Tammy had cancelled her appointment for Thursday afternoon. Kate was about to breathe a sigh of relief when the receptionist informed her that the client had rescheduled for Friday.

Damn!

Pauline said, "Are you okay, dear?"

"No not really, but thanks for asking." Kate went into her office to eat her lunch, and to contemplate whether she should refer Tammy to another therapist. It wasn't a good sign when you were glad a client had cancelled and disappointed when she rescheduled.

Audrey was Kate's last client of the evening. She hadn't been able to get a sitter so she could come in during the day. The downside to cutting off contact with her parents was that it was now harder for her to find a babysitter. So far it was the only downside Audrey had reported.

The abuser's face was still fuzzy in her memories, but Audrey told Kate that it didn't seem to matter all that much anymore. It was either her father or his look-alike brother, and she had no intentions of having anything to do with either one of them again.

"It's possible that you're not getting a clearer image of the abuser's face because those details weren't recorded in the first place," Kate pointed out. "We tend to think of human memory like it's a camera, but it's not. It only records the details of an experience that we actively pay attention to. As a child you may have been *avoiding* looking at his face, because you didn't want to think about how this man, who was supposed to love you, was hurting you instead."

Audrey nodded. "The voice, when he talks about... the lollipop, it sounds like my old man, but again his brother's voice is similar. Oh, speaking of my asshole uncle, my mother called this afternoon. Without thinking I picked up the phone. Forgot to screen the call. I was about to hang up when I realized what she was saying.

"She'd thought she had my father talked into dropping the lawsuit, but then dear sweet Uncle Phil convinced him not to. Mother started trying to guilt-trip me into letting her see Alicia. Playing the martyr who can't control what her husband does."

"How did you deal with that?" Kate knew Audrey was more susceptible to her mother's manipulations than to her father's efforts to control her.

"I surprised myself. I didn't feel the least bit guilty. I told her she's an autonomous adult and she can refuse to participate in the lawsuit, and that until it's dropped, I'm not even going to discuss the possibility of her seeing Alicia."

Kate sat forward in her chair. "That's great that your mother's guilt trip didn't work. But don't let the lawsuit against me affect your decisions about yourself and your family."

"Oh, I have no intention of letting her see Alicia anyway, not until she gets it that there *is* abuse in this family and it's her job to protect her granddaughter from it."

"Okay, that's the right thing to be negotiating with her. The lawsuit is my problem. The agency's behind me. We've got malpractice insurance, and the insurance company has a whole army of lawyers to defend me."

Kate was fibbing here. If the insurance company thought they could get a settlement that would be cheaper than going to court, she suspected their lawyers wouldn't hesitate to throw her and her reputation under the bus.

But she needed to get her client to stop trying to protect her. "I only went along with Rob's idea that you sue them because that's what you had wanted to do in the first place."

"I understand all that," Audrey said. "But as far as I'm concerned my parents' attacking you is an attack against me. They're only doing it to mess with me, to try to control my life. And you're the one helping me get through this crap. Without you, I don't think I could face it."

Kate paused for a moment. "Okay, putting myself in your shoes, I can see where you're coming from. A threat to me is a threat to you because I'm part of your support system."

"A huge part. I need your support as much as I need Ted's."

When Audrey left and Kate had to refocus on her own life, she discovered that she felt a lot better than she had that morning. She was exhausted, but it had been a satisfying day. Her job might be difficult at times, and it opened her up to things like malpractice suits and anonymous threats. But she still loved it.

She hated that Amy and her family had been caught in the crossfire, but she decided she wasn't going to let some crazy fanatics stop her from using her skills to help people. She was not going to take a leave of absence.

Having made that decision, Kate felt better still. She had found her equilibrium again.

———◦———

Skip was waiting on her front porch when she got home. Shadows from the porch light accented the tension and fatigue on his face.

Guilt jabbed at her heart. He probably wasn't sleeping well, from worrying about her.

He opened the door for her and followed her inside. Maria descended from the second floor, with a freshly-bathed Edie in her arms.

"Go on home, Skip. You look beat," Kate said over her shoulder as she took her sleepy child from the nanny.

"I think that falls into the pot callin' the kettle black category, darlin'."

Kate gave him a small smile, then wished the nanny a goodnight and headed for the nursery.

When she emerged fifteen minutes later, she was pleasantly surprised to see Skip sitting on the sofa. "You're still here!"

"Yeah, I'm still here." His voice sounded as tired as he looked. "Made the mistake of sitting down and couldn't work up the energy to get up again."

"Well, if you're that tired, I guess it's safe for me to sit down next to you."

"Not sure I'm quite *that* tired." He gave her an exaggerated leer.

Kate plopped down on the sofa anyway, just a few inches from him. She had made another decision.

"Uh, I know we suspended the four-foot rule over the weekend," Skip said, "but we probably need to reinstate... What are you doing?" There was alarm in his voice as she wiggled closer, the soft wool of her slacks brushing against the side of his jean-clad thigh.

"Just sitting down to talk." Her tone was casual, but she was feeling a powerful surge of self-doubt. She'd been putting him off for so long. What if his interest had waned? Her eyes stung at the thought. He'd jokingly leered at her, but maybe that was just his way of segueing into the request that they reinstate the four-foot rule.

"But if you're too tired..." She let her voice trail off, giving him an out if he didn't want her anymore. Her chest ached.

Skip had been sitting very still for several seconds. Now he twisted around to face her. "Is what I think is happening here, is that what's *really* happening here?"

"Yes," she whispered, suddenly unable to catch her breath as his eyes locked on hers.

A smile spread slowly across his face. It was the sexiest smile she had ever seen.

He picked up her hand and brought it to his face, then turned it over and kissed her palm, a feathery touch of warm lips against her skin. She sucked in her breath.

"That wasn't exactly the reaction I expected," she managed to gasp out. "But I like it," she hastily added.

"Oh don't worry, darlin'. I'm gonna get to the kissing your lips part soon. But first I need to ask you something." He was holding her palm trapped against his cheek.

She cupped her hand slightly under his jaw and tried to pull his face down toward hers, but he resisted. "Is it okay if I ask you something first?" he repeated softly, his face and voice serious.

"Yes," she whispered. Her hand was still trapped under his against his cheek. He tilted his head so he could touch his lips to the soft skin on the inside of her wrist.

She heard a small strangling noise and realized it had come from her own throat.

"Actually two questions, darlin'. Where exactly is Maria's bedroom? I know it's upstairs somewhere, but how *far* upstairs? And how soundly does she sleep?"

She smacked him on his thigh with her free hand. "Third floor, has her own little apartment up there." Then her voice dropped to a husky whisper. "She's off duty. She won't come out again tonight."

"So we have an entire story of the house between ourselves and Maria, as a sound buffer," he said softly. His lips drifted closer to hers.

Then he pulled back a little. "Nope, better not kiss you yet. Once I do, there'll be no pausin' to consider logistics, and I'm way too big a man to make love on a couch." He smiled at her, the gold flecks flashing in his eyes. "May I suggest we move to the bedroom?"

Dear God, Kate prayed. *Get us past this next bump and I think I can take it from there.*

"Well, there's just one little problem," she said out loud, dropping her gaze to the diamond ring and wedding band on the hand that was resting on his knee.

Of its own volition, the hand moved a bit up the warm surface of his jeans, stretched tight across his muscular thigh.

He sucked in his breath. "Half an inch further," he growled softly, "and it'll be the damn couch after all."

She gave him a small smile, then said quietly, "I'm afraid we won't have an *entire* story between us and Maria." She tilted her head to the side, in the direction of the hallway that led to the master bedroom. "Not *that* bedroom."

His response was quick and self-chastising. "Of course not. How stupid of me!" But then her first words sank in. "You have another bedroom in mind? On the second floor?"

"Guest suite. Only a queen-sized bed, but it has a lovely adjoining bathroom." She realized she sounded like a sales brochure for a bed and breakfast inn.

He tilted her chin up so he could look down into her eyes, then his face broke into a wide grin. "Second floor suite, it is then. We'll just have to be quiet."

Disentangling himself, he pushed to a stand, pulling her up with him. He leaned down and whispered in her ear, "Would you like me to sweep you off your feet or would you prefer to walk?"

"Uh, just hold on to me in case my knees give out. They're a little wobbly at the moment."

Arm around her shoulders, he moved her toward the stairs.

Her arm slid around his waist, bumped up against the butt of his gun in its waistband holster, and moved up a bit on his back. She veered over toward the nursery to retrieve a small plastic box from the table beside its door. "Sorry," she said, holding up the baby monitor. "Comes with the territory."

He grinned down at her. "Of course. *Now* can I sweep you off your feet?"

She grinned back. "Sweep away."

He had her in his arms and was halfway up the stairs before she could take another breath. On the second floor, she pointed toward the guest room door. Once through it he put her down on her feet.

But before he could kiss her, she tilted her head toward the bathroom and said, "Uh, I'll be right back."

He nodded, but his smile had vanished.

"I'll only be a minute," she promised and slipped into the bathroom, closing the door. It actually took less than a minute to do what she needed to do, which included removing Eddie's rings from her finger.

She opened the door. Skip had turned off the overhead light. The bedroom was bathed in the soft glow of the small lamp on the dresser.

Intentionally leaving the bathroom door open, she moved slowly into the darker bedroom. The semi-sheer negligee drifted softly around her, backlit by the bathroom light. A soft hiss came from the direction of the bed.

She walked toward him. He was sitting on the side of the bed in nothing but his jeans. But he wasn't looking at her now. His head was hanging down between his broad shoulders, soft brown hair a curtain hiding his face.

She sat beside him and ran her hand up his bare arm to the shoulder. They both sucked in their breath.

Then he said in a strangled voice, "Kate, we can't do this."

She froze. "Why not?"

He turned to her, anguish in his eyes. "I don't have anything with me, you know, to protect you."

Her breath rushed out on a bubble of laughter. Leaning over to put her lips against his ear, she whispered, "Top drawer of the nightstand."

He turned and gently grabbed her shoulders. "You planned this, didn't you?"

She couldn't tell in the dim light if he was angry. "Well, not exactly this particular moment. But I figured this moment would happen eventually, and a little pre-planning might be helpful."

He laughed out loud, then pulled her against his chest. "You are somethin' else, darlin'."

He let her go, then turned to the nightstand to extract the needed object from the drawer. Unbuttoning his jeans, he pushed them off his hips and onto the floor, then turned slightly away from her as excited fingers struggled with the small package.

"Not exactly the most romantic way to get things started," he muttered under his breath.

Kate pretended she hadn't heard him. She used his distraction to move around the bed, peeling off the negligee before sliding between the sheets. Fair is fair. If he was starting out buck naked, so was she. This drawn-out anticipation was losing its appeal.

His task accomplished, he slipped between the sheets and turned to her. She moaned softly when he touched bare skin.

"What happened to the negligee?" he whispered, as his hand slid across her rib cage and then slowly down her belly, stopping just above her navel.

Distracted by the heat coursing through her, it took her a moment to remember what the question was. "Figured it had served its purpose."

She turned on her side to face him. His hand settled in the valley between ribcage and hip. In the dim light, Kate feasted her eyes on his broad chest, the muscles smooth and strong but not unnaturally bulging. She bit her lower lip and ran her hand over the curve of shoulder and down, coming to rest on his solid bicep. She heard a soft groan and felt his skin quiver, which set off a responding quiver down the core of her body.

"Kate?" he whispered.

"Hmm."

"Can I kiss you now?"

She looked up into his eyes, a small smile on her lips. "What are you waiting for?"

He knew he had to go slow, even though it was exquisite agony. He had learned long ago that he was too big and strong to let himself lose control. He could all too easily hurt a woman. So he took his time, savoring the slowness, now that he could finally hold her, stroke her, kiss her, and then do it all again.

Kissing her was everything he had imagined it would be. When their mouths met and her lips parted slightly, he slipped the tip of his tongue between them, nudging them further apart. He lost himself in that warm place, slowly exploring it.

Her arms wrapped themselves around his neck and she moaned deep in her throat, arching her back to press against him. That was almost his undoing.

Patience, patience.

He stroked his hand down her side and then up again to cup her breast. As his tongue made another lazy circuit of her mouth, he flicked his thumb across her nipple.

She jerked a little. Another moan deep in her throat. She broke away from his lips just far enough to gasp out his name.

Heat raged through him. Slow was becoming difficult.

He moved his head down and touched his lips, feather soft, to her breast, and then claimed it with his mouth.

She sucked in her breath. A shudder ran down the length of her body arching against him.

His body trembled in response, desperate to merge with hers.

Then her fingers were in his hair, tugging gently.

He took that as a signal. Briefly reclaiming her mouth, he rolled her over onto her back. He pushed up off her chest so she could breathe and locked his elbows.

Her eyes, now a smoky indigo in the soft light, locked onto his, and her well-kissed lips slowly spread into a smile.

"What *are* you waiting for?" she whispered, opening her legs just far enough for his hips to fit nicely between them. Her back arched and her eyes glazed over as he moved into her.

With great effort, he kept his movements slow. Her legs were now entwined around his. Her hands ran down his arms and back up to his shoulders. Then they were tracing fire across his skin as they explored every inch of his body. He struggled not to lose control.

She hit a ticklish spot on his side and he wriggled slightly away from her touch. She smiled.

Then suddenly her arms were wrapped around his waist, forcing him deeper inside of her.

And he was gone, lost in a sea of sensations stronger than he'd ever felt before. With the few brain cells that were still functional, he knew he needed to drop down on his elbows, before he forgot to keep them locked and ended up crushing her.

His forearms along either side of her head, he could feel her breasts pressed against his ribs. Her lips, warm and soft, were skimming little kisses across his chest. His skin burned in their wake.

He groaned aloud. Her fingers ran up his back and down again, trailing fire.

She held on tight as wave after wave of pure sensation washed over them. He was soaring, all connections lost except the one with her. She surrounded him, filled him, every corner of his being.

Slowly, with a twinge of loss, he drifted back to earth.

His thigh muscles were quivering from the strain of holding his weight off of her. Rolling onto his side, he brought her with him, still welded together, as he kissed her again—a long, slow, delicious kiss.

Their bodies peeled away from each other as he rolled onto his back. Another twinge of loss when cool air flowed over sweaty skin. He gathered her in against him. On her side, one leg thrown over his, an arm lying across his stomach, she rested her cheek on his chest.

He heaved a sigh of contentment.

Her fingers searched for and found the ticklish spot. He wriggled a little but he didn't want to pull away from her. The fingers stilled. He could feel her mouth spreading into a grin where the side of her face was pressed against his chest.

"You're gonna use that against me at some point in the future, aren't ya, darlin'?" he whispered into her curls. She didn't say anything but he felt the grin grow wider against his skin. He tightened his arms around her.

He couldn't make himself wait any longer. He tilted her head up. "I love you, Kate." Then he touched his lips to hers. They kissed until they were both desperate for air.

She sighed and settled her cheek back against his chest.

He held her, marveling at his good fortune. He was thirty-eight years old and had never truly been *in* love, before now.

After things had gone sour with Carrie, he'd stopped looking for love, although he still dated. He enjoyed the company of women and had no desire to be a monk. But he'd come to the conclusion that this great passionate falling-in-love thing that people talked about, that songs and movies and novels were written about, that it didn't really exist. It was an adult version of Santa Claus and the Tooth Fairy.

And then this woman had snuck up on his heart. Or maybe there really was some naked cherub out there, flinging arrows randomly at people, for he knew she had no more intended to fall in love with him than he had with her.

Hot moisture on his chest. It took him a second to realize what it was.

Panicking, he turned onto his side and pushed up on one elbow. "My God, Kate! Did I hurt you?"

Tears were streaming down her cheeks, but she shook her head.

"What's wrong? Tell me what's wrong!"

She shook her head again, struggled to get words out. Finally she whispered, "Eddie just said goodbye." Her face crumpled.

The pain in his chest was so sharp, for a second he thought he was having a heart attack. It had been too soon after all. Now how was she going to feel about him? Would she push him away?

Stop being so selfish.

He gathered her into his arms and held her, whispering, "it's okay, sh, sh, sh, it's okay."

When her tears slowed, he kissed the top of her head, then said in her ear, "I'm afraid I don't have a handkerchief to offer you. No pockets at the moment."

Rolling onto her back, still encircled by his arms, she looked up into his eyes and gave him a lopsided smile.

"What does this mean?" he asked, trying to keep the anxiety out of his voice. He brushed damp curls off her cheeks.

She stared up at him for a long moment. "It means... it's okay now," she whispered haltingly, "...to move on. I might miss him at times, but it's okay now to..."

She reached up and put her hands on his cheeks, then pulled his face down to hers. "I love you, Skip Canfield," she murmured against his lips.

He lost himself in her again.

CHAPTER FOURTEEN

Kate was awakened the next morning by a ray of sunshine sneaking through a crack between the curtains. It only took a second of staring at the ceiling to know where she was. She had imagined this moment enough times that finding herself in this bed was not disorienting. Recalling the evening before, in glorious technicolor detail, she savored the array of tingling sensations in her body.

Slowly, so as not to disturb Skip if he was still asleep, she rolled over on her side.

He wasn't there.

She sat up and started to pull the sheet up over her breasts.

Oh, come on, girl.

He'd seen them last night, more than seen them actually–the tingling got stronger–he might as well see them in broad daylight. He would just have to get used to whatever imperfections age and nursing a child had imprinted on them.

"Skip," she called softly in the direction of the slightly ajar bathroom door.

No answer.

She swung her feet around and sat on the side of the bed. She glanced at the nightstand. The baby monitor was gone. Confused, she looked down to see if it had gotten knocked off onto the floor. Nope.

She looked around the room. It was on the nightstand on Skip's side of the bed.

What's it doing over there?

She stretched across the tousled bedding to grab the little plastic box. It had been turned off.

Her mind registered the angle of the sunbeam streaming across the bed. Panic shot through her. The baby never slept this late, and Skip had turned the monitor off.

She jumped up and started for the door, then realized she couldn't race downstairs stark naked. Running into the bathroom, she grabbed the terrycloth robe from the hook behind the door. Hastily wrapping it around her, she raced across the bedroom.

She was looking down, tying the sash, when she ran head on into the front of Skip's shirt. Bouncing back a couple inches, she looked up at him.

He wrapped his arms around her, smiling down into her eyes, until her expression registered.

"Skip, the baby! Why isn't she awake yet?"

"She is. She's fine! She's had her morning pony ride around the living room and is now in her highchair, finger-painting with her oatmeal."

Kate sagged against him, her knees gone weak with relief.

He gathered her closer and said into her hair, "I'm sorry. I didn't mean to scare you. I just wanted to let you sleep in a little, since I kept you up half the night." He took her by the shoulders and held her away from him, then dropped one hand to pull loose the half knot in the sash of her robe.

A new feeling jolted her, but the heat coursing down the core of her body was making it hard to sort out.

He took her face between his hands and leaned down to kiss her, then stopped halfway there. He eased back. "If you're still worried about her, we can go check on her. But Maria seemed to have things under control."

"No, it's not that. It's... I'm not sure what..." She was discovering she couldn't think and talk at the same time, at least not when he was standing this close, his hands on her cheeks, his body radiating the medley of scents she had come to associate with him—the cottony fragrance of his shirt, the lingering whiff of citrus aftershave and the smell of warm male skin, *very* warm male skin.

She reached up and touched the stubble on his cheek. It was a shade lighter than his hair, almost blond. Heat and energy shimmered through her. "I just felt, uh, realized..."

Skip ended her struggle to think by covering her mouth with his own. Her knees melted. She sagged into him.

Wrapping one arm around her to pull her closer, he continued to explore her mouth. His other hand slid inside her robe to do some exploring there.

She wrapped her arms around his waist. It took a long moment for it to register that something was missing. She broke the kiss. "Where's your gun?"

He looked across the room. She followed his line of vision. His .38 was lying in its holster on the nightstand.

"Careless of me," he said. "I forgot to take it downstairs." While guarding Edie, he usually kept it on top of an antique china cabinet in the living room, well out of the baby's reach but close at hand if he needed it.

"We'll need to do something different. Maybe get a gun cabinet," Kate said, still looking at the gun. "Edie will be walking soon."

He took her chin and turned her face back toward his. "Kate..."

"What?" she murmured, looking up at him. Her hands had somehow moved around to stroke his chest. His skin quivered under her touch.

"I love you," he whispered. "Now shut up." And he kissed her again.

They had finally had breakfast and were sitting on the living room sofa, not touching, Skip's arm was draped across the back of the sofa, behind Kate's shoulders.

She figured he was leaving it up to her to explain the change in their relationship to Maria.

Of course, the fact that we spent half the morning upstairs is probably a giveaway.

Kate watched Edie pull herself to a stand by grabbing the edge of the armchair seat. She let go, took a step, then fell down. She immediately crawled back to the chair and repeated the process all over again.

Her little girl was learning to walk.

Kate, on the other hand, wasn't sure she would ever be able to walk again. Her legs felt like rubber and there was a relaxed, warm feeling all over her body. It felt like her joints, bones and muscles had melted into one flowing sensation of contentment.

Skip glanced at his watch. "Don't you have a lunch date with Rob today, darlin'?"

"No, he's in court."

Maria was in full housekeeping mode, bustling around between the kitchen, master bedroom and nursery, first with a laundry basket in her hands and now with a feather duster. She stopped in front of them and opened her mouth to say something.

But Kate didn't give her a chance. "Maria, Skip's going to be staying at night, in the guest room, to keep us safe."

"*Si. Muy bien. Señor* Skip stay." Maria's grin was about to split her face and her head was moving up and down like a bobble-head doll. She bustled off to dust the master bedroom.

"How will we ever overcome her disapproval, darlin'?" Skip drawled in her ear as he dropped his arm onto her shoulders.

She turned and smiled up at him. "Is that okay with you? I guess I'm kind of taking liberties here..." her voice trailed off.

"Darlin', you can take liberties with me *any time you want.*"

They heard a shrill cry from across the room. Edie had taken two steps away from the armchair and had fallen face first on the rug.

Kate started to get up but Skip put his hand on her knee. "I'll get her."

Before she could respond, he stood up and scooped the crying baby into his arms. He brushed dark curls off her chubby wet cheeks. "It's okay, little one. Let Uncle Skip kiss the boo-boo and make it better." He kissed her tiny nose.

The baby gave him a solemn look. Then she blessed him with a snaggle-toothed grin and said, "Uh Ski."

Skip glanced across at Kate, a big smile spreading across his face. "She said my name."

Kate didn't respond. She stared into space, once again trying to sort out the feeling she'd had earlier.

"Did I do something wrong?" Skip said, his voice worried.

She shook her head. "No, you're fine."

He returned to the sofa, Edie in his arms. Her tumble seemed to already be forgotten. She sat on his lap and played with the buttons on his shirt.

Then the baby suddenly pushed herself backward along one thigh toward his knee. He grabbed her hands just before she slid off onto the floor. Edie chortled and started bouncing up and down.

Skip jiggled his leg and made giddy-up noises, holding onto her plump little arms.

Softly, Kate said, "That's the realization you wouldn't give me time to sort out this morning."

"What's that, darlin'?" He was watching the baby to make sure she didn't jiggle off his knee.

Now that she'd brought it up, Kate wasn't sure she should have. "Well, that..." She hesitated, considering and rejecting different words, unable to think of a way to say it that wouldn't sound presumptuous. What she had felt earlier, when she'd realized he had gotten up to take care of the baby so she could sleep in, was the lifting of some of the weight from her shoulders. Weight she'd gotten so used to carrying the last eleven months that she'd forgotten it was there, until some of it was gone.

He glanced over at her. "Are you gonna share this realization, darlin'? Or is it a secret."

"Uh, I realized that... I'll have to, uh, get used to sharing some of my parenting tasks." Those were most definitely *not* the right words. They implied way too much permanency.

"Is that a bad thing?" he asked.

"Oh, no, it was kind of a relief," she said, then was sure she had gone too far. She hadn't meant to convey an expectation that he continue to carry part of the burden–a burden he couldn't even know existed yet, since he'd never had children.

Skip gave the baby one final bounce, lifted her up to kiss her again on her little nose and then put her down on the floor. "Go play, little one, while I talk to your mama."

He turned sideways on the sofa. "Let's get something straight here. I'm in this for the long haul. That is, if that's what you want?"

She looked into his eyes, then nodded. Her arms, of their own volition, circled his neck. Their lips met.

The sound of someone clearing their throat brought them back to their senses before they started to make love right there on the sofa.

Maria stood in front of them, hands on her hips, feather duster sticking out to the side like a lopsided rooster's tail. She was trying to look stern but wasn't quite pulling it off. "You two, go! Pretty day. Go out. I clean here now. You in way. *¡Fuera de aqui!*" She made shooing motions with her hand.

"Let's take Edie for a walk," Kate said.

Skip frowned. "Uh, I'm not sure that's a good idea."

"Sweetheart, remember that conversation we had last summer?"

"Which one? We've had *so many* conversations."

She chuckled a little. "True. I mean the one about fear, how I'm not willing to let it rule my life. I don't take unnecessary chances. I'm not a rash person. But I'm not going to stay cooped up in my house, because some kook is running around out there. Besides, whoever's doing this is probably going to lay low for a while, after last weekend. And if they *are* around, they're not going to try anything if we're with you, in broad daylight."

"Okay, you talked me into it." He got up and pulled her to a stand.

"It'll just take a minute to change her."

Skip started talking to Maria in Spanish while Kate picked Edie up and took her into the nursery. For once the baby lay relatively still while her mother changed her diaper.

The actions were so rote that Kate's mind wandered. She couldn't believe her good fortune to have this man love her. Without conscious forethought, the words slipped into her mind, *How did I get so lucky, Eddie, to find two wonderful men in one lifetime?*

Her hands froze as she was tucking Edie's arm into the sleeve of her little jacket. The baby squirmed and brought her mother back to task. Kate held her breath, waiting for an answer, while she finished getting the child into her jacket and fastened the strap of her hat under her chin.

No answer came. Kate let out her breath.

A wave of sadness swept through her, closing her throat and threatening to buckle her knees. Eddie was truly gone.

Then she could have sworn she felt someone press lips against the top of her head.

An image popped into her mind of Eddie, sitting on the edge of a cloud and smiling down at her and their daughter. She couldn't help smiling herself at the silliness of the image, but she knew he wanted her to move on and be happy again—and provide a flesh-and-blood father for his daughter, not just stories of a dead man told to her by her mother.

Kate's throat closed again.

Edie started to fuss, unhappy about lying on the changing table. Her mother picked her up and turned around.

And collided once again with Skip's chest. She jumped.

He grabbed her shoulders to steady her. "Sorry. Didn't mean to startle you."

"Not your fault. I was thinking about other things and didn't hear you come in." She smiled up at him.

He cupped the side of her face and gently ran his thumb across her cheek. "What were you thinking about, darlin'?"

"How lucky I am."

He cocked his head to one side.

But Edie chose that moment to pat her mother's other cheek. "Ma muh."

"We better go," Kate said. "She doesn't stay happy for long if she isn't moving."

"I've noticed that."

"Would you grab the stroller. It's in the closet by the front door."

Once Edie was strapped into the stroller, they started down the sidewalk. Skip put his arm around Kate's shoulders, but his hip kept bumping against the side of the stroller handle. Stopping, he pointed at the handle. "Mind if I do that?"

"Help yourself," she said. They switched places and he planted his big, right hand in the middle of the stroller handle, then scooped up Kate's hand with his left.

They started moving forward again. "Much better," Skip said.

Kate thought so too, but the tingling sensation running up her arm was making it hard to think. Searching for a subject that didn't require much concentration, she recalled how he'd snagged his pistol off the top of the china cabinet as he'd moved through the living room a few minutes ago. He'd tucked it into his waistband holster in one fluid and well-practiced movement.

"I have a question for you," she said.

"Shoot."

She laughed. "Actually that's what the question's about. Why do you carry your gun in your waistband, instead of using a shoulder holster? Isn't that uncomfortable?"

"Technically that's two questions." He smoothly swerved the stroller away from a bush that Edie was determined to defoliate. "Question number two. I'm used to it, hardly even notice it's there most of the time. Question number one. It's just as easy to get to quickly, but a shoulder holster requires wearing a jacket to hide it, year round."

"You still carry it there this time of year though, when you're wearing a coat anyway."

"Gotta be consistent. Don't want to be reaching around to my back, and my gun's not there, 'cause I'm wearing a shoulder holster that day."

They had reached the end of her street and turned the corner to go around the block.

Kate realized that her light topic of conversation wasn't so light after all. Before this, her mind had shied away from thinking about the dangers of his job. The times when she'd seen him pull his gun in the past, he had been protecting her. She thought of those incidents as aberrations in her life. But for him, they were his bread and butter.

He broke into her thoughts. "My work isn't as dangerous as one might think."

She looked up at him. In a teasing tone, she said, "I'm not sure I can be with you after all, Skip Canfield. It's rather disconcerting that you seem to be able to read my mind."

He chuckled. "Not usually a good mind reader. Just with you."

"I didn't think I was all that easy to read." She knew she wasn't. Her work required that she be able to hide her thoughts and feelings, unless and until it was therapeutically beneficial to share them.

He glanced down at her upturned face. "You're not. But I tend to pay closer attention to you than most folks would."

"I hope you keep on paying close attention to me." She grinned up at him.

"You bet. It's something my daddy taught me. 'Pay attention to your woman, son, and she'll love you forever.'" He squeezed her hand.

"Very wise man, your daddy... So what did you mean?"

"About what?"

"That your work isn't as dangerous as I might think."

"It's not the same as being a cop. I don't go looking for the bad guys, or at least not the violent ones. PI work is mostly computer searches these days and when you are doing field work, it's usually to catch a cheating spouse or a person pretending to be disabled to defraud an insurance company. And even then I don't have to confront them, just snap some pictures."

She snickered a little as they turned the next corner. "Hard to visualize you hiding in the bushes with your camera. Have to be a mighty big bush."

He smiled down at her, then his expression grew serious again. "Yeah, sometimes my size can be a disadvantage, but it's also another thing that keeps me safe. When I'm acting as a bodyguard, I'm mostly a deterrent. The bad guys tend to decide against trying whatever they had in mind, when they see me coming."

All that made sense, but she knew of at least two occasions when he *had* been actively looking for the bad guys, and one of those times, he'd almost ended up dead.

"Don't worry, Kate. I'm not only a very patient man. I'm also a very careful one."

She punched him lightly in the arm. "Will you *stop* reading my mind."

"Not in this lifetime." He grinned down at her.

"So what were you and Maria talking about, while I was changing Edie?"

Skip's grin widened. "Well, I was going to surprise you but... I asked her to call Rose to see if she's available for some guard duty tonight so we could go out."

She matched his grin. "And here I was thinking that your fluency in Spanish was yet another good reason for keeping you around. But now I'm not so sure, not if you and Maria are going to conspire behind my back."

He lifted the hand he was holding to his lips and kissed her fingers. "Pretty lady, will you have dinner with me tonight?"

The zing of electricity that shot up her arm made it hard to breathe for a moment. "I would be delighted," she finally managed to say. "Although it may be hard to keep from creating a scandalous scene."

"Why's that, darlin'?"

"Cause we seem to have great difficulty keeping our hands off each other."

They rounded the next corner. "At least now that's only a problem *in public*. In private, I can have my way with you." He looked down at her with a lascivious grin. "You have no idea how hard it's been to keep from grabbing you and kissing you the last few months."

"Oh, I most certainly do. I was having the same problem. It's a good thing that you can't *always* read my mind, 'cause I was fantasizing about ripping your clothes off on more than one occasion."

He stopped moving and brought her hand to his lips again. This time he turned it over and kissed her palm. Her knees almost buckled under her.

He leaned down to kiss her, but Edie chose that moment to fuss.

Kate chuckled. "Afraid that's something you'll have to get used to, having to compete with my daughter for my attention."

"It would never occur to me to think of it as competition." He started the stroller rolling forward again.

————◇————

They walked in silence for a few minutes. Skip was struggling with his feelings. He had loved this woman for months without being able to declare that love. Now he felt so good, he wanted to say "I love you" every five minutes. But she'd only said it once, last night when emotions were running high.

He realized he was terrified. What if he said too much too soon, moved too fast and scared her off? The thought that he could still lose her... He swallowed hard.

He wasn't used to feeling insecure like this. Or at least not in the last couple decades. He'd been a late bloomer and the scrawny sixteen-year-old inside of him had never quite gotten used to the idea that he'd grown up to be a hunk.

But being handsome had its advantages in the world of relationships. In his senior year of high school, he had gone from the guy no girl would consider dating to being able to have just about any girl he wanted. He'd never particularly worried about getting his heart broken before, but then he'd never felt like this before.

Damn it, one of the things he loved about Kate was that she was such a straight-forward person. She didn't play games. It would be okay to just ask. Or would it?

Kate squeezed his hand, making him realize that he'd tightened his grip.

"What's the matter?" she asked.

He stopped moving and looked down at her. "I've been holding back for so long, it's hard for me to go slow now. I... I'm afraid I'll push too fast." He turned his face away, staring off into the distance. "I don't want to lose you, now that I've finally got you."

She reached up and turned his face back toward her, then brushed his hair back out of his eyes. The touch of her fingers sent a frisson of energy through him. He groaned softly.

"Sweetheart," she said softly, "you're not going to lose me. I don't spook easily, and I'll let you know if you're moving too fast."

He breathed out a sigh, then tensed again. "Would I be moving too fast if I asked if you love me?"

She looked up at him, laughter in her eyes. "I thought we'd established that fact last night."

"Yeah, well, I wasn't sure that... maybe that was just the passion of the moment."

She gave him a gentle smile. "Sweetheart, I told Liz Franklin weeks ago that I was in love with you."

His heart did a funny little flip. "You did?"

"I did. I love you, Skip Canfield." She wrapped her arms around his neck to pull his face down. She kissed him.

After a moment, the stroller handle started jiggling in his hand. Without breaking the kiss, he looked at Edie out of the corner of his eye. She was bouncing up and down, her arm stretched as far as she could reach, trying to grab the branch of a pine tree sticking out over the edge of the sidewalk.

He pulled away from Kate and nudged the stroller handle to keep the branch out of the little girl's reach. "Oh, no you don't, little one. I suspect pine needles are not part of your approved diet."

He started them moving again. They turned onto the sidewalk leading to the front porch.

At the bottom of the steps, he reached for Kate before she could take the baby out of the stroller. But he didn't kiss her. He just held her gently against him. Her arms slid under his jacket to wrap around his back. He kissed the top of her head, then rested his cheek against her hair.

They stood that way, content to just hold and be held, breathing in each other's scent, until Edie started fussing.

Skip let Kate go so she could undo straps and lift the baby out of the stroller.

She hefted Edie onto her hip. "Time for your nap, little girl."

"Oh, I like the sound of that." He leered at Kate. "Do the adults get to take naps too, while babies are sleeping?"

She chuckled and started up the steps. Over her shoulder, she said, "So this is going to be my fate, huh? You're going to want to make love to me every time we don't absolutely have to be doing something else."

"Are you objecting to that plan?"

"Not in the least." She grinned down at him.

Kate unlocked the door while Skip wrestled the stroller into submission and carried it up the steps. By the time she walked inside, the baby had already fallen asleep on her shoulder. Fresh air tended to have that effect on her.

While Skip was figuring out how to get the folded-up stroller back into the tiny closet, Kate went into the nursery and gently laid Edie on her back in her crib. She undid the hat and got it off, then unbuttoned the jacket but decided to leave it on rather than risk waking her. She flipped the switch for the overhead fan so the child wouldn't get overheated.

Kate went into the kitchen. Dropping her coat on a chair, she went to the refrigerator and got out a bottle of water. She twisted off the cap and took a long pull as she turned around.

Skip had walked up behind her. He put his arms around her waist. She offered him the water bottle.

He took a drink, then put the bottle on the counter. Taking her hand in his, he brought it to his lips and gently kissed the inside of her wrist. Her joints melted.

"I love you, Kate," he whispered, then swept her up into his arms and turned around.

He stopped in mid-stride.

Maria was standing in the kitchen doorway, her face pale. "Oh, Kate, *Señor* Skip, I so glad you back." Then she burst into rapid-fire Spanish.

CHAPTER FIFTEEN

As Maria talked, Skip's arms tensed around Kate.

She clung to his neck, not understanding a word but knowing something was very wrong. "What's she saying?"

"I'm not sure, She's going too fast for me." He set Kate down on her feet. "*¡Maria, no hables tan rapido, por favor!*"

Maria repeated what she had said, at a somewhat slower pace.

"Where is it?" Skip interrupted, his voice sharp. She pointed with a trembling hand at the kitchen table.

He closed the distance to the table and looked down at a piece of paper lying there.

Kate moved up next to him. She grabbed his arm as she read the words. YOU NEED TO LEAVE OTHER PEOPLE'S FAMILIES ALONE. OR I'LL MAKE YOU PAY. I'LL MAKE <u>YOUR</u> FAMILY PAY.

A vice clamped around her chest, making it hard to breathe. "How'd they get into my kitchen?" She heard and hated the tremor in her voice.

Skip put his arm around her shoulders. "They didn't. Maria found it between the screen door and the inside door, when she took some rugs outside to shake out. It must have been propped up there, so we would see it when we came back."

He asked Maria something in Spanish and she responded.

"She looked up just in time to see someone walking away toward the street. They went around behind the big pine tree just as she glanced up. But she thought it was the same person, the one that came here posing as a lady collecting for a church."

He again said something to Maria. She brought him a gallon-sized baggie and a table knife.

Skip let go of Kate and opened the bag. He slipped the knife under the note, maneuvering it into the bag without touching it. "We're calling the police this time."

"What can they do?" Kate's fear morphed into anger. "Protect and serve. Bullshit! They can't do anything until an actual crime's been committed. Hell, even after a crime *had* been committed against Amy, they still couldn't do anything because her crazy mother wouldn't cooperate. They probably won't even take it seriously since the person didn't break into the house."

"Yes, they will," Skip said, his jaw tight. "I'm not letting them wait until Edie's face is on the evening news!"

Fussing came from the nursery. They had forgotten to keep their voices down.

As Kate had predicted, the police took their sweet time getting there. Threatening note left on a front porch didn't rate a very high priority. She was kicking herself for not getting Detective Randolph's phone number on Friday.

Skip had called the precinct and asked for Randolph but was told he was not in his office. Did the gentleman want to leave a message for him? When Skip had explained about the note, he was told that officers would be dispatched.

So now they had to convince the responding officers to contact the detective.

Skip didn't even let them get past the entranceway. As soon as the two officers stepped over the threshold, he handed them the note inside the baggie and succinctly told them how and where Maria had found it.

The older and shorter of them produced the expected response. No law had been broken other than trespassing. They would certainly file a report.

Skip interrupted him, pointing out that this was related to several earlier incidents involving threatening actions against Mrs. Huntington, her daughter and her niece. A Detective Randolph had handled the kidnapping of the niece. His voice sounded calm on the surface, his words clear and succinct.

But Kate could see the tension in his body from where she stood across the living room. Her arms were wrapped protectively around her daughter.

Her throat hurt from the realization that the happy bubble they'd been living in for the last twenty-four hours had been burst.

The senior officer still seemed hesitant about calling the detective. Skip loomed over the older and much shorter man and roared, "Someone is threatening that little girl!" He pointed to Edie. "You need to call that damned detective. Right now!"

Adrenaline shot through Kate's system. She frantically looked around for Maria to hand Edie off so she could intervene.

But Maria wasn't fond of *la policia*. She'd made herself scarce.

The older cop had taken a step back and was saying, "Calm down, sir. I'll call him."

But the younger one, a man almost as big as Skip, had failed to take his cue from the senior officer. Hand on the baton in his belt, he stepped forward instead.

Skip, his fists and jaw clenched, showed no signs of backing down.

The older officer reached out a restraining hand.

A compact woman suddenly inserted herself between the two big men. "Step back, Officer," she barked at the young cop.

The older one yanked his partner back and stepped in front of him, just inches from Rose. "Sorry, sir, he's a rookie," he said over her head, then looked down. "Hello, Officer Hernandez, I didn't recognize you at first, out of uniform."

"Hi, Officer Lindsey." Rose flashed him one of her brief but stunning smiles.

When he didn't react, Kate assumed he knew Rose better than their formal greetings implied. Men usually had their mouths hanging open for a moment or two the first time they experienced one of Rose's high wattage smiles.

"These folks are good friends of mine and I know the background on the situation. There's a real threat here, and that little girl..." She tilted her head in Kate and Edie's direction. "She's my goddaughter. Detective Randolph responded last time, but he couldn't do anything but file a report, 'cause the niece's mother wouldn't cooperate. But the girl had been kidnapped. Looked like she'd been given roofies. No visible injuries but the mother wouldn't allow an exam."

Kate had moved to Skip's side. He drew her up against him. In her arms, a wide-eyed Edie was watching the adults. Kate was amazed that she hadn't started crying when Skip had yelled.

Officer Lindsey didn't say anything in response to Rose's summation. He just keyed his portable radio. "Can you contact Detective Randolph, 10-17 at 2610 Linden Lane," he said into it.

"He'll be here as soon as dispatch can track him down, sir," he said to Skip. "We'll wait outside for him." The officer, who looked to be in his mid-forties, smiled down at Rose and touched the front of his hat in a small salute. "See ya 'round, Officer Hernandez."

Mac's growling voice came from behind him. "She *ain't* available, Officer." The younger cop spun around, hand going to his holster.

"Cut it out, Mac," Rose said. "We're just end-of-shift drinking buddies."

Mac stepped around Lindsey and put a possessive arm across Rose's shoulders.

Lindsey's grin grew wider. "This is him, huh?" He directed this to Rose and then said to Mac, "Don't mind my partner. Guess he didn't hear you approach."

Rose's cheeks currently matched her name. She elbowed Mac in the ribs before he could respond. "Yup, this is him. And you didn't hear him 'cause he didn't *want* you to hear him."

"I recall you mentioning that he was Special Forces," Lindsey said pleasantly. The older man seemed to be enjoying Rose's discomfort, but it had a good-natured, ribbing-amongst-colleagues feel to it.

Rose's face, despite the blush, remained blank. Kate suspected Lindsey would be receiving some kind of payback in the future.

"We'll fill the detective in when he gets here and then be on our way. Try to have a good evening, folks." The officer motioned his partner out the door and pulled it closed behind him.

Maria appeared and took Edie from Kate. "*Bebé* hungry." She moved off toward the kitchen.

"I'm calling Rob." Kate followed Maria into the kitchen to get the phone.

"I'll handle this, Kate," Skip called out, his tone sharp.

She was already punching in the number as she came back around the corner. "I didn't say that you weren't, but we could use some reinforcements. In addition to Rose's timely intervention." She smiled gratefully at her friend.

Skip scowled at Kate.

"Take a deep breath and calm down," she said quietly. "You almost slugged a cop."

"No, the asshole was about to take a swing at me. And *then* I would have slugged him!"

"And he would have richly deserved it." She decided not to add, *but you would be in jail.*

The ringing in her ear stopped as the call rolled over to voicemail. "They're not home yet." Kate hit end, then punched in Rob's cell phone number.

Skip watched her, clenching and unclenching his fists at his sides.

She walked over and stood on tiptoe to kiss him on the cheek. "Calm down, sweetheart," she whispered near his ear.

He deflated and wrapped his arm around her shoulders.

She said into the phone, "Hi, Rob. Sorry to disrupt your evening, but we have a situation here." She raised her face and quickly pecked Skip's cheek again. "I'll be right back, sweetheart."

Walking toward the master bedroom, she said, "No, dear, I was talking to someone else." She wanted some privacy. It had occurred to her that she should fill Rob in on a few things, to give him time to digest them a little before they talked to the detective.

In the bedroom, she quickly told Rob about the newest note and that Detective Randolph was on the way.

Without her having to ask, he said, "You want my help dealing with him?"

"Yes, if you don't mind coming over. We had some trouble convincing the uniforms to even call him, until Rose arrived and gave them the background information, one cop to another."

"I'll be right there."

"Wait! Uh, Rob..."

"Yes."

"Skip and I are, uh... We've dropped the four-foot rule."

"Okay... I'm happy for you."

She didn't say anything.

"Kate, it's no surprise. Everybody's known for *months*, that you two would get there eventually. You practically vibrate whenever you're within ten feet of each other."

"Uh, there's something else."

"Yes?"

"He yelled at one of the cops and almost slugged the other one. He's a little intense right now. Can you be kind of a buffer, but not take charge completely?"

Rob didn't respond.

"He's just trying to protect us..." Kate said into the silence. Then her throat closed up on her. She couldn't figure out how to reassure Rob when she wasn't real sure what was going on with Skip herself.

"I know, sweetheart. I'm leaving the office now. Be there in about ten minutes."

———————◆———————

Rob disconnected.

Laid-back Canfield blew up at the cops?

He felt the familiar twist in his gut.

And they had finally stopped dancing around each other. He'd have to sort out how he felt about all that later.

Right now, Kate needed him to referee.

CHAPTER SIXTEEN

Back in the living room, Rose, Mac and Skip were sitting on the sofa and chairs, leaning toward each other. As she entered the room, they stopped talking.

Skip turned to her. "Maria's putting the baby to bed for you, darlin'. She figured with all the excitement and having her nap cut short, she could use an early bedtime."

Kate went over and sat beside him on the sofa. "Are you okay?" She put her hand on his thigh.

"Yes. I've calmed down, *dear*." He picked up her hand in his.

Was the emphasis on *dear* her imagination? Maybe they needed to have a quick chat about Rob and endearments.

"Uh, I need to talk to you for a minute." She jumped up and tugged on Skip's hand. "Be right back, guys," she said over her shoulder, as she dragged him toward the master bedroom.

Once the door was closed, she said, "Look, there's already enough tension tonight so I need you to understand something, because we can't afford for you and Rob to be distracting each other."

"*Distracting* each other?"

"Okay, maybe not the best words, but here's..." She made herself stop and take a deep breath, then began again. "Rob calls his daughters *sweetheart* or *dear,* and somewhere along the way he started calling me by those endearments as well. But it just means that he cares about me as a friend. He calls Liz *hon* or *honey,* or sometimes *darling.* He never calls me any of those things and he never calls her *sweetheart* or *dear.* And I call him *dear,* or sometimes *dear heart,* when emotions are running high, but never *darling* or *sweetheart.* Is this making sense?"

"Yes, darlin'. I get it. Different names for different folks."

"Oh, and while we're on the subject, try not to call me *love* or *my love*."

He stepped in close to her and took her hands between his, holding them against his chest. "Because that's what Ed called you, right?"

"Right," she whispered, looking at his hands encircling hers.

"What did you call him?" Skip asked, his voice gentle.

"*Darling* or *love*," she pushed past the lump in her throat.

Skip wrapped one of his big hands around both of hers and used the other to tip her chin up. "Which is why you don't call me that."

She nodded.

"Okay, I think I've got it." His voice took on a teasing note. "Did y'all sit down one day and figure this out?"

"No, it just evolved that way. We never even paid attention to what we were calling each other, until Rob calling me *sweetheart* almost got us arrested for Eddie's murder, when that jerk detective decided we must be lovers, trying to get rid of our spouses."

"Okay, but I may need a crib sheet to keep all this straight. What happens if I get it wrong?" He wiggled his eyebrows suggestively above a mock scared look. "Are you going to *punish* me?"

Catching on that he was trying to lighten the mood, she said, "Hmm, I'll have to come up with something appropriate." Pulling one hand free, she found the ticklish spot on his side. "How about this?"

He wiggled away from her, grinning. "Hey, I'm bigger'n you, remember?"

Kate breathed a small sigh. She wasn't real sure who that other guy was who'd yelled at Officer Lindsey, but her Skip was back.

Out in the living room, Rob was ushering Detective Randolph toward one end of the sofa. He sat down on the other end.

Maria was nervously perched on the edge of an armchair. In her country, the police were often corrupt, and it was dangerous to have anything to do with them. Kate felt a swelling of gratitude and fondness for this little woman who was so devoted to Edie she would endure questioning by the dreaded *policia*.

Rose and Mac came out of the kitchen, each carrying a wooden chair. Rose set one beside her cousin and sat down on it. Mac positioned the other next to the empty armchair. He then stepped back and leaned against the wall.

Catching Kate's eye, he winked at her. "Take the easy chair, sweet pea. You look a bit knackered." Kate gave him a small smile as they sat down, Skip on the kitchen chair beside her.

———◇———

With her cousin Rose translating, Detective Randolph walked Maria Hernandez through the finding of the note and the description of the person who had apparently left it.

Then he turned toward Canfield. This was the guy the uniforms said had yelled at them. Mr. Franklin, who'd introduced himself as Mrs. Huntington's lawyer and friend, had said this Canfield fellow was also a friend, and a private investigator.

The guy was big and looked a little rough–unshaven, his clothes rumpled. Why would he have gone ballistic over a note? Something didn't quite add up here.

"I understand there have been other notes. You've been investigating their source, Mr. Canfield?"

"Yes, sir. One of those notes *was* actually left inside the house. Since then, I started coming over during the days that Kate works, to protect the baby and Maria."

"So you've been providing bodyguard services."

"Yes, but today I was, uh, visiting with Kate. We took the baby for a walk, and when we came back, Maria told us how she'd found the note."

Mrs. Huntington filled Randolph in on the other notes. "Maria thinks the person today was the same one who left the note in the baby's playpen, and–"

He held up a hand and turned back to the nanny. He asked her a couple questions, through her cousin, about the woman who had delivered the first note. Satisfied with her answers, he turned his attention back to Mrs. Huntington.

She said, "The notes are tied to what happened to my niece."

He cocked an eyebrow as she told him about the phone call from her sister-in-law, and the note in young Amy's pocket. He switched eyebrows at the news that the note had been destroyed.

Now the pieces were starting to fall into place.

"It would help tremendously," he said, "if you could convince your brother and sister-in-law to file a complaint regarding the kidnapping."

"I doubt that's going to happen, Detective. I've already pushed them to do just that, and to get Amy some counseling. I didn't get anywhere."

"I see." Randolph turned back to the lawyer. "Without that incident reported officially as a crime, what we have here are several notes, none of which actually make direct threats, except this last one."

"And the one in my niece's pocket," Mrs. Huntington said.

"Unfortunately we only have your statement, ma'am, that the note your sister-in-law described even existed."

Canfield leaned forward in his chair. "Are you *questioning* the validity of that statement, Detective?" There was steel under the surface in his deceptively calm voice.

Franklin jumped in. "No, Skip, but that's considered hearsay evidence. There's no way of proving it's true, since it's coming from a third party. Kate never saw the note. She was just told that it existed."

"I understand your concern, Mr. Canfield," Randolph said, "for the safety of your friend and her baby, but–"

Canfield clenched his fists and shook his head. "No, sir, I *don't* think you understand."

Randolph braced himself. The guy looked like he was about to explode.

"Kate's not just a friend, she's the woman I plan to marry!"

The others stared at Canfield with shock on their faces. Mrs. Huntington's eyes had gone wide. At the same time, her lips had thinned into an angry line.

Randolph suspected there would be hell to pay for the poor man later. Hell of a way to have to announce your engagement.

"Well then," he said, "your concern makes that much more sense. I can certainly understand how you must feel–"

Canfield interrupted again. "Detective, do you have children?" The steely calm was back in his voice.

Both eyebrows shot up. He nodded, wondering where the hell this was going.

"Okay, then it's possible that you *can* understand, but I don't think you're quite there yet. Have you *ever* had some person, some unidentified person, threaten to harm your child, to *destroy* your family?"

Randolph sat still for a long moment, digesting that.

As he opened his mouth, the lawyer jumped in again. "Detective, I am *quite* sure you *do* understand Mr. Canfield's level of concern. So the current question is, *what* is the Baltimore County Police Department planning *to do* to catch this unknown person before he or she harms Edie?"

The detective sat back. He glanced at Canfield. The man's jaw was still tight but he seemed under control. Now it made a lot more sense why he was wound so tight.

"Okay, folks, you deserve the unvarnished truth. Mr. Canfield, please hear me out before you react."

Canfield just nodded, showing no visible signs of relaxing.

"Officially what we have here is a series of anonymous notes, only one of which is overtly threatening, and a teenage girl who disappeared for several hours and turned up under the influence of drugs. And the only thing tying those two situations together is a third-party report that a note, consistent with the others, was found in the girl's pocket. Normally we would file a report, tell you all we'd look into it and to be careful, and send this latest note to the lab–"

Canfield ground his teeth and leaned further forward.

"Let him finish, Skip," Franklin said, a touch of anger in his voice.

Randolph had spelled all that out so they wouldn't be too shocked if his lieutenant, due to the department's limited resources, eventually pulled the plug on the investigation he was about to launch.

"But," he said, "looking beyond the official facts, there's a serious threat here. Anyone who's willing to kidnap a teenager in a crowded mall is probably capable of hurting an infant. I'd like to catch 'em before that happens. I'm gonna have some uniforms canvass the neighborhood. See if anyone saw the person who left the notes, either this time or before. Maybe we can get a better description."

Canfield pointed out that he and his partner had done that after the note was left in the baby's playpen. "But it occurs to me, Detective, that if this is a man, he could be coming into the neighborhood dressed normally, then when he's close to the house, he puts on a disguise to look female. So when we've asked around using Maria's description, we got nothing."

Randolph nodded. "I'll instruct my officers to ask about *anyone* your neighbors have seen that they didn't recognize, and especially anyone carrying a bundle or bag that could hold a disguise."

Canfield's partner gave a synopsis of her investigation of the false memory group, including a description of the leader. "Harris has admitted to me that they do sometimes send anonymous notes to therapists, but I haven't been able to link anything specific to this case."

Randolph glanced at Canfield. The man's posture had relaxed considerably.

He turned to Mrs. Huntington. "I'm going to put some pressure on your brother and his wife to let me question your niece, in connection with *this* investigation. She may remember something about her assailant, from before she was drugged... I need the other notes. Do you still have them?"

"I have the one from the playpen, sir," Rose Hernandez said. "Had a buddy run it through the lab, as a favor. No clear prints except Kate's."

"My boss has the others, in a folder in her office," Mrs. Huntington said. "Some came through the mail but two were dropped off when no one was around. Maybe someone else in the building saw who delivered them." She gave him her boss's name and the office address.

"Okay, I'll check it out. Mr. Canfield, until we catch whoever's doing this, I suggest you stick like glue to your fiancée and the baby."

Canfield glanced sideways at his fiancée. A grin spread across his face. "Not exactly hardship duty, sir," he drawled.

Randolph couldn't suppress a grin of his own. "Congratulations on your engagement." He stood up. "I'll touch base with you all soon. Goodnight."

Franklin rose to see him out.

As soon as the door closed, Kate jumped up, her hands on her hips. But nobody was paying attention to her.

Mac had grabbed Rose out of her chair and was waltzing her around the living room. "She's gettin' married in the mornin', ding, dong the bells are gonna ring," he croaked out in his gruff voice.

Rose, having no affinity for dancing, was struggling to stay on her feet, but she was grinning. Maria was holding her sides and laughing at the sight of her cousin being dragged around the room.

Rob came back from the door and made a beeline for Skip, hand extended. He too was grinning. "Congratulations, Skip."

Skip stood up to shake his hand. "Thanks."

Rob slapped him on the shoulder. "Ouch! I gotta remember not to do that." He shook his hand in the air. Skip grinned at him.

"I think this makes us friends-in-law," Rob said. They both laughed.

Skip slapped Rob on the back. He mock staggered across the room.

"Now wait just a damned minute!" Kate's raised voice cut through everyone's frivolity.

The baby wailed from the nursery. Maria muttered something and jumped up to go to her.

Kate looked at Rose.

"Now look what you've done," Rose translated.

Kate decided Edie was in good hands and she had other issues to address. She turned to Skip, hands back on her hips. "I do *not* recall, *Mr. Canfield*, that you *ever* specifically *asked* me to marry you."

"I was going to, once we'd had a few more real dates. When the timing felt right."

Kate heard the anxiety in his voice and most of her anger melted away. Of course he hadn't intentionally sprung this on her in front of their friends.

"We were going to have one tonight, remember? We can still go, Kate. It's not that late. Everybody's going to help out. Maria's gonna take care of Edie, and Mac and Rose said they'd stay to guard them."

"I'll stay too, if it'll make you feel better," Rob offered.

Maria came out of the nursery and eased the door closed. "You go, Kate."

"Wait, you're ganging up on me," Kate protested, then remembered the conversation that had ended abruptly when she'd entered the room earlier. Her eyes narrowed, she looked around the room at them. "You all had this planned, didn't you? So what's with the fake expressions of shock?"

"Just the date," Rose said. "We didn't know he was going to *propose* tonight."

"*I* didn't know I was going to propose tonight," Skip muttered under his breath.

"Go on, sweet pea," Mac said. "Go out with the man so he can propose proper-like."

Kate turned back to Skip. She wanted to give in to the pleading look in his eyes, but she couldn't. "Sweetheart, I'm sorry to disappoint you, but no matter how many people stay here tonight, I wouldn't be able to stop worrying about Edie."

Skip sighed and reached out for her hand. "Why is it, darlin', that nothing ever quite happens like it's supposed to when I'm around you?"

He startled her when he dropped down on one knee in front of her.

"Kate, will you marry me?"

For a long, agonizing moment, she debated with herself. She had promised to tell him if he was going too fast. But she knew damned well that they would have ended up here in a few months, or maybe even a few weeks. It wasn't his fault that today's events had brought them to this point prematurely.

She looked down into his anxious eyes and gently brushed tousled hair off his forehead. "Yes, Skip, I'll marry you."

CHAPTER SEVENTEEN

When Kate woke up in the guest bedroom on Thursday morning, once again alone, her mind was confused but not because of her location. She could faintly hear the deep rumble of a male voice and the echo of a childish giggle from the living room below her.

Glancing at the clock on the nightstand, she realized Edie would not have been up for long. But Skip had once again grabbed the monitor and turned it off before it could wake her.

Swinging her legs out of bed, Kate headed into the bathroom where she indulged in a long shower. The hot water pelting against her skin cleared the cobwebs of sleep from her brain, but did nothing else to help with her mental overload.

As she vigorously rubbed shampoo into her curly mop, she realized that her heart was quite clear on the subject of her sudden engagement. Her head, however, was reeling.

She had been way too tired and overwhelmed to sort it all out last night. But apparently not too tired for other things. Her skin tingled now at the memory. She wasn't quite sure how this man managed to turn every cell in her body into warm, quivering...

Stop that.

She dried off and towel-dried her hair. Then she dressed in the sweater and tailored slacks she'd brought upstairs the night before.

When she descended to the first floor, she stopped on the bottom step and watched Skip and Edie through the kitchen doorway. He put one small chunk of banana at a time on the highchair tray. The little girl ate the first two, then squished the third one in her chubby fist and smeared it across her cheek.

Kate was smiling as she walked into the kitchen. She sat down at her place at the breakfast table. Something winked at her from the middle of her plate. Indulgent feelings shifted toward annoyance.

"Rather presumptuous of you, Mr. Canfield, to buy a ring before actually proposing. Or did you run out and get it while I was in the shower?"

She had trouble maintaining her frown as she looked across the table at him.

The previous evening, Rose and Mac had stayed at the house with her while Skip made a quick trip back to his apartment for clean clothes and his razor. Freshly shaven, he now wore a crisply ironed white shirt, jeans, and that sexy smile.

He reached over to take her hand. "I didn't buy it. It's my mother's."

That took her by surprise. Why would his widowed mother *not* be wearing the engagement ring her husband of thirty-nine years had given her?

He picked up the ring and slipped it on her finger. "She wanted me to give it to you, darlin'. On Thanksgiving, she was giving me the 'when are you gonna settle down and give me more grandchildren' routine, so I told her about you, and Edie. She took off her ring and handed it to me, and said, 'It's about time, boy!' I've been carrying it around ever since, scared to death I'd lose it."

Kate stared at the ring on her finger, trying to sort out her jumbled feelings.

"That ring's got quite a history," he said. "It was my grandmother's. She died when my dad was in his teens. A few years later, when he told his father that he'd asked my mother to marry him, but he couldn't afford a ring, his father gave him *that* ring to give to my mother."

This was the grandfather after whom Skip's father and Skip himself had been named. Kate thought about the diamond ring she'd taken off, along with its matching wedding band, in the upstairs bathroom two nights ago—the diamond she intended to someday pass on to her daughter.

Her heart warmed toward her future mother-in-law. She was a far cry from the stiff and jealous Edith Huntington.

Maria began serving up the sumptuous breakfast she had prepared in celebration of their engagement. She piled scrambled eggs, refried beans, and sauteed plantains onto their plates and placed a platter of warm corn tortillas on the table.

Then she picked the baby up from the highchair and started out of the room. In the doorway, she turned and actually winked at them.

Laughing, they dug into the feast.

After a few minutes, the silence was broken by a contented sigh from Skip. She glanced up.

He was watching her from across the table. "Despite all the chaos and crap that's going on in our lives, I'm the happiest man alive right now."

She noted his choice of words. The threatening notes, the malpractice suit, the problems in her family—these were no longer things happening in *her* life that he helped her deal with. She felt more weight lift from her shoulders.

As Kate reached for another tortilla, the diamond on her finger sparkled in the sunlight streaming through the kitchen windows. She pulled her hand back empty and put it in her lap.

"Skip, before I say what I need to say, I want to reassure you that I am *not* changing my answer to your proposal. My heart knows that I want to marry you. But my head is *screaming*, 'Slow down, What the hell is going on?' I just can't wrap my brain around how fast things have moved in the last twenty-four hours."

He smiled at her and drawled, "Does kinda feel like we're on a runaway stagecoach, don't it?"

"Yeah, and whoever the hell the driver is, he's falling down on the job!"

"Oh, I think he got throwed off quite a few miles back, darlin'."

Kate couldn't stay serious, with the image he had just planted in her mind. "Oh, Mr. Skip, save me!" she said in a high-pitched exaggerated Southern accent, picking up her napkin and rapidly fanning herself. "Yuh have ta save me, sur."

He laughed out loud and leaned across the table to capture her hand in his. "Don't worry. The horses'll run out of steam eventually."

Then he brought her hand to his lips and kissed the knuckle of her ring finger, just below the sparkling diamond. "I do love the way that ring looks on your finger, darlin'."

His warm lips, even on that small patch of skin, sent a jolt through her system. "I do too," she said softly.

Skip let her hand go so she could finish her breakfast.

After a few minutes, he said, "Actually I was thinking about that this morning. About how fast everything happened yesterday." He snorted.

"And right after we'd had that talk about not rushing things. But if we'd been truly dating for the last five months… If the relationship had been able to evolve a bit more naturally, I think we'd be about here by now. We're really just catching up with ourselves, in a way."

"You would have asked me to marry you after dating just five months? You, the guy who'd never even seriously *considered* marriage before."

"Yes, I would have asked you to marry me, after five months of knowing I was madly in love with you."

She realized her mouth was hanging partway open and closed it. "You fell in love with me five months ago?"

"Yup! Head over heels, that day I kissed you last summer, and by the end of that week, I knew I wanted to marry you." He quietly added, "The feeling's only gotten stronger since then."

Kate stared across the table at him. She had known he wanted her, had been fairly sure that he loved her, and he'd said he wanted a serious relationship. But she'd assumed he was *hoping* the relationship would grow in that direction, not that it was already there, on his end at least.

His words shed a different light on his actions last night. They weren't those of an impulsive, out-of-control man. How much more control could one ask for than five months of that kind of patience?

Once again he read her mind. "I'm sorry I lost it with the cops. I hate it when I lose control like that."

"It was a bit of a shock."

"Don't worry, I only blow like that about once or twice a decade. Last time was right after my dad died, when I told my captain to 'take this job and shove it.' I'd just gotten the call from my sister. I went to Johnson to arrange for the time off to fly to Texas. He wanted me to come back right after the funeral. Wouldn't give me a few extra days to stay with my mom and make sure she was okay, help her get the practical stuff sorted out. And my sister was pregnant at the time, with two little rug rats already. I wasn't gonna just dump everything on her and race back here.

"He had the gall to suggest that I needed to get my priorities straight, at which point I told him, in a *very* loud voice, that I *did* have them straight. My family comes first." Skip reached across the table and took her hand again. "And it always will."

She smiled at him. "That's good to hear."

"Darlin', you better stop lookin' at me like that," he drawled, "or I'm gonna be throwin' you over my shoulder and haulin' you back upstairs."

"And that wouldn't be fair to Maria, to leave the dirty dishes after she cooked us such a feast," Kate said. They got up and started clearing the table.

While he was loading the dishwasher, Kate rummaged in the junk drawer where she kept rubber bands, carry-out food menus and various other minutia. When she found what she was looking for, she slipped it into the pocket of her slacks.

Taking Skip by the hand, she led him into the living room. Maria was coming out of the nursery, the baby in her arms. They thanked her for the delicious breakfast and Kate took the baby from her. "I have a little while before I have to leave for work. I'll watch her for a few minutes."

"You got good time," Maria said. "I just change diaper. Phew!" She held her nose.

Kate smiled at her. "Yes, I do have good tim*ing* then."

She sat down on the living room rug with the baby. Edie immediately crawled off her lap to dig through her pile of toys.

Skip flopped down on the sofa with a groan. "I ate too much. I keep hanging around here, I'm gonna need to work out a lot more often."

"Speaking of hanging around here." Kate reached into her pocket. "At the risk of whipping up the stagecoach horses, I figure if we're engaged, you might as well have this." She handed him a house key. It was one part practical gesture and one part a token of permanency. Not quite as flashy as a diamond ring, but...

Skip grinned, his eyes acknowledging the implied message. He took out his key ring to add the key. The baby zeroed in on the shiny, jangly treasure and crawled rapidly in his direction.

"Watch out. She loves keys."

He inspected the key ring to make sure there was nothing on it she could get loose and choke on, then he handed it to the child. She sat up and started shaking it vigorously.

Over the clamor, Kate said, "Actually, I think we need to shoot those damned horses. Now that we've caught up with ourselves, as you put it, we need to take some time to sort out some things. There's a lot of stuff we need to talk about."

"Kate, talking to you is the *only* thing I've been allowed to do for the last five months. Is there *anything* we haven't talked about?"

"Believe it or not, yes," she said with a chuckle, but she was now choosing her words with care. "There are still things we need to figure out."

Like where we're going to live. She wasn't ready to give up the old Victorian that she and Eddie had so lovingly renovated.

Or how we're going to manage my million-dollar brokerage account, and that I might not be able to provide your mother with more grandchildren.

It had taken six years of trying before Edie was conceived.

"What things, darlin'?" Skip was asking.

"I don't even want to list them, because then we'll start talking about them. It's nothing all that earth-shattering," she fibbed. They *were* potentially earth-shattering, which was why she didn't want to go there right now. "Just some things that we would have normally discussed along the way, before we got to the getting married stage."

"I guess I shoved the cart in front of the horse, didn't I? I'm sorry I rushed things."

"I'm not. Now that I'm getting used to the idea. Dancing around the subject of commitment was already getting a little tricky, and I was kind of expecting we would move fast once we repealed the four-foot rule." Kate let out a little snort of laughter. "I told Liz that I was afraid we'd go from zero to sixty, but it ended up being more like zero to a hundred."

The baby had lost interest in the keys. She dropped them and crawled back toward her toys.

Skip scooped them up as he slid off the sofa to sit beside Kate on the floor. "My engine's still idlin', darlin'," he whispered in her ear, "whenever you're ready to take another ride."

She punched him in the shoulder, and then leaned against him. She was reminded of the first time she'd leaned against that solid shoulder, on a steaming hot day five months ago. "I think last summer I was already in love with you, but I was afraid to admit it even to myself."

"Because it was *too soon*. How I've come to hate those two words."

"Well they're gone from our vocabulary now." She looked up into his eyes. "I love you, Skip."

His face broke into a grin. "I like those words much better."

———— ◆ ————

By Friday morning, Kate was somewhat less sleep deprived, but she was still trying to wrap her mind around the sudden turn that her life had taken. Driving to work, she was thinking, *This is crazy!*

Then she looked at the diamond winking at her from the ring finger that had remained naked for less than forty-eight hours. Crazy or not, it felt right.

On top of all the other adjustments involved, both practical and emotional, she was having a bit of an identity crisis. "Guess I'm gonna have to stop thinking of myself as a widow," she said out loud, barely catching herself before she added "Eddie."

She held her breath for a second, but she suspected he wouldn't answer her. A wave of sadness, not quite as strong as the one on Wednesday, washed over her. Then she saw Eddie in her mind's eye, sitting on the edge of his cloud, an indulgent smile on his face as he slowly shook his head at her.

Kate laughed. *I really do have an over-active imagination.*

When she arrived at the center, Pauline informed her that Tammy had cancelled again, and this time she had not rescheduled. Kate could only hope the woman was gone for good.

Then she had an idea. She gave Rob a quick call before her first client of the day arrived.

"Hey there, are you free for lunch today, since we missed our normal Wednesday get-together? My one o'clock client cancelled."

There was a pause as Rob checked his schedule. "Yeah, actually I can do that. And I have something to talk to you about, so good timing."

Her curiosity was peaked, but her first client would be in the waiting room by now. "Okay, see ya later."

———— ◆ ————

When Rob arrived at Mac's Place a little after one, Kate had already claimed their favorite booth. After they ordered, he said, "Got a call first thing this morning from Wells. He's suggesting a, quote, 'reasonable settlement' might be possible."

"I'm not willing to settle with these people," she said. "That's rewarding their behavior, and then lawyers like him are encouraged to pursue more of these suits. And quite frankly I'm not sure I can handle dealing with that sleazeball right now."

Rob studied her eyes, always the best barometer of her stress level. They were the washed-out gray that indicated she was in overload. "I understand, but if he calls the insurance company, they may jump on a settlement to avoid the possibility of having to shell out even more if you lose in court. I think we need to hear him out, so the insurance company sees you as being cooperative."

He reached out and took her hand. "And you don't need to deal with him. He was pushing for a meeting quickly, so I agreed to go by his office today at two, since I'm going to be in that section of town anyway for another appointment. I'll tell him you couldn't get free on such short notice but I'm there to listen to what he has to say."

Kate squeezed his hand. "Thank you for being willing to take care of it for me."

"Happy to. I'll call you tonight with his offer." He squeezed back, then let go of her hand as the waitress arrived with their food. He snitched her pickles to add to his own on his crab cake sandwich.

They ate in silence for a few minutes.

He was working up the nerve to broach a subject he knew might get touchy. Trying to sound nonchalant, he said, "I am truly happy for you, but aren't you guys moving kind of fast?"

Kate snorted. "Skip's analogy was a runaway stagecoach."

Rob hesitated. A lot of his reservations about Skip Canfield had been assuaged Wednesday night. The man seemed to genuinely care about Kate and Edie, but... "He was the one who seemed to be pushing things forward the other night."

"That wasn't his original intention," Kate said. "Life events have picked us up and carried us along lately. First there was all that mess last weekend. When Amy was kidnapped and then Phyllis and Michael..." She stopped and shook her head in frustration. "I needed him there so badly, Rob, and he *was* there for me. And it just seemed ridiculous to keep on holding him at arm's length. And then..." Her voice trailed off.

Guilt clouded her eyes. "I'm sorry, Rob."

It sounded like a *non sequitur*, but he knew what she meant. She hadn't called to fill him in on what had happened to Amy until Saturday morning.

"It's okay, sweetheart. If Ed were alive last weekend, he would've been the one you leaned on first. And then you would've told me about it later. It may take me a little while, but I'll get used to being a close second in your life again."

"I don't know that it's first or second. It's just different." She paused. "I had an insight awhile back, about you and me, our friendship. We've always said we're like siblings. But after Eddie died, after all we've been through together, it's more like we're twins."

Rob looked at her for a moment, digesting that idea. Then he grinned and shook his head a little. "You've got to analyze everything until you have it pinned down, don't you, sweetheart?"

"Occupational hazard, I'm afraid," she said with a small smile.

"Actually I agree with you. That is a good way to describe us."

"Twins. About as connected as two people can be, but still not the same kind of connection one has with a mate," Kate said, coming back to her original point.

"No, Liz is..." He thought about the woman he had lived with and loved for two and a half decades. His voice dropped to a tender whisper. "Liz is my soul."

Rob took a bite of his sandwich to cover his embarrassment. He didn't normally talk about his feelings for Liz, even with Kate.

When he glanced up, he stopped chewing.

A strange look had come over Kate's face—confusion mixed with wonder. "Soul mates," she breathed. "I always thought that concept was so corny..." She fell silent again.

Then she chuckled. "I guess I'm not that great an analyzer after all. Why didn't I see that sooner?"

"You're too close to it," he said.

She nodded and stabbed a chunk of tomato from her salad plate.

"So it's definitely not too soon? Before, you said you were afraid of feeling guilty or disloyal to Ed," Rob said, referring to a discussion they'd had the previous summer.

"I get an occasional twinge of guilt. And now I think I understand why." She put her fork down. "Eddie was the love of my life. If anyone had ever asked me if he was my soul mate, I would have sworn that he was." She dropped her gaze to her plate.

"But he wasn't." Her voice was barely above a whisper. "That's what I feel guilty about. That I sometimes feel *closer* to Skip than I did to Eddie."

Rob's chest ached. He put his sandwich down and took her hand in both of his. "Sweetheart, Ed was the closest male friend I've ever had. And I *know* that he was thrilled to be the love of your life. The love, and the life, that he had with you..." He choked up a little. "It was all he ever wanted or needed."

Tears filled her eyes. Several broke loose and wandered down her cheeks. He handed her his handkerchief.

She just sat there, staring down at the white cloth in her hand, while the tears kept coming.

"I'm sorry, Rob." Her voice was thick with emotion. "I knew you were friends, but I never realized how close you were." A tear dropped off her chin, making a spreading gray circle on the snowy whiteness of his handkerchief. "You loved him, too, didn't you?"

"Yes."

"I'm so sorry... that I wasn't there for you when you were grieving for him. I didn't even realize..."

Rob let go of her hand to gently lift her chin. "Sweetheart, I intentionally hid my grief from you. You already had too much to deal with, and I had Liz to lean on."

Her face crumpled. She buried her face in the handkerchief in her hands. Sobs shook her body.

Rob's insides turned to jello. He quickly dug out his wallet and dropped some money on the table. "Come on, sweetheart. Let's take a walk."

He gathered her up from her side of the booth and draped her coat around her shoulders.

As he turned her toward the front of the restaurant. Mac, came through the kitchen door. He took in their faces and froze.

"She'll be okay," Rob said in a quiet voice. "Just a little residual grief. Could you hang onto my briefcase for me."

Mac nodded. His Adam's apple bobbed in his throat as he swallowed hard. "Take care, sweet pea."

Kate hadn't seemed to hear either one of them.

The expression on Mac's face was almost Rob's undoing. The blow of Ed's death hit him again, as hard as it had the day his friend had been killed. For a moment, he couldn't breathe.

Then he shook himself. He put an arm around Kate's shoulders and steered her out of the restaurant.

They walked the short distance to the park in front of the courthouse, and sat down on a bench.

She looked down at the piece of cloth clasped in her hands. "He gave you his, remember? His handkerchief. When Liz was in the hospital, and we were afraid she wasn't going to make it."

Rob's throat tightened. "I remember."

"He didn't have... well, yes he did, but he didn't care about any damned meeting the next morning. He just figured you and I were closer... and I... that you would be able to talk to me easier."

She looked up at him finally, tears again streaming down her face. "He was the sweetest man who ever lived."

"Yes, he was." Rob's eyes stung.

"Dear God, I loved him so," she whispered.

"I know, sweetheart. So did I." He wrapped his arms around her, resting his chin on top of her head. They held each other for several minutes.

Then she sat back and dried her eyes.

Rob was worried about her. He'd *never* seen her lose control in public before. Cry, yes, but not lose it completely, not even at Ed's funeral. But when he considered all the stressors in her life right now, he was surprised she was still walking around upright.

"Do you have to go back to work this afternoon?" he asked.

"Yes, but I've only got one client, and she's easy to work with. And then I'm going to indulge in some retail therapy." Her face brightened. "I have a little surprise planned for Skip. So, this afternoon I'm gonna drag Rose with me to get the supplies I need."

Relief washed through him. She might still have some grieving to do, but it didn't seem to be affecting her feelings for Skip.

She smiled as she held up the soggy ball that had been his handkerchief. "And I need to do some laundry."

CHAPTER EIGHTEEN

It was hard for Rob to make the transition from grieving with Kate in the park to dealing with Phillip Wells.

He just kept saying, "I'll have to consult with my client about that."

Then Wells got to the last stipulation for settlement.

Rob struggled to maintain his court face. "I seriously doubt that my client will agree to that, but I will ask her."

"The offer's only on the table for a short time." Wells gave him a sly smile. "Be good if you got back to me, say, by tomorrow. Or my brother and sister-in-law might change their minds."

Rob wanted to kill the man with his bare hands.

This wasn't something he wanted to discuss over the phone, so Rob swung by Kate's house after his last meeting of the day.

Skip answered the door. "Come on in the kitchen. We were just sitting down to eat. Join us?"

"Did Kate cook it?"

Skip laughed. "No, Maria did."

"Hmm, then I really hate to turn down that offer, but Liz is expecting me home soon."

They went into the kitchen.

Skip sat down at the table. Nudging an empty chair, he said, "Have a seat. You want some iced tea?"

"Sure."

Maria had jumped up and was taking a plate out of a cabinet. Skip spoke to her in Spanish. She put the plate back and turned to the refrigerator to get out the pitcher of tea.

Rob paused for a moment, taking in the sight of the three of them, Kate and Skip sitting at the oak table with the baby in her highchair between them. The little tableau, as well as the soft glow that shone through the fatigue on Kate's face, warmed his heart.

But then, despite their conversation earlier at lunch, he felt a small pang of something. Not jealousy exactly. Displacement? Since Ed had died, he and Liz had adopted Kate and Edie into *their* family. It would take some adjustment to think of her as a member of a *different* family again.

Maria brought him his iced tea, then she sat down and they started eating.

Rob hated to ruin their good mood, but it couldn't be helped. "I met with the plaintiffs' lawyer in the malpractice suit today," he told Skip, then turned to Kate. "I'm not even going to start with the amount he mentioned, because there's another stipulation I'm pretty sure you won't like. They'll only settle out of court if you agree to remove yourself from the client's case. They want you to refer her to someone outside the center."

"I can't do that." Kate tossed her fork onto the table. "I'm not about to abandon her, right in the middle of her recovery process. And it would be highly unethical for me to do so." She pushed her barely touched plate away.

"*¡Dios mio!* You need eat," Maria said.

Kate just shook her head.

"I knew you would say that," Rob said. "This isn't totally a bad thing–"

"Wait a minute," she interrupted. "Was there someone specific they want me to refer her to?"

"Yes, but I don't remember his name. I didn't even bother to write it down because I knew you weren't going to accept that stipulation."

"Wasn't Dr. Zebulah Simpson by any chance, was it?"

"Actually yes," Rob said.

Kate ground her teeth. "Those sons of–" She stopped, glanced at the baby. "He's one of the big proponents of the false memory theory. They want him to *de-program* their daughter. And they want *me* to talk her into going to him!"

Rob's face broke into a grin. "Excellent."

Both Skip and Kate looked at him as if he'd lost his mind.

"They've overplayed their hand, guys. The insurance company can't make you accept a settlement that would breach the code of ethics for your profession. Trying to force you to abandon your client and support an action you believe would be harmful to her, those are rather blatant breaches. And the insurance company might have settled otherwise because the plaintiffs are offering to settle for thirty grand. Which is probably less than it would cost them in attorneys' fees if we went to court, win or lose."

Kate had calmed down but she hadn't resumed eating.

Skip nudged her plate back in front of her. She ignored it.

He and Rob exchanged a glance.

Rob shook his head slightly. "Something the lawyer said makes me think the thirty grand's going mostly to him."

"That jives with what the client reported," Kate said. "At one point, the parents were talking about dropping the suit but the uncle talked his brother out of it."

Disgusted, Rob shook his head again. "The sleazeball's trying to make a buck off his own family's misery."

Skip picked up his fork and took another bite of food, but Kate didn't follow suit.

"So I tell him no and we go to court," Rob said. "He'll want to depose you but I'll try to stall him until after Christmas." Seeing Kate's face tighten, Rob amended his statement. "Strike that. I'm going to *make* him wait until after the holidays."

He stood up. "Try not to worry too much about it, guys."

"Finish your dinner, darlin'," Skip said, also rising. "I'll walk Rob out."

He followed Rob outside, closing the door behind him, then gestured toward the porch steps. The two men descended and walked to the street.

They were beside Rob's car before Skip spoke. "I'm getting a little worried about her. When she came home today... I've never seen her quite so worn down."

Rob nodded. He wasn't about to tell the man that an unexpected bout of grief for her late husband had played a major role in how worn down Kate was. "I can count on the fingers of one hand," he said instead, "the number of times I've seen that woman lose her appetite."

"The only time I've ever seen it, before all this happened, was when *you* were in danger two years ago."

Rob's heart pounded at the memory.

"But she wasn't like this back then," Skip said. "She took charge."

"Liz said she even cowed her poor father into following her lead."

Skip nodded. "Yeah, she was something else."

"There's your answer. She was able to *do* something then. She's the one who pointed out to me afterwards, that helplessness is the most... *debilitating* I think was her word. It's the most debilitating emotion humans can have."

Skip shook his head, then ran long fingers through his hair, shoving it back out of his eyes.

Rob was surprised by the doubt in those eyes. He'd never known Skip Canfield to be anything but confident.

"I'm glad you two are finally together," he told the younger man. "You've got more patience than most men I know."

Skip shook his head again. "I can't help thinking I wasn't patient enough, that I took advantage of her in a weak moment, when she was still upset about Amy–"

Rob intentionally interrupted. "Did you seduce her?"

"Hell, no! I don't need to seduce women."

Even in the dim light, Rob could see Skip's cheeks flush.

"I guess that sounded kind of obnoxious."

Rob snorted. "No, I get what you mean."

Skip shook his head. "She clearly gave me the green light, but..."

Rob laughed and slapped him, gently, on the shoulder. "Then I can guarantee, my friend, that she was doing exactly what she wanted to do, and had thought about it long and hard."

"Yeah, she has an annoying habit of doing that. Especially the long part." Skip's voice was light, but his face was still tight with anxiety. "Then I went and rushed things by blurting out that I wanted to marry her, in front of a room full of people, and a cop to boot."

Rob put his hand on the other man's shoulder. "Skip, I thought the way you handled Randolph was masterful. You got him to take the situation seriously, to look at it as a father rather than a cop. I'm not sure you could've done that without claiming Kate, and therefore Edie, as your family... And there's one thing that I'm totally, one-hundred percent sure about. *You* are not part of the problem. You're the best thing that's happened to Kate in a long time."

Skip grabbed his hand and shook it. "Thanks, coming from you that means a helluva lot."

Rob held the handshake for an extra beat. "Hang in there, man."

Skip nodded. "Thanks," he said again, then turned and loped back toward the house.

As Rob unlocked his car, he realized that he might or might not develop the level of friendship with this man that he'd had with Ed Huntington.

But he and Skip were forging a bond, based on the fact that they both loved the same woman, although in different ways.

After breakfast on Saturday morning, Skip pulled Kate to her feet. He trapped her hands against his chest with one of his.

The reassuring thump-thump of his heart made her smile.

"I'm afraid I've got to work today, darlin'. Surveillance job. Lady thinks her hubby's having a Saturday rendezvous with his mistress, instead of working overtime like he claims." He skimmed his other hand through his hair. "Man, I can't wait until Rose and I are established enough that we don't have to take these kinds of cases. But until then, another cheater, another check."

Kate wondered if this was a good opening to bring up her money.

Skip glanced at his watch, then grimaced.

Maybe not.

"I better get a move on," he said, "but speaking of Rose. She's off duty today. So if you need to go out for any reason, you call her, okay?"

She nodded, looking up at him.

He squeezed her hands tighter against his chest. "Darlin', if you keep looking at me that way, I will definitely be blowin' off this job and staying here."

She shook her head, trying to hide her relief. Unbeknownst to him, she and Rose had plans for today, and for once she didn't want him around. "No, sweetheart, you go. Do your manly thing and bring home the bacon. I'll call on Rose if I need her, uh, to go out with me."

Skip leaned down and touched his lips to hers. She relaxed against him. He wrapped his arms around her and kissed her a little longer. Finally he broke away and left for his job.

Rose stood in the middle of the master bedroom, looking around.

Kate came out of the bathroom, towel-drying her curls. "Did I get all the paint out?" She leaned over.

Rose inspected her friend's hair. "Yup." Then she looked around the room again, admiring their morning's work. They had gotten a lot more done than she'd expected they would.

They'd moved most of the furniture upstairs for temporary storage. Then with Maria watching the baby, they had gotten the rest of the morning's tasks done in record time. The walls that had been a pale yellow were now a medium shade of blue, and the old flower strewn border at the ceiling had been covered by a new one, a geometric print in shades of blue and burgundy.

In the middle of the stripped-down bed, which was now on the opposite wall from where it had been, were three Kohls bags. They contained the linens and curtains that Kate had bought the previous afternoon.

In the adjoining bathroom, a new burgundy shower curtain was already hanging around the footed bathtub, and striped towels—navy, burgundy and white—were on the towel rack.

Rose shook her head slightly at her friend's need to color-coordinate everything. But she had to admit the new decor looked good, and she suspected Skip would like it.

After they grabbed a quick lunch, if he still wasn't home yet, they would start moving the furniture around. Kate wanted to switch most of the things from this room with those in the guest suite.

They headed for the kitchen to get lunch. When the doorbell rang, Kate changed directions. Rose followed her.

Kate looked through the peephole. Excitement in her voice, she said, "It's police detectives. Maybe they've found out something." She unlocked and opened the door.

The tall, fiftyish white man and the short, stocky, forty-something black woman were both dressed conservatively. They looked like Jehovah's witnesses.

Rose cleared her throat.

The woman held up her hand and flashed a detective's shield at them. "I'm Detective Jones." She gestured toward the guy. "This is Detective Bradley. Which one of you is Kathleen O'Donnell Huntington?"

"I am." Kate turned and led the way into the living room, waving a hand toward the sofa. She perched on the edge of one of the armchairs. Rose took the other one.

"Have you found out who's sending the notes and kidnapped my niece?" Kate asked.

Detective Jones arched an eyebrow. Her partner cocked his head in confusion.

"Mrs. Huntington, we need to ask you some questions," Bradley said.

Something about these two was giving Rose a bad feeling. She didn't think they were here about Amy's kidnapping. "Questions about what?" she jumped in, her tone sharper than she'd intended.

"And you are?" Detective Jones aimed her arched eyebrow in Rose's direction.

"Officer Rose Hernandez. Off duty at the moment. Helping my friend do some painting." She was hoping that her status as a police officer might get these detectives to be more forthcoming.

It worked with Bradley. "You with Baltimore County?"

"Yes, sir. Robbery division."

Bradley smiled at her and nodded. "That's probably why we haven't crossed paths then. We're..." He clamped his mouth shut when his partner gave him a repressive look.

Jones turned to Kate. "Ma'am, where were you between three o'clock yesterday afternoon and eleven this morning?"

Kate looked at Rose, her expression now wary.

"What's this about, Detectives?" Rose's sharp tone was intentional this time. She locked eyes with Jones.

"Mrs. Huntington," the woman said without breaking the staring contest, "we need to speak with you alone."

Kate didn't respond.

Rose said, "I think we need to call Rob."

Kate was already on her feet. She headed for the kitchen.

Jones's head swiveled, her glare following in Kate's wake.

"Rob as in Robert Franklin, the lawyer?" Bradley said.

"And why exactly do you think your friend needs a lawyer, Officer Hernandez?" Jones asked.

"Because I don't particularly like the fact that you won't tell us what this is about."

"You're very protective of your friends, aren't you, Rose? May I call you Rose?" Bradley's voice was gentle.

Rose resisted the temptation to roll her eyes. Did they really think they could play good cop-bad cop *with a cop?*

"We'll answer your questions when Mr. Franklin arrives," she said evenly.

In the kitchen, Kate finished whispering an explanation of what was going on into the phone.

"I'm on my way," Rob said. "Don't say anything until I get there."

Kate disconnected, then punched in another number.

CHAPTER NINETEEN

Skip had a little bounce in his step as he walked out of the Sheraton. He didn't care for these sleazy adultery cases, but it still felt good to have done a job well. And he was particularly pleased with the way the tiny digital camera he could hide in the palm of his hand had worked out.

He had trailed the husband from his office to the hotel, then up to the room. He'd gotten a shot of the guy going into the room. The room number on the door was crystal clear in the photo.

Two hours later, a room-service waiter arrived with a cart of food.

Skip had bribed the waiter to let him take the cart into the room. He'd worried a bit that the occupants might question his attire. Waiters didn't usually wear jeans.

But they'd been so preoccupied with each other, they hadn't noticed.

The man had given him a little added bonus. He'd slipped Skip a twenty and an expensive looking bauble with whispered instructions to put it on the lady's plate. Skip had done so, his back turned to the occupants of the room, and then had snapped a quick shot of the pearl necklace before hiding it under the folded napkin.

At the door, he turned back toward the couple, now sitting together at the little table by the window. He was able to discreetly snap a shot of them making goo-goo eyes at each other. The woman wore a flimsy satin robe, hanging partway open, lots of cleavage and the top of a sheer negligee showing. The man was naked from the waist up.

The twenty had gone to the desk clerk in exchange for a photocopy of that morning's page in the hotel register. The jackass had actually registered under his real name.

Oh, yes, a very satisfying few hours of work, indeed. He was calculating in his head what he would charge the betrayed wife, when his cell phone vibrated in his pocket.

Kate's tense voice said into his ear, "We're safe, but can you come home?"

"I'm on my way. What's the matter?"

She had already disconnected. He sprinted to his truck.

He and Rob pulled up in front of the house within seconds of each other.

Rob paused at the foot of the porch steps, waiting for Skip to catch up with him.

"You know what's going on?" Skip asked.

"Police detectives showed up. It's not about the notes, but they won't say what it is about."

Skip nodded and got out his house key as they climbed the steps.

Inside the house, Rob surreptitiously looked the two detectives over as he introduced himself and shook their hands. He gestured toward Skip. "And this is Skip Canfield, Mrs. Huntington's fiancé."

Skip nodded to them and moved to Kate's chair. Perching on the overstuffed arm, he took her hand in his.

Detective Jones looked around the crowded room and narrowed her eyes. She stood up and said to her partner, "I think we need to take this to the station."

"Detective, *I* think you need to tell us what this is about," Rob said in a firm, even voice.

Rose stood up and stepped behind Kate's chair.

Rob took the armchair she'd abandoned. He caught movement out of the corner of his eye and turned his head.

Maria was coming down the stairs, the baby in her arms. A quick spate of Spanish from Rose. She turned around and went back up.

"Now, Detectives," Rob said pleasantly, "I suggest we start over. What is this about?"

Jones had resumed her seat. Her lips were pressed together. Finally, she said, "Phillip Wells was found dead in his office, at eleven o'clock this morning."

Kate gasped.

Rob barely managed to keep his court face in place.

Bradley was watching them carefully.

"What do you need to know from us?" Rob asked.

Jones looked around and pursed her lips again. "Mr. Franklin, we need to speak with you and your client alone."

Skip shot a glance his way and tightened his grip on Kate's hand.

"Detective," Rob said. "I think, unless this is an official interrogation of a *suspect*, that we need to keep things informal."

Jones' annoyed expression didn't change as she glanced at her partner. He closed his eyes slowly, then opened them again.

Jones turned to Kate. "Where were you, Mrs. Huntington, between the hours of three o'clock yesterday and eleven this morning?"

Rob nodded that she could answer.

"I had a client until three, left the office about fifteen minutes later." Kate looked pleadingly at Skip. "I went shopping. Rose was supposed to go with me, but she's not all that into shopping, so I, uh, insisted she go home."

Skip's jaw tightened but he didn't say anything. Rob figured there'd be hell to pay later.

"I got home a little after five-thirty last night," Kate said. "I've been home here, either with my fiancé or Rose, from then until now."

"Where did you go shopping?" Detective Bradley asked.

"Kohls and Home Depot."

"I didn't leave," Rose said. "I waited in my car, until I saw Kate come out of Kohls. Then I followed her to Home Depot and went in after her. Watched her from the next aisle over."

For the first time, Jones's face showed something other than irritation. Her eyes went wide as her partner blurted out, "Why the hell were you spying on your friend?"

Rose's eyes flicked toward Rob.

He jumped in. "Okay, let's back up for a minute." He explained to the detectives about the notes and Amy's kidnapping. "So you can understand why we're all feeling a little paranoid."

Bradley's expression had relaxed.

But Jones still looked skeptical. "How long was Mrs. Huntington in each store, Officer Hernandez?"

"Hour and a half at Kohls. About forty minutes in Home Depot."

"Did you buy anything, Mrs. Huntington?"

"Yes, at both stores. I have the receipts."

"May we see them, please?"

As Kate headed toward the master bedroom, Jones turned to Skip. "And where were you, Mr. Canfield, between three yesterday and eleven this morning?"

"Yesterday afternoon, here, with the baby and the nanny. Around three-thirty, I stepped outside to speak to a client, out front on the sidewalk."

"A client?" Bradley said.

"I'm a private investigator."

"Why were you consulting with a client on the sidewalk?" Jones asked.

Skip hesitated for a beat, then said, "The client called my cell phone. She was... upset.. Insisted on seeing me immediately to discuss a development in her case. Because of the notes, Amy's kidnapping, I wasn't willing to leave the baby and the nanny unprotected. So I told the client to come here."

"The name of this client, Mr. Canfield?" Bradley asked.

"I'd rather not say. This client's a bit..." Skip paused again. "Uh, let's just say she's high-strung. And also quite rich. She wouldn't take kindly to the police showing up at her door, asking questions."

Jones frowned. "Client names are not privileged information for private investigators."

"Yeah but, Detective, this lady will totally freak out if you show up, asking to verify my alibi, not to mention that her cheatin' husband might be home at the time, which would definitely complicate things."

"Tell ya what, son," Bradley said. "It's early on in the investigation. We don't really have much reason to suspect you or your fiancée at this point. Her case was one of several that the victim was involved in. So you give us the woman's name and we'll hold off talking to her, unless and until we have more reason to think you could have been involved in this."

Rob suspected that was the best deal they were going to get. He nodded to Skip.

"Tammy Wingate," Skip said. "Husband's Mark Wingate."

Bradley had been taking notes in a small pad. He wrote down the names.

"How long were you outside talking to her?" Jones said.

Skip thought for a moment. "Probably half an hour, maybe a little longer. She was pretty upset."

The detectives exchanged a glance.

"Wells' office is about fifteen minutes from here," Jones said.

"Did you leave the house at any other point during that time frame, son?" Bradley asked, acting as if his partner hadn't spoken.

"No, sir. Not until this morning. I left about nine. To do some surveillance, same case."

Kate returned to the room as Jones was saying, "So I don't suppose anyone will be able to verify your whereabouts then," her voice took on a snide tone, "while you were lurking in the bushes."

Skip's jaw tightened again. "It was actually a stairwell, in a rather swank hotel."

Rob was impressed by how calm his voice was.

"But you're right. The only proof I have of what I was doing would be the photos I snapped. They'll be date and time stamped. First one would have been right around eleven."

"We'll need the camera, son," Bradley said, his voice apologetic.

Skip's expression was pleasant. "Not real comfortable with that, sir. Client confidentiality again. But you can watch while I upload the first two to my computer and I'll print y'all copies of them. They're fairly innocuous."

Bradley nodded. He and Skip went back to the desk in the office area to do that.

Kate handed Detective Jones two slips of paper.

Jones studied the receipts for a moment, then put them in her jacket pocket and turned to Rob. "According to his secretary, you had a two-thirty appointment with Wells. What happened during that meeting, Mr. Franklin?"

"We had a short discussion about the possibility of settling out of court."

"And how did that discussion go?"

Rob shrugged. "He made an offer. I told him I would have to consult with my client and get back to him." He knew the detectives would have already listened to the victim's voicemail messages, so he added, "I called later and left a message that my client wasn't interested in his offer."

"Your rejection of the offer was rather vehement," Jones said.

"Yes. I believe I said she wasn't interested in his *damned* offer. I don't mind telling you that Wells is... was the kind of lawyer that gives the rest of us a bad name. I didn't particularly like the guy."

Bradley gave Rob a friendly smile as he and Skip came back into the room. "Then it's a good thing Wells' secretary brought him a cup of coffee after you left, before she went home early to get ready for a date."

Skip sat down again on the arm of Kate's chair.

Jones gave her partner a repressive look that Rob suspected was part of the good cop-bad cop routine.

"Where were you, Mr. Franklin, during the rest of that time frame?" she asked.

"Went from Wells' office straight to a meeting with a corporate client in Timonium. That lasted a couple hours. Then I swung by here to discuss the offer with Mrs. Huntington. Went home and ate dinner with my wife. Been at home since then."

"Alone or was your wife home the entire time?"

"Mostly alone today. My wife was in and out all morning running errands." Rob resisted the temptation to point out that if he killed off every colleague who annoyed him, after a while he'd be the only lawyer left standing.

"We'll need the name of that client in Timonium," Jones said, then turned her attention to Skip. "Do you have a license to carry concealed, Mr. Canfield?"

Skip nodded.

"I'm afraid we'll have to take your gun, son," Bradley said, "to test if it's been fired recently."

"What caliber was the bullet?" Skip asked.

"Won't know until ballistics get's done examining it," Bradley said. "Might never know. It was pretty messed up, imbedded in the wall."

Jones gave her partner another repressive look.

"How could a bullet kill Wells and then end up in the wall?" Kate asked.

"It went through him," Bradley said. "Did enough damage on the way by that he bled out."

The color drained from Kate's face. "Sorry I asked."

Rob glanced at Skip, wondering how much he would resist the inevitable, ready to intervene if he did. The man's jaw was clenched again, but then he shrugged. He stood up slowly, lifted his shirttail and turned around.

Detective Bradley walked over and removed the pearl-handled .38 from its waistband holster.

"Detectives," Kate said, "that pistol has great sentimental value to my fiancé. It was his grandfather's. I trust that you will be very careful with it and get it back to him as soon as possible."

Jones started to say something but Bradley cut her off. "Of course we will, Mrs. Huntington." He smiled at Kate as he slipped Skip's gun into an evidence bag he'd pulled out of his pants' pocket. I've got some of my granddaddy's guns myself. I understand."

Bull hockey.

Bradley put the gun, wrapped in the bag, into his pocket.

Rob wondered how safe it was to do that with a loaded pistol. He knew nothing about guns. Did the pistol have a safety? Was it on? He considered saying something, but didn't want to show his ignorance. Besides, he wasn't sure he minded if this guy accidently shot his dick off.

"We'll need to talk to the nanny, son," Bradley said.

"She doesn't speak much English but Rose or I can translate for you."

"That won't do," Jones said. "We'll take her to the station and use a police translator."

Rose jumped in. "I wish you wouldn't do that, ma'am. She's my cousin and a recent immigrant from Guatemala. The police there are often corrupt and everyone has good reason to be afraid of them."

Jones opened her mouth but her partner cut her off again. "I think we can trust this young man to translate for us, Stella. Don't want to give the poor woman a heart attack."

Jones's eyes lit up, while the rest of her face remained grim. After a pause, she shrugged.

Rob knew enough Spanish to follow the gist of Maria's interview. Skip's translation seemed accurate to him.

Maria confirmed that *Señor* Skip had been home all day and evening the day before. She hadn't really noticed how long he had been outside Friday afternoon. And yes, her *patrona* had come home around five-thirty and had been here ever since then. *Señor* Rob had come over last night but he didn't eat any of her good food because his wife was waiting with dinner for him at home.

The two detectives exchanged a glance and a slight nod, confirming Rob's suspicion that at least one of them spoke Spanish.

"I think that does it." Bradley stood. "Thanks for your cooperation, folks. We may have a few more questions as the investigation proceeds."

They were almost to the door when Bradley turned around, an apologetic look on his face. "Oh just one more thing we forgot to ask."

Who the hell does this guy think he is, Colombo?

"When was the last time either of you saw Mr. Wells?" Bradley said to Kate and Skip.

Kate answered for both of them. "Neither one of us has ever met the man. All of my dealings with him have been through my attorney."

"I see. Well, thank you for your time, folks. Have a good afternoon."

They all waited until Rob had closed and locked the door before breathing a sigh of relief.

Skip turned to Rose. "Can you stay here for a little while. I need to go to my place and get my back-up piece."

Rob knew they should have turned that gun over to the detectives as well. But he didn't say anything. With a nutcase running around threatening Kate and Edie, Skip needed to be armed.

Sunday morning Kate was surprised to find Maria in the kitchen cooking breakfast, wearing one of the brightly colored, shapeless dresses she normally wore around the house. Kate looked at the kitchen clock.

"You're going to be late for church, Maria. I can make us breakfast."

"No go today. *Señor* Skip ask me stay. Help with Edie."

"But it's your day off."

"Iz okay. I tell *Señor* Skip I no mind stay home."

Kate thought about arguing with her but decided to take that argument elsewhere. She went looking for Skip. He hadn't been raised Catholic but she had. She knew Maria would be in a confessional later this week to be absolved of the sin of skipping church.

She found him sitting on the living room floor, watching Edie play.

"Skip, you shouldn't have asked Maria to stay home today. It's her day off."

"Don't worry, I'm gonna pay her overtime. Time and a half."

Hands on hips, she said, "That's not the issue."

He got up off the floor and wrapped his arms around her. Keeping his voice low, he said, "It occurred to me that it may not be safe for her to be wandering around in the world by herself. Whoever is sending the notes might decide to get to you by hurting her. But I didn't want to scare her, so I just told her we could use some extra help today."

Kate's anger deflated. "I hadn't thought of that." She shuddered at the thought of Maria being harmed. "I'll pay her overtime. You need your income to keep the agency going."

"I can afford it." His jaw clenched slightly.

He's been doing that a lot lately.

"Okay, Mr. Macho, how about we split it?" she said out loud, going for the compromise that usually worked with Rob. "We'll each pay half."

Skip grinned down at her. "Okay, Ms. Independent, you got a deal." He was leaning down to kiss her, when she caught a flicker of movement out of the corner of her eye.

She jerked her head around. Edie had her little fist wrapped around the cord of the lamp on the end table.

Skip leapt across the room and grabbed the lamp just before the child pulled it off onto her head. "Never a dull moment around here."

Redirecting the little girl's attention back to her toys, Skip sat down on the floor next to her again. "I hate to go out today, darlin', but the lady I was doing the job for yesterday, she's been leaving voicemail messages on my phone for the last twenty-four hours. Each one a little shriller than the last. I need to take my report to her, and collect my money."

Kate hid a smile. She'd been wondering how she could get him out of the house so she and Rose could finish the bedroom project.

"We'll be okay. We'll stay inside and I'll set the alarm."

Having Maria available to watch the baby turned out to be quite helpful. Once Skip had gone on his way, Kate called Rose.

They quickly rearranged the furniture. Eddie's dresser, along with the small tables that had been on either side of the king-sized bed, were switched with the chest of drawers and nightstands from the guest room. The antique rocker was replaced by an upholstered wing chair from upstairs. Then they hung the new curtains and made up the bed.

Earlier in the week, Kate had switched the closets around, taking Eddie's old one as her own. She didn't want Skip standing, taking clothes in and out, turning to talk to her, from the same spot where Eddie had done those things.

She wanted no ghosts in this bedroom.

They finished just in time. The rumble of a male voice came from beyond the closed bedroom door.

Rose grinned at Kate. "I'm outta here."

After Rose had said her goodbyes to Maria and Skip and left, Kate gave Skip a peck on the cheek. "Close your eyes. I've got a little surprise for you."

She turned him around three times so he would be less likely to figure out where they were headed. Taking him by the hand, she led him toward the master bedroom.

He held his other hand out in front of him as he shuffled along. "Where are we going?" he asked, laughter in his voice.

"You'll see. No peeking."

The smell of fresh paint assailed her nostrils as she opened the door. She led him to the center of the room. "You can open your eyes now."

His mouth hung open a little as his eyes scanned the room. "Wow. When did you do all this?"

"Yesterday and this morning."

"You got all this done in a little over a day?"

She nodded, grinning. "This is what I was shopping for on Friday."

He frowned.

Oops! Shouldn't have reminded him of that. He never had gotten around to yelling at her for ditching Rose.

She grabbed his hand again and led him toward the bed, figuring that was the best way to distract him. She sat down on the edge, and pulled him down beside her.

Skip looked around the room again. "This looks great."

"I didn't like being upstairs, so far away from Edie. But I had to do all this first." She swept a hand in an arc to encompass the room. "Before *we* could sleep here. Uh, the closet on the right is empty, if you want to bring a few things over."

"Whoa, isn't that riling up the horses, darlin'?"

"Skip, can you imagine us spending a night apart?"

"Not really."

Kate stared into those hazel eyes. "I love you, Skip Canfield," she whispered, her voice husky. She shook her hand free from his and slid it under his shirt and up his chest. She wrapped her other hand around the back of his neck.

He sucked in his breath. "I take it this means we're gonna christen the new bedroom now."

"That was my plan. Maria's watching Edie."

She pulled his head down. When their lips touched, she parted hers, inviting him in.

He eased her back onto the bed, unbuttoning her blouse as they went. He had it half off and her bra unhooked when he froze.

Glancing at the nightstand next to the bed, he smiled.

"Yeah, it's the one from upstairs," she whispered.

His hand stopped exploring under her loosened bra and reached over to open the drawer. Blindly, he pawed around inside it, while his mouth went back to kissing her.

He suddenly broke the kiss. "The drawer's empty."

"Damn," she said. "I forgot to check that they were in there."

"I might've dropped the box on the floor last night." He let out a low chuckle. "Returning the condoms to their proper place was *not* my top priority at the time."

They lay there for a few seconds, Skip propped up on one elbow above her, both of them breathing hard.

Kate made what was for her a hasty decision. With her infertility problems the odds of her conceiving were slim anyway.

He groaned and began to push himself up off the bed.

She wrapped an arm around his waist and pulled him back down beside her. "Never mind. I hate that barrier between us."

His hand had found its way to her breast again. She gasped as his thumb grazed her nipple.

He was looking down into her eyes, that slow grin of his spreading across his face.

Oh, crap, he thinks we're gonna make a baby.

But she wasn't about to break the current mood with the disappointing news of how unlikely that was.

He flicked his thumb again and she sucked in air. Heat flared, her skin tingled. Her back, of its own volition, arched toward him.

His grin grew bigger.

"Skip, what *are* you waiting for?"

CHAPTER TWENTY

Monday morning, Rose called Skip for some guidance. "Got that meeting tonight. But I'm not real sure what to do from here. Kate said something awhile back about handwriting analysis. Been racking my brain trying to think of a way to get a sample of Harris's writing. Got any suggestions?"

"Hmm, it would be better if it were all caps as well, but people don't usually write that way." Skip thought for a moment. "I might have an idea. You think Mac would be willing to do a little job for us this afternoon?"

"Probably. What'd you have in mind?"

Skip told her.

At two-twenty, Mac and Skip were sitting in Skip's Explorer halfway down the block from Harris's bar. Mac was dressed in brown work clothes, fresh off the rack from Walmart. They had been watching the bar for a little over an hour.

Mac wiggled in his seat. Damn new clothes were scratchy.

"Here we go," Skip said.

Mac looked up and saw a delivery truck coming toward them. As it pulled into the curb across from the bar, Skip jumped out and jogged up the sidewalk.

The driver stepped down from the cab, clipboard under his arm. Skip started talking to the guy, gesturing toward the Explorer.

"Now don't we just have the luck of the Irish," Mac muttered. The driver was wearing a *brown* uniform with a *brown* cap, the beer company's red logo emblazoned on it. Skip traded the man a fifty-dollar bill for the cap and a clipboard. The driver climbed back into the cab of the truck.

Mac got out and loped up to the truck.

"It's Miller Time," Skip said with a grin, handing him the cap.

A few minutes later, Mac was backing a hand truck loaded with cases of beer through the door under the *Girls, Girls, Girls* sign. He had the cap pulled low on his forehead, just in case this bozo had gotten a good look at him that night.

The Irish luck was holding. Harris was sitting at the bar going over some paperwork.

"Can I get ya to sign here, sir?" Mac said, handing him the clipboard containing the delivery slip. Harris took it and absently scribbled his name on the line at the bottom. He started to hand the clipboard back.

"New rule, sir. We're supposed to get ya to print your name as well, under yer signature. All caps, they said."

Harris gave him a funny look.

Mac shrugged. "Some restaurant dude swore it wasn't his signature and refused to pay. Now they want the name real clear, in the person's own hand."

Harris nodded and wrote on the slip, then handed the clipboard back to Mac.

"Where ya want these, sir?"

"Cooler's in the back. Susi'll show ya," Harris said, already refocused on his paperwork.

Back out on the street, Skip neatly cut off the bottom of the delivery slip. He scrawled an indecipherable signature across the middle of the slip and handed the cap and clipboard through the truck window to the driver.

Back in the Explorer, Mac drove while Skip called Detective Randolph to tell him they had a present for him.

—◇—

The operatives of Canfield and Hernandez were feeling quite good about their day's work, until Rose went to the meeting at Harris's house that evening. Her ears perked up when the group started discussing their plans to picket a therapist's office the following week. Harris mentioned the address.

Rose barely managed to maintain her cop face. It was the trauma center's building.

An hour later, she was ringing Kate's doorbell.

Skip answered the door. "Hey, Rose, what's up? Come on in. Kate's putting the baby to bed."

She followed him into the living room. Kate was coming out of the nursery.

Rose took a deep breath. "Afraid I've got some bad news, guys."

———◆———

Kate's Tuesday was off to a bad start. She was sleep deprived after a restless night.

First thing, she had called her boss and relayed Rose's bad news. That hadn't made Sally's day either.

And now Kate was facing a long day of clients. When she arrived at the center, Pauline informed her that Tammy had called and asked to see her as soon as possible. After saying a few choice words inside her head, she told the receptionist to plug Tammy into the hole in her schedule at three.

She waited until she was in her own office, the door closed carefully behind her, before she allowed herself to groan out loud.

That afternoon, Tammy seemed somewhat calmer than she'd been in a long time. So when Kate asked the client how things had been going, she was shocked by the answer.

"Well, my marriage is over," the woman said, in a matter-of-fact manner. "I was right. Mark's having an affair. And he had the gall to lie about it when I confronted him on Thanksgiving. But now I have proof. I kicked him out of the house and I've already met with my lawyer."

Kate tried to hide her horror that this woman had acted so precipitously. "What proof is that?"

"I don't really want to talk about that," Tammy said, her tone now crisp. "That's not why I'm here today. I came in one more time to tell you face-to-face that I'm not continuing therapy with you. If you had done your job, my marriage would not be over."

Kate bit the inside of her cheek to keep from saying out loud that she was not responsible for the Wingates' lousy marriage. This time, it would be easy to go with the resistance. "I can give you a referral then. There are several competent people in the Towson area that you could see."

"No need. I've already found a new therapist. And she's wonderful! She totally gets what's going on with me."

"I see. Who is that?"

"I don't think that's any of your business actually," Tammy said.

Kate hoped it wasn't one of her colleagues that she particularly liked.

"I just came in today to tell you, in person, that your reputation as a good therapist is richly *un*deserved!"

If Kate had any lingering doubts about Tammy's diagnosis, they were gone now. This was a typical borderline reaction. You were wonderful until they felt you'd disappointed them. And then you were the devil and they found someone else to cast in the angel role.

Kate stood up. She wasn't about to sit there and take verbal abuse from this woman for another forty-five minutes. Schooling her face into a neutral expression, she said, "Well, I appreciate you telling me that you were transferring to another therapist. Otherwise I would have been worried about you when you didn't reschedule."

Tammy also stood and delivered her parting shot. "Don't bother billing me for this appointment."

Kate didn't respond. She just wanted the woman out of her office.

As she heard the outer door slam, Kate was tempted to break out in song. Better not. People in the waiting area might hear her. She settled for a fist pump in the air and a whispered, "Hallelujah!"

For the first time in her career, she was happy to be filling out insurance forms for the rest of the hour.

———◦———

Tuesday afternoon, Skip received a call from Detective Randolph.

"Had a long conversation with Michael O'Donnell this morning. Got him to override his wife's objections and let me interview Amy."

Skip was surprised. From Kate's description of events on Thanksgiving weekend, his future brother-in-law sounded like a total wuss. "How'd you manage that?" he asked.

Silence for a beat. "Guilt-tripped him. Said I hoped he could live with himself if anything happened to his baby niece."

Skip winced.

"Unfortunately," the detective said, "we didn't get much useful information from the young lady. Said she was thirsty so she stopped to get a soda. Somebody bumped into her as she was opening her wallet and she dropped it. She bent down to pick up the stuff that fell out on the floor, finished paying for her drink and started strolling toward the main entrance. Last thing she remembers is window shopping as she drank her soda."

"So that's probably how they drugged her, put something into her drink," Skip said.

"Most likely. Paramedic said the symptoms pointed toward roofies. Timing does too. They take about fifteen minutes to kick in. Brother isn't due for a bit so the girl's taking her time. Just about when she got near the main entrance, the roofies would've hit her and then the perp took her."

"She see who bumped into her?"

"Nope. Food court was packed with people. She said she didn't think anything of it. Didn't even turn around to try to see who it was."

Randolph also told Skip that the canvassing of Kate's neighborhood and tenants in Kate's office building had come up empty.

"Got some partial prints on the notes that are unaccounted for, but the system didn't cough up any matches."

"What about the analysis of Harris's handwriting?" Skip asked.

"Results aren't back yet. I'll let you know when they are."

When Kate got home that evening, Skip saw no point in telling her about the call from Randolph. She hadn't slept well the night before, after the visit from Rose and the news about the false memory group's plans. She didn't need to be upset again this evening, just before bedtime.

Maria had already retired for the evening, after giving Edie her bath. Skip was holding the yawning child tucked into the crook of his arm.

Kate gave him a tired smile as he handed her the baby, who was now rubbing her eyes with her chubby fists.

"Be back in a few minutes," she said, taking the little girl into the nursery.

When she came back out, she dropped down next to Skip on the sofa.

He put his arm around her shoulders, pulling her up close beside him. Deciding that a happy topic was called for, he said, "So how long do you think it'll take us, at the rate we're going, to make Edie a little brother or sister?"

There was no response. He looked down at her. Her head was down. He couldn't see her face. Had she fallen asleep?

With a finger under her chin, he turned her face up. Tears were pooled in her eyes.

"Skip," her voice was barely above a whisper, "would you be terribly upset if there weren't any little brothers or sisters?"

For a moment, Skip was at a loss. Then his father's voice echoed in his head. *When a woman asks you a question and you're not sure what she wants you to say, don't answer her. Ask for more information.*

"What do you mean?"

"It took six years for me to get pregnant with Edie. We don't have six years. I'll be forty in February." She looked down at her lap.

Skip's brain scrambled to process what she was saying, and why she was so upset about it. She had trouble getting pregnant. There might not be more babies. Okay, he got that. Mildly disturbing.

"The problem could've been Ed's."

Kate shook her head. "We both got tested. He was fine. It's me. I'm not very fertile apparently." She looked up at him, pain and worry in her eyes. "I'm sorry, Skip. I should've told you this sooner."

"No, now hush, it's okay." Skip pulled her onto his lap. "This was one of those things that was in the cart that got before the horse, wasn't it?"

She nodded mutely.

"Kate, I've been capable of fathering children for two decades. If I'd wanted a family, I could've had one years ago. I never particularly wanted one, until I met you. And now I have my family. You, me and Edie."

"You won't be disappointed if I can't... give you a child of your own?"

He smiled down into her still worried eyes. "Kate, I *have* my family," he said again. "I adore Edie, and you, you're... " Words failed him. How could he explain to this woman what she meant to him?

"At the risk of sounding like a corny love song, you're my life, my heart, my soul. I can't imagine living a day without you." He tenderly kissed away the tears that had broken loose and wandered down her cheek, then he moved on to her lips.

When they came up for air, he said, "You know, I was actually trying for something light and happy to talk about. That didn't work out quite like I thought it would."

———•◦•———

Kate snuggled against his chest. After a moment she said, "I love sitting in your lap."

Actually, Skip was the first man she'd ever been romantically involved with whose lap was big enough for her to sit in. She'd always been attracted to lean, lanky men like Eddie–men who were attractive enough, but not so attractive to be conceited.

She was reminded of the conversation she'd had with Skip the previous summer, when he'd told her about the short, scrawny teenager he had once been–harassed by bullies at school because of his nickname, until he'd had a late growth spurt.

She sat up on his lap and leaned back slightly to gaze into his eyes. "Skip, I gotta tell you something else."

He looked a little scared.

She grinned at him. "I do *not* love you for your body."

He chuckled. "Okay, what the hell does that mean?"

"I would love you even if you were still a scrawny little dude named Skippy."

He laughed, then kissed her again. This time when they came up for air, they decided it was time to retire for the evening.

They walked into the master bedroom. Or rather Skip walked. Kate floated. She had told him about her infertility and he didn't care.

One cart-before-the-horse issue down, two to go.

The money seemed like too much to tackle tonight, but maybe the house. Standing in the middle of the bedroom, she said, "Where do you want to live, after we're married?"

He looked at her in confusion. "I assumed we would live here. Is that okay?"

"Of course it's okay with me. But are you sure it won't feel strange for you?"

He stepped over to her and took her hands, holding them against his chest. After a moment, he said, "Since I didn't know you before Ed died,

I've always thought of this as your house. And I can't really imagine you anywhere else. This place suits you, Kate. It's your home."

She smiled up at him. "*Our* home, and we're putting your name on the deed after the wedding, so it's truly yours too."

He paused again. "I don't need my name on the deed to feel like it's my home." Then his voice went from serious to teasing. "I started feeling that way after you let me move outta the guest room."

She smiled, but her brain was scrambling to figure out what it meant that he didn't need his name on the deed. Was he resisting the idea because it smacked of taking money from her, or was he saying it didn't matter one way or the other to him?

"What's the matter, darlin'?" Skip gently touched her lips with his fingertips.

She realized she'd been gnawing on the lower one. Looking up into his face, it struck her that what they had was more important than the damn money. If it bothered him when he found out he was marrying a wealthy woman, she'd put all the money in a trust fund for Edie.

Ignoring his question, she said, "I'm thinking we can let those horses have free rein now. How's this for a happy note to end the evening, when and where shall we get married?"

He grinned at her without answering, then lifted one of her hands and kissed her palm.

Her breath caught in her throat. When she could talk again, she said, "I think the where should be Texas. Most of my family's scattered all over the country anyway. Just as easy for them to fly to Texas as Maryland."

"My part of Texas is right purty in early May, ma'am," Skip drawled.

"May it is then."

He wrapped his arms around her. She reached up to brush back the hair from his forehead. He closed his eyes and groaned softly as her fingers caressed his skin. The sound sent a wave of shimmering warmth down the core of her body.

She rested her hand against his cheek. "Skip," she whispered, "there's one more thing I should tell you tonight. *You* are my heart and soul!"

Then a snicker escaped her lips before she could catch it. "You're right. It does sound like a corny love song."

He grinned and swept her up in his arms to carry her to bed.

On Wednesday, Kate was changing her clothes to go meet Rob for lunch, when the doorbell rang. She heard Skip's footsteps and figured he would answer the door.

She smiled as she put on her jewelry–her watch, simple silver studs in her ears, and of course the diamond ring. She couldn't wait to tell Rob that they had set a date for the wedding.

Skip came into the bedroom, his face grim. "It's Bradley. Wants to talk to both of us."

Out in the living room, the detective pulled Skip's pearl-handled revolver out of his pocket and handed it to him.

Skip broke it open and spun the empty cylinder.

Bradley dropped a handful of bullets into his hand. "Clean as a whistle, son. I don't think we'll need to be troubling Mrs. Wingate about your alibi."

Kate froze.

The detective extracted a folded sheet of paper from another pocket and handed it to her. "Search warrant, ma'am. Hate to bother you, but I need a hair sample from you."

She took the paper and stared down at it, her mind reeling from the name she had just heard him say.

"Your hairbrush in your bedroom?" the detective asked in a pleasant tone.

She nodded, still staring at the paper in her hand.

"And that would be where?"

Skip cleared his throat.

Kate looked up. "What?"

"Down the hall," Skip answered the detective's question, pointing in the direction of the master bedroom.

Bradley came back in less than a minute, sliding a small evidence bag into his coat pocket. "Thanks for your time, folks," he said, and left.

As soon as the door closed behind him, Kate turned to Skip. "Mrs. Wingate, as in *Tammy* Wingate?"

CHAPTER TWENTY-ONE

"Yeah, do you know her?" Skip said.

Kate debated for a moment, but she really couldn't *not* tell him. "She is... was my client too, until yesterday."

"That's weird."

"More than weird. Let me call Rob and ask him to come here for lunch. There's something we need to hash out, and we need to tell him about the search warrant."

Skip just gave her a curious look as she headed for the kitchen. She grabbed the phone and punched in Rob's cell phone number.

Skip had followed her into the room. She said to him, "Could you ask Maria to take the monitor, in case the baby wakes up from her nap."

He nodded.

Rob answered and Kate explained to him in vague terms what was going on.

She disconnected as Skip came back into the room. "He's on his way." She started dragging things out of the refrigerator to make sandwiches.

Skip stepped over took her hands to steer her to the table. "I'll do that. You sit and relax for a moment."

"Oh, come on, even *I* can make sandwiches."

He grinned at her. "Yeah, but my daddy used to say 'Wait on the woman, now and again, son...'"

"And she'll love you forever," Kate finished for him, grinning back at him from her chair. But her mood sobered as she tried to sort out what this meant, that Skip just happened to be the private investigator Tammy had hired to follow her husband.

When Rob arrived, Skip asked him first about the significance of the police wanting a sample of Kate's hair.

"I wouldn't worry too much about it," Rob answered. "They must have found some hairs at the scene that looked similar to Kate's. But I seem to recall that Wells' secretary had dark curly hair. Longer than yours, Kate, but not quite as curly."

"There's something else we need your take on," she said.

Without saying their names, she and Skip filled Rob in on the Wingates, and the unlikely coincidence that the wife had hired her therapist's fiancé to spy on her husband. Kate was also weighing her words carefully, trying not to reveal anything that Skip didn't already know about the couple.

"At first Sally and I wondered if the husband might be sending the notes, trying to back me off because he saw me as supporting his wife's side and maybe making their arguments worse, which I wasn't. But then the notes started talking about destroying families and that sounded more like the way the false memory people would talk."

"This guy's an average-sized man," Skip said, "so bundled up the way Maria described the church lady... Yeah, I can see him disguising himself as a woman that way."

"The attack on Amy doesn't really fit though," Kate said. "He's a Type A businessman. Works practically 24/7. I just don't see him taking a whole day off to follow us around Towson Town Center looking for a chance to snatch one of us."

"The tone of the notes changed some around then," Rob said. "Became more directly threatening."

"There's another thing that doesn't fit," Skip said. "According to the e-mails from the mistress that the wife stumbled on, he was already having his torrid little affair a little while before Thanksgiving, and maybe didn't care quite as much what his wife was doing."

Kate hesitated. She really shouldn't discuss anything more specific with them. Then she remembered that the notes were making threats against her daughter.

She blew out air. "The wife fired me yesterday as her therapist. After she got the goods on her husband from you, Skip, she tossed him out on his ear... Wait a minute, she said she first confronted him *on Thanksgiving!*"

She ran a hand through her hair, thinking it through. "I take it back. He could've come unglued when he realized that his affair had been discovered and he was about to lose his family. Yeah, under those circumstances, I can see him coming over here the next day and spying on me, and following us to the mall. Especially if he'd been blaming me all along for stirring her up.

"And the wife's definitely blaming me for the break-up. She said, point blank, that if I'd been doing my job, their marriage wouldn't be over."

"That's pretty crazy," Skip said, then paused for a moment. "So could be the husband, but another possibility just occurred to me. The husband could've started off sending the notes, told the wife about them at some point, and maybe even planted the seed in her mind that the marital problems were because of you. Then Tammy kidnapped Amy and delivered this last note."

She winced at his use of even the woman's first name.

"Kate, do you think this woman is capable of sending threatening notes to her own therapist?" Rob asked. He was the only one who had eaten any of his sandwich.

She had a sick feeling in her gut. This was so against the rules, and she'd already said more than she should have. But Edie was at risk, and it was totally weird that Tammy just happened to hire Skip when she was looking for a private investigator.

Another thought made the blood drain out of her face. "Skip, you've got to be really careful. This woman's blaming me for the collapse of her marriage. The absolute best revenge against me would be to take away the man I love."

"She did come on to me some when I took her the report on Sunday."

Kate shook her head. "That's not what I mean. She could try to hurt you. Maybe that's what the more recent notes about destroying my family are referring to. Not Edie, but *you*."

"And by using you to spy on her husband," Rob said, "she's established a professional relationship with you. So you would be relaxed around her, wouldn't have your guard up."

Skip snorted. "I don't think any man would ever be completely relaxed around Tammy Wi..." He stopped when Kate shot him a sharp look.

"Come on, darlin'. We can't be worrying too much about confidentiality at this point. If we're going to sort this out, we need to have all the information on the table. It won't go beyond this room."

She sighed. "Skip, you need to understand the seriousness of confidentiality in my profession. Beyond the ethical issue itself, it's the quickest way to get sued, and Tammy would go there in a heartbeat. She'd have a damn good case too. At best, I'd lose my job and probably would never be able to get malpractice insurance again. At worst, I'd lose my license."

"Rob and I are both used to being discreet regarding confidential information." Skip's voice was gentle.

"You never did answer me, sweetheart," Rob said. "Is this woman crazy enough to send threatening notes to you while she was still in therapy with you?"

Kate looked across the table at them. These two men and her daughter were the most important people on the planet to her. As much as she loved her work, she could handle losing her license better than losing either Skip or Edie.

"Okay, okay, yes, she could be angry enough, and distorted enough in her perceptions to do that." She sighed again. "Tammy has borderline personality disorder. She has volatile moods, and does something called *splitting*. People with this disorder have a very all-or-nothing view of the world, and other people. They can't integrate the idea that someone might be a good person and care about them, but might also be imperfect and sometimes let them down. And their perceptions of others' motives are often skewed.

"So, yeah, it's possible that Tammy could have written at least the last two more blatantly threatening notes. By that point, she was pretty pissed off at me, because I was pushing her to do certain things... things she didn't want to do. And I think she was already looking for a new therapist by then."

"Are these folks often violent?" Skip asked.

"Well yes and no. Most of the time they get depressed easily and do self-harm things, like cutting, or attempting suicide. But they are full of rage about the things that were done to them as kids. This is a disorder that is most often caused by fairly bad child abuse. And they have poor impulse control. So yeah, they can sometimes become physically aggressive. Especially if they see someone as having betrayed them, or as thwarting their efforts to get their needs met, which are legion. They are very needy people."

Skip grimaced. "It must be hard for you to work with these people."

"Most therapists hate dealing with this disorder. But I actually, *usually*, like my borderline clients, even though they're tough to work with. Underneath all the annoying symptoms, there's an innocent, and often very sweet child, who's been horribly wounded and is just trying to get her needs met. But they're going about it all wrong because adults aren't supposed to be clingy and demanding and volatile. We accept it if children are that way, because we know they don't know any better and can't really control themselves yet. But adults are supposed to be more mature than that."

"So you could put up with this lady because you saw that sweet child inside of her," Skip said, a new note of respect in his voice.

"Well, truth be told, I was relieved when Tammy fired me yesterday. In her particular case, her inner child's a spoiled brat."

Skip flashed her a grin.

"Well, if either she or her husband were the source of the notes," Rob said, "now that you're not seeing her anymore as a client, the notes may stop."

Skip shook his head. "Yeah, but if this is about one of them blaming Kate for their problems, they may take action now that the marriage has collapsed."

"So time will tell," Rob said.

Kate picked up her sandwich and took a bite, even though she had no appetite.

They ate in silence for a few minutes.

A new thought hit her, closing her throat. She managed to swallow the food in her mouth, then said, "Guys, these two get physical with each other when they fight, slapping and throwing things. Or at least that's all Tammy's reported. In her case, I think it's out of frustration over... uh, the state of their marriage. But I don't know him nearly as well. He could have an abusive personality."

"In other words," Rob said, "he could be capable of violence in general."

"Yeah." Kate gritted her teeth. "Damn, there's got to be a way to check this out. Can we somehow find out what these people were doing the day Amy was kidnapped?"

Skip paused, his sandwich in midair. "I can probably find some excuse to talk to the wife again, see what I can find out."

"No!" Kate said. "You can't go alone."

Skip shook his head. "She's not likely to be open with me unless I'm alone. But I can have Rose wait in the car. We'll figure out some way for me to signal her if I need back-up. And if Tammy tries something, that'll tell us she *is* the culprit, and we can put an end to all this."

Kate had mixed emotions about that idea.

Before she could respond, Rob said, "Can we get Detective Randolph to check out the husband? Maybe question him directly, ask him about his alibi for that day?"

Kate sighed. "We can't tell him about them without explaining why we suspect them, and then I'd be breaching confidentiality."

"Let's see what I can find out," Skip said. "Try not to worry, darlin'. This is what I do. I know how to protect myself."

She sighed again. She wasn't just worried about him. She was also frustrated that she couldn't do more herself to investigate. She did *not* like the idea that they might never know who had made these threats, or whether or not the danger was truly over. Eventually they would let down their guard and...

Skip changed the subject to the false memory group's picketing plans for the following week.

Kate was grateful. As stressful topics went, it was a lesser evil than thoughts of someone kidnapping or hurting Edie.

"We can't stop them from picketing out front," Rob said. "But I can probably get a restraining order to keep them out of the back parking lot. That's private property. I'll talk to the landlord." He turned to Kate. "I'd suggest you all tell your clients to come in the back way, but the picketers may try to block that entrance too."

"A half dozen beefy guys should be a good deterrent for that," Skip said. "I'll make some calls, and I'll see if Rose can tag some of her police buddies to do some off-duty work."

"I'm paying for them, Skip. No arguments." Kate shot Rob a quick look. "This is to protect my workplace and my clients."

Rob interpreted the look accurately. "I'll talk to my partners," he said, as Skip opened his mouth to protest. "The firm can help cover some of the cost. The pickets would affect our business as well. The landlord may pitch in too."

"I just hope this doesn't get the center evicted," Kate said.

"We'll cross that bridge if and when we come to it." Rob stood up. "Thanks for the lunch, guys."

Kate got up to walk Rob to the door. Once out of Skip's earshot, she brought up something that had been gnawing at her all during lunch.

"Rob," she whispered, "can you write up a legal document naming Skip as Edie's guardian should I be unable to care for her?"

"Sure, but why?"

"If I get arrested, Social Services may come and try to put her in foster care. My folks would be able to get her back, or I would if the judge lets me out on bail, but I don't want her to be exposed to that, even temporarily."

"You're not going to be arrested. You've never been to Wells' office. Never even met the man. The police aren't going to be able to tie you to his death."

"Rob, please! I'm not willing to risk that she might have to spend even one night torn away from everything familiar, suddenly in the care of strangers, maybe in a situation where she could be abused. They screen foster parents carefully but some abusers fool them, or other foster kids in the family could..." Kate's throat closed at the thought. "Skip needs a piece of paper he can wave in their faces and say, 'You can't take her, she's mine.'"

"You're getting a bit paranoid, sweetheart."

She tried to grin but didn't succeed. "Just because you're paranoid doesn't mean they aren't out to get you."

"Okay, if it will make you feel better." He leaned down to kiss her forehead. "But I don't think you have anything to worry about."

Kate tried to convince herself that he was right.

CHAPTER TWENTY-TWO

Skip called Rose to discuss recruiting some muscle to back off the picketers. Once they'd ironed out the details, he said, "I don't think you should have any more contact with Harris. If he figures out you've been spying on him–"

"I already talked to him. Found out that the case related to the picketing is one of Sally's, that is unless there's another black counselor at the center."

"What do you mean?"

"He used the N word."

Skip felt his jaw tighten. "Son of a bitch!"

"I know. I'd like to pound him into the dirt," Rose said.

"Has he been obnoxious to you?" He willed his clenched fist to relax.

"No, but he's pretty condescending to a Mexican-American couple in the group. He's nice to me 'cause he thinks he's got a shot at getting me into bed with him."

"All the more reason for you to stay away from him at this point."

"Skip, you've got to steer clear of him, too. He'll recognize you from the bar."

"Damn! You're right. Are you supposed to see him again?"

"He thinks I'm gonna be one of the picketers. That's how I got him to give me the additional info, by pretending I wanted to participate. But I just won't show up and I'll tell him later that I got sick."

"*Call* him later," Skip said. "No more face-to-face contact for now. Is this guy typical of the rest of the group?"

"Yes and no. He's the most extreme, but some of the other men are controlling like him, especially where their families are concerned. There are a few couples who seem genuinely at a loss. Can't figure out why their kids are accusing them of abuse."

"Kate said that false accusations do sometimes happen, for a variety of reasons."

"Yeah, there's one couple I feel bad for," Rose said. "They really seem to be hurting, but whenever they talk about making amends with their daughter, Harris bullies them back into line."

"*Bully* is a good word for Harris." Skip changed the subject. "Rose, are you off duty tomorrow morning? I need back-up for something."

"Off all day. What's up?"

"Uh, I can't tell you. At least not yet."

After a beat of silence on the line, Rose said, "Okay. Want me to tag Mac to stay with Edie and Maria?"

"That'd be great. It shouldn't take more than about an hour."

Skip had expected her to push for more information. After disconnecting, he remembered that she'd been in the army for six years, before becoming a police officer. She knew when to not ask questions.

At nine-thirty the next morning, Skip pulled his truck up in front of an impressive stone-faced house in one of the ritzier sections of Towson. He took out his phone and punched the speed dial number for his partner.

Rose, sitting next to him, answered her ringing phone and held it to her ear.

Skip slid his own phone into his shirt pocket, with the connection still open. "Can you hear me?"

"Muffled but yeah. Raise your voice a little."

"Can you hear me?" he said louder.

"Clear as a bell."

Skip got out of the truck and walked up to the front door to ring the doorbell. A melodious chime echoed inside the house.

He was a little surprised when Tammy Wingate herself answered the door. He gave her his excuse for being there, that he thought he might have left his jacket when he'd delivered his report on Sunday. "I wanted to talk to you about something else as well." That got him in the door.

"It's the maid's day off. Would you like something to drink? Iced tea, coffee?" Tammy said over her shoulder as she headed down the sumptuously decorated hallway.

"Coffee'd be good." He had no intentions of drinking it but he needed to prolong the meeting.

"I didn't see your jacket lying around, but I'll ask the maid when she comes in tomorrow."

Skip followed her into a spacious kitchen, with all the latest gadgets.

After pouring coffee from a carafe into two white china mugs on the counter, Tammy turned to reach into the cabinet above her head and bring down a sugar bowl. Her body was blocking his view of the mugs.

"Cream or sugar?" she asked, without turning back around.

"Black's fine."

He heard a spoon clinking against china. Was she adding sugar to her own coffee or something else to his?

She waved toward the kitchen table. He took a seat. She brought the mugs over and sat down across from him.

Skip pretended to take a sip of his coffee. "So how'd your husband react when you confronted him, if you don't mind my asking?"

"He denied it at first, until I showed him the pictures. For a minute I thought he was going to hit me, but then he just turned on his heel and stormed out."

"When did all this happen?"

She gave him a curious look. "Sunday evening. Why do you ask?"

He shrugged but otherwise ignored her question. Pumping a touch of alarm into his voice, he said, "Has he been violent with you before? Is it safe for you to be here alone?"

"Oh, don't worry. I paid a locksmith double time to come out Sunday night and change the locks. I am done with that bastard!"

That answered his second question, but didn't tell him anything about how violent the husband tended to be.

"I'm surprised, after you confronted him on Thanksgiving, that he didn't stick close to home and try to reassure you that everything was okay." Tammy hadn't actually told him about the Thanksgiving confrontation but Skip hoped she wouldn't remember that.

"Hell, no, he went into work every day that weekend, just like always. Or he said he was going to work. No doubt, he spent some of that time with his slut."

"He didn't even take that Friday off? Most people do." Skip knew he was pushing his credibility, but so far she'd only seemed mildly curious about his strange questions.

She snorted. "He even went in for half a day on Thanksgiving itself, or at least he said he was going to work but I think he went to see *her*."

"That must've been a lonely weekend for you." That probably sounded like he was coming on to her but he had to risk it.

"Nope." Tammy lifted her mug to her lips and smiled at him over the rim. "I went shopping and spent a bunch of his money." She took a sip of coffee. "So what was the other thing you wanted to talk about?"

"Uh, I hope you won't be pissed at me but, uh... Well, my fiancée's involved in a lawsuit, and the opposition's lawyer got himself killed. Police came to question both of us and, see, he was killed around the time you and I were talking last Friday outside my house. I'm afraid they insisted that I give them your name."

"I thought all that was confidential." Tammy's tone was sharp.

"Well, it is, normally. But like I said, they insisted. I really didn't have much choice."

Her expression softened. "I guess not. Hey, you're not drinking your coffee. Is it okay?"

"Oh, yeah, it's fine."

She was watching him so he had to drink some. Randolph had said it took roofies about fifteen minutes to kick in, so he'd better get out of here.

He stood up, then lifted the mug and faked another sip. "It's great, but I have to get going. Thanks for being so understanding, Mrs. Wingate."

"I thought I told you to call me Tammy," she said, as she followed him to the front door.

Before he could open it, she wrapped manicured fingers around one of his wrists and tugged him around to face her. Running her other hand down his shirtfront, she purred, "I do wish you didn't have to run off. I'm awfully lonely today."

Skip lifted the arm that she was still attached to and gently peeled her fingers loose from his wrist. He held her hand in his for a beat. "Tammy, ma'am, I would be sorely tempted to stay and keep you company, but I *am* engaged."

And unlike your husband, I believe in fidelity.

Out loud, he said, "Besides, my fiancée is waitin' in the car."

She pushed her lips out into a small pout.

Skip turned and opened the door. On the porch, he paused for just a second and thanked her again for the coffee, then tried not to run as he headed to the truck. He waved at Rose.

The door slammed behind him.

Was it his imagination or was he feeling a little dizzy? Probably the former, since one sip of doctored coffee would be unlikely to have much effect on his large body, especially not this soon.

Rose lowered her window.

"Just to be on the safe side," Skip said, "you'd better drive."

She cocked one of her expressive eyebrows at him, then slid across into the driver's seat.

Once in the truck, Skip fished a plastic bag out of his glove box and spat into it. He could still taste the coffee, so hopefully any drugs in it would show up in his saliva.

He held the bag out to Rose. "Think your buddy at the police lab would be willing to test that for traces of Rohypnol?"

"Probably." She eyed the baggie without taking her hands off the steering wheel. "I like you, partner, but I'm not putting your spit in my pocket."

He chuckled and set the bag down on the console between them.

"You gonna tell me what this is about?" she asked.

"Wish I could, but I can't. Not unless that comes back positive for roofies."

Kate was greeted at the door that evening with a hug and a long kiss.

Mmm, I could get used to this.

She let herself relax against Skip's solid body.

When they came up for air, he led her over to the sofa. "Best I can tell, neither of the Wingates have an alibi for the day Amy was kidnapped. He told Tammy he was going to the office. She went on a vengeful shopping spree. She offered me coffee, but I only drank a little. Rose is going to try to get her–"

Kate tensed.

He held up his hand. "I didn't tell Rose anything. Just that I needed my saliva sample tested for roofies."

As Skip was giving her the details of his conversation with Tammy Wingate, the doorbell rang.

She followed him to the door. He leaned down and looked through the peephole, then cursed under his breath. "It's Jones and Bradley."

Kate's stomach clenched.

Skip opened the door.

The detectives were no sooner in the living room then Jones began reciting the Miranda warning. "Mrs. Huntington, you have the right to remain silent..."

Kate stared at the detectives as Jones droned on. Finally she found her voice. "Are you arresting me?"

"Not yet, lady," Jones said. "But we need some answers to some questions. Some straight answers this time." She took a step toward Kate.

Kate instinctively took a step back.

Skip inserted himself between them. "We're more than happy to cooperate, Detectives. We'll follow you to the station."

Jones opened her mouth but Bradley cut her off. "You lead, son. We'll follow. Seventh precinct."

"I need to tell my nanny what's going on," Kate said.

Jones narrowed her eyes at her.

Anger surged. Kate glared back at the woman. "I'm assuming that's permissible, since I'm *not* under arrest."

She found Maria in the nursery and told her that she and Skip needed to go out. "Be sure to set the alarm after us."

Maria nodded, her eyes wide and anxious.

Skip led the way down the porch steps, nonchalantly jiggling his keys. But his tight jaw told Kate he was faking it.

Once they were in the truck, he said, "Call Rob. I'm gonna get Rose to come over and guard Maria and the baby."

At the police station, Rob found Skip sitting on a bench in a hallway. The big man stood up. Both his jaw and his fists were clenched.

Rob put his hand on the younger man's shoulder. "I can only begin to imagine how upset you are but you've *got* to keep your cool. That little girl needs at least one of you to come home to her this evening."

He handed Skip a folded piece of paper.

"What's this?"

"Names you as Edie's legal guardian should Kate not be able to care for her." He'd taken the liberty of forging Kate's signature, but Skip didn't need to know that. "Anybody with the baby, besides Maria?"

Skip nodded. "Rose should be there by now."

"Okay, I don't think this is going to happen..." But then again, he hadn't thought Kate would become a serious suspect either. "Just to be on the safe side, call Rose and tell her that if Social Services shows up, she's not to let them in the house if she can help it. She's to tell them that she is the child's godmother and the child's soon-to-be stepfather, who has been named as guardian *by* the mother will be home soon."

Skip's expression went from angry and worried sick to conflicted and worried sick. "Maybe I should go home then."

Rob shook his head. "Social Services won't push it. They'll just want to know that there's someone responsible taking care of the baby. Sit tight for now. Once I get a handle on what this is about, we'll get it straightened out, I promise."

Skip just nodded and swallowed hard.

"It'll be okay. I'll take care of it," Rob said. Then he went to find Kate, knowing he had just made a promise he might not be able to keep.

Once Rob, Kate and the two detectives were gathered around the table in a cramped room, Jones pointed out that the interview was being taped. For the record, she stated who was in the room and what their role was. Then she told her partner to mirandize Mrs. Huntington again.

"Now I don't think that's necessary, Stella," Bradley said. "We already explained all that to the lady. I'm sure she'll stipulate that for the record."

Rob wanted to tell them to cut the crap. Did these two really think they were that stupid? But hostility was probably not the best approach.

Jones handed him two pieces of paper. "Search warrants, for her house and the fiancé's apartment. They're being executed now."

Kate turned to Rob in horror.

He put a hand on her arm. "It's okay. Rose is there, and Skip has the paperwork we discussed."

She sagged in relief.

Jones gave them both a hard look. "Mrs. Huntington, do you want to rethink your answer to the question, when was the last time you saw Phillip Wells?"

Kate's eyes filled with confusion. "No. As I told you, I've never even seen the man."

"So when you went to his office to talk to him," Jones said, "I guess you kept your eyes closed."

Bradley shook his head slightly. "Now give the lady a chance to explain. I'm sure you have a good explanation, Mrs. Huntington, for why your hair was found in Wells' office."

Rob held up his hand. "Don't answer that yet, Kate. You can't possibly have DNA results back this soon."

"No but we do have a match," Jones said. "The old-fashioned way. Color, thickness, follicle structure. The DNA test will just confirm it."

"Perhaps, but the old-fashioned way has been wrong before, as we are now discovering in some cases where DNA tests are exonerating incarcerated people."

Jones ignored Rob. "Mrs. Huntington, how do you explain your hair being in Wells' office?"

"I can't, because I was never there," Kate said.

Rob sat up straighter in his chair as it dawned on him how the hair got there. "I can explain it. I had lunch with Mrs. Huntington, just before going to Wells' office last Friday. Her hair must have been on my clothes, and it fell off in his office."

"How convenient." Jones sneered at him. "Her hair just jumped across the lunch table and onto you. Or are you telling us that there's more to your relationship with Mrs. Huntington than friendship?"

Rob gritted his teeth, but he kept his voice calm. "*My wife* and I have been good friends with Mrs. Huntington *and her late husband*, for years. As I told you before, there have been anonymous threats made against her child. She was upset when we met for lunch." Resistant to giving them any more information than necessary, he let them assume that the notes had been the cause of her distress. "We took a walk. I had my arm around her shoulders, to comfort her. A few hairs could have very easily ended up on the sleeve of my coat."

"Do you have witnesses to this?" Bradley asked.

"Yes, a restaurant full of people, and the owner."

"Mr. Franklin," Jones said, "I think you need to call another attorney to sit in on the rest of this interview. You are a person of interest in this case yourself. Your presence in this room is interfering with our ability to question Mrs. Huntington effectively."

Rob glanced sideways at Kate. Her eyes had gone wide, but otherwise she was hiding her feelings.

"My client has the right to select any attorney she chooses and she chooses me." He managed to maintain his neutral lawyer tone, despite his rising anger.

Jones narrowed her eyes at him. "You know that witnesses and suspects are always interviewed separately. So they can't feed each other information, or plausible explanations, like you *just did*."

"If you try to exclude me from this room, I will see that the detective's shield in your pocket is removed from your possession." Rob was no longer trying all that hard to hide his anger.

"Are you threatening a police officer, Mr. Franklin?"

"No, ma'am, just pointing out the consequences should you violate my client's legal rights."

Bradley raised his hands in a placating gesture. "Now everybody calm down."

Jones sat back in her chair. "I don't take kindly to threats."

"No one does, Detective." Rob's voice was now mild. He knew he'd won that round when Bradley intervened. "But I like to warn people of the consequences of their actions *before* they act. Saves a lot of grief later."

After a brief pause, Bradley said in a conversational voice, "Mrs. Huntington, I've been wondering why you were so upset when I came to your house yesterday to get the hair sample."

Kate hesitated. "Uh, I was actually reacting to something else."

Rob's brain was scrambling. She couldn't admit that her shock when she heard the detective say Tammy Wingate's name was because the woman

was her client. Therapists weren't allowed to even acknowledge that someone was seeing them.

"And what was this other thing you were reacting to?" Jones asked.

"I can't tell you because it relates to a client of mine and that's privileged
information."

"Not if it's related to a murder investigation, it's not," Jones said.

"Oh, I beg to differ," Rob jumped in. "Mrs. Huntington could be sued
for malpractice even under these circumstances, unless you subpoenaed
her. And since you have no idea whether or not her answer is related to
this case, I doubt a judge would allow such a subpoena. I assure you that
you would be wasting your time because what she was upset about in that
moment is not related to this case."

"How would you know? She wouldn't be able to tell you what it was
either," Jones said.

Rob had painted himself into a corner, but better him trying to explain it
than Kate. "She did tell me what had thrown her, because she could explain
it to me without revealing who the client was."

"Then she can explain it to us the same way," Bradley said, looking
genuinely confused.

"Unfortunately not. I am truly sorry, Detectives, that we can't be more
forthcoming on this. But we are already skating on thin ice regarding my
client's ethical obligations. All we can do is reassure you that the issue Mrs.
Huntington was upset about has nothing to do with your investigation. It
has to do with the notes she's been receiving."

"Mrs. Huntington, this isn't making any sense," Jones said directly to
Kate. "You *could* tell Mr. Franklin, but you *can't tell us* why you were
upset?"

Rob put his hand up. "Stop right there, Detective. We've said all we can
legally say on the matter."

Bradley shook his head sadly. "Well, it does make Mrs. Huntington look
more suspicious."

"That is unfortunate, but we have no other choice," Rob said in a firm
voice. "Could we move on, please? I, for one, am tired and hungry and
would like to go home soon."

The two detectives looked at each other. "I think we'll be requesting that
subpoena, Counselor," Jones said.

Rob shrugged. "It's your time to waste."

"We need to speak to Mr. Canfield." Jones stood up. "That will be all for now, Mrs. Huntington, but I suggest that you not leave the area until further notice. If you do so, we will view that as suspicious and as potential grounds for arrest."

Kate's eyes went wide and her mouth fell open. "But Christmas—"

"No problem, Detectives." Rob took a firm hold on her elbow and pulled her to a stand. "We'll deal with that later," he whispered, as he hustled her out of the room.

When Skip saw them coming down the hall, he jumped up and met them halfway. He moved to wrap his arms around Kate.

Rob shook his head at the man.

Skip froze and cocked his head.

"He's right," Kate said in a low voice. "If you hug me, it will be my undoing."

"Here comes Jones," Rob said out of the corner of his mouth.

"We need to speak with you, Mr. Canfield."

"I'll be right with you, Detective. I just need to talk to my fiancée for a moment."

"Out of the question," Jones snapped. "We cannot allow you to confer—"

Skip interrupted her. "I was just going to reassure her that our friend Rose is staying with our daughter and the nanny." He gave Kate a peck on the cheek.

A fake smile plastered on his face, he turned to Jones. "I'm all yours, Detective. Lead the way."

In the small interrogation room, Skip leaned his chair back, balancing it on its back legs.

His body looked relaxed, but Rob was learning the signs that Skip Canfield had moved from laid-back to intense. His jaw was tight, his normally hazel eyes a brooding mud color.

Jones started reciting the Miranda warning.

Skip waved his hand in the air. "I was on the job for eleven years. I know my rights. My lawyer is present. I'm happy to answer your questions."

Bradley began this time. "We did check out your alibi this afternoon, son. Mrs. Wingate was happy to verify it for us. Said to tell you to come by and see her again when you get a chance." He gave Skip a man-to-man wink.

The muscle in Skip's jaw quivered, but his face remained neutral.

"And there wasn't any problem with the husband. She informed us that she'd thrown him out on his ear."

"So, Canfield," Jones said, "you've helped contribute to the demise of another marriage."

Skip's expression remained bland. "I didn't cheat on the woman, her husband did. Quite frankly, I can't wait to get established enough that I don't have to take adultery cases. They do kinda stick to your shoe and smell bad."

Rob leaned forward. "So if his alibi checked out, why are we here, Detectives?"

"Well, that part checked out okay, but we have some concerns about the rest of that afternoon," Bradley said. "See you all are each others' alibis and yet you all have a reason to want Wells gone so that lawsuit would go away."

"Oh come on," Rob said. "Are you trying to say that both of us are lying to cover for Kate? You seem to forget that Rose Hernandez was keeping an eye on her all afternoon."

"Well, I don't think you all are lying," Bradley said. "But my partner here tends to be more skeptical than I am. Occupational hazard, I'm afraid, after you've had enough criminals try to bullshit you."

Jones frowned. "It's not Mrs. Huntington's alibi we're discussing at the moment. It's yours, Mr. Canfield. We only have your fiancée's word, and the nanny's, that you didn't go out of the house between the time you met with Mrs. Wingate and when Mr. Franklin arrived. We timed it. You could make the trip to Wells' office in fifteen minutes, blow his brains out and then get back home well before Mr. Franklin here arrived."

Skip brought the front legs of the metal chair back to the floor. The crash made Rob jump. But to their credit, the detectives didn't flinch.

"Are you accusing my fiancée of lying?"

"Now, son," Bradley said, "just calm down. We're not saying that at all. You would have had enough time to do all that and get back before she got home. And we can't help but notice that you're very protective of her."

Before Rob could stop him, Skip blurted out, "Of course, I'm protective of her. I love her and she's been under a lot of stress lately."

"Because of the lawsuit," Jones said. "So maybe you figured to take out the lawyer and then the suit would most likely go away. We took a closer look at the lawyer's case file. He was suing on behalf of his brother and sister-in-law and was offering to settle for a paltry amount. And his case was so weak, Mr. Franklin, that you turned down that settlement. It's unlikely another lawyer would agree to take the case."

"Gotta admit, son, she's got a point," Bradley said. "Lawyer who's doing it *pro bono* goes away, lawsuit goes away. And after all, the guy was a sleaze bag. It wasn't like you were killing someone who actually deserved to live."

After a pause, Jones leaned forward. "We discovered you have two other weapons registered to your name. Bet you never go anywhere without one of those little babies tucked in your waistband."

"You are welcome to check those weapons as you did his .38," Rob interjected.

"Oh, we will," Bradley said. "But he's had plenty of time to clean them since last Friday. You know that, Counselor."

"So no one can prove, one way or the other, that those guns have been fired recently," Rob said. "I take it the bullet was indeed too mangled for the caliber to be identified?"

They ignored Rob's question. "What I'd like to know," Jones said, "if your client here is so innocent, why didn't he voluntarily produce those guns as well, when we asked for the one he was carrying?"

Skip opened his mouth, but Rob put his hand up. "Those guns are registered. It's public record that he owns them. So why didn't you ask for them sooner? Jury's going to wonder why you put that off."

Jones's eyes narrowed. "We thought your clients were unlikely suspects until the hairs matched," she snapped.

Bradley held up his hand in a sharp gesture that negated their attempts to imply he was the junior partner. "Now Stella, don't let the good counselor get under your skin. He's just doing his job."

"And what exactly do the hairs have to do with Mr. Canfield's alibi?" Rob asked.

"We're getting to that, Counselor," Bradley said. "You see your little theory also works for Mr. Canfield here. The hairs could've been transported to Wells's office on his clothes."

"Again, we're back to the DNA test results are not back yet," Rob said. "And you seem to be discounting the nanny's verification that my client was home all day and evening."

"Well, now we got a little problem with that as well," Bradley said. "Ms. Hernandez was very nervous."

"Maybe she was intimidated into saying Canfield was home," Jones said.

Rob stifled a sigh. "As Officer Hernandez explained, in their country of origin, *any* encounter with the police is likely to produce an anxiety attack."

"Yes, how convenient that she said that, so we wouldn't wonder why the nanny was nervous," Jones said. "Just because she's a cop doesn't mean she wouldn't cover for her friends. We heard her talking to her cousin earlier. Who knows what she told her to say."

Lady, you just plucked my last nerve.

"I'm not even going to dignify that with a response. I know damned well at least one of you speaks Spanish." Rob stood up. "Come on, Skip, I've had enough of these people insulting my friends. This interview is over."

"Sit down, Counselor," Jones ordered. "We'll say when this interview is over."

"Now everybody just calm down." Bradley held both hands out, patting the air.

Rob stayed on his feet.

Bradley leaned over toward Skip. In a sympathetic voice, he said, "Son, I'll bet you just wanted to talk some sense into the man and things got carried away. That'd only be second degree. We might even be able to get it knocked down to manslaughter."

Rob noted the tight jaw, but otherwise Skip looked calm. He opted not to intervene.

"Detective, I was a state trooper for eleven years. During that time I only discharged my weapon twice, both times during a pursuit, when the S.O.B. didn't stop like I told him to. Missed one of 'em, got the other in the leg. Since I've gone private, I've had to draw my gun a few times, but I haven't needed to shoot it. I've never killed anything bigger'n a rattlesnake in my life, and I hope to God I never have to."

Rob figured that was an excellent exit line. He gestured to Skip.

Jones barked, "I told you to sit down, Counselor."

Skip took his cue from Rob. Rising slowly to his feet, he stepped around his chair to lean against the wall, crossing his arms on his chest.

Rob looked at Jones. "Detective, you know you can't make us stay here. Unless you're ready to arrest my client, we're leaving."

He probably wouldn't have called their bluff like that with Kate. But he knew damn well they didn't have enough to hold Skip. Really, they had nothing. These cops were just trying to shake Skip's tree, to see what might fall out.

He gestured to Skip again.

Once his client was out the door, Rob turned back to the detectives. "Part of me wishes you *would* try to charge him. I'd really enjoy mopping up a courtroom floor with you two, when all you've got is somebody *else's* hair at the crime scene and you're claiming that *four* people, one of whom is a police officer and another an officer of the court, are conspiring to cover for him."

Out in the hall and several long strides away from the interrogation room, Skip quietly said, "Damn you're good!"

Rob grinned at him as they kept walking. "Thanks. I thought it was one of my better performances myself."

CHAPTER TWENTY-THREE

On Saturday, Skip was once again tailing Mark Wingate, while Kate did some computer research. He called her at twelve-thirty to check in.

"Got the name and address of Wingate's secretary," she said. She gave him the information.

"Thanks, darlin'. See if you can find out who rents apartment 309 at the Cedar Grove Apartments on Belmont Road. That's where our man is having lunch today, and I've got a sneakin' suspicion it's his girlfriend's apartment."

"Okay, I'll check it out."

Skip continued to shadow the man for the rest of the day. He ended up at the Sheraton Hotel again. This time it took a fifty to pry the information out of the desk clerk that Wingate was renting a suite by the week.

Interviewing the two women on Sunday did little to pin down Wingate's activities. His secretary had been off the Friday after Thanksgiving, the day Amy was kidnapped. She said her boss had planned to be in the office, but she couldn't verify that. When asked about the Wednesday afternoon when the latest note had been delivered, she couldn't remember for sure but she thought Mr. Wingate had gone to a meeting at a client's office. He hadn't told her which client.

The girlfriend swore she hadn't seen him either day.

The women would no doubt tell Wingate that someone was questioning his movements on those days. Kate and Skip could only hope that it would scare him into backing off, if indeed he was the note sender.

Skip had also talked to Tammy's maid when her boss wasn't at home, again using the lost jacket excuse. Tammy had been out most of the day on both that Friday and the following Wednesday.

So neither of the Wingates had an alibi for either incident.

Sunday evening, Skip was pacing the house like a caged animal, not at all comfortable with the idea that neither he nor Rose could be at the center the next day to supervise the response to the picketing.

"Come on, sweetheart," Kate said. "Let's make up the guest list for the wedding."

"It's still five months away."

"I know but focusing on what we *can* do something about beats the hell out of worrying about what we can't control."

He nodded. "Like anonymous note senders and crazy picketers."

"Exactly."

"I'll be with you in a minute. I want to check in with Rose one more time."

Kate rolled her eyes at him as he punched his partner's number into his cell phone.

"Hernandez."

"Hey, Rose. Just wanted to double-check that we've got things covered for tomorrow. How many men do we have lined up?"

"More than enough," Rose said. "Ben Johnson's doing a little freelancing with us. I put him in charge."

"Good." Ben worked for the same PI and bodyguard agency that Skip had recently left.

"You remember Bill Lindsey?"

"Who?"

Rose snorted into the phone. "The cop you yelled at."

"Oh, yeah."

"He's off duty tomorrow and I signed him up. He said he's hoping that Harris tries to violate the restraining order, so he can have the pleasure of arresting him."

Skip smiled for the first time all day. "Thanks, Rose, for organizing these guys."

"*De nada*, partner."

"*Buenos noches, mi amiga.*"

The picketers showed up bright and early, but the men Rose had recruited had gotten there even earlier. They were lined up on the sidewalk blocking access to the back parking lot. When Harris and a couple others tried to do an end run, they suddenly found three mountains standing in front of them.

Ben Johnson was built like a grizzly bear, with thick dark hair and a beard to complete the image. He pulled a folded sheet of paper out of his pocket. "Restraining order," he growled, handing it to Harris. "Back lot's private property."

The picketers marched back and forth in front of the building, waving signs and yelling obnoxious comments at anyone who went in or out of the front doors. But only a few brave souls picketed on the back sidewalk, in front of the line of he-men standing at parade rest.

Those picketers quickly learned there was no point in trying to stop cars from turning into the lot. As soon as they did, a blockade of thick muscular chests was shoving them back out of the way.

The men never said anything. Their faces remained expressionless, and they never lifted their hands, which could be construed as attempted assault. They just herded the picketers aside with their bodies.

By late afternoon, everyone but Harris and three others had lost interest and had gone home.

Ben called Skip with a final report for the day. "Me and a few guys'll stay on the back parking lot until the center's closing time, just in case folks come back after supper."

"Thanks, Ben."

Skip's satisfaction with the day's results was dampened when Detective Randolph called to tell him that Harris's handwriting was not a match with the notes. Of course, that didn't eliminate the other members of the group.

He called Rose and they exchanged bad news.

"My buddy didn't find anything but coffee in the saliva sample. And he says that's the last freebie. Have to hire a private lab from now on."

"Did you tell him it's not for a client?"

"Yeah," Rose said. "Not sure he believed me."

"So we're back to square one on the notes." Skip ground his teeth. "You got enough guys lined up for the center tomorrow?"

"Got it covered, partner."

———◆———

Kate was pleased that Sally had decided to be proactive. She had called a press conference for first thing Tuesday morning.

Kate went into work early to support her boss.

Impeccably dressed, with her staff lined up behind her, Sally was at her dignified best as she addressed the reporters crowded into the center's small conference room. She gave what Kate thought was a very balanced overview of the false memory controversy, acknowledging the pain that families affected by this issue endure and conceding that false accusations do sometimes occur.

Then she pointed out that therapists have no way of knowing if their clients' memories are true or not, nor is it their job to make that determination. The therapist's job is to support the client through the process of analyzing those memories. Clients ultimately have to determine for themselves whether they believe their memories are valid.

That's as far as Sally got.

"Bullshit!" a man yelled from the back of the group of reporters. "You damn shrinks are fillin' our kids' heads with lies!"

Two men appeared on either side of him.

Even though he was in civvies, Kate recognized one of them as the senior cop who had come to the house.

Smiling, Lindsey produced a pair of handcuffs. "Mr. Harris, you have the right to remain silent, and I do hope that you exercise that right."

Sally paused until Harris, shouting and cursing, had been dragged from the room.

Her voice still calm and dignified, she said, "I believe, ladies and gentlemen, that the man with the red face has clarified what we are dealing with in this particular case." She then turned and left the room.

Sally's parting comment made an excellent sound bite for the noon news as her dignified bearing was juxtaposed against the image of an angry man being led away in handcuffs.

By the time Harris made bail that afternoon, Rob had requested a restraining order specifically prohibiting him from coming within one hundred feet of the building's property line. Since Harris had violated the first order, the judge was inclined to grant Rob's request.

With no leader to goad them on, the picketers dwindled down to two or three at a time, showing up sporadically.

At five o'clock on the Tuesday before Christmas, Kate closed her office door and walked over to the loveseat where her clients normally sat. Settling into one corner of it, she kicked off her shoes and put her feet up. She had a whole half hour to relax, before her first evening client was due.

She heaved a sigh. Finally, things had settled down and she was getting some sense of sanity back in her life.

Their investigation into the notes had hit a dead end, but there hadn't been any new ones in over two weeks. And the picketers hadn't shown up at the center in a while. She said a silent prayer of thanksgiving that the agency had dodged a bullet that could have been fatal.

Her two toughest cases weren't so tough anymore. Tammy was no longer her client, and Audrey was doing much better. The young woman had confessed in her last session that she hadn't had any issues with sex recently. Kate suspected the uncle's death had a lot to do with Audrey's progress. One of her potential abusers was gone, and the other no longer had any power over her. As Detective Jones had predicted, Audrey's father had been unable to get another lawyer to take their shaky case. The malpractice suit had been dropped.

Kate had also dropped her lawsuit against the Wells, but Audrey was debating about her own. Rob was holding off on further action for now.

Phillip Wells' murder case was still a dark cloud hanging over them. But the detectives' subpoena had been quashed. The judge deemed the justification for it too vague to require a therapist to reveal privileged information.

Unfortunately, that had pissed Detective Jones off. She had been uncooperative when Rob asked about Kate's Christmas travel plans. Although the police have no real authority to restrict the movements of someone who isn't under arrest, Rob had suggested they not push the issue. He'd reassured her that, even if the hair was hers, the detectives had a weak case. But with the DNA results due back any day, Rob felt it was a bad idea for her to be out of town should they want to talk to her again.

She'd long ago requested the week between Christmas and New Year's off, and she'd decided to leave that part of the plan intact. Miraculously, her clients were all relatively stable and as ready as she could get them to deal with the holidays.

Her parents were now coming to Maryland for a few days after Christmas.

Once she'd gotten over the disappointment that she wouldn't see her siblings, Kate had decided there was something to be said for a quiet holiday at home, just the three of them, on their first Christmas as a family.

Excitement bubbled in her chest.

Family... My family!

Neither she and Eddie as a couple nor she and Edie as mother and daughter had felt completely like a family to her, not after growing up in the crowded and boisterous O'Donnell household. But now she had a real family, with a mom and a dad and a child.

The thought that it would always be just *a child* poked a pin in some of the bubbles of excitement.

Get a grip, woman!

She'd accepted long ago that she would never have more than one child. What was different now?

Edie has a father, that's what's different. And we're a family.

The bubbles were back. Kate smiled and glanced at the clock. She dropped her feet to the floor. Time to shift mental gears for Audrey's appointment.

The young woman was beaming as Kate ushered her into the office. Once the door was closed, she dragged Kate into a hug. "I'm pregnant!"

Kate ignored the twinge of envy that momentarily squeezed her heart.

Leaning back, she put her hands on Audrey's shoulders. "Wow! That's terrific. How far along are you?"

"Not very. I used a home pregnancy kit." She crossed the office and settled onto the loveseat. "I've got an appointment with my obstetrician for the Saturday after the holiday. We're not telling anybody but you until the doctor confirms it."

Kate took her own seat and asked how things were going otherwise.

"Good overall. I did have a short anxiety attack a few days ago. Alicia's going through a phase. I swear she's reverting to the terrible twos. She wanted candy when we were in the grocery store and I said no. She threw a tantrum and started screaming, 'I want a lollipop' over and over again."

"Oh, no. I can see how that would be triggering."

"It was all I could do to get her and myself out of the store. I abandoned my cart right in the middle of an aisle. But once we were in the car, I took a couple deep breaths and did one of those relaxation techniques you taught me, and I was fine... It actually worked out good with Alicia. She must have thought I yanked her out of the store as punishment. She was good as gold for a whole day afterwards."

"So have you talked to your mother lately?" Kate asked. "How are things going there?"

Audrey was still refusing to have anything to do with her father, but she had started talking to her mother again by phone. The woman, desperate to see her granddaughter, seemed to be developing better listening skills. Audrey had finally agreed to meet her for lunch occasionally, bringing Alicia along so grandmother and granddaughter could have some semblance of a relationship. They'd had one such meeting so far.

"She's been a bit more pushy lately, with the holidays coming up," Audrey said with a grimace. "She wanted us to get together as a family. I told her I wasn't willing to be around my father. Then she started in on how he never would have hurt me, he loves me, my abuser had to have been my uncle, yada, yada. And then she slid right into why couldn't I let Alicia come over and stay with them for a weekend, now that Uncle Phil was dead."

Kate was shaking her head.

"Oh, don't worry. I'm not about to let Alicia stay with them. I told Mother that I couldn't leave Alicia with them even if I wanted to, because then my therapist would have to report to Child Protective Services that a child was at risk. And then the old man would be investigated." Audrey grinned. "Mother changed the subject real fast."

"I *would* have to report it," Kate said, "but they probably wouldn't investigate. The situation's a little too fuzzy, and CPS is so overwhelmed with cases that they only investigate what they call a first party report, from someone who has been abused or has personally witnessed concrete evidence of abuse."

It was the only thing she disliked about the law mandating that professionals report suspected abuse. She had to breach confidentiality and make the report, even if it was against the wishes of the client, which it sometimes was. But her reports were considered third party and only merited opening a file and keeping an eye on the situation. She knew it was the best that Child Protective Services could do with their limited resources, but she wondered how many children continued to be abused, even after the situation had been reported.

"Yeah, but Mother doesn't know all that," Audrey said. "And it's a moot issue because I have no intention of letting my father get within a hundred feet of me or Alicia. Even without the possibility of sexual abuse, he's been plenty abusive in other ways."

"Have you given any more thought to your lawsuit?" Kate asked.

Audrey sighed. "I hate to let the old man off the hook, especially considering all the money we've spent on my therapy. But I'm thinking I'll drop it for now. I don't need to be stressed out while I'm pregnant. And Rob said there's no statute of limitations on sexual abuse in this state, so I can file again later if I want to."

Kate suppressed a sigh of relief. "I think that's a wise decision."

"I'm a little worried about that grandparents' visitation issue, though. What if the old man tries to force me to let him see Alicia?"

"Usually those cases are filed by in-laws when one of the parents dies," Kate said. "Or in a divorce situation where the noncustodial parent drops out of the picture, but his or her parents still want access to their grandchild. Rob checked the Maryland case law. There's only been one case so far in this state where a grown child refused to let her own biological parents see her children. Rob said it was a long drawn-out battle but the ruling eventually was that the daughter was within her parental rights to decide who her child would be exposed to. With that precedent established, Rob doesn't think your father would have a prayer."

As the session wound down, Kate reminded the client that she would be on vacation the following week but would be available for emergencies.

"I don't think I'll be having any of those any time soon," Audrey said, flashing a big smile. "And hopefully never again. Merry Christmas, Kate."

———◦———

The center closed at noon on Christmas Eve. After the last of the clients had left, Kate gave Pauline her usual Christmas offering, a sampler of chocolates. Then she knocked on Sally's half opened door and peeked in.

Sally looked up from the papers on her desk. "Come on in, Kate."

"I know we don't usually exchange gifts but you've been so supportive these last few months that I had to get you this." She pulled a two-pound box of chocolate-covered cherries from behind her back. "A little bird whose name starts with a P told me these were your favorites."

Sally broke out one of her rare smiles as she took the box. "Thanks! I'll have to pace myself with these. Just let myself have a few a day, so I don't end up in a sugar coma."

Kate smiled. "Grant proposal?" She gestured toward the papers on the desk.

Sally sighed. "Yeah. I wanted to finish it this afternoon but it's even more convoluted than most of its breed."

"Well don't work too late. After all, it's Christmas Eve." Kate turned toward the door. "Merry Christmas."

"Same to you, Kate. Lock the outer door for me, would you?"

"Sure thing."

———◦———

Sally struggled with the grant proposal until her eyes started to cross. She sat back in her desk chair and sighed.

She hated Christmas. She had no family and only a few friends, none of them close enough that it would occur to them to include her in their Christmas festivities. She would be spending this evening and tomorrow alone in her apartment. Well, not completely alone. She did have a cat.

Girl, you need to get a life.

Especially since the Trauma Recovery Center, that had been her life for over two decades, was now at risk. They had stopped the picketers, but some harm had still been done. Several of the clients had been afraid to come in for their sessions, not willing to run the gauntlet, even with the bodyguards holding the picketers back. Sally couldn't blame the clients.

The anger emanating from the picketers was too reminiscent of the very abuse they were trying to recover from.

The press had been mostly sympathetic toward the center, but not completely. The sliding-scale fees the clients paid covered only a small portion of salaries and overhead. The small agency depended heavily on grants. If those who dispensed the grants decided there was something inappropriate going on... The center, with its already squeaky budget, could very well go under.

Well, at least she had chocolate-covered cherries to console her. That had been very sweet of Kate to think of that, and to take the time to ask Pauline what she might like. She really did have a great bunch of people working for her. The other three counselors were gems as well.

Okay, you're gettin' sappy, girl. Time to go home to the cat. But first...

Sally tore the cellophane off the outside of the box, lifted the lid and inhaled the luscious fragrance. She selected one and popped it into her mouth. The rich chocolate slowly melted on her tongue as she stood up and gathered her things to head out.

She crossed the outer office, turning out lights and checking that file cabinets were all locked. As she neared the outer door, she finally bit down. The pocket of sweet cherry juice exploded in her mouth. She rolled her eyes in pleasure.

Looking down as she reached for the door handle, Sally nearly choked on half-chewed cherry and chocolate. Gagging, she stepped back away from the door. She coughed up a gooey wad into her hand.

An icy shiver ran down her spine.

She pulled herself together and grabbed a tissue from the box on Pauline's desk to wipe her hand. Then she took out her wallet and extracted the detective's business card.

She didn't touch the envelope on the floor—addressed to SALLY—that someone had slid under the door.

CHAPTER TWENTY-FOUR

Once he had taken several pictures of the envelope where it lay on the floor, Detective Randolph put on latex gloves and lifted it by one corner. Using the letter opener from the receptionist's desk, he slit it open and pinched the edge of the folded paper inside to slide it out.

Then he dropped the envelope into an evidence bag. Handling the note as little as possible, even with gloves on, he unfolded it and slid it into another evidence bag. He sealed the bag and only then did he read the words.

He turned it around so that Mrs. Huntington's boss could read it.

I TOLD YOU TO FIRE HER. NOW IT'S TOO LATE. IT'S YOUR FAULT.

Sally Ford stared at the note for a long moment. "What do you think it means, Detective?"

"Don't know. Doesn't really fit with the false memory fanatic theory. No mention of families. And why would it be too late?"

"It almost sounds like the sender is giving up. Because the damage, as they see it, has already been done," Ms. Ford said, but her voice didn't sound hopeful.

"Maybe. Or they're about to act on the threats. I need to alert Mrs. Huntington and her fiancé."

Ms. Ford shook her head, her lips set in a grim line. "It's going to ruin their Christmas."

When Randolph called Mrs. Huntington's house, Canfield answered. The detective told him about the new note.

The young man swore into the phone for a few seconds, then blew out air. "So much for a peaceful holiday... Hey, is there any way we can hold off telling my fiancée until after tomorrow? Let her enjoy Christmas Day at least."

Randolph hesitated. "I understand the sentiment. But I need to talk to both of you, to see if this new note gives you any more of a hint as to who this is."

"Actually I do have an idea about that," Canfield said.

"I'm on my way."

"Uh, Detective, can you call my cell phone when you get here, and I'll come out to your car. Kate's out doing some last minute shopping right now. If she comes home, I don't want her walking into the middle of our discussion."

Randolph paused. "I'm not promising that I won't need to talk to her."

"I know. I, uh, have a good reason for wanting to talk to you alone first."

Even though there hadn't been any notes for several weeks, Skip had asked Rose to go Christmas shopping with Kate. Rose had agreed, mainly because she'd put off her own shopping until the last minute.

Now she was wishing she'd said no. The stores were mobbed and her normally decisive friend was dilly-dallying over every purchase.

Gift cards for everyone on her list were starting to have great appeal for Rose. Her cell phone rang. Praying the call would give her an excuse to abandon this retail nightmare, she pulled out the phone. "Hernandez."

"Don't let on that it's me," Skip said in her ear. "There's been another note."

Shit!

Rose's hand tightened around her phone. She glanced at Kate, who was digging through a pile of sweaters, looking for one she thought Maria would like.

Skip gave her the details, then said, "I don't want to tell Kate yet. But I wanted you to be on guard."

Rose didn't respond. She really couldn't say much since Kate was standing right next to her.

Into the silence, Skip said, "It's our first Christmas, and the baby's. Kate's been so excited about it. I want her to be able to enjoy tomorrow."

"Okay." She tried to think of something else to say and came up blank. Settling for a simple "*Adios*," she disconnected.

"Who was that?" Kate asked.

"Just *mi madre*, reminding me what time to show up for dinner tomorrow."

Rose hoped her partner knew what he was doing. There would be hell to pay if Kate found out they were keeping things from her.

Skip sat in Detective Randolph's unmarked Crown Victoria, across the street and half a block down from the house.

He had been thinking about his approach while waiting for the detective to arrive. He hoped Randolph would agree to his plan.

"Detective, I'm between a rock and a hard place here. The wording of this new note fits with someone I think may have sent the notes, either she or her husband, and one of them may have kidnapped Amy. The wife was a client of mine. Unfortunately, I can't tell you why I suspect her, because of confidentiality issues."

Randolph looked at him, one bushy eyebrow at a sharp angle. "You're concerned about client confidentiality, son, when your future step-daughter's at risk?"

Skip grimaced. "Well, see that's the rock, sir. If this woman is the one who's threatening Edie, then I'll do whatever has to be done to stop her. But the hard place is that there's some, uh, overlap between my case and one of my fiancée's psychotherapy cases. And she takes client confidentiality very seriously. So if she knew I was talking to you about this, Edie might not end up being my stepdaughter 'cause there might not be a wedding."

He sucked in a deep breath. "So here's what I propose. I've got an idea for how to get this lady's fingerprints and a sample of her handwriting. If we can link either to the notes, then I think Kate will say to hell with confidentiality. But in the meantime, I gotta ask you to take my word for it that this lady's a viable suspect, and to keep all this just between us."

The detective was silent for a moment, then he said, "What's your idea, son?"

Skip tried not to visibly wince. He liked this guy, and Randolph might be old enough to be his father. But after the police interrogation last week, he wasn't sure he'd ever be okay with being called *son* again.

"You go to this lady's house, pretending you're from the PI licensing board, checking up on the quality of my work because my license is up for renewal. Have some kind of bogus checklist that you go over with her. Then ask her to sign it and also print out her name, in block letters so it's real legible. Hand her your pen. Hopefully you'll get prints on that and the paper."

Randolph nodded. "Should work, but it won't be admissible in court."

"No, sir, but it will tell us if it's her. Then I can tell you why I suspect her, and you can bring her in and officially fingerprint her and get a new handwriting sample."

"And if we don't get a match, what about the husband?"

"I actually have a copy of his handwriting. Photocopy of a hotel register page." Skip handed the detective the copy he had kept for his file.

"Uh, there's something else... I don't want it to throw you off if this woman brings it up. Kate was involved in a lawsuit and the lawyer on the other side got himself killed. Homicide was checking out people involved in all his current cases, I guess, 'cause they talked to us. This lady–Tammy Wingate is her name–she was part of my alibi for time of death so the homicide detectives have been to see her recently."

Randolph had gotten out his notepad to write down the woman's name. "Can't go to see the lady 'til Monday. It'd look pretty strange to be coming around with a routine survey on a holiday weekend."

Skip nodded. "I won't let Kate or the baby out of my sight until I hear back from you. I really appreciate your being willing to handle it this way, sir. I know it's a bit unorthodox."

"Well, son, as long as it's not unethical, I believe in doing whatever works."

This time, Skip wasn't fast enough to catch the wince.

The corners of Randolph's mouth twitched. "The homicide detectives you talked to wouldn't happen to have been Bradley and Jones by any chance?"

"Yup."

Randolph gave him a half smile. "Their good cop-bad cop routine's a bit transparent, isn't it?"

Skip grinned at the detective. "Yup."

Randolph's face sobered. "Don't let that fool you. They're good at their jobs."

Skip nodded. He'd known a few cops like Bradley and Jones when he was a trooper. Not brilliant investigators necessarily, but tenacious enough that they closed their fair share of cases.

The two men shook hands and Skip got out of the car.

Before pulling away, Randolph lowered his window. "Try to have a good Christmas, son."

Skip didn't wince this time. "Thanks. Merry Christmas, sir."

Even though it was freezing cold, Skip sat out on the porch for a few minutes, to make a phone call that he didn't want even Maria to overhear.

"Franklin," Rob yelled over the Christmas music blaring from the stereo in the family room.

"Are you at a party?" Skip said.

"No, but I hope you're calling with some legal emergency that will take several hours to resolve. Get me out of this madhouse! My womenfolk take Christmas way too seriously."

Skip chuckled.

Rob could barely hear him, especially since Samantha was now singing along with the Christmas carol, loudly and slightly off key.

"Only a small emergency, I'm afraid," Skip said. "It'll just take a few minutes."

"Hold on a sec." Rob climbed the stairs and went into his study. He closed the door, then went over and dropped into his desk chair. "There that's better. What's up?"

His stomach clenched at the news that there was a new note.

Skip filled him in and then described his conversation with Randolph. "I don't want to tell Kate about this, at least not yet. But I wanted to ask you about the confidentiality issues should Randolph get a match and either of the Wingates is the note sender."

Rob paused, then decided to come back to the not-telling-Kate part. "If Randolph's got a concrete reason to believe they've committed a serious crime, and kidnapping a minor is about as serious as it gets, then he can go to a judge and ask for a subpoena for Kate's records. If she's subpoenaed, then it's not breach of confidentiality."

"You sure the judge would give him the subpoena?"

"Most likely, especially if Kate didn't fight it. Skip, are you sure you want to keep this from her? She'll be royally pissed when she finds out. Have you seen her when she's royally pissed?"

"Once, briefly. Mostly, I've managed to only annoy and irritate her occasionally. But I can imagine what full-blown royally pissed looks like. Does she hold a grudge?"

"Not forever. She'll just make you miserable for a while."

"Rob, she's gonna be pissed anyway, when she finds out I even hinted to Randolph that Tammy Wingate might also be her client. If Randolph gets a match and one of them's our perp, then Kate will forgive me. If there's no match, then no harm done. Tammy will never know that the guy with the PI survey was really a police detective, and hopefully Kate will never find out that I told Randolph about her."

"I hear ya, and I understand your motivation. But you're in dangerous territory."

"What else can I do, Rob? What would you do? I love that baby. She's *my* child now. Maybe the only child I'll ever have. I can't..." A pause, then Skip continued in a choked voice. "I can't bear the thought of anything happening to her. And I can't imagine what it would do to Kate if something did."

Rob swallowed hard himself. "You're right. The stakes are high. I'll do what I can to help calm her down if it blows up in your face."

"Thanks, man."

Rob disconnected, then sat back in his desk chair for a few minutes to think. Skip's plan was actually a good one, except for the part about keeping secrets from Kate.

Apparently she'd told Skip about the infertility issues at least, but yesterday at lunch she'd admitted that she still hadn't found an opportunity to tell him about her million-dollar brokerage account. She had a plan, she'd said, for telling him on Christmas.

Hell! What's with these two with their secrets and their plans!

Then he laughed at himself. It was a sign of how long he'd been married that he'd lost touch with the dance of a new relationship.

"But I know what ammo I'm gonna use with you, Kate Huntington," he muttered. "If you give your man too much grief about keeping secrets."

Later, when the frenzy of cookie-baking, present-wrapping and tree-trimming was over and they were getting ready for bed, he told Liz about the conversation with Skip. The younger man might be willing to risk his woman's wrath by keeping secrets, but Rob had been married for a quarter of a century. He knew better.

Liz shook her head. "I love Kate dearly. But sometimes I think we should get combat pay for being her friend."

Rob laughed out loud, then gathered his wife into a hug. He leaned down and whispered in her ear, "I love you, Lizzie. Merry Christmas!"

CHAPTER TWENTY-FIVE

Skip knew Kate was disappointed that she couldn't be with her parents and siblings, but he was secretly pleased to have his new little family all to himself. And Kate's disappointment was short-lived. They had a great Christmas.

Edie had no concept of what was going on, but she was all for new toys—one of which was her first little rocking horse. Skip had a baby-sized cowboy hat to go with it that he had bought in Texas. They joked that it was a half-gallon hat.

There were also wrapped presents from the grandparents and aunts and uncles. Skip helped the little girl rip the wrapping paper off the boxes. She was then much more interested in playing with the colorful scraps than with whatever was inside the boxes.

Maria was spending Christmas with Rose's family, but she had cooked a turkey breast with the trimmings for them to heat up, along with several Guatemalan Christmas treats--*tamales* stuffed with cheese and fruit, and *buñuelos*, little balls of fried dough sprinkled with cinnamon and sugar.

After they had finished the feast and had washed the cranberry sauce out of the baby's hair, Kate took her into the nursery to put her new Santa's elf pajamas on, sent by her grandparents.

They had decided to wait until Edie was asleep to exchange their own gifts. While Kate was putting the baby to bed, Skip was making a nest of blankets and pillows in the middle of the living room floor. He would let her believe that he was just being romantic. But he was also guaranteeing that no one could get to Edie without coming through him.

When she came out of the nursery, he was sitting in the nest. He patted the bedding in front of him. She smiled at him and sank down to lean back against his chest. His arms encircled her from behind.

They sat like that for a while, watching the lights sparkling on the tree–their first Christmas tree. The bottom two layers of branches were looking a little ragged where Edie had pulled off clumps of needles and tried to eat them. Fortunately, they'd been able to thwart these attempts to add extra fiber to her diet. Most of the unbreakable ornaments that Kate had put on the lower branches were now on the floor.

"Next year maybe we should get an artificial tree," she said.

"Hopefully by next year she'll have a better concept of what's edible and what's not."

"Don't count on it."

He chuckled and tightened his arms around her, sighing with contentment. He nudged a brightly wrapped box with his toe. "That's from my mom."

Kate pushed his arms apart so she could scoot over and pick up the box to unwrap it. Inside was a sweater, the same shade of blue as her eyes. "Oh, it's beautiful!" She pulled it out of the box and held it up in front of her.

"Looks like it should fit. She asked me a bunch of questions and then I e-mailed her a picture of you." That palm-sized camera was definitely a handy little gadget.

"This looks handmade."

"Yup."

"She made this in three weeks!"

He nodded. "She can make those knittin' needles fly."

"I think I already like my new mother-in-law." She pulled her black top off over her head, exposing a lacy black bra.

Skip sucked in his breath and reached for her.

She slapped his hands away. "I want to try it on." The blue sweater was on in less than a second.

"Damn! You're too quick for me. You keep flashing flesh at me like that, and we'll never get to my present for you." He grinned at her as she rubbed her hands up and down her arms.

"It's so soft! Feel it." She held an arm out toward him.

"I'd better not, or we'll be exchanging Christmas gifts on New Year's Day."

———◦———

Kate laughed as she picked up a shirt box, wrapped in silver paper. It felt empty but in it were two pieces of paper as heavy as a million dollars in gold.

She moved around to sit cross-legged facing him and handed him the box. Biting her lower lip, she prayed that this was the right thing to do.

Skip hefted the light box. He looked at her quizzically.

She gave him a small smile. "Open it."

Inside, under a thick layer of tissue paper, was a sheet of stationary. He pulled it out and read, "Dear Mrs, Huntington, As per your request, we have added the name of Reginald William Canfield, III, as co-owner of your brokerage account. Enclosed is a statement showing the current balance. Congratulations on your upcoming wedding..."

"I've been looking for a good opening to tell you," she said. "That life insurance policy Eddie had..."

Skip had picked up the second sheet of paper from the box. His eyes went wide when he saw the figure. "It's over a million dollars."

"It's down a little from what it was." Kate was talking fast now. "Eddie's old partner's been advising me on investments. He says it'll be back up fairly quickly, unless I have to hire guards again to discourage picketers." She tried to laugh but it came out sounding more like a strangled cough.

"What the hell," Skip said under his breath.

Kate bit down so hard on her lip, she tasted blood. This had been a big mistake. She hoped she hadn't ruined their first Christmas together. "Please don't be mad. This is the last of the things in that cart, you know, the one we got before the horse."

His expression was still stunned but he reached out and touched her lips with his fingertips.

She relaxed them under his touch.

"Why would I be mad, darlin'?"

"Because I didn't tell you sooner. And you seemed to be kind of sensitive on the subject of money, you know, when I tried to pay for things, or help you out with the start up of the agency."

"Darlin', that was when I thought you were trying to support yourself and Edie with a part-time job and whatever you were getting from Ed's half of the accounting firm's profits. I never dreamed you had this."

"I'll put it in a trust fund for Edie, if it bothers you."

"I'm not bothered by it, just surprised. What were you so worried about?"

"I... I was afraid this might change things, somehow come between us. I kept putting off telling you about it. And the longer I put it off, the harder it got to tell you. I wasn't sure what to do. I didn't want to lose you, so I made it *our* money. But–"

"Kate." He put his fingers on her lips again. "I'm honored that you trust me this much, to put my name on this before we're even married. And you will never, *ever* lose me."

Her voice barely above a whisper, she said, "I've already trusted you with my heart and my child. The money seemed pretty unimportant next to those two things."

Skip pulled her onto his lap. He tenderly kissed her bottom lip, a bit swollen now from being chewed on.

She parted her lips and invited him in.

They lost themselves in the kiss for a while. Then he laid her back in the nest of bedding, and made love to her.

It was a long time before they got around to his gift.

When Skip woke the next morning, he extracted himself carefully from their nest so as not to wake Kate. It took him a moment to find his jeans in the jumble of bedding and clothes. Finally he spotted the darker, duller blue hiding under his mother's gift to her future daughter-in-law.

The sweater was indeed quite soft. He paused for a moment to recall the sensation of slipping it slowly up and off Kate's lovely body, as he'd trailed kisses up her torso.

He sucked in his breath, then felt a little strange. Should he be thinking about his *mother's* gift in such sexual terms?

He silently laughed at himself. He might not like to think of his mother as a sexual being, but she had been married to his father for thirty-nine years.

The father who had advised his son to love his woman on a regular basis, until her eyes rolled back in her head. Skip was pretty sure he'd accomplished that goal at least twice last night.

The beginnings of baby-waking-up noises coming from the nursery brought him back to the present, and the reality of a sopping wet diaper. If he was lucky, it would *only* be sopping wet. He grinned as he headed for the nursery to take care of the child before her fussing got any louder.

Ten minutes later, he placed a freshly diapered and now only slightly cranky baby on the floor near her mother, who was still asleep under the blanket tucked around her.

It had made a major dent in his savings account to buy the necklace that was currently the only thing she was wearing under that blanket. The diamond sparkled from the hollow at the base of her throat.

It had been worth every penny. His mother's ring, with all its family history, belonged on her finger. But he had wanted to give her a diamond that was just from him.

Of course it was easier to contemplate his depleted savings now. All the money in that brokerage account only meant one thing to him though—security, for *his* family.

His reverie was interrupted when Edie crawled over to her mother and patted her cheek. "Ma muh."

Kate's eyelids flickered.

Skip scooped up the baby and whispered, "Shh, little one. Let's let your mama sleep a little longer."

It was Skip's turn to get his cheek patted. "Unk Ski."

"No, Edie," came a sleepy voice from the floor. "Dada."

On Monday afternoon, Skip received the call he'd been waiting for.

"Your plan worked like a charm," Detective Randolph said. "Got a good handwriting sample from Mrs. Wingate, and the prints of the thumb and first two fingers of each hand." Unfortunately, the lab had told him that he'd be lucky to get the results by the first of the year. Between personnel taking time off to be with their families and an increase in certain crimes this time of year, they were backed up.

Randolph reminded Skip to stick close to his fiancée and the baby until they got the lab report.

"Still not hardship duty, sir," Skip said with a small chuckle.

But after he disconnected, his mood sobered. Recalling Rob's words and Rose's disapproving silence, he debated whether he should tell Kate about the latest note at this point. Several more days of keeping her in the dark did not bode well for her reaction when he finally did tell her.

He definitely couldn't tell her about his conversations with Randolph until they got the results back from the lab. If there was no match, he'd never have to tell her. And if there was a match, he was fairly sure she'd forgive him. She'd be too busy being relieved that they now knew who was sending the notes and could do something about it.

But keeping the note itself from her, that would be perceived as protecting her, and he knew she hated that. Could he tell her about the note without blurting out the rest of it? Probably not. He could lie when he had to, in order to do his work, but he was a lousy liar when it came to dealings with the people he cared about.

And if he told her about the note without the more optimistic news that Randolph might soon know the identity of the sender, Kate would be terrified. How long would he be able to watch her worried face, feel her tossing and turning beside him at night, before he'd blurt out what he had done?

Okay, now he *was* trying to protect her.

Or was he mostly trying to protect himself? He snorted.

Face it, Skippy, you're a coward!

He'd rather fight off several two-hundred-fifty pound men at one time, than deal with one hundred-thirty pound Irishwoman in a full-blown state of royally pissed.

I'd better tell her, at least about the note.

He headed for the living room where she had been playing with Edie a little while ago. But the room was now empty. He heard her voice, full of excitement, coming from the kitchen.

Standing in the kitchen doorway, he watched her as she jiggled Edie on one hip and talked into the phone.

"Okay, see you soon then." She turned to Skip, her face bright with pleasure. "Dad and Ma's plane was early getting in. Dad's renting a car, so we don't have to pick them up. He said it'd be nice to have their own transportation while they're here. They're going to do some visiting with friends."

Kate pecked him on the cheek as she rushed by. "Come on, Edie, let's get you into that new outfit Grandma sent you."

Skip realized that there wouldn't be much chance to talk privately for the rest of the day.

I'll tell her tonight, after her folks have gone to bed.

But at bedtime, he lost his nerve.

CHAPTER TWENTY-SIX

On the first Saturday of the new year, Kate was feeding her now one-year-old daughter her breakfast cereal, and daydreaming about the holiday vacation that was, sadly, coming to an end.

Her parents had arrived a couple days after Christmas. Mac, Rose and the Franklins had joined them on the twenty-ninth, for a small party to celebrate Edie's first birthday. That was the only day Kate had really missed her siblings, especially her sister Mary.

Her folks were thrilled that Skip was to be their new son-in-law. Her father hadn't stopped beaming the whole time they were here. They had flown home late yesterday afternoon, to get back in time for a big *shindig*, as her father had called it, at their retirement community this evening.

She was brought out of her reverie by the ringing of the phone. She reached over to grab the portable out of its charger on the counter.

It was the answering service. "Lady wouldn't give her name, just her number, but she said she was a client of yours. Sounded pretty upset."

Kate sighed as she got up to get paper and pencil and jot down the number. She figured she should consider herself lucky there hadn't been any emergencies before this. The number seemed vaguely familiar.

Turning the baby over to Maria to wipe her sticky hands and face, Kate punched the number into the phone. After a moment, she realized the sobbing woman on the other end of the line was Tammy Wingate.

Kate made calming noises while trying to figure out what she should do. She did not particularly want this difficult client back in her caseload. Especially since the woman and/or her husband might have been the sender of those notes.

"I know I have absolutely no right to ask this of you." The woman's voice was thick with emotion. "But I really need to see you. I'm falling apart, and I have no one else to turn to. Please, please, can I see you today, just for a few minutes?"

Okay, the fact that she gets it that she has no right to ask is a good sign.

"Can you tell me what this is about?" Kate asked.

"Oh, I made such a mistake leaving you. I hope you'll forgive me and let me come back."

Kate dodged the question by asking one of her own. "What happened to change your mind?"

"That other therapist I was seeing, she turned out to be horrible. The first few sessions, when I was mostly complaining about Mark and about, uh... she was great then. But when I finally got up the nerve to tell her about the things my father did to me, she didn't believe me." Tammy started sobbing again.

So now this other therapist is the demon, and I'm the angel again.

"Kate, I'm so sorry to bother you like this," the woman choked out. "I tried so hard to wait until Monday, for the center to open. I was going to call and make an appointment. But I started thinking about what was in my medicine cabinet that I could take, to get away from the loneliness once and–"

"Calling me was the right thing to do," Kate gently interrupted. "Give me a minute, okay? I need to think through the logistics here."

"Okay." Tammy's voice was soft and timid.

Kate shook her head. Could even a borderline be so clueless that she'd try to get her previous therapist to work with her again, after sending her threatening notes?

Maybe. But either Tammy didn't send the notes, or she did and now regretted it. And with the state of mind the woman was currently in, if she did send them, she would probably confess to the deed if confronted directly.

Which is exactly what I'm going to do. Enough is enough!

But would Tammy react to such a confrontation with violence?

Maybe, but Kate doubted it. The woman was much more likely to storm out of her office and then do something sneaky later. And in the unlikely event that Tammy did try to hurt her, she was fairly confident she could protect herself. She'd taken several self-defense classes through the years, and she exercised regularly.

Another thought struck her. If she didn't see Tammy and the woman killed herself, she'd be facing another lawsuit. Knowing a client was suicidal and not doing enough to prevent it was one of the most common reasons therapists got sued.

At the very least, she would have to call Tammy's contact person, who was Mark, and warn him that his wife was suicidal. Yeah, and if he was the note sender, that would stir him up again.

Facing Tammy seemed the lesser of those two alternatives, and maybe, just maybe, she could find out some information about the notes.

"Kate?" The small voice again.

"Sorry, it's a little complicated, but I think I can shake free. Can you meet me at my office in half an hour?"

"Oh, yes. Thank you so much, Kate."

She disconnected, hoping she wouldn't end up regretting this. Now the question was what to tell Skip.

Despite the lack of notes for almost a month, he was still being very protective. He was not going to like the idea of her going to the office alone, but she could hardly show up with him in tow. Who knows what that would set off in Tammy's psyche if she didn't already know that the investigator she'd hired to spy on her husband was the fiancé of her therapist.

Maybe Skip would be satisfied if Rose went with her.

Kate found him in the living room, where Maria had deposited Edie next to her toys. After telling him that she had an emergency, she said, "I think Rose is off duty today. Maybe she can follow me over to the office, so you can stay here with Edie and Maria."

Skip looked at his watch. "Actually she's doing some surveillance work in a little while. But she probably hasn't left yet."

She couldn't ask Rose to stay in the waiting room then. No way was she further disrupting the operations of the infant PI agency.

"Maybe she could take you over on her way to this job," Skip said, "and then I could come pick you up when you're done. I'll pile everybody in the truck and then we'll go do something fun as a family."

Kate would have preferred to take her own car, but she didn't have time to argue.

Skip pushed himself to a stand. "Uh, darlin', I should tell you something."

"Can't it wait? I need to change my clothes." She started for the bedroom without waiting for an answer. "Call Rose for me, would you?" she said over her shoulder.

Audrey woke up Saturday morning with a smile on her face. Her appointment with her obstetrician was this morning. She couldn't wait to hear the doctor confirm that she and Ted were going to have another baby!

Crawling carefully out of bed so as not to wake Ted, she went into the bathroom to take a shower. She'd been lucky to get a Saturday appointment, so Ted could stay with Alicia. She needed to ask her friends about reliable teenagers in the community, now that she could no longer just call her mother whenever she needed a sitter. It was a shame that Ted's family all lived in other states.

When she came back into the bedroom, her robe wrapped around her, Ted was sitting up on the side of the bed.

"Bad news, babe. Pete just called. I've gotta go in." Pete was the weekend foreman at the small manufacturing company where Ted was the new Vice President of Production. The plant was currently going full tilt to meet a government contract deadline.

"Crap," Audrey said. "What am I going to do with Alicia, then?"

"Can you reschedule?"

"Yeah, but I won't be able to get a weekend appointment any time soon."

Ted grimaced. "Can you take her with you?"

Audrey sat down next to her husband to think about that option. She didn't relish the idea of trying to discuss serious issues with her doctor—such as the risk of birth defects now that she was older—while also trying to keep Alicia under control. The child had been such a handful lately.

"Here's another idea," Ted said. "How would you feel about asking your mother to come watch her over here?"

She contemplated that possibility. Her mother had been much more subdued and cooperative the last couple times she'd talked to her. And as desperate as she was to see her granddaughter, Audrey was fairly sure she'd jump at the chance to babysit.

"I'd be okay with that, if Mother's available."

Ted's face brightened. "Call her and see. I'm going to grab a shower." He shoved up off the bed.

Audrey threw on her clothes and hustled Alicia out of bed and into the hall bathroom to brush her teeth. Then she grabbed the phone to call her mother.

⸻◦⸻

Frances Wells always tried to resist the sin of lying. She had to improvise fast. She wasn't about to pass up a chance to see Alicia, but she'd had a different agenda for this morning.

She quickly adjusted a knob on the stove and slid a cake pan into the oven. "I'd love to, Audrey, but I'm in the middle of baking a cake. Why don't you bring her over here? Your father's going to be occupied all day. Some sports thing. He said he'd be home around four."

She could sense her daughter's hesitation on the other end of the line. "Audrey, I do get it. I don't believe your father ever did anything to you. But I'd never jeopardize my grandchild's safety."

"Oh, Mother," Audrey's voice sounded choked. "Those are the words I've been waiting to hear. We'll be there in twenty minutes."

Frances hung up the phone and went into the living room where her husband was watching the golf channel. "Dear, I hate to ask but I just realized I may need more vanilla extract, and I've got a cake in the oven. I've got to bake another one today, 'cause I promised Joanne at church that I'd bring at least two for the bake sale tomorrow. If you'll run out and get me some more vanilla, I'll bake your favorite coconut cake for dessert tonight." She smiled at him, praying that he would, for once, be cooperative.

He grumbled a bit but then turned off the TV and got up to fetch his car keys.

Smelling something burning, Frances raced into the kitchen and turned off the oven. Grabbing an oven mitt, she pulled the cake pan out.

The empty, scorched pan was unsalvageable.

Riding to the office in Rose's car, Kate was feeling guilty. She probably should have told Skip who she was going to see. Well, ethically she wasn't supposed to. But she had told him she wasn't a rash person, didn't take risks. So what was she doing now?

But then again, she most likely didn't have anything to fear from this woman herself. The threats in the notes had been aimed at Kate's family. If Tammy was the note sender, she probably wouldn't attack her directly. Especially since she needed her at the moment.

That is, unless Kate poked the hornet's nest too hard. Maybe she shouldn't confront the woman after all.

But she wasn't willing to keep living like this, having to be guarded, and on guard all the time, constantly worried about the safety of her loved ones.

Rose turned into the back parking lot of her building.

Kate saw Tammy getting out of her car. "You can let me out here and watch to make sure we get into the building okay."

"Be sure to lock yourself in the center, and *stay there* until Skip comes to get you."

"Okay, *Mom*, and I won't let the boys take advantage of me either."

Rose flashed her a quick grin. "Seriously, he's not just being over-anxious here. We don't know that the threat is gone."

Kate thanked her for the ride and got out to escort her client into the building. As they neared the door, Rob's admin assistant pushed it open and stepped outside.

"Hey, Fran, is Rob being a slave driver and making you work on Saturday again?" Kate said, as the woman held the door open for them.

"Yeah, big court case next week. I'm going on a donut run. Stop by and say hi later."

"I might do that. Happy New Year, Fran."

Tammy managed to hold it together until they were actually inside the center, then she burst into tears in the middle of the empty waiting area. Kate put her arm around the woman's shoulders and herded her into her office and over to the loveseat. She handed Tammy the tissue box.

While the woman was dabbing at her eyes, Kate quickly went over to lock her door.

"Oh, Kate, that woman was so horrible." Tammy launched into a blow-by-blow description of her last session with the other therapist.

Kate interrupted her. "Who is it you're talking about? Who were you seeing?"

"Sylvia James."

Kate managed to keep her face neutral. Sylvia James was a novice therapist with whom she had crossed paths at a conference a few months ago. When she'd identified herself as a trauma recovery specialist, the woman had bluntly declared that half the people with *supposed* PTSD just had lively imaginations, especially if they were claiming they had been abused as children. James had then expounded on the fallibility of human memory and how easily it could be influenced by suggestion. When Kate had attempted to politely insert that, yes, memory was fallible but nonetheless child abuse was a very real phenomenon, James had talked right over her. Kate had finally walked away from the woman while she was in mid-sentence.

Tammy had gone back to her blow-by-blow narrative.

Kate interrupted again. "Tammy I know this woman. Your perceptions of her are accurate."

That brought the client up short.

Kate hid a smile. "This time, you are not over-reacting. Sometimes people really are..." She caught herself. She shouldn't be slamming a colleague to a client, no matter how much she disliked that colleague. "Well let's just say, even intelligent people can be misinformed."

"Oh Kate, I felt so awful when I left her office on Wednesday that I wanted to kill myself. And then I had to spend New Year's Eve by myself, and I missed Mark so bad, even though the son-of-a-bitch broke my heart... I tried to do the right thing, not be so needy. That's what Mark always said, that I was just too needy, that I drove people away. And he's right. I've been driving the people I love away ever since I was a kid." Tears were once again pouring down the woman's face.

Hmm, despite the emergency call and the suicidal thoughts, that insight showed real progress. And Tammy was taking responsibility for her actions.

Kate leaned forward. "You may not be ready to hear this, but I'm going to say it anyway. As long as you were trying to save your marriage, I was supportive of that goal, but now I'm thinking that you're actually doing *better* without Mark."

There was a flash of something in the woman's eyes—was it anger? Then Tammy started to protest, "But I miss him—"

"Of course, you miss him. But missing him is not the same thing as needing him back. In time, you'll get over missing him. I know that's hard to believe right now, but you will. And here's what I'm seeing. You were handling life okay, even got through Christmas without him, until your therapist let you down. And even then you tried not to interrupt my holiday, which I appreciate.

"Quite frankly, the Tammy who was living with Mark Wingate was much more selfish than that. You've been so wrapped up in trying to get him to meet your needs, that you were becoming more and more that desperate, self-centered child."

Kate knew she was pushing the woman a bit with her bluntness. She was bracing for the shift, when Tammy would turn her anger on her for being a bad therapist.

One part of her mind was mulling over which of her colleagues she would refer Tammy to. There were a couple who could *probably* work with her, although Kate figured whichever one of them Tammy ended up with, that colleague might never speak to her again.

But the shift didn't happen. Tammy seemed to actually be listening. Kate was beginning to wonder if this emergency might end up being a teachable moment.

"Tammy, I think you're better off without Mark," she said again.

The young woman sniffled. "You may be right. But how do I let him go?"

"It will take time, and it will hurt for awhile. But the thing about feelings is that they *always* change. They either get worse or they get better. There are things we humans can do to make them better, *or* to make them worse. Because you didn't know what else to do, you've been doing a lot of the things that actually make the feelings worse. But now I think you're in a place to learn how to make them better."

The woman's expression brightened a little. "Really, I can learn how to do that?"

"Yes, but first you have to learn how to be a good student. I'm not saying we therapists always know what's right for a client. We're human, we make mistakes, and we can be misinformed, like Sylvia James. But we're trained to help people learn how to make their lives better. So when a therapist tells you something, you need to listen with an open mind. Think about what they're saying, see if it fits... Just like you're doing now. But you need to remember to do that even when what the therapist is saying is hard to hear."

"But how do I get over Mark? It hurts so much." Tammy's eyes welled up again.

"Oh, right. Back to that lesson." Kate intentionally used a matter-of-fact tone, as she handed the client more tissues. This emergency session was turning into a marathon. She wasn't going to encourage any more venting of grief today.

"To get over Mark you need to do two things. First, you need to acknowledge the grief and let yourself feel it, knowing that it will go away eventually, and the sooner you let yourself feel it, the faster it will go away."

"Are you sure? It feels like it'll never go away."

"I know it *feels* that way now, but like I said, feelings never stay the same forever. The other thing that will help those bad feelings go away faster is to get angry, and *stay* angry. Reminding yourself of why you threw the cheatin' son-of-a-bitch out of your life in the first place will strengthen your resolve to let him go, so you can get on with your life."

This time the anger in Tammy's eyes was more than just a flash.

When Audrey pulled up in front of her parents' house, she was relieved to see only her mother's car in the driveway. She helped Alicia out of her booster seat and led her by the hand to her mother's kitchen door.

Frances opened it before she could knock. "Come on in, Alicia. Grandmom's baking today and you can help me make cupcakes."

"Thanks, Mother, for doing this, at the last minute and all," Audrey said, and then quietly, so the little girl who had run ahead of her into the kitchen couldn't hear, she added, "You're sure Dad won't be home until after I get back?"

"Yes, dear. He said he'd be home around four."

"Okay, I'll see you in a couple of hours then. Bye, Alicia, Mommy'll be back soon."

"Bye, Mommy." The little girl was already pulling the cupcake pan out of the cabinet where she knew her grandmom kept it.

Audrey smiled and shook her head indulgently as she headed back out the door. Alicia had once told her that she loved cupcakes the *bestest* of all.

———

When John returned with the vanilla, his face broke into a big grin at the sight of his granddaughter standing on a stool, happily stirring batter in a big bowl.

Seeing that smile, Frances knew she was doing the right thing.

"I'll finish making the cupcakes, sweetheart. Why don't you go play with Granddad?"

Frances washed the unused batter down the garbage disposal. It would be ruined by the time she got back. She'd make some more then. She put the new bottle of vanilla in the cabinet, next to the almost full one that was already there.

Grabbing her purse and her coat off the hook next to the kitchen door, she went into the living room. Alicia had dragged out the tea set from the toy chest they kept for her in the corner of the living room. Her granddad was sitting on the floor, pretending to drink imaginary tea out of a tiny cup.

"John, I just realized I have an appointment I forgot about." She patted her hair to imply that it was a hairdresser's appointment. "Can you watch Alicia for a little while? I'll have to finish my baking when I get back."

"Sure," her husband said. "We'll have a ball, won't we, peanut, just you and me!"

Frances hurried out to the driveway. She started for her car, then remembered it was low on gas. There was no time to make a stop. She needed to get where she was going and get back before Audrey returned.

She climbed into John's car instead and checked the gas gauge. Half a tank. She started the car. While backing out of the driveway, she fumbled one-handed in her purse for her cell phone. She was running behind schedule.

CHAPTER TWENTY-SEVEN

Finally, Tammy seemed stabilized enough that she would probably make it through the rest of the weekend. The second time the woman asked about becoming her client again, Kate couldn't duck the question any longer.

"Before I answer that, I need to ask you about something else." She paused to make sure she had Tammy's full attention. The woman tended to zone out when the topic of conversation wasn't about herself. "For quite some time now, I've been getting strange anonymous notes, and they've been getting more and more blatantly threatening, not toward me but toward my family, if I didn't stop doing something I'm doing with one of my clients. Trouble is the notes never specify which client or what exactly I'm supposed to stop doing."

Tammy was watching her intently, her forehead furrowed.

"All this started around the time that you and Mark were beginning to have serious problems, and I can't help wondering if yours was the case the notes were referring to."

Tammy's eyebrows shot up. "What? You think Mark was sending them?"

"Either him, or possibly you," Kate said evenly, bracing herself for an explosion.

But Tammy looked hurt instead. "You think I'm that crazy?" she said in a small voice.

"Not now. You seem more stable now, but as things were deteriorating with Mark, you were getting more and more volatile. The notes kept referring to me tearing families apart, destroying them, and you told me point blank, the last session we had, that if I'd been doing my job, your marriage wouldn't be destroyed."

Tammy straightened in her chair, blinking rapidly. Her voice was child-like as she said, "I didn't send those notes, Kate, but I guess that answers my question. I... I'd appreciate a referral." She looked down at the wad of tissues clutched in her hands.

Kate's heart ached for that scared, hurt child. And she was even liking the adult Tammy better than she had. "Actually I will consider working with you again, on one condition."

Tammy's head jerked up.

"The condition is that you go to the in-patient treatment program I recommend. When you finish up there, we'll meet and I'll reassess whether I'm the best therapist for you at that point."

An array of emotions passed across Tammy's face. Finally she said, "What exactly are these programs like?"

"Hang on, let me get out the literature on the one I have in mind." It was one in California that specialized in borderline personality disorder. Kate was amazed that such a facility even existed. She worked well with borderlines, but she tried not to have more than a couple clients with the disorder in her caseload at a time. They were exhausting. She couldn't imagine working exclusively with people with that diagnosis, and 24/7 at that.

With her back to the client, Kate rummaged through her file cabinet, looking for the brochure for Clearview Women's Center. Meanwhile, she was trying to decide if she believed Tammy's claim that she hadn't sent the notes.

Was the woman that good an actress? Yes, Kate decided. As melodramatic and manipulative as Tammy could be at times, she was indeed a good actress.

She found the brochure and turned toward the woman.

———◦———

Maria stood in the kitchen doorway, indulgently watching *Señor* Skip play with the baby in the living room. The phone rang. She picked up the portable lying on the kitchen counter. "*Hola.*"

As soon as she determined that the caller was asking to speak to her boss, Maria gave her standard answer. "She no home. I no speak English good. Call later pleeze."

She'd started to disconnect when the caller said, "Where is she? I've got to talk to her." Maria didn't understood the rest of the English but she caught the word *client*, and the voice sounded desperate.

¡Dios mio! She felt so bad for her *patrona*'s clients who did not have a loving *familia*.

"She go office. You got number? *Muy bien.* You call her there."

Skip balanced the baby on her new rocking horse, placing her little hands on the handles on either side of the horse's head. "Hang on, Edie." He started rocking the horse gently back and forth.

Edie gave him a big grin.

When she seemed to be getting the hang of how to keep the horse rocking, Skip leaned back against the sofa, long legs stretched out on the floor in front of him. He glanced at his watch. Kate had been gone for over an hour.

He was growing increasingly uncomfortable with the idea that she was in her office on a holiday weekend, when it was unlikely other tenants in the building would be working overtime. Of course, she had her client with her. But once the emergency session was over, she would be alone until he got there.

He had started to tell her about the new note before she left, but she'd been in such a rush. And then he'd thought better of it. Not a good idea to upset her just before she went into a session with a client in crisis.

He took out his phone and called Rose's cell.

"Hernandez."

"Hey, Rose. Uh, I'm starting to get worried about Kate. What if the emergency call was a fake just to get her by herself?"

"Call had to be legit. I saw the client get out of her car. Kate waved to her and then went over and walked with her into the building."

Rose's words should have reassured him, but he still had a bad feeling about the whole set-up. "The client, what'd she look like?"

"About Kate's height. Wasn't close enough to see her face all that well, but I'd say early to mid-thirties. Thin. Good dresser. Long straight blonde hair."

Skip's heart stopped. Rose had just described Tammy Wingate.

"No time to explain, but that client might be who's been sending the notes. How far away are you from Kate's office?"

"A good forty-five minutes. Call Rob's cell. I saw his admin assistant coming out as Kate was going in. Might mean he's in his office. He can go check on her until one of us gets there."

Neither of them bothered to say goodbye.

Skip searched the contacts on his phone for Rob's office number while he told Maria he was going over to check on Kate. She was to set the alarm system after he left and not answer the door for anyone, no matter what.

Skip hit *send* on his phone and raced out the door.

When Rob answered, Skip quickly explained. Rob said he'd go right down to the center and make sure Kate was okay.

Skip tried Kate's cell phone. It went straight to voicemail. Either she was still in session, or something–or someone–had prevented her from turning her phone back on.

"Tammy, there's just one other thing that I need to clear up."

The client looked at her expectantly.

"You hired Canfield and Hernandez to follow Mark."

"Yeah." Tammy cocked her head to one side, her expression confused.

"Skip Canfield is my fiancé."

Several emotions crossed the woman's face in rapid succession, too fast for Kate to interpret them.

"Wow! Congratulations, Kate. He's a hunk."

Kate stifled a laugh. "How'd you happen to hire him?"

Tammy tilted her head again. "I picked up his card out in the waiting room."

This time, Kate had to stifle the urge to smack herself in the forehead. She'd completely forgotten that she'd put Skip's cards on the end table in the waiting area, way back in August.

She smiled. "Well, that solves that little mystery."

Tammy's face clouded. "Is that why you thought I'd sent the notes?"

"No, it was just a weird coincidence that clouded the issue." Kate rose from her seat. "I'll call the place in California to see about availability."

Tammy rose as well, looking hesitant.

Kate's heart swelled with the familiar feeling she usually had with borderlines. She took Tammy's hand and squeezed gently. "You're on your way now. You're going to be okay."

Tammy's eyes filled with tears. "You really think so?"

Kate pulled her into a hug. "Yes," she whispered in her ear.

CHAPTER TWENTY-EIGHT

Escorting Tammy out of her office, Kate was startled to see a figure huddled in the far corner of the waiting room. She assumed it was a woman, based on the length of the mostly gray hair and the fact that the rather shabby winter coat was yellow. A homeless person, perhaps, who'd managed to find her way into the building hoping to stay warm.

Kate realized that she must have forgotten to lock the outer door when she'd been trying to get a distraught Tammy into her office.

"I'll call you when I hear from the place," she said to her client.

"Thanks a million, Kate." Tammy smiled at her, then went out the door.

Kate took a step toward the hunched-over figure. "I'm very sorry, but you'll have to leave. I need to lock up."

A frisson of fear ran down her spine.

But before her brain caught up with her instincts, the person stood and turned toward her.

"Kate Huntington, I need to talk to you."

The outer door opened. Rob stepped into the reception area. "Kate, are—"

⎯⎯⎯◆⎯⎯⎯

Rob's paralegal met Skip at the office building's back entrance. She held the door open for him. He raced past her.

"Should I call the police?" she yelled after him.

He hesitated a second. "Yes." Then he slammed through the fire door to his left and bolted up the stairs, his gun already in his hand.

He paused to listen at the center's outer door. Hearing nothing, he cautiously pushed it open. The waiting area was empty.

Kate's door was ajar. Skip walked quietly toward it. Two feet away, he heard a woman's raised voice and froze.

"Now pick up the note. I want your fingerprints all over it." The hysterical edge to the voice made it hard to tell if the speaker was Tammy.

"You're not going to get away with this." Rob's voice, sounding calm. But Skip detected the current of fear under the surface.

"Everybody who knows us is going to swear that note is a fraud. They *know* we're not lovers and never have been."

The voices gave Skip a sense of where Rob and the woman were located. He could only guess that Kate was at her desk.

"It's in her handwriting with her prints on it. They'll just think you've had them fooled."

Skip raised his gun and adjusted his stance so he would be facing in the correct direction. He reached out his left hand toward the door.

The woman's voice became accusatory. "If you hadn't stuck your nose in here, I wouldn't have to do this. It's your own fault that I have to kill you too."

Skip nudged the door open.

The woman's gun was aimed at Rob's head.

The roar of the gunshot was deafening in the small office. Skip knew he would never forget that sound.

Audrey pulled into her parents' driveway and again was relieved to see only her mother's car there. She went to the kitchen door and knocked.

After a moment, she knocked again. When no approaching footsteps could be heard, she tried the knob. It wasn't locked.

Stepping into her mother's kitchen, she heard the sounds of a children's cartoon coming from the living room. Mother must be watching TV with Alicia. That's why she hadn't heard her knocking.

Audrey walked across the kitchen and was almost to the open doorway when she heard a male voice. It took her a second to realize it wasn't coming from the TV.

"Come here, sweetie. Granddad's got a lollipop for you."

CHAPTER TWENTY-NINE

The parking lot behind Kate's building was teeming with police cruisers, an ambulance and an unmarked Crown Vic. Rose slammed on her brakes and jumped out of her car. A van pulled in behind her. On its side was the emblem of the medical examiner's office.

That meant somebody was dead.

Rose's heart pounded as she raced through the back entrance of the building and up the stairs, flashing her badge at the uniforms who kept trying to stop her. In the center's outer office, she elbowed her way past more uniforms and two paramedics standing idly next to an empty gurney. An officer tried to grab her but she ducked under his arms.

She stopped at Kate's office doorway, her eyes frantically scanning the room. They came to rest on Skip and Kate huddled on the loveseat in one corner, their arms wrapped around each other. Skip's head was down, his forehead on Kate's shoulder. Her face was buried against the side of his neck. They were both visibly shaking.

Rose could hear Kate crying.

The pearl-handled .38 was lying on Kate's desk, in an evidence bag.

Rose's knees started to buckle in relief. Someone grabbed her arms from behind and steadied her. She spun around, her badge held up in the palm of her hand.

But it wasn't a cop behind her. Her knees wobbled again.

Rob looked over her shoulder toward the other end of Kate's office. She turned and followed his line of vision.

Detective Stella Jones was crouched down a few feet past Kate's desk. Bradley stood near her. Between the two detectives lay a dead woman.

Middle-aged. Not Kate's client.

As Rose turned back to Rob, she realized that it wasn't Kate who was crying.

Her eyes locked on Rob's. His Adam's apple bobbed in his throat as he swallowed hard.

Rose winced, wishing for a way to block out the sound of her partner's sobs.

Kate huddled into her coat, ducking her head as the cold wind blew hair across her face. She rushed toward the door of Mac's Place. January had been particularly brutal this year, but at least it was coming to an end.

Rob wasn't there yet, so she grabbed their favorite booth. The waitress came and asked what she wanted to drink. Kate hesitated. "Water will be fine, no ice." She decided to order the crab soup for a change, on such a cold day.

When Rob arrived, they greeted each other without their usual enthusiasm. The gray skies outside were only part of the reason for their subdued mood.

Once they had ordered their food, Kate asked, "Have you talked to Audrey yet? She was going to call you."

"Yeah. I think I've talked her into waiting to file the civil suit until after the criminal case is decided. If her father's convicted, we'll be on a lot firmer ground."

"What do you think the chances are that he'll be convicted?"

Rob shrugged. "I'd say 50/50."

"What? She caught him in the act!"

"True, but a good defense attorney will claim that she misread the situation. Or her father may just flat out lie and say she made the whole thing up. His lawyer will try to postpone and drag things out as long as possible, so the little girl's memory gets foggier over time. Her testimony's pretty crucial to the prosecution's case. No doubt they've videotaped her telling what happened. But if she isn't able to remember at least the gist of it at the time of trial, they'll have to get in experts to explain about the limits of a four year old's memory."

"Can't the prosecutor push for a speedy trial?" Kate asked.

"Sure but that doesn't mean he'll get one. With the courts backed up the way they so often are these days, a speedy trial may be six months from now."

"That's a long time for a four year old to remember something. Auto-biographical memory is still iffy at that age, and especially since Audrey and Ted aren't allowed to talk to her about it. The memory won't get consolidated... What about Audrey's journals?"

Rob unrolled the napkin that was wrapped around his utensils. "They'll help, assuming the prosecutor can get them admitted into evidence." He fiddled with his fork. "That's where your testimony will be crucial, to establish that those journal entries were written long before that day. But the defense attorney's going to try to twist it around that you have an axe to grind against Wells, because of the malpractice suit."

Kate nodded. She wasn't looking forward to the day that case went to trial.

"How's the little girl doing?" Rob asked.

"The play therapist I referred them to did an evaluation. She said she thought the girl had not been abused, that this was probably the first time the grandfather had tried anything with her."

"Well, that's a relief. But why wouldn't he have abused the girl sooner?"

Kate shrugged. "The motivation for when abuse starts is often hard to figure out. We think four or five is about when Audrey was first abused as well. Could be that was the age her father was when he was abused. It's pretty much a given that abusers were themselves abused. That's how they learn such an aberrant behavior."

She picked up her own bundle of utensils, then put it back down. "Or maybe babies and chubby toddlers have no appeal for him. But when the child slims down a bit, looks less like a baby, then he's attracted to them."

Rob shuddered. "How can a man be attracted to a four year old?"

Kate had no answer for that.

The waitress appeared with their food. After she left, Rob asked, "Is it weird, working with Audrey, after all that's happened?"

"Not as weird as I thought it would be."

Audrey had begged her to continue as her therapist, despite the awkwardness of the situation. And she had expressed no animosity toward Skip, the man who had killed her mother. Indeed, at the beginning of each of her sessions, Audrey asked how Skip was doing.

Kate always lied and said he was fine.

"Hey, I just thought of something." She ate a spoonful of crab soup as she pondered the enormity of the insight.

Rob was piling pickle slices on top of his crab cake, while he waited for her to continue.

"I'm thinking about the earliest notes," Kate finally said. "If I remember correctly, Audrey hadn't told her mother anything about abuse at that point. She was just distancing herself from her parents as much as possible. And then when she did say something to her mother about it, she pretended that the abuser was someone outside the family."

Rob's eyebrows went up. "So why say in the notes that her daughter lies and accuse you of destroying families?"

"Because the woman *knew*, on some level at least, that her husband had abused her daughter when she was little." Kate put her spoon down and sat back against the bench. "She knew the truth was about to come to light, and that truth would destroy her family."

"And she was trying to get you fired, or scare you off before that happened," Rob said, nudging the edge of her soup bowl.

She dutifully ate another spoonful. "I need to tell Skip this. He thinks he killed a poor misguided woman who was just trying to protect her family."

"When she was really protecting a sexual abuser."

"While putting her own grandchild at risk. Yeah, I think that might help Skip put things in perspective." Kate ate another spoonful of crab soup, and actually tasted it this time. It was delicious. The cold spot in the center of her being was beginning to thaw.

Spoon halfway to her mouth again, she stopped. "Damn! *Can* I tell Skip this? The confidentiality issues with this case have gotten so murky."

Rob was shaking his head. "This isn't something your client told you. It's an insight you just had about a woman who tried to kill you, tried to kill *us*. And now Skip's suffering because of that woman's actions. You have every right to tell him, and you wouldn't have to go into any details about what Audrey told you."

Kate smiled at him. "Has anyone ever told you that you'd make a great lawyer?"

He grinned, then nudged her soup bowl again.

"Eat your own food, Mr. Pot Calling the Kettle Black."

He gave his untouched sandwich a chagrined look, then picked it up and took a bite.

They ate in silence for a moment, then he asked, "How's Skip doing?"

"Not great, but a little better. He's still having nightmares, but not quite as often... How are you doing with it?"

"No more nightmares," Rob said. "Not since the first week, but I find myself thinking about it. A lot. Whenever I'm not distracted by other things. I can't get what she said out of my mind."

"Me neither." Kate looked down at the table. She repeated the woman's dying words. "'I didn't want to hurt you or Phil. I just wanted my family back.'"

"How about you? How are you doing?"

"Some flashbacks, and I'm still kind of jumpy. Monday, I was bringing groceries into the house and the wind caught the door, slammed it shut with a bang behind me. The entranceway ended up covered in food. Broke the eggs." Kate shook her head. "What a mess..."

Her mouth went dry as her mind flashed to the image of that gun pointed at Rob's head. She jumped a little in her seat at the sound of the gunshot that she had believed, for one horrible second, had taken her dearest friend's life. Then she shuddered slightly, as she once again saw the woman who was holding the gun slowly crumple to the floor.

Kate hadn't even realized that Rob had put his hand over hers on the table. "Are you okay?"

Her eyes came back into focus and she looked across the table at him, turning her hand palm up to tightly grasp his. "I thought I'd lost you..." Her throat closed up on her.

"But you didn't, sweetheart. I'm still here. We're all still here."

She nodded mutely and looked down at the table again, composing herself.

After a moment, she squeezed his hand, then let it go so he could eat. "At least we don't have a possible murder charge hanging over our heads anymore."

Rob picked up his sandwich. "I'm not sure Jones and Bradley would have believed us, even after the lab found the residual blood on her coat, if Audrey hadn't told them that her mother had a motive for killing her uncle. That he was the obstacle to dropping the lawsuit so Audrey would let her see her granddaughter again."

"And getting rid of him worked. Audrey was letting Alicia visit with her grandmother again." Kate picked up her fork and halfheartedly stabbed at her salad.

"I can't quite understand why the woman came after you at that point," Rob said.

"I think it's because of something Audrey told her. She was trying to get her mother to back off, so she told her that I'd have to call Protective Services if she let Alicia spend the night with them."

"Having no idea just how unglued the woman had become."

Kate nodded. "Her mother probably also figured she'd get Audrey to come back into the family fold, once she was out from under my supposed influence."

"Is Skip going to continue his PI work?" Rob asked.

"Yeah. After a few days he realized that this had nothing to do with his work. He was protecting us."

"Indeed, if he wasn't a PI who carries a gun, we'd probably be dead now."

Kate swallowed the lump clogging her throat. "Rob, I'm scared to death he'll hesitate, if he's in a situation again where he has to draw his gun, or actually shoot it. And that hesitation could be fatal."

He took her hand again. Her anxiety was reflected in his face.

"I finally convinced him to get some counseling," she said. "I pointed out that if he wanted to protect *me* from pain, then he needs to protect *himself* from harm. He's only had one session so far, but he did smile yesterday."

She smiled a little herself at the memory.

"Counseling should help with the nightmares," Rob said. He'd had first-hand experience with his own PTSD symptoms in the past.

"Would you look for an opening to talk to him, man to man? If he knew you'd been in counseling before and that it helped, that would make a big difference, I think. He really respects you and considers you a friend."

"As do I him, on both counts. Yeah, I'll talk to him. He's a hell of a guy. I'm really happy for you, that you've found another good man."

Her eyes filled with tears, happy ones for a change. "It's amazing, with all the jerks in the world—and trust me there's lots of them, most of them related to my clients—and here I've managed to cross paths with three of the healthiest and most wonderful men out there."

"Thanks for the compliment, sweetheart." Rob let go of her hand to reach in his pocket for his handkerchief.

She took it and dabbed at her eyes. "If Liz ever gets tired of washing and ironing these, let me know. I'll take over the chore. I don't ever want my men to stop carrying cloth handkerchiefs."

"How sexist of you." He grinned at her. "What makes you think that Liz irons them?"

"You!? You iron them?"

"Yeah." His face grew serious. "I go through them pretty fast sometimes. I see a lot of misery in my job, too. I can't help people in quite the same way as you do, though..." He trailed off.

She was grateful that he didn't continue the thought. She wasn't in the mood for a pep talk about the importance of her work. She stabbed again at her salad.

"Have you decided anything about taking a leave of absence?" Rob asked after a moment.

"I don't know. I'm really torn about that. I love my work, most days. But this is the second time that one of my cases has put the people dear to me in jeopardy. I keep telling myself that it's a fluke. Ninety-nine percent of therapists go through their entire careers without anything disrupting their personal lives, except an occasional middle-of-the-night emergency call."

Kate lowered her gaze to her plate, then shook her head. She didn't want to think about that anymore right now. And this was as good an opening as she was likely to get.

She looked up and gave Rob a smug smile. "It looks like I'll be able to put off that decision for a while. I'll have an excuse to take a leave soon anyway, for a different reason. Oh, by the way, we're moving the wedding date up to March."

Rob's look of confusion morphed slowly toward comprehension. His eyes went wide, then a big grin spread across his face. "How long have you known? Why didn't you call and tell us right away?"

"Just since yesterday. I wanted to tell you in person," she answered his questions in order. "And I thought it would be appropriate to tell the baby's *father* first. *That's* when he smiled."

AUTHOR'S NOTES

If you enjoyed this book, please take a moment to leave a short review on the book retailer(s) of your choice. Reviews help to sell books and sales help keep the stories coming! You can readily find the links to these retailers at the *misterio press* bookstore (https://misteriopress.com/bookstore).

The next novel in this ten-book Kate Huntington Mystery series is *CELEBRITY STATUS*. The book before this one is Book 2, *ILL-TIMED ENTANGLEMENTS*. And I am currently writing a spin-off series of police procedurals, featuring a secondary character from the Kate books. The C.o.P. on the Scene Mysteries has two novels out so far. (All my series are listed in the front of this book.)

This book was proofread by multiple sets of eyes, but proofreaders are human. If you noticed any errors, please email me at kass@kassandralamb.com so I can have them corrected.

Heck, email me anyway. I love hearing from readers!

And you may want to sign up for my newsletter at https://kassandralamb.com to get a heads up about new releases, plus special offers and bonuses for subscribers. You will also receive a free novelette, *The Tell-Tale Bark*, the prequel to my Marcia Banks and Buddy cozy series, AND a free novella, *Sweet Sanctuary*, the prequel to this series, the Kate Huntington Mysteries.

Also, *misterio press* now has a readers' group on Facebook (www.facebook.com/groups/misteriopressmysteries/) where we chat with readers and also offer giveaways, contests and other goodies. Please stop by and check it out!

Let me ramble for a page or two and then I will give you a synopsis of the next adventure in the lives of Kate, Skip and the Franklins.

I feel that I have not sufficiently thanked the people who make my books a reality. I have a wonderful group of beta readers who help me transform the raw material of my first draft into the polished version that you read. Thank you, thank you, thank you to Angi, Sue, Jonathan, Gina, Ralph, Virginia, Judy, Juanita and Ann (I hope I haven't forgotten anyone!). And a special thanks to my good friends, Angi, Dot and Mary, for all their encouragement and support.

God bless my long-suffering husband, who is also my proofreader. Although an avid reader of many things in the non-fiction spectrum, he never reads fiction so it is a very real sacrifice for him to wade through my books to make sure all the T's are crossed and the I's are dotted.

And how could I forget my good friend and co-owner of *misterio press,* Shannon Esposito, who helped tremendously with the final polish of this book and is one of the best hand-holders I've ever known. She has talked me down off the ledge more than once when I was ready to chuck it all and go back to being a retiree. I can't thank you enough, Shan!

Also a big thanks to the priests, Louann Loch and Allen LaMontagne, of my two Episcopal parishes (in Florida and in Maryland) and to all the wonderful folks in both parishes. Bless you all for your amazing support.

And thank you, Ma, for the gift of this plot concept. In 1995, I had started the first novel in this series. One day, my mother, who wrote travel articles and children's books, called me up. "I have a great idea for a novel," she said. "But I know I'll never get around to writing it before I die, and it would fit in nicely with your Kate and Rob series." She told me her idea and I agreed that it would work in my series.

Unfortunately, life happens. That first novel, one third finished, languished in my hard drive until 2009–six years after my mother's death. Once retired, I could focus on my writing, and my mother's idea has finally become Book 3 in the Kate Huntington mystery series.

Last but not least, may I express my gratitude to Marcy Kennedy, the editor who has taught me so much. During this past year (2014) I've re-released the first three books in this series, after an overhaul to correct the newbie author mistakes made in these earlier works. I didn't change the storyline or any of the characters, just cleaned up the writing a bit. Once

Marcy had taught me the right way to do things, the perfectionist in me couldn't leave things alone.

All the characters and groups mentioned in this book are fictional (my deepest apologies if a name I have randomly picked for one of my bad guys/gals happens to be your name). The "false memory" movement, however, is very real. It provides an excellent example of how a noisy minority–ill-informed and with their own agenda–can distort reality for the majority of society.

The proponents of the so-called "false memory syndrome" have done a lot of damage to innocent people, both sexual abuse survivors and the trauma recovery therapists trying to help them. And they have sometimes rubbed salt in the wounds of families already devastated by incest.

As Sally Ford acknowledges, false accusations do occur. And in the early years right after sexual abuse came out of the closet, there were zealots who–out of naivete, not malice–pushed beyond the limits of what we knew about traumatic memory and trauma recovery in the 1980's.

But science has since caught up and there is now considerable proof of the validity of traumatic amnesia, although delayed memories, like any other memories, are far from infallible. Human memory is susceptible to suggestion, and is not always recorded accurately in the first place. But traumatic memories operate somewhat differently, research has found. Contrary to what we might expect, they actually tend to be a bit *more* accurate than normal memories, perhaps because they are seared into our brains so dramatically at the time of the event.

On the other hand, there is absolutely no scientific evidence that a "false memory syndrome" exists. In the medical and mental health fields, the word *syndrome* refers to a group of symptoms that occur together and are thought to be related to a common cause, i.e., it is a synonym for the words *disorder* or *disease.* Thus, post-traumatic stress *syndrome* involves nightmares, flashbacks, intrusive thoughts, exaggerated startle response, etc. all related to the trauma the person has experienced.

There are no symptoms in this supposed "false memory syndrome." There is only a conflict of opinions as to what has happened during a person's childhood. The grown child believes one thing happened; others believe differently.

The false memory movement was one of the main reasons I retired when I did. After twenty years as a childhood abuse specialist, I felt it was time to get out while I was ahead. There were some people I was unable to help but I had many successes as well, and I had never lost a client to suicide and had never been sued for malpractice. When the climate of our society shifted from one of respect for the intense work that I did to one of skepticism and assumptions that I was planting false memories in my clients' heads (in order to keep them in therapy and make more money—excuse me while I grind my teeth), I decided it was time to bail.

Okay, enough of that gruesome subject.

Let me point out again, as I did at the end of *Ill-Timed Entanglements*, that these two books are set in 2006, making Kate and Skip members of Generation X (the generation between the Baby Boomers and the current crop of thirty-somethings).

I also have another reason for setting it in that year. There are four more books in the series between this one and the current year of 2014. *Celebrity Status* (Book 4) jumps three years to the spring of 2010; I decided the characters needed a break to enjoy life for a while before more bad stuff came their way. *Collateral Casualties* (Book 5) is set in the fall of 2011. Book 6, *Zero Hero*, involves the ten-year anniversary of 9/11 and is set in 2013.

And now, as promised, here is a summary of the next book in the series.

CELEBRITY STATUS, A Kate Huntington Mystery

Kate Huntington is now married to the *very* patient man who has courted her through the last two books in the series. Life is good. She has her own private practice, the kids are thriving and the PI agency Skip co-owns is steadily growing.

But perhaps Canfield and Hernandez, Private Investigations, is doing a little too well. They have attracted their first celebrity client, and they soon come to hope she's their last.

Pop singer, Cherise Martin, is being stalked by an anonymous fan with a twisted concept of love. Before Skip realizes just how twisted, he involves first his psychotherapist wife and then their lawyer friend, Rob Franklin, in the case.

Soon their mundane lives as everyday citizens are being reported, and distorted, all over the tabloid press. Nothing they try—not restraining or-

ders, threats of lawsuits nor even Skip's imposing size–seems to be suffi-
cient to stop the unrelenting paparazzi. Or the stalker.

Skip Canfield is a strong man, emotionally as well as physically, but
everyone has their limits. When hints of his wife having an affair with Rob
are added to his feelings of helplessness over being unable to protect his
family, the big man is terrified he will lose the life he loves–his wife, his kids,
his dreams.

ABOUT THE AUTHOR

Kassandra Lamb has never been able to decide which she loves more, psychology or writing. In college, she realized that writers need a day job in order to eat, so she studied psychology. After a career as a psychotherapist and college professor, she is now retired and can pursue her passion for writing.

She spends most of her time in an alternate universe with her characters. The portal to that universe, aka her computer, is located in Florida, where her husband and dog catch occasional glimpses of her.

Kass has completed the ten-book, traditional mystery series, The Kate Huntington Mysteries (set in her native Maryland, about a psychotherapist/amateur sleuth), plus four Kate on Vacation novellas (with the same main characters). She is also the author of the thirteen-book Marcia Banks and Buddy cozy mystery series, about a service dog trainer and her sidekick and mentor dog, Buddy, set in north central Florida.

And she has started a new series of police procedurals, with Lieutenant Judith Anderson from the Kate Huntington series as the main character in the C.o.P. on the Scene Mysteries (two books out with more to come).

To read and see more about Kassandra and her books, please go to https://kassandralamb.com. Be sure to sign up for the newsletter there to get a heads up about new releases, plus special offers and bonuses for subscribers (and free stories).

Kass's e-mail is kass@kassandralamb.com and she loves hearing from readers! She's also on Facebook and Goodreads and she blogs about psychological topics and other random things at https://misteriopress.com.

Kassandra also writes romantic suspense under the pen name of Jessica Dale.

~~

Please check out these other great *misterio press* series:

Karma's A Bitch: Pet Psychic Mysteries
by Shannon Esposito
Multiple Motives: Kate Huntington Mysteries
by Kassandra Lamb
The Metaphysical Detective: Riga Hayworth Paranormal Mysteries
by Kirsten Weiss
Dangerous and Unseemly: Concordia Wells Historical Mysteries
by K.B. Owen
Murder, Honey: Carol Sabala Mysteries
by Vinnie Hansen
Payback: Unintended Consequences Romantic Suspense
by Jessica Dale
Buried in the Dark: Frankie O'Farrell Mysteries
by Shannon Esposito
To Kill A Labrador: Marcia Banks and Buddy Cozy Mysteries
by Kassandra Lamb
Lethal Assumptions: C.o.P. on the Scene Mysteries
by Kassandra Lamb
Never Sleep: Chronicles of a Lady Detective Historical Mysteries
by K.B. Owen
Bound: Witches of Doyle Cozy Mysteries
by Kirsten Weiss
At Wits' End Doyle Cozy Mysteries
by Kirsten Weiss
Steeped In Murder: Tea and Tarot Mysteries
by Kirsten Weiss
The Perfectly Proper Paranormal Museum Mysteries
by Kirsten Weiss
Big Shot: The Big Murder Mysteries
by Kirsten Weiss
Steam and Sensibility: Sensibility Grey Steampunk Mysteries
by Kirsten Weiss
Full Mortality: Nikki Latrelle Mysteries
by Sasscer Hill
ChainLinked: Moccasin Cove Mysteries

by Liz Boeger
Maui Widow Waltz: Islands of Aloha Mysteries
by JoAnn Bassett

Plus even more great mysteries/thrillers in the *misterio press* **bookstore** .

www.ingramcontent.com/pod-product-compliance
Lightning Source LLC
Chambersburg PA
CBHW050403260626
47156CB00003B/844